RHOMBUS

RHOMBUS

BOB GORE

HUNTINGTON PRESS • LAS VEGAS, NEVADA

Rhombus

Published by
  Huntington Press
  3687 South Procyon Ave.
  Las Vegas, Nevada 89103
  (702) 252-0655 Phone
  (702) 252-0675 Fax
  e-mail: books@huntingtonpress.com

Copyright© 2000, Bob Gore

ISBN 0-929712-88-9

Cover Design: Bethany Coffey Rihel
Interior Design: Bethany Coffey Rihel
Production: Laurie Shaw

Printing History
1st Edition—October 2000

DEDICATED TO

Feona, the angel who shares my life.
—and Homer McCormick, wherever you are.

ACKNOWLEDGEMENTS

Christum and Juanita Gore, the best parents a kid ever had. Eugene and Dorothy Smith, the couple who raised my angel. Bill Branon, novelist, the best teacher I ever had. Greg Kolligian and Bruce Redditt, who never lost faith in *Rhombus* and kept me moving forward. Barry Becker and Kevin McKinley, my business partners who graciously tolerated my absence to tend to my writing. Deke Castleman, my editor, who both amazed me and became my friend. Bethany Coffey, Huntington Press cover girl and marketing wonder. Anthony Curtis, Huntington Press head genius and bulldog. Michele Bardsley, who persevered a year to "sell" Anthony on *Rhombus*. Chuck Masters, who helped me invent the airplane. Rudy Miller for … I forget. All with whom I served my country—who understand the meaning of honor and the sting of sacrifice. Blue Flight, for their inspiring devotion. The Boy Scouts of America for the value of others above self.

1983
SPECTER

The beam from a lighthouse on the horizon swatted the misty night with a slow tedious rhythm. Black waves capped with a turquoise luster rose from the Pacific, marched beneath the full moon, and collapsed on the beach where they became glimmering, foam-edged sheets that erased a trail of footprints left by an old man.

He walked near the water where the footing was firm and held his grandson in the crook of one arm. They didn't hear the explosion high above them in the black sky. "It a cold place, Dappy," the little boy said.

The old man noticed the cooling sea breeze and felt the child shiver. He wrapped his arms around him and held him close. "You're almost too big for me to carry."

"Yep," the boy said as he rubbed the stubble on his grandfather's cheek. "I a big boy." He jerked away and pointed up. "Look, Dappy! Look!" The old man saw a thin, sparkling streak of light, the hand of God striking a bar of flint across a wrought-iron sky. "Make a wish, Dappy. Make a wish."

A huge, wounded war machine on the edge of space pitched its nose down and tore through the night toward the safety of a runway that lay farther up the beach.

A mile away an off-duty naval officer sat in his Jeep Cherokee at the end of the runway at Naval Air Station, North Island. He saw the sparks, too, but like the old man and the little boy, he dismissed them as natural. He zipped up his windbreaker, closed his eyes, and inhaled the ocean fragrance that mingled with the scent of dune flowers.

"What the hell?" The officer grabbed the steering wheel. It vibrated.

Head cocked, the man strained at a noise he didn't recognize. It was deep and intense, like thunder, but not loud.

The dashboard shuddered.

Coins in the ashtray rattled.

"What the hell!"

He jerked at the handle, threw his shoulder against the door, jumped out and away.

But the sound wasn't in the Cherokee—it was out here!

He looked up the beach, toward the resonant violence that bore down on him.

He saw nothing, but it came at him.

It came for him.

The low, thunderous growl surrounded him.

"What in God's name!"

He threw himself to the sand, thought of how dying would feel.

The sound moved over him.

He looked up to see his attacker, raised a fist, defiant. He shouted.

Stars moved one way and the other as a huge pane of imperfect glass passed overhead. The whispering thunder moved with it and disappeared into the night—toward the runway that lay on the sand between two rows of white lights.

A second later the officer heard the ripping noise made by the small tornadoes that trail from the wingtips of heavy airplanes.

His shout echoed in his ears.

Then—silence.

He got up, didn't brush the sand from his clothes, and stared at the two lines of white lights.

His breath was ragged; his lips quivered.

He spun toward the Cherokee. Warm light from the open door spilled across the sand, and the door chime beckoned.

He raced to the jeep, got in, and slammed the door.

A shadow to his left, outside.

He fumbled for the ignition.

The shadow. Larger!

Just as he heard the muffled shot, part of his brain blew out in a red mist.

He pitched sideways; his head bounced on the right seat.

His dying eyes focused on a white Toys R Us bag that sat on the floorboard. It held a gift for someone who would miss him.

His world spun away.

His last memory of it was that sound—the sound of whispering thunder.

1972

WARRIOR

1972, Tuesday, 4 April
1814 Hours (6:14 PM)
Yankee Station, South China Sea
USS Kitty Hawk

The metal hatch on the outside of the aircraft carrier's superstructure flew open and banged the steel bulkhead. Lt. Mike Christum bounded into the sunlight and stopped at the rail of the bridge deck that overlooked the flight deck. The run from his fighter made him breathe hard. His six-foot frame was clothed in a gray flight suit, G-suit, nylon survival vest, and a .38 service revolver with bandoleer. The warm wind hardly moved his dark, sweaty hair.

He focused on a black dot just above the horizon behind the ship, above the waves tinted pink by the setting sun. Closer the dot came, until he made out the large engine intake and the distinctive, stocky shape of the A-7 fighter.

The A-7 clawed for altitude. In the cockpit, Christum's wingman and bunkmate fought for life.

The fighter's wings rocked at the edge of a stall.

"Eject, damn it! Ejeeeect!" he shouted at the airplane.

He waited, anxious, hoping to see the flame of the rocket that launched the ejection seat away from the fighter.

Veins bulged in his neck and spit sprayed in the wind as he screamed, "Eject, Danno! Get the hell out!"

The A-7 bore on.

Its engine howled.

Smoke poured from rips in the fighter's sides and flowed along its skin. The engine exhaust blasted the smoke against the sea where it flattened and spread, a rolling black fog.

The jet's nose crossed the edge of the flight deck.

Too low!

Christum flung himself to the steel deck plates, fingers meshed behind his head, shielding himself from the flying metal, from the flames, from Danno's body as it tumbled in pieces after being ripped from the airplane. The scythe of the Grim Reaper hissed; its shiny edge flashed. He braced himself.

The A-7 hammered the flight deck below. The bridge deck jolted and stomped the air from his lungs. He gasped.

He waited.

The only sound he heard was the melting whistle of a jet engine shutting down. He peeked from under his raised elbow. Nothing. He grabbed the rail and eased himself up.

The A-7 sat below, its hook snagged to the first cable. It leaned to the side. A wheel and other pieces of the landing gear lay against the carrier's superstructure. Fire-extinguisher foam arced through the air and splashed on the fighter's torn skin as smoke and steam poured away. The cockpit was open—and already empty.

1972, Tuesday, 4 April
1931 Hours (7:31 PM)

For the past five months the aircraft carrier had cruised the South China Sea, its bow making never-ending surf that rolled from the giant ship. Its tireless catapults shot warplanes over the water where they climbed into the sky, joined up, and disappeared over the western horizon. Later, like honeybees returning to the hive, they lined up to land. One by one the airplanes slammed against the carrier's flat top, protected from destruction by their long landing gear. Tailhooks snagged one of four wire cables strung across the deck. Those that hooked the cables were the lucky ones, because they had made it home from the hard hot skies of North Vietnam. Home was a giant complicated machine. Home was the USS *Kitty Hawk*.

The *Hawk* was gray throughout with pipes and conduit running down halls called passageways and through rooms called spaces. In this floating catacomb, men, mostly young, worked and lived in a timeless world where the metronome of life ticked from one meal to the next, from one letter to the other. Some worked deep within the ship's engineering spaces and for months never saw the sun nor smelled the sea, a sacrifice of their own choosing. They all lived without caressing soft skin, firm breasts, and rounded hips. They dreamed the conscious dreams of young men.

Living spaces were divided between enlisted men and officers. The latter lived in an area called Officer Country that was marked by blue linoleum glued to the decks. They enjoyed the luxury of living only two to a room that measured about ten by ten. In one of these staterooms, Mike Christum lay in the top bunk, one arm at his side and the other across his face to cover his hazel eyes, straight nose, square jaw, and a thin pink scar that ran along his jaw to a nick on his earlobe. His dark hair was still matted from wearing his helmet, and the gray flight suit was unzipped to his waist, revealing another scar on his chest. The scars accounted for two Purple Hearts. Dog tags on a beaded chain lay over his shoulder. He wore white socks, grayed on the bottom from walking on the linoleum deck. His flight boots sat on the floor at the foot of the bunk, still warm and humid from the day of combat. His exhausted body twitched each time the giant catapult piston shot from one end of its cylinder to the other as it sent another man and his airplane into the maw of the war monster. The catapult jarred the stateroom with a thump that sounded like a giant, rubber-coated sledgehammer hitting a heavy steel table.

Nearly two hundred and fifty times before, Mike had lain like this after flying through a sky that was filled with bullets, flak, and missiles. While Daniel "Danno" Riley, his idiot bunkmate who had just crashed on the carrier deck, escaped the pressure of the day by listening to classical music in the ship's library, Mike escaped by daydreaming about the green mountains of his boyhood home. His thoughts rolled back to the small town of Hinton, West Virginia, a little burg built on one side of the New River Gorge at the edge of a whitewater river more challenging than the Colorado. Ancient commercial buildings sprouted sumac saplings from dirt that accumulated in the corners of their flat roofs. Old homes and churches built along brick streets in the railroad heydays hid under canopies of maple and oak trees. Windowsills held Folgers and Maxwell House cans filled with earth that grew pink and red geraniums and yellow pansies. People waved hellos from passing cars, grade-school boys hid in alleys and gagged at their first taste of chewing tobacco, while girls pulled fallen cakes from too-hot ovens and the smell of burnt chocolate drifted among the honeysuckle trellises. Hinton resembled a toy village set up on a wide staircase, filled with people who seemingly led toy lives.

The tension from the hot day of combat washed away in the memories of cool summer nights, the delicate roar of the river, and the scent of summer flowers that wafted through the window above his childhood bed. Dozens of plastic airplanes dangled from his bedroom ceiling on threads. Fueled by his imagination, the fighters flew daily at supersonic speeds and fought off MiGs and Yakolevs. They won every battle, too. Over time, though, his diminutive air fleet took serious losses from its greatest single enemy, Mom and her dust cloth. Mike grinned as he thought of the woman who was the nemesis of his boyhood air force.

He remembered wading in the river with his beloved dad

as they flung spinning lures from the tips of their fishing poles at bass that cruised the rocky banks. His reverie turned to his burr-headed little brother, Scott, who tagged along to explore a universe of creeks and valleys, mountaintops and old hollow trees, leaves in the gutter, and ants warring in the backyard. They crept to the kitchen windowsill where Mom cooled her blackberry pies. With a small fishing hook they'd pull out some of the fruit through the holes in the middle of the crust. She never noticed. Mike was an adventurer who encouraged an often reluctant but admiring brother into his dreams. His most energetic plan was to build a raft and sail it down the river to the sea, but his brother resisted. Scott was happier stomping along an old logging road that snaked along Barton Ridge or overturning rocks in Madam's Creek to watch the crawdads scamper. Scott heard the look-homeward call of the mountains, while the sirens of the sea lured Mike with the flirting song of the river.

A soaked towel whizzed through the air and smacked cold against his face, shattering the daydream of his childhood. "Brother," he said as he pulled it off and flung it back without looking. He opened his eyes to see the gray steel ceiling just above his nose. The catapult hammered again. "I see you made it back," he said, angry.

"Nice shot!" The muffled voice came from behind the sloppy towel that wrapped around Danno Riley's head. He peeled the towel from his face and tossed it in the sink. It smacked the porcelain. "Yep. Kept it in the air and snagged the number-one wire. The Air Boss spent the last hour chewing on me. Thinks I should've punched out."

"You should've, you idiot." Softer words now. "No airplane's worth your life, Danno."

Danno stood, silent. His physique was much like Mike's. He had a broad, handsome face and a youthful cut of almost-black hair that spilled over his forehead and covered his straight eyebrows. White teeth shone behind the boyish grin. "You saw it?" he asked, almost proud.

"Oh, sure. You dragged your butt across five miles of ocean

and barely"—Mike held a thumb and forefinger just apart—"barely made it back."

Danno remembered the time he'd watched Mike wrestle his own airplane onto the deck while the blood from Mike's face painted a lengthening red streak down the side of the fighter. He opened his mouth to say something about setting a bad example, but he knew Mike's anger came from concern—and that made it OK. "Mail, Super Jock."

A letter dropped on Mike's chest. He fought off a smile. "Damn, Danno. I have an easier time staying mad at a puppy." A smile broke through. "What'd I do to deserve you, anyway?" He rolled on his side, dog tags jingling. His quick hand grabbed the letter before it fell off the bunk.

"You're a lucky man, that's why," came the answer from below, muffled by the mattresses. Mike peered over the edge. All he could see of Danno was his back and rear. A long salt stain ran on either side of his spine. He was rummaging under the bed, shaking both bunks as he did.

"What're you doing?" Mike asked.

"Lookin' for somethin'." The bunk moved. "Ah ha!" Danno stood. "I found it!" He beamed and held up a rather large but thin book titled *Scottish Art and the 17th Century*.

"How do you sleep on all that stuff?"

"It's all this stuff that helps me sleep," Danno said, serious.

Mike nodded. He rolled on his back, careful to hold the precious letter. "Here I am, senior in rank to you and sleeping on the top rack because of your art books."

"Wanna trade places?"

"You kidding? I'm safer looking down Ho Chi Minh's gun barrel than I am sleeping under all your stuff."

"Also," Danno raised a finger, "if you were killed by my books falling on you, it would be difficult to justify you for another Navy Cross." Danno looked in the mirror above the sink and dragged a forefinger across his teeth.

"Hot date?"

"Headed to the library. Never know who'll be there."

"No doubt Sophia Loren between the pages of some Italian art book."

Danno patted Mike's arm. "If you don't spend more time in the library, you can change your last name from Chris-tum to Chris-dumb."

"I have something to read, thank you very much." Mike sniffed the letter.

"Showoff."

"Wanna go to the movie tonight?"

"Yeah. What's on?"

"Does it matter?"

"Good point." Danno closed the door as he left.

"Hey!"

Danno cracked the door and looked back in.

Mike's eyes softened. "Good to see you, Danno."

"Yeah. I know." The door closed.

Mike swung his legs over the side of the bunk and put the pink envelope on the skimpy pillow. The *Hawk* swallowed another catapult shot. He jumped to the deck and stripped off his flight suit, underwear, and socks. He stuffed the clothes into a nylon mesh bag. Standing naked on stout legs, he pushed his feet into rubber shower sandals and pulled a towel from a rack. His sandals flop-flopped as he walked down the passageway to the head.

The head smelled vaguely of old soap, urine, and puke. The puke was usually from a new guy who had just flown his first combat mission, sometimes from an old guy who'd barely made it back.

He stepped into a shower stall so small that if he dropped anything, he'd have to step out to pick it up. "Damn," he said as he hit his head while trying to bend over far enough to reach his knees. He ran only enough water to wet his body. He lathered with a soap-on-a-rope, then turned on a stingy stream to rinse. He combed his hair, repacked his dop kit, and walked back to his stateroom, leaving wet spots on the blue linoleum passageway.

He put on a fresh pair of jockey shorts and a T-shirt and

climbed into his bunk. He fluffed the pillow against the bulk-head. Nothing gave him greater pleasure than the letters from Kachina, his best friend, soulmate, lover, and wife of four years. He pressed his lips on the upside-down stamp. He pictured her sitting on the edge of their high granny bed after writing the letter. Her smooth round bottom caused folds in the thick comforter as soft light from the country lamp revealed the sheen of slender legs that reached the floor on tiptoes. The beige nightie flowed off a shoulder and around her curves. A postage stamp lay beside her. Her hand reached for it, and she picked it up as though plucking the reflection of a star from the surface of a pond. She looked over her breasts—down at herself, long eyelashes brushing high cheekbones. Her legs spread apart. She lifted the ruffled edge of her garment and pressed the stamp against her wet place. "O-o-o-h," he said, without knowing it. Kachina placed the stamp on the enve-lope. He remembered—and he could feel her body as it pulled him into a world of warm, moist, pliable ripples that engulfed his soul and floated him on rolling waves of impossible plea-sure. Pain fluttered across his face as he imagined things he couldn't touch. His body ached as Kachina leaned from the letter and sighed, her breath a warm breeze around his heart.

The catapult thumped.

He jerked up.

His head banged against the overhead and bounced back to the pillow. He threw a forearm across his eyes and wished the ship would just go away. He wished he were magically flown back to the granny bed where he could fall asleep—nothing more, just fall asleep as he held her.

1972, WEDNESDAY, 5 APRIL
0955 HOURS (9:55 AM)

The sky was clear and blue with round clouds evenly spaced apart at the same altitude. Shadows from the clouds made large dark blue polka dots on the sea from horizon to horizon. The water between the dots sparkled in the brilliant sunlight, and the wind blew cozy over the waves.

The *Hawk* turned her massive bulk into the wind. The ship was so ponderous and her turn so steady that it was impossible to feel it move, as if the carrier were stationary and the world turned around it. Two A-7 fighters composing Canasta Flight stood ready for takeoff. Mike was Canasta 301 and flew flight lead. Danno was Canasta 302.

Mike sat in his open cockpit with arms resting on the canopy rails, waiting for a hookup to the left catapult. The scratchy sounds of his radio; the smell of plastic and sweat; the bite of straps, belts, snaps, pistol, and helmet; and the sharp taste of anticipation assaulted his senses. He scanned the expanse of the *Hawk's* flat top. Steam wafted from the catapult and rolled a few feet down the deck before it disappeared into thin air. Men wore helmets and vests of different colors and moved around with hurried, deliberate purpose. In all directions, the black deck broke off in crisp edges and sharp angles. Mike felt like he was in one of his toy airplanes that sat on Mom's black coffee table as it moved across the blue living-room carpet.

He glimpsed the sleek outline of a cruiser cutting the water two thousand yards away. Its job was to protect the battle group from enemy airplanes. Beyond the cruiser, a frigate maneuvered as the carrier's first line of surface defense. A frigate was so small that none of its crew would survive a hit by a modern torpedo. In the galley of that little ship were cooks who were as brave as anyone who manned a gun, and in as much danger.

Mike rolled his head against the headrest and breathed in the scent of the sea. He closed his eyes and pictured a blanket spread on the ground in the Appalachian woods. He knelt there as Kachina lay beside him, blouse open and skirt raised around her hips. White panties were a small memory at her side. Sunbeams filtered through the sugar maples and dappled her breasts. The sound of her breathing folded with the breeze that glided among the wildflowers. Her sweet musky fragrance mingled with the aroma of the rich earth. He straddled her, took her face in his hands, and kissed her forehead. Lissome arms wrapped around his neck as he kissed each cheek and felt her—

What! … Who? A deck hand stood in the middle of a steam cloud and motioned him to move. Mike flinched as the sight of metal warplanes on the steel deck punched his reverie away. He looked to his right. Danno was there, in his A-7, smiling as always. Mike gave a thumbs-up.

Danno nodded, returned the thumbs-up, then attached his oxygen mask and lowered his canopy. Mike followed suit. He advanced his throttle and responded to the deck hand's directions.

The deck crew positioned the fighter's nose gear over the catapult's shuttle. They locked it in.

Mike saluted and forced his head hard against the headrest. He was ready.

In less than a second, the pressure in the catapult's piston reached its trigger level.

The shuttle broke its restraining device and tore toward the end of the deck, taking the A-7 with it. In the time it takes to swat a fly, Mike and his bomb-laden airplane were doing more than a hundred and forty nautical miles per hour just above the sea. A second later the *Hawk* shot Danno and his A-7 off the deck, too. The fighters were now in their element, flying in the blue sky among the shafts of sunlight and over the dark blue polka dots.

Mike glanced over his shoulder. Danno's airplane was a few feet away. He gave a thumbs-up. Mike returned the gesture and brought his attention back to the cockpit. He pressed buttons that displayed his route to the target and showed what ordnance he carried. He ran a finger down the target sheet and studied a topographical navigation map. His mind raced ahead to the target and the coming images of billowing fire and streaking tracers; tiny people in black pajamas shooting rifles at him; his own 30-millimeter cannon shells streaking toward the ground, cutting human beings into pieces.

Behind, on the flight deck, the memory of Kachina swirled with the steam of the catapult, then vanished. In the cockpit, her husband's lips hardened and creases formed between his eyes. Mike Christum put on his game face.

Ahead lay a savage storm, a storm that rained fire and steel.

1972, WEDNESDAY, 5 APRIL
1810 HOURS (6:10 PM)

Tiny ringing sounds filled the dim stateroom. Mike hunched over the foldout desk, writing. Light from a small lamp slanted across him and sunk into the dark corners. The beam shone hard on his red eyes, the craggy lines on his face, and the salt stains that ringed the armpits of his flight suit. Behind him, on Danno's bunk, sat two open cardboard boxes. One was filled with clothing that included a flowered Hawaiian shirt folded beside a flight suit. The other box contained letters, books, and other personal things. *Scottish Art and the 17th Century* was on top.

Built into the bulkhead at the foot of the bunks were two tall wall lockers. The door of one was open, and it swung back and forth with the rolling of the ship. Inside the locker, empty coat hangers pivoted on the rack and touched their ends together. They made the ringing sound.

A month before this day, a 37-millimeter anti-aircraft shell was built on the outskirts of Leningrad in a factory run by a father of three. It was packed in a wooden crate by the mother of a little girl and sent by ship to Haiphong, North Vietnam. When it got there, it was off-loaded by a crew of teenagers and trucked to People's Defense Site #23 by the son of a farmer. This morning a former college student shot it from a gun. It left the barrel at three times the speed of sound and arced to a rendezvous with an A-7. It entered the airplane that was crafted by people in Texas who had tucked their children in their beds a few hours earlier. Tomorrow they would start a new day building more A-7s.

The shell didn't explode as it entered the fighter. It broke apart and sprayed white-hot shrapnel into the main fuel tank.

The cockpit bulkhead split.

Flaming jet fuel curled around the ejection seat and Danno Riley before it splashed against the instrument panel.

Fire tore away Danno's clothing.

Nylon parachute straps melted and flowed down his chest and between his legs in tiny rivers that popped and flamed with black smoke.

He jerked at the ejection handles.

The seat failed.

He jerked again, and again, and again, while his airplane yawed and pitched through the sky.

As his helmet visor became a sheet of molten bubbles, Danno put his hands back on the stick and the throttle. The A-7 stopped its gyration and rolled in a sweeping arc toward Earth. He would not die like those in the photos—distorted, Picasso-like figures whose silent, charred mouths shrieked their last agonizing seconds of life while their bowels squirted from their cindered buttocks. He would die as a man, as a pilot, as an American warrior.

He jammed the throttle forward.

He dove while he watched the jungle rush up. The A-7 shot through the humid sky leaving a lazy trail of burned fuel and seared flesh.

Flames licked across his visor, and fire sliced through his oxygen mask and pulsed into his throat, turning pink lung to black rubber.

A silent explosion of white light filled his vision, and his pain vanished. "Please, God, tell them I love—"

Danno and his airplane blasted through the branches of the jungle trees and buried themselves among the shadows.

Mike stopped writing and held the stationery closer to the light. With hard eyes he read what he had just written. "Damn." He rolled the sheet into a ball and threw it to the side where it landed near two identical paper balls. He pulled another sheet from a drawer.

Dearest Alice,
Only God knows how I hate having to write this letter and pack these boxes. Today was a bad day. You lost your husband, your kids lost their father, and I lost my friend.

He bowed his head while the *Hawk* thumped another airplane toward North Vietnam. He continued:

Danno was special and he meant so very much to so very many.

Mike's hand covered the paper and ground it in his fist. Another paper ball bounced on the floor.

He opened the drawer again. One sheet remained. He laid it on the desk and poised his pen above it. He stared somewhere in the distance as he thought about the day. In one of the ten thousand horrors of the Vietnam War, he and Danno were sent to bomb a small bridge that crossed a small river near the small town of Thanh Son. To get to the small bridge, they flew over large ships that carried large battle tanks to the large harbor of Haiphong. Danno died while the two of them carried bombs through the most hostile sky in history to bomb nothing but a little bridge. Mike used a knuckle to wipe beneath one eye. He wrote:

Dearest Alice,
This morning we received intelligence reports that tanks were moving south to assault a Marine position. I tried to get through low clouds to stop them. I couldn't, so Danno went in. I saw the flashes of his bombs, but he never came up. This afternoon we got word that he stopped the tanks.
Danno saved a lot of lives today. Dan Junior and

Teri are too young to understand, but someday they will know that their father gave his life so others could live. I pray that those in our country who hate us for what they've asked us to do can appreciate that. Kachina will call you.
My love to you all,
Mike

He threw the pen down. What am I supposed to tell them, anyway, that her husband and their daddy lost his life while bombing a footbridge?

He picked up the pen again. At the bottom of the letter he drew a hand with the thumb, forefinger, and pinkie outstretched, the two other fingers folded against the palm. Danno had been teaching Uncle Mike how to sign, and this was a special message for Teri. It said, "I love you." He imagined her, sitting beside Alice, as her mother read this letter—tiny little tennis shoes on outstretched legs not reaching the edge of the sofa, a large hearing aid behind each ear, and pretty brown eyes made huge by thick glasses—wondering what was happening.

Mike put the letter on the flowered shirt. As he closed the box flaps over the letter, he thought of dirt falling from the sides of a grave. "Bye, Danno," he said as he stretched masking tape over the box.

The coat hangers in the empty wall locker pealed for another young man's clothing.

1972, MONDAY, 11 APRIL
2110 HOURS (9:10 PM)

"Excuse me. Lieutenant Christum?" The voice came from behind. "I'm Lieutenant JG Billy Jones, your new bunkmate."

Mike stood alone in the Ready Room and stared at a vacant white movie screen. Beside him, a film projector hummed while its take-up reel twirled a length of film that slapped the table several times a second.

"Lieutenant Christum?" Jones' hand touched Mike's shoulder. Mike spun around and glared. The young man staggered back a half step, eyes wide.

Mike's face softened. "I … I'm …"

"You OK, sir?" the Junior Grade asked.

"I'm sorry." Mike put his hand on the man's shoulder. "Please don't take this personally. We'll be fine. I just can't talk right now." He pushed by the JG and left the room.

Billy watched him walk down the dim passageway, then looked at the running projector. He stopped the machine, rewound the film, rethreaded it, and pressed "Start." It was a news clip. War images moved on the screen, then changed to swearing young Americans waving North Vietnamese flags while they urinated on Old Glory. The last scene was of a movie star squinting through the sights of a 37-millimeter anti-aircraft gun. She looked up at her North Vietnamese Army hosts, her face gleeful. She mouthed, "Oh, how exciting!"

Billy stared at the vacant white screen while the tail of the film moved through the projector and twirled again on the take-up reel.

1972, MONDAY, 15 MAY
0515 HOURS (5:15 AM)
WAILUA
KAUAI, HAWAII

Mike stood behind the rain-spattered sliding glass door and watched the pre-dawn sky change color. The horizon wiggled as waves bounced on the edge of a far reef. "Thank you, God," he whispered. "Of all things you have blessed me with, this woman is the most precious." He leaned his forehead against the glass. "Thank you. Thank you. Thank you."

There was a rustle behind him. Kachina rolled beneath the sheet, exposing her shoulder. He turned away from the slider, leaned down, and eased the sheet to cover her exposed skin, then tucked it beneath the pillow and caressed her hair.

He looked back at the brightening sky. Rose-colored light bathed his face with warmth that conflicted with his growing melancholy. It seemed like yesterday that they met at the Honolulu airport, she having flown from home via San Francisco and he from the *Kitty Hawk* via Manila. Washington let its Vietnam soldiers, sailors, marines, and airmen take two weeks in the middle of the war for R&R, rest and relaxation. It seemed like a good idea two weeks ago. Now, Mike wasn't so sure. Two weeks ago I destroyed a convoy and killed people. Today I'll make love to Kachina. Tomorrow I'll kiss her goodbye. Day after tomorrow I'll kill again. This makes no sense. He turned his back on the sunrise and shook his head to force the thought away, to defend himself against the depression that rushed at him with the sun as it rose above the reef to both give and steal another day. He thought about dinner last night.

He assured himself the restaurant's tablecloth hid his hand as he inched it between her legs to lift the edge of her panties away from her inner thigh. He touched her with a fingertip and her soft skin yielded its wet fold. She closed her eyes, held her breath. He withdrew his hand and immersed his fingertip in his water glass, then drank. "Chateau Kachina, vintage year." He winked.

Kachina opened her eyes and looked at him as he held his water glass with curled fingers, debonair cool. "I think … you just … drank your finger bowl."

He blushed as he put his hand to his forehead. "What a bozo," he whispered.

He watched the rhythm of her breathing as she lay there. He loved her the instant he saw her, that first time, in Pensacola. His heart blew away, a dandelion on the honey wind, as he knelt beside her to pick up the tomatoes, oranges, and grapefruit that rolled on the sidewalk in front of the grocery store. "It happens all the time," she said, her cheeks glowing with embarrassment. "I'm such a klutz."

Her parents had died some years before. She had worked her way through college and was on her way to a master's degree in business. They stood before the Justice of the Peace two weeks later, and Mike's parents had accepted her, not just as an in-law, but as a daughter. Life with her was full of love, laughter, and passion—interrupted only by carrier cruises and the silence that came after the occasional shattering of a dropped dining plate on the kitchen floor. "I'm such a klutz," she'd always say.

Her name came from the Pueblo and meant "spirit of life." She had more good in her than any person he'd ever known— good that glowed from her soul and through her beautiful features and bathed him with a spiritual and loving warmth. He often felt inept because he couldn't find words that satisfied him—satisfied him that he was expressing the depth of his feelings. So he improvised ways to show his love for her. He didn't know it, but Kachina understood his love language better than he did. No words he could speak carried deeper meaning than the boyish ingenuity of his I-love-you schemes.

His eyes softened as he looked at the red hair that flowed around her face and across the pillow. She had small hands with elegant fingers. Her eyelids closed over the only midnight blue eyes he had ever seen. The skin on her face had a luster that accentuated high cheekbones and the gentle hollows of her jaw. Her right cheek held a dimple—her left cheek held none. He often imagined the wry smile on God's face as He plucked back the dimple on her left cheek in an impulsive last-minute touch of creativity.

Mike picked up the edge of the sheet and pulled it toward the foot of the bed, careful not to wake her. Kachina lay motionless and watched him through barely open eyelids. She fought off a giggle. The receding fold revealed round breasts with small nipples that were slightly darker than her skin, a wondrous color of cream blended with buckskin. The fold moved farther down and exposed a discrete sprinkling of softhued freckles. A band of more closely spaced freckles lay across her hips between her pubic area and her belly button to form the most natural of bikini bottoms. The sheet lifted along her hairless legs and fell to the floor at the end of the bed … all without waking her. Boy, was he good.

She smiled.

"Nuts," he whispered.

He thought that God must have created Kachina on His day of rest while He listened to His favorite records on the stereo. To Mike Christum, the Seventh Day was more creative than all the others put together.

"I have a surprise for you," he said.

"Oh, Michael, really. I think I know all your tricks by now." She rolled to her back and revealed the full length of her body while she stretched.

He opened a dresser drawer and withdrew a small box from which he retrieved a single pearl with no mounting and no chain. She cocked her head, a question on her face. He sat on the bed beside her and, with the pearl between his thumb and forefinger, held it between them so that he looked past the pearl into her eyes. "I want you to wear this," he said.

"When?"

"Now."

"How? There's no chain."

He put his hands under her knees, lifted, and spread them apart. He touched the pearl to her most private place. She relaxed and allowed Mike to push the pearl into her while she enfolded his finger with warm wet pressure. He watched her eyes close and her hands claw the bed sheet into knots.

They made love with the pearl inside her as the sun rose from the ocean, pushed the laughing rain away, and spread its golden glow over the vaulting green mountains that rose toward rich rolling clouds.

1972, Tuesday, 16 May
1313 Hours (1:13 PM)
Honolulu International Airport, Hawaii

The airline ticket agent had just made the last boarding call on the PA system. Mike and Kachina stood, holding each other. Tears glided down her cheeks, and her quiet sobs rolled through both their bodies. His head was lowered to her shoulder, and his face was buried in her hair.

"We have to hurry," Mike whispered. "Here, I have something for you." He eased her away, reached into his pocket, and pulled out a familiar ring box. He opened it and retrieved a delicate chain that was threaded through a mounting that held …

"The pearl!" Kachina gasped, eyes wide. "I forgot. … How did you? … When did you? …"

"Shh." Mike spun her around. He draped the chain around her neck and fastened the clasp while she held a damp ball of Kleenex. He turned her back and centered the pearl in her cleavage. He touched a finger to the tip of her nose. "My number-one goal in life is to make you a choker."

"Ohhhh," she moaned as she threw her arms around his neck and squeezed until her knuckles were white. He closed his eyes as he held her. She felt so fragile.

He heard a cough from his right. The ticket agent stood beside an open jetway door.

Kachina pulled her face away. She sniffed at her wet ball of Kleenex. With a scolding frown she pointed at his nose. "When did you? …"

"Superglue," Mike said, beaming.

"That and a congenital sneakiness," she sniffed.

The ticket agent mouthed, "Ple-e-ease."

Kachina started to speak, but Mike interrupted her. "You have to go, honey. We both have to go."

She kissed him on the lips and pulled away. Her hand drew a line down the scar to his chin. He kissed the end of his finger and pressed it on the tip of her nose. He watched her walk down the long square tube … watched her walk away and wondered if this would be the last time he'd ever see her.

"Sorry," the agent said as she eased the big door closed.

Mike stood at the terminal window and watched the 747 climb from the runway and turn out over the Pacific. Countless times since the war began, many United airplanes had taken off late because of lingering goodbyes, some of them the last goodbyes. United always found a way to make up for the lost time.

He stared into the wistful sky as the big jet got smaller. An elastic gossamer thread of his imagination stretched between them as she flew away, and in some way physically bound them and gave him a measure of comfort. Finally, the airliner disappeared above a cloud and the thread snapped—evaporated. He was alone. He held his fingertips to his nose, first the front of his fingers and then the back, and sniffed her lingering scent.

He walked away, down the long concourse, headed back to the *Kitty Hawk*, back to war.

1972, SATURDAY, 29 JULY
1940 HOURS (7:40 PM)
CHARLIE STATION, SOUTH CHINA SEA
USS KITTY HAWK

"What the heck's gotten into you?" Lt. Billy Jones asked. Mike sat beside him on the lower bunk, his hands trembling as he stripped the cellophane wrapping from the wooden box. "Here, let me help," Billy said as he reached for the box.

"I got it. I got it." Mike flung the clear crinkled plastic toward the wastebasket in the corner, but it made it only halfway before it expanded and fell to the floor.

"Do they sell those things at the geedunk?" Billy asked, referring to what can best be described as a 7-Eleven on a Navy ship.

"Naw. Got 'em from one of the guys."

Billy scratched his head. "One minute you're reading a letter from your wife, and the next you're acting like an idiot."

"Not an idiot," Mike said as he opened the box, withdrew

an ugly cigar, also wrapped in cellophane, and jammed it into Billy's open mouth. "I'm gonna be a daddy." He disappeared out the door and down the passageway. "Hey guys! Hey guys!"

Billy removed the cigar from his mouth and stripped away the saliva-covered plastic. He bit off the end and spit it at the wastebasket. It went in. "Hmmmm," he said as he leaned back. "Nice shot for both of us."

1983

SHAMAN

Sunbeams streamed between the leaves of a tree and through the window, and splashed off brass picture frames. The photos in the frames chronicled fifteen years of marriage and the gathering and growth of precious faces. One face was that of a red-haired boy whose image progressed from babbling innocence to boyhood mischief. They called him Scotty, after Mike's little brother. He was born following Mike's last Vietnam cruise. The other young face was Lisa Marie, now fourteen months old. Her blonde hair swirled around a delicate face punctuated by a small button-like nose. Scotty posed with a ball, or a bat, or something to hit something else with—the family jock. Lisa struck dramatic poses, like a midget opera singer—the family ham.

Mike and Kachina lay entangled, he on his back and she

on her side with her head on his chest. She stroked his graying hair. He caressed her skin. The passion of their lovemaking had melted into relaxed breathing. They fell into and out of sleep. A rosy glow brushed their cheeks. A peaceful smile deepened Kachina's dimple.

The irritating noise of the bedside phone scratched itself into their reverie. They ignored it. It stopped. Then the phone rang again. "It might be about Scotty, honey," Kachina pleaded.

Mike kissed her and reached for the phone. "Commander Christum," he answered. Mike said nothing. Finally, "Aye, aye, Skipper."

He put the phone in the cradle and rolled back to Kachina. He blew a rasping sound between her breasts while he held them against his cheeks. She tapped him on the head, a playful slap. "How come you always do that when you have to go somewhere?"

"Would you rather I do this?" he asked, straddling her and tickling her sides.

"Oh, I hate that," she laughed. She slipped a slender leg from beneath him, placed her foot on his chest, and shoved. He rolled backward, off the bed. His body thudded on the floor.

He lay still.

He waited for her to show concern. He opened his eyes just enough to see. Above him, just over the edge of the bed, Kachina peered down. "I'm on to that one, too, big boy." A splash of ice water hit him between the eyes. He gasped, sputtered, then stood. She rolled back on the bed to put the glass on the end table. She reached for the sheet. He snatched it from her grasp and held his arms out, his fingers moving like pincers. "Michael Christum, don't you dare!" She pulled her knees beneath her chin and wrapped her arms around her shins.

He dropped his outreached hands, and all his mock aggression melted away. He smiled at how she looked in her defensive posture. The curves of her buttocks blended into sleek calves and her breasts bulged against her uplifted thighs. Red hair flowed across her face and brushed her buckskin-tinted shoulders. A blue eye opened. She smiled. She released her shins and relaxed her legs. She lay back and spread her arms. He lay upon her. She wrapped her arms around his neck. As he kissed her, he glimpsed the clock. He pushed away.

"I gotta go."

She locked her legs around him. "Tell the Navy I need you more than they do."

"I know you do, but the Navy can send me to jail."

"I can make things worse than that," she cooed as she kissed him on the cheek, then smacked him on the butt. "Anchors aweigh, sailor."

Mike hit the shower, hustled into his khakis, and headed out the door after kissing her goodbye.

Kachina lay on her side and stared at nothing. When he'd carried her to the bedroom, she'd expected an afternoon alone with her husband. Small orgasmic aftershocks still stirred her body, but she was surrounded by loneliness. She rolled her head back as she remembered how it felt to have her husband hold her, how it felt to run among the stars as he moved within her. From the hallway of her mind, his "I love you" echoed, as it had moments before from the hallway of their home. She sniffed at the lingering scent of his aftershave and pictured his loving eyes as they looked at her from beneath the bill of his cap just before he left. For an instant she wondered about his eyes as they stared through a gunsight. Did they squint? Did they flinch as he pulled the trigger and killed people whose names he didn't know? Did they show fear as they watched a friend die? She blinked the vision away.

Memories, she knew, were like footprints on the beach, and she fought the erosive wind of time that blew across them. She fought to savor the feelings, smells, sights, sounds, tastes, and thoughts of the time they had just shared. She had done this so many times—so many times. The cold steel of a chain-link fence of the past pushed its way into her memory. It put red marks on her fingers as she clutched the interwoven wire. She stood there and watched as her beloved and his airplane hurled down the runway and into the sky, flame and thunder behind them. She knew that everything he touched or saw, everything that moved him faster or slower, everything that sent him up and held him down tried to kill him. How was it possible that his great joy of flight was her great fear? How was it possible that their marriage and their love could survive the partings? It all frightened her, a fear she could never reveal to him. Kachina pulled the sheets to her bosom, folded her knees to her chest, and touched the still-warm depression on the pillow next to hers.

Mike pulled into the parking space beside the squadron building reserved for him as squadron Executive Officer, or second in command. The parking lot was empty except for one other car and a Harley-Davidson Sportster parked in the Commanding Officer slot.

Chris Patterakis' motorcycle gleamed in the sun, and a steady drip of oil added to an old black spot that got a little larger each day. The cycle was unique, like its owner. While the exhaust notes of the Japanese-made "crotch rockets" that other men owned blended with the sounds of the jets on the base, Patterakis and his Harley thumped around, sprinting dinosaurs on missions of importance. The word dinosaur fit Patterakis. He was an outstanding leader and a superb aviator—a warrior to the core. However, it was peacetime, and Patterakis' direct apolitical manner with his superiors seemed to relegate him to a place in history—or a place in the future—rather than the present. He was the kind of man the peacetime military would have liked to store in a glass case with a sign that read "In Case of War, Break Glass." If the truth were known, that's the way Patterakis would want it, too. Of course, the glass case would have to be big enough to hold the Harley.

Mike walked to the squadron building under a blue canopy. He pressed the button beside the front door. A petty officer pushed the door open and held it with the panic bar. "Afternoon, Commander Christum."

"Hi, Sandy. You and the Skipper the only ones here today?"

"Yes, sir. Skipper's in his office," Sandy said as she tugged on the door until the latch set.

"Thanks." Mike walked down a long unlit hallway, his footsteps making the only sound in the building. Sunlight came through an opaque window at the end of the hall and accentuated the slight bumps and dimples in the linoleum. Near the end warm light from an open door spilled out. Mike walked by his own office, turned at the light, and knocked.

"Come in, XO," came a voice. The office was typical of military self-help decoration. Sailors from years gone by had painted the walls light blue. Framed lithographs of Navy ships and airplanes broke the blue tedium, but added a monotony of their own. A block of teakwood was front and center on the desk, with Chris Patterakis carved into it. Beneath the name was his call sign, Harley. When the carver questioned why the call sign wasn't Zorba or Greek, Patterakis growled, "Because I'm an American. That's why." The carver didn't ask again.

Patterakis sat behind the desk, trim and muscular. Gray streaks made tight swirls in his curly black hair. He started to say something but stopped. He grinned as he stood and tugged at his waistband, an old habit. He pressed a button on his phone. "Petty Officer Cook. Commander Christum and I are not to be bothered until further notice."

A metallic voice shot back, "Aye, aye, sir."

Patterakis motioned. "Follow me, XO. You're either going to love or hate this."

He stopped at a door on the other side of the office and realized Mike wasn't following. "Well?"

"You want me to follow you?" Mike frowned at the door that led to a small closet.

"Well you never hesitated to follow me before," Patterakis said with a smile.

"You never asked me to share a closet with you, either."

"You'd rather follow me into combat than into a small closet?"

Mike thought for a moment. "Damned right I would. You're Greek."

Patterakis laughed. "Come on. I'll behave." He opened the wooden door while still chuckling, then tugged at the shelves inside. The shelves swung away, and behind them was another wooden door. Patterakis pulled on the second door's handle. As it opened, Mike saw that it was disguised, steel, and about three inches thick.

"Here, watch out," Patterakis said, a finger pointed to a high metal sill. "Knee knocker, there."

Mike stepped over the high steel threshold. Patterakis closed the hatch behind them and took a chair behind a small desk. Mike sat in a chair in front of the desk. The little room reminded him of a space aboard a carrier with its gray walls, linoleum floor, and a naked lightbulb that shone through the metal grate of an industrial-type fixture mounted in the center of the ceiling. A scrambler telephone sat on the edge of the desk. "This is a little weird, Chris," he said, amused.

"Think so?"

"How long has this—"

"I'm shipping out in a week and you're coming with me," Patterakis interrupted. His face was impassive as he considered the man who was the best pilot he had ever known.

"Skipper, we just got back from cruise," Mike said, more firmly than he should have.

"We're not going on cruise," Patterakis responded. He paused as if not knowing how to begin. Finally, with a what-the-hell shrug, he continued. "Mike," he said, "this is a 'quiet room.'"

"Got that."

"The CIA built it."

"Really." Slight sarcasm from Mike.

"I just made Captain."

Mike jerked with surprise. "Well, that's great!" He extended his hand. "Damned good news. Nobody deserves it more than you do, Skipper."

Patterakis shook Mike's hand, but didn't smile. "I'm getting a new command, and you're coming with me."

Mike was bewildered. Normally, when a CO moved on,

his XO took his place. Mike's chance to have a command just evaporated, at least for a while. "Skipper?"

Patterakis held up his hand. "Don't get upset. Yet." He picked up the scrambler phone and dialed. After a few seconds he spoke.

"Rhombus."

A few more seconds.

"Alpha."

Patterakis withdrew a code booklet from a drawer and opened it. He also retrieved a thin metal device about the shape and size of a half-foot ruler. The device had a notch along one side and three square holes in it. Placing the notch over one of the code letters in the book's margin, he studied the letters revealed by the holes. He spoke into the phone, "I authenticate Romeo Golf." Patterakis listened, then, "He's here. Yes, sir. Here," he said as he handed Mike the phone. "Someone wants to talk with you."

Mike put the phone to his ear. His eyes widened, and his jaw fell slack. "Yes, sir. Yes, sir. Well. Yes, sir. Goodbye, sir." Mike lowered the phone to his lap. Patterakis pointed to the receiver. Mike blinked himself back to reality and handed the phone back. "I'll be damned." Then, looking at Patterakis, "I'll be damned."

Patterakis grinned, relishing Mike's response to the phone call. "How does it feel to be so popular?"

The shock fell away, and Mike squinted. "You're having a good time with this, aren't you?"

"Yeah. I guess I am." Patterakis pointed to Mike's chair. "A month or so ago I sat there," he said, then pointed to his own chair, "while an Admiral sat here. Sitting here is more fun than sitting there, I have to say." Patterakis frowned. "Besides, it makes up for your lousy Greek jokes."

"You sure?"

"No," Patterakis responded. "But it's a start. You have a long way to go." His smile evaporated. "You and I, especially you"—he pointed at Mike—"are headed into the jaws of the devil, and we're taking every man, woman, and child in this country with us. The bottom line is, we're at the brink. You and I are either going to bring down the Soviet Union or we're going to start World War Three."

Mike's face blanched. Patterakis' preposterous statement became very real when put in the context of the telephone conversation. A chill oozed from the room's steel walls and sank into his bones. The afternoon of lovemaking and military repartee had become foreboding. The only movement in the room was that of their chests as they breathed.

Breaking the silence, Patterakis said, "Will you bear with me for a moment? I want to go over something very elementary with you to make a point. OK?"

"Aye. Sure," Mike responded.

"What is the war doctrine that keeps us and the Soviet Union from fighting each other?" Patterakis asked.

"MAD. Mutually Assured Destruction."

"And why does it work?"

"Because it's suicide."

"Why?"

"Because," Mike said, "our power is roughly in balance with theirs. If either of us launches against the other, the other side will see the launch and retaliate. About ten minutes after the first launch, forty or fifty thousand warheads will be passing in space while we mark the rest of our lives on an egg timer."

"Illustrate that, if you would," Patterakis said.

"Well …" Mike thought for a moment. "It's like you and I were each sitting on an armed bomb. Under my butt is a trigger attached to your bomb, and under your butt is a trigger attached to mine. So if you shoot me, I fall off my bomb, release my trigger, and blow you up. You won't shoot me because it's suicide for you. You can't win."

Patterakis nodded.

"Well," Mike continued, "ever since the Cuban missile crisis, we and the Soviet Union have not directly confronted each other because of MAD, so it's worked."

"But," said Patterakis as he held up a finger for effect, "what if you discovered a gadget that would disable the trigger I have to your bomb?"

"I'd build it."

"Why? So you could blow me up?"

"No, because if I discovered the secret, so could you, and I can't let you have it if I don't."

"Paranoia?" Patterakis asked.

"Perhaps, but I think a better description is prudence."

"So it's prudent to go ahead and build your gadget?"

Mike nodded.

"And what if I find out that you have the gadget?"

Mike was quiet for a moment. "Uh oh."

"Why uh oh?" Patterakis asked.

"Because, if you discover I have it and you don't, you have only one defense against me."

"What's that?"

"You have to shoot me," Mike responded.

"But if I shoot you, you'll fall off the trigger and set my bomb off."

"You have to take that chance. If you wait, I can kill you when I choose. If you shoot, maybe my trigger won't work. No matter how you look at it, shooting me is the only play you've got."

"So," Patterakis said, "you have no choice but to build the gadget once you've discovered the secret."

"Right."

"And I have no choice but to shoot you if I discover that you have it, right?"

"Right."

"Now, if the United States discovers the secret gadget, what are the odds we can keep our discovery from the Soviet Union?"

"None," Mike responded. "No matter how hard we try, they'll find out, eventually."

"So what you're saying is, the countdown to World War Three begins from the moment we discover a gadget that can render Soviet defenses useless."

"Yes," Mike responded. He looked at Patterakis and waited

for another question. Something nagged him … the secret room, … and that phone call … and what was it Patterakis said about the two of them either bringing down the Soviet Union or causing World War Three? The marrow in his bones froze. "No-o-o," he said. He sat at attention. "No-o-o-o-o."

"Yes." A firm response.

"We have the gadget?"

"We have the gadget."

"Dear God. Help us." Mike's shoulders fell.

"It gets better or worse, depending on how you see it," Patterakis continued.

"How should I see it?"

"From its cockpit."

"From its cockpit? I don't under—"

"You know that gadget we've been talking about?" Patterakis interrupted.

"Yes."

"You'll be flying it."

Mike's emotions bounced to the extreme, steel balls ricocheting off the side of the pinball machine, bells ringing with the promise of adventure and the prospect of danger.

The pilot-child in him laughed with the thought of flying what few, or perhaps no one, had ever flown before. Oh, the rapture of flying higher, farther, faster, of seeing things unseen, and feeling things unfelt, and hearing things unheard. It was joy beyond comprehension.

The father in him recoiled at what his wife and children would feel as they watched the nuclear fire of his creation. What scene would glint from their eyes as they awaited the coming blast wave? Where would they turn as Armageddon lunged for them with open jaws? Mike didn't know whether to rejoice or throw up.

Patterakis knocked on the door of his thoughts. "The airplane is called Rhombus, Mike." He knew Patterakis was talking, but his body wouldn't respond. His brain wouldn't shatter the image of the crimson blast wave tearing the clothes off Kachina and their children as it broke their grasp on each other and hurled them away, each dying alone on a different part of the boiling street as they wondered where Daddy was.

"Mike," Patterakis said. Mike didn't respond. "Hey! You with me?"

Mike exhaled hard as he let go of the breath and the image he'd been holding. "Oh …" Composure returned. "Aye, Skipper, I'm with you."

Patterakis raised an eyebrow.

"I'm fine," Mike reassured him. "Want me to insult you with a Greek joke as proof?"

Patterakis shook his head. "I've been meaning to ask you," he said. "Did you know that a West Virginian invented the toothbrush?"

Mike squinted. "And?"

"If anybody else had done it, they'd call it a teeth brush." Patterakis beamed, satisfied.

Mike stared. "I'd like to register your insult on my heritage with the appropriate authorities." He and Patterakis broke into snickers like two men pouring shots of Jack Daniels to break the tension.

"We're moving," Patterakis said, pulling things back to business. "You and I and a select few others will move our families to Las Vegas. Everyone not connected with Rhombus will be told we're working with the Air Force and flying A-7s at Nellis Air Force Base. Actually, we'll shuttle between Nellis and a secret facility called Groom Lake Base, which is about a hundred miles north of Vegas. In most cases, we'll live at Groom Lake during the week and be home on weekends. We'll be involved with Rhombus for up to five years. People who are selected for this assignment won't be transferred nor will they be allowed to resign from the Navy."

"They can't force us to stay in the Navy, can they?" Mike asked.

"Yes, they can," Patterakis responded. "Think of Rhombus Ops as being in a state of war with the Soviet Union."

Mike blinked, silent.

"And forcing us to stay in the Navy isn't all they can do in a state of war." Patterakis paused. "Which brings me to my next point." He pulled a folder from a drawer and let it flop onto the desk where it sent a little puff that ruffled a small stack of papers. "Yours," he said, tapping the folder with his index finger. "That gentleman you just talked with has a copy, too. He also has a file on each man involved with Rhombus. I'm telling you this because you need to understand that everything you do, everything you say, and everywhere you go for the next five years may be monitored by someone else. An elite network of security people has been set up. Its only responsibility is to keep Rhombus secret. That network is called the Tango Team."

Mike said nothing.

"Mike." Patterakis took a deep breath. "Do you understand what it means if someone without clearance finds out about this airplane? It means that soon after the secret gets back to the Soviet Union, twenty-four thousand nuclear warheads will be headed our way."

Mike nodded. "Yeah, I get the picture." The images of Kachina and their children rushed back.

"It means something else, too. It means that any American ..." Patterakis paused. "Anybody without a clearance who discovers Rhombus will be executed—on the spot, if possible."

Mike stared at the floor and picked at his fingernails. The room was filled with the hum of the ventilating fan. The fan worked because somewhere an American monitored a plant that made electricity. That American and about 250 million others were going about their lives unaware that he and Patterakis sat in a small room in Alameda, California, and discussed how everyone was going to die.

"Damn," he said. "There was a time when we went off to war and said goodbye to our wives and kids. I think we've brought the war to them."

"Sure have," Patterakis responded. "War at our doorsteps." He sat for a moment and watched Mike. "Maybe that's what we need to stop the insanity." Mike didn't respond. "You'll have your orders on Monday. Go home. Tell Kachina you love her. Hug your children. Call God on the private line and ask him to help us do this right, to help us through the night. Whether this leads to war or a better world depends on us, a little luck, and, mostly, the grace of God." Patterakis looked away and, as though Mike wasn't there, mumbled, "God have mercy on us." Then back to Mike. "See you Monday morning. That is all."

Mike stood to leave.

"Two more things," Patterakis called after him. Mike's hand paused on the hatch. "One, drive around until you get that shocked expression off your face. And two, your new assignment brings you a new call sign."

"It's taken me twelve years since flight training to get used to Hillbilly."

"Well," Patterakis said, "your new call sign is spelled S-H-A-M-A-N. I don't know if you pronounce it shay-man or shaw-man."

"I know the word," said Mike. "Kachina taught it to me. Did you know she's part Cherokee?"

"No."

"She pronounces it shaw-mun, with the accent on the first syllable. The term is used by Native Americans to describe the tribal member who acts as a medium between the visible world and the invisible spirit world."

Patterakis shrugged.

Mike grinned. "Medicine Man to you."

"Oh," Chris said as he closed the folder. "Sounds like a promotion to me." He smiled. "See ya Monday, Shaman."

"Aye, aye, Skipper."

"Hi, Sailor," Kachina purred as she threw her arms around Mike's neck.

"And what've you been doing while I've been with Patterakis?" Mike asked.

"Stock market."

"Yeah? How we doin'?"

"The market's not super, but we're doing great." She put a finger to the tip of his nose. "We'll have our little home on the high meadow, Michael."

He kissed her forehead. "That brain and the business degree are an awesome mix. Sure you don't want to go back to work?"

"Nope." She tossed her head. "Not until the kids are raised and gone. Besides, our stocks don't take much of my time." Mike felt like weeping. How was it God made someone like this? Beauty, brains, dedication to being a mother—sexy as all hell. He put his arms around her and held her. Not so much as a lover, not so much as a husband, but as a friend with deep admiration and loving respect. He didn't know what he'd done to deserve her. It saddened him somewhat that how she was put together was a mystery he'd never solve. She pulled back. "And what was so important that Patterakis couldn't wait till Monday?" she teased.

"The President's busy Monday." He swooped her up and carried her down the hall, into the bedroom. "You and I are going to have another powwow."

Kachina nibbled his earlobe.

"By the way," Mike said, "we're moving again."

"What!" She took off his cap and swatted him with it.

"Ow!"

"Where to?"

"Las Vegas."

The playfulness in her eyes vanished. "No kidding." It wasn't a question.

"No kidding."

She put his cap back on his head, crooked. Mike's face strained a bit as he put her down. They sat together on the bed, legs dangling over its edge, two kids who had just missed the bus to Disneyland.

She put her hand on his thigh, then looked away, toward the brass-framed pictures. Tears welled in her eyes while her lips hardened. "What did you volunteer for this time?"

"I didn't. I—"

"I don't want to go to Las Vegas."

"The Navy needs—"

"Both these children have allergies, and—"

"I know it's an Air Force town, but—"

"And I don't know about the schools. What kind of place is that to raise children, anyway. I mean—"

"Besides, anything is better than going on cruise. Right? I think we'll enjoy—"

"Neil and June—you remember Neil and June? They were billeted there, and their sons had awful allergies. One was so bad that they—"

Then, silence.

They looked at the floor. "We did that thing again," Mike said.

"What thing again?"

"We talked past each other."

She stood. "Good thing we're not unpacked from the last move, yet." She strode across the room, dragged a box from the closet to the dresser, opened all the drawers, and threw socks, underwear, negligees, a jogging suit, and a stream of other items into it. She reached for the jewelry box.

Mike leapt from the bed and stood beside her. He held her hands around the box, firm but gentle, so she couldn't let go. She looked at where they touched—at the contrast between the color and texture of their skin, the difference between his strength and her delicacy, their wedding bands. "I don't want to do this," she said as she leaned into him, her head against his chest.

With one hand he eased the jewelry box onto the dresser. "I'm not sure I do, either."

Mike always thought that launching from an aircraft carrier at night was life's most dramatic leap of faith. While hooked to the catapult, you see nothing but a few lights that faintly define the deck and give glimpses of the deck crew. In a blink, the ship disappears behind you as steam shoots you off the bow. When you leave, you're sure of only two things: blackness and faith. The blackness is certain, absolute. Faith is something else. Faith is a bond between you and the sailors on the deck who launched you … between you and the folks who built your airplane, its engines, its wing flaps, its instruments, its hydraulic pumps, its fuel pumps, its control surfaces, its rivets, and a million other parts. All the years of learning to trust your body to tell you which way is up or down or left or right have to be replaced with absolute faith in the genius of man. Instruments alone tell you how fast you're going, how high you're climbing, and which way your airplane is pointed. Instruments alone tell you whether you're ascending into the sky or descending into the path of the ship and its propellers. You do this thing because of your faith in the friends that you know and those that you don't know—friends who risk their lives above and below deck to send you off and bring you back. You do it because you love them—and your country.

"Will you hold me?"

As Mike lay with his arms wrapped around the woman he loved, his heart prepared for war again. As he inhaled her scent and listened to her breathing, he smelled the gunpowder and heard the drumbeat. War was at their doorstep, and she was going with him as he launched them both on his wings of faith and into the coming brittle night.

1983
BLOOD BROTHERS

1983, MONDAY, 2 MAY
0530 HOURS (5:30 AM)
NELLIS AIR FORCE BASE
LAS VEGAS, NEVADA

Mike, wearing a crisp khaki uniform, walked across the concrete ramp, each stride one step closer to a great discovery and one second further along in an unfolding adventure. The old 727 that waited sported the markings of Eastern Airlines, not quite obliterated by a sloppy application of white paint. He looked to the southwest at the vast Nellis parking ramp that held angular shapes of F-15s and F-16s. The famous lights of Glitter Gulch and the Strip were blinking off as Nellis came to life. Mike and a few dozen sailors entered the 727 up a stairway that extended beneath its tail.

The airplane taxied onto the runway, then accelerated toward Las Vegas. After it became airborne, it raised its gear and flaps and banked to the north, away from the city. It climbed out of the Las Vegas Valley and flew past Gass Peak and snowcapped Mount Charleston.

Thirty-two minutes later, Mike stepped off the airliner at the secret base at Groom Lake. This was it. Dreamland, Area 51, the cutting edge of the Cold War. At the bottom of the ladder, Chris Patterakis stood ramrod straight in whites, his black hair contrasting with his uniform. Mike saluted as his feet hit the ramp. "Good morning, Skipper."

Patterakis returned the salute. "Follow me." As the two men walked toward a hangar, they exchanged light conversation about their respective moves from Alameda. They stepped into the empty hangar and walked to a blue door at the other end. The door led to a lounge area.

A man dressed in rumpled khakis sat at a beige Formica table. His elbows rested on the table and he held a Styrofoam cup and a cigarette in one hand. He used his other hand to pick at his teeth with a metal, rubber-tipped, dental tool. In front of him was an ashtray whose bottom had long disappeared under a growing mound of Camel butts. His brass belt buckle was half obscured under the slight bulge of his belly. His feet rested on their toes under his seat and revealed pale legs between baggy socks and short pants. His attention was on the wall-mounted TV set. "Brian," Patterakis said to the man.

The man didn't hear. He watched college baseball scores scroll across the screen.

"Commander Davis," Patterakis said, louder.

The man jumped up and spilled the contents of the cup. A sheet of coffee spread across the Formica, and his dental tool clattered on the floor. "Oh, sorry, Skipper," Brian said as he dragged the last possible smoke from his cigarette and crushed it in the ashtray. "My son played yesterday, and I was trying to catch the score."

Behind his weight, Brian was a powerful man about five feet eight inches tall. His curly hair was short, and his smile revealed capped teeth that were yellowed by years of cigarettes and coffee. His eyes had an honest look and he carried himself with the countenance of a confident man. The silver oak leaves of a Commander were pinned to his collar. Above his left pocket were tarnished gold wings and faded stained ribbons. The ribbons included the Medal of Honor.

I'll be damned, Mike thought. That's Brian Davis.

"Brian Davis, this is Mike Christum," Patterakis said.

Brian extended his hand. Smoke rolled through his smile.

"Hi, Brian. Nice meeting you," Mike said.

"Same here." Brian motioned to the table. "Seat?"

"No, thanks." Patterakis left the room.

"Is he OK?" Brian asked. "I hear you know him."

"Yeah. Something's on his mind, that's all. Sometimes he's brusque, but don't take it personally. In a few weeks you'll think he's the best CO you ever had."

"Good. I'm the sensitive sort."

Mike eyed his new friend. "I'll bet you are."

Brian mopped up the coffee with cheap, white, dispenser napkins and rammed them into his cup. He muted the TV.

"Been here long?" Mike asked.

"Yep. Got here yesterday. Spent a year here last night," Brian responded.

"Really. It's that boring, huh?"

"Worse than a carrier."

"No kidding."

"Well," Brian said, "at least on a carrier, if things get bad enough, you can jump overboard. Swimming with sharks is somewhat … stimulating? But I got so bored last night, I tried to strangle myself."

"You weren't successful—obviously."

"Every time the lights went out, I lost my grip," Brian said. "Tried it several times, too."

"I admire persistence."

"Thanks. It's one of my better attributes."

Mike glanced over his shoulder. "Would you excuse me?" he said, pointing toward the vending machines that sat across the room. "I didn't have breakfast." Brian nodded. "Want anything?"

"Nope."

Mike returned with a bottle of Pepsi and a bag of peanuts. He opened the nuts, formed a funnel around the bottleneck with one hand, and poured the nuts into the bottle. It fizzed brown foam.

Brian curled his lip.

"What's the matter?" Mike asked. "Never met a Southerner before?"

"Where you from?"

"West Virginia. Southern West Virginia."

"I thought West Virginia fought for the Union."

"Not my part of West Virginia," Mike said as he took a drink of his peanut-Pepsi. He chewed while he studied Brian. "Am I going to be seeing much of you?"

"Yep."

"Why?"

"Because I'm your co-pilot." He raised an eyebrow in a mock flirt. "And your new roommate."

Mike coughed. Pepsi burned his nose.

Brian considered Mike's glance at the ashtray. "Don't worry about the smoking." He pulled out a Camel, tapped it against the face of his watch, and placed it between his lips. "It won't bother you."

"How do you know?"

Brian's fresh cigarette bobbed up and down in the Zippo's flame as he talked from the side of his mouth, eyes squinting. "'Cause," the Zippo closed with a hollow clink as he exhaled a blue cloud across the table, "my drinking problem's so bad that you won't notice my smoking."

1983, MONDAY, 2 MAY
0958 HOURS (9:58 AM)
GROOM LAKE BASE, NEVADA

Mike and Brian walked together down the center aisle of the briefing room and took seats in the first row. Like church, the rows closer to the front had fewer occupants than the rows near the back. Mike looked behind him. He nodded to a few familiar faces that belonged to maintenance men he'd met over the years. They nodded and smiled back. He turned to Brian, puzzled. "Isn't this supposed to be a flight and maintenance crew briefing?"

Brian nodded.

Mike continued, "See any other aviators here?"

Brian put his arm behind Mike's chair for leverage and turned to look for other officers wearing the gold wings of a Naval Aviator. "Nope."

"Meaning what, Brian?"

"Meaning we're the only pilots here."

"I know it's unusual, but isn't it strange?" Mike asked.

"Yep."

"Attention on deck!" came a command from the back of the room. Every man stood erect, unmoving, eyes to the front.

Chris Patterakis walked by and up three steps to the small stage. He faced his men, serious for a moment. These weren't recruits. He'd handpicked these men during many late hours of reviewing thousands of personnel records. He'd interviewed all the officers and the senior enlisted men, known as chief petty officers. A Navy chief was the counterpart to an Army master sergeant. The chiefs were the Navy's backbone.

Patterakis broke into a broad smile, proud. "At ease," he commanded. The theater echoed with the thumping of seats and the rustle of people making themselves comfortable.

Patterakis waited for the noise to fall off. "Over the next several months, you'll be exposed to something you cannot now imagine. Only one thing stands between success and failure: what you may say to anyone who does not have a security clearance for this project. Should word of what we're doing leak to the Soviets, it will bring an end to both countries, resulting in the deaths of several hundred million people, maybe billions.

"As of now, we, as a unit, are at Defense Condition Two— DefCon Two—which means hostilities are imminent. Consider yourselves combatants and act accordingly. You have all been briefed on the specifics concerning security and the consequences of breaching that security. This is all I am saying on the subject."

Patterakis waited for his words to settle. "As you know, the airplane you're here to fly and maintain is called Rhombus. You're here to make it combat ready. One Rhombus airplane exists now. The contractor will build one every three months until we have a total of twenty. The security measures you have been briefed on are the strictest ever undertaken by our country. You will learn exactly why forty-five days from now. That's when you'll see Rhombus for the first time.

"Between now and then, you will learn only the basic systems of this airplane. After Day Forty-five, you will learn the classified aspects and will begin to see Rhombus as a weapons system. I encourage the free exchange of information among you all. Speculate all you want, but keep all discussion confined to this base. Department heads carry out the orders of the day. That is all."

The men stood at attention again.

Patterakis left the podium and walked up the aisle. He stopped beside Mike and Brian. "Notice anything different?"

"Yes, sir," Mike and Brian responded together.

"Follow me."

Patterakis walked into his office, trailed by Mike and Brian. "Close the door. Take a seat." Patterakis sat behind his desk. "We have a Rhombus on base. Other than the company people, I'm the only one who's seen it. In fact, I'm the only military guy who's ever seen it. Because this thing is so secret, it'll have only three pilots. You two are its crew. I'll train as a backup in case one of you gets killed or sick. The United States of America already has more than fifteen billion dollars sunk into this single airplane."

"Fifteen b-b-billion?" Brian asked.

"Well," Patterakis answered, ignoring Brian's clowning, "all the research and development costs are borne by the first airplane. By the time all twenty are built, the cost for each will be under one billion."

"Billion?"

"Billion." Patterakis smiled. "Are you guys ready for the responsibility of flying a fifteen billion dollar airplane?" Mike nodded.

Brian picked at a tooth with his tool. "Well, Skipper, I see it like this. If I get there alive, the rest of the airplane will, too."

1983, Monday, 2 May
1030 Hours (10:30 A M)
Groom Lake Base, Nevada

George Koisumi was dressed in a white lab coat. His flat nose barely supported thick-rimmed eyeglasses that sat beneath a thatch of black hair. He held a clipboard as he walked in front of Mike and Brian down the long chilly hallway. Their footsteps tapped the hollow floor that covered a channel filled with computer cables. "This place is about as cold as his personality," Brian whispered to Mike, loud enough for Koisumi to hear.

Mike grimaced and held a finger to his lips.

They stopped at a door with a sign that read "WST."

Mike tapped a finger on the sign. "I give up."

"Weapons System Trainer," responded Koisumi as he pushed his eyeglasses up with a forefinger.

"Ah, so!" Brian again. "This is a sim-u-rator." Mike fired an elbow at him.

"They used to call it a 'Link Trainer,'" Koisumi deadpanned.

"Ah, so. The Rink Tlainer. Pattelakis the Gleek will be velly pleased."

Koisumi faced Brian, angry. Mike moved his arm between the two just as Brian held up his arms and called, "Hey, Chunky-moto!"

Koisumi held up his arms and called, "Hey, Brian-flake!" After a moment of backslapping, they pointed at Mike.

"Gotcha!"

"We haven't seen each other since college," Brian said. "I get off the airplane the other day, and guess who's at the bottom of the ladder?" He smacked his old friend on the back. George coughed and his glasses fell to the tip of his nose. Both men chuckled while they pointed at Mike's disgusted expression.

"I see," Mike said, "that neither of you have grown up since then, either."

"True," both responded.

"Yeah," George said, "so last night we cooked up this little show for you."

Mike's face was rigid.

George added, "You know, kind of a welcome to the WST, uh, kinda thing."

Brian's joyful expression melted away.

Mike frowned. His eyes darted from one man to the other. "Well, hell, Mike. We didn't—" Brian fumbled

"Gotcha!" Mike said, then cracked a bright smile.

"Oh, man!" George said.

Brian pointed at Mike. "You shouldn't joke around like that. It's immature." Grins returned all around.

"Speaking of the WST," Mike hinted, nodding at the door.

"Oh, yeah. That." George lifted a card attached to a chain around his neck. He inserted the card in a slot and put his hand in a tight recess to punch digits on a keypad. At the loud buzz George smiled as though relieving himself after a long car ride. "Ahhhhh, don'tcha just love gadgets?" He pushed the door open with one arm, and with the other made an underhanded theatrical motion toward the inside. "Gentlemen," he said, "it's show t-i-i-ime."

Mike stepped through the threshold. "My-o-my, I'm home," he said, his face a mixture of awe and respect. The white room was sterile and measured about 100 feet to a side and 30 feet high. A huge American flag hung against the far wall. In front of them was a large U-shaped console that held an array of CRTs, short for Cathode Ray Tubes, the technical description of TV screens. Lighted buttons in groupings of various sizes filled in the spaces between the CRTs.

Beyond the console, a large, white, box-shaped device the size of a houseboat perched on six, telescoping, hydraulic legs. Snaking from jacks were hoses that led to a junction box on the floor. Mike and Brian knew that an exact duplicate of the Rhombus cockpit was inside the houseboat. Instead of cockpit windows, the WST had CRTs on which a computer displayed the outside world as seen from a real cockpit. At the touch of a keypad, the cockpit could be placed at Los Angeles International, Andrews Air Force Base, Heathrow International, or on the Washington Monument for that matter. A technician at the console could put the crew in any situation. Ice on the wings, smoke in the cockpit, an attack run up the Volga River while dodging MiGs, an attack by a Good Humor ice cream truck. The WST could duplicate almost anything.

George pushed a button. Hydraulic motors whined in another room and the houseboat kneeled to the floor.

"Gentleman," George said with a grin, "your airplane has arrived."

"Fond memories," mused Brian. "Last time I was in a houseboat, it seated twelve and slept twenty-four." George smiled while he opened a section of the floor-mounted safety rail that surrounded the WST. He opened a door in the rear of the houseboat and allowed Mike and Brian to lead. The two aviators stepped in and stood in reverence.

"What's the matter, boys?" George asked. "Cat got your tongues?"

Two ejection seats dominated the cockpit. On the right side of each seat was a joystick like those used on video games. On the left side of each seat were four throttle levers.

"It's got four engines!" Brian's eyes were wide.

"We added two engines when we found out you were going to be flying it," George said as he eyed Brian's paunch. Brian sucked it in.

Between the seats was a large console that contained radio panels and a small CRT. Outboard of each seat and against the side of the cockpit were consoles that contained items such as oxygen-system and intercom controls. An overhead console held switches for fuel management, lighting, and other systems. In front of the seats, on the main instrument panel, was a grand sweep of nothing but black glass.

"Where're the gauges?" Brian asked.

"Yeah," Mike agreed. "Where are the gauges?"

"Oh, sorry." George reached forward. "Watch." He flipped a switch on the instrument panel labeled "Main." The black glass came alive with a rainbow of color that scattered into straight and curved lines, then organized themselves into the forms of buttons, numbers, gauges, and other instruments. The black glass was an array of CRTs that displayed flight, engine, and navigational information.

"What kind of engine instruments do you like?" asked George. "You like these?" He pressed a button. Round dials displayed themselves on one of the CRTs. "How about these?" Vertical instruments were displayed. "Or maybe these?" Up popped a display that was unfamiliar. "The ultimate toy!" said George triumphantly. "Rhombus will be whatever you want it be and whatever the bad guys don't want it to be."

"Meaning?" Mike asked.

"Ah ha!" George waved a finger. "For that answer you will have to wait until Day Forty-five, just like Captain Patterakis said." He chuckled. "I'll be watching you on that day. I can't wait to see your faces when you see your airplane for the first time."

"You're a ruthless person," Brian said.

Mike spoke. "OK, what are we doing standing in the middle of an Air Force base, and what the hell are we doing flying an Air Force airplane?"

"The Air Force is asking the same question," George replied.

"Is there an answer?"

"Yes. It basically goes like this. The Air Force says, 'It's our airplane.' The Navy says, 'Yeah, but it's our technology.' The Department of Defense says, 'The Navy's right.' Besides, the

Ruskies would never believe the Navy was flying something as big as Rhombus. It helps keep the secret, I guess."

"And what does Congress say?" asked Mike.

"Congress doesn't know about it."

"You gotta be kidding."

"Nope, Mister Aviator," George responded. "You're now standing in what's known as the 'Black World.' It's a world of inventing and building weapons that Congress votes money for, but doesn't want to know about. They send the money and say, 'Come back in five years and tell us what you've done.' I guess it's the only way they can keep a secret." He glanced back and forth between Mike and Brian. "Sometimes I'm amazed that you flyboys don't know how your best stuff is made."

Brian put his hand on George's shoulder. "You gotta help me, Chunky-moto. Here we are in Nowhere, Nevada, a hundred and twenty-five miles from anywhere, getting ready to fly an Air Force airplane whose only reason for being is its Navy technology, and it's being paid for by a Congress that doesn't want to know about it. I got that about right?"

George shrugged. He slid two stacks of books off a table in the rear of the cockpit and handed one to each pilot. "I'll see you boys in two weeks, after you study a bit." He pinched Brian's cheek. "Welcome to the Black World, Brian-flake."

1983, MONDAY, 16 MAY
1930 HOURS (7:30 PM)
GROOM LAKE BASE, NEVADA

"Well, it sure is pretty, isn't it," Mike said as he strapped himself into the left seat of the WST's houseboat.

Brian scanned the array of CRTs with flight and engine instruments displayed on them. "When's the game on?" he asked.

"Which one?" Mike asked. "Professor Koisumi," he turned

his head to the back of the houseboat, "would you step into my office, please?"

"Yes, sir." George leaned between the two pilots.

"We know how the aircraft systems work," Mike said, "at least those things that aren't highly classified. We know how the cockpit's configured, and how the CRTs work, and we know things like the ejection seats and survival gear." Mike tugged at George's sleeve, pulling him closer. "We're getting ready to fly this simulator and only have a guess at how much this thing weighs and how much thrust it has. That would be important to know before we fly, don't you think?"

"Worried about crashing the WST?" George asked.

"No." Mike stiffened a bit. "I've never crashed anything, not even a simulator." He pulled George closer. "What I worry about is not having enough information to learn something. We're not taking this thing off the ground, so to speak, until we know something about how it's going to fly. Wouldn't you agree with that?"

"It's enormous," George responded, pulling back.

"We know."

"It weighs one hundred and twenty-five thousand pounds with two pilots and lubricants on board."

"Holy—" Brian reached for his calculator. Naval aviators were not used to numbers like these when it came to airplanes. "That's, let's see, roughly sixty-three tons. Dear God."

"It carries two hundred and thirty-five thousand pounds of fuel."

"Don't have to be formal, here," Brian said. "We call it gas." He punched in more numbers. "OK, that's more than thirty-six thousand gallons of gas."

"Enough," George offered, "to carry you halfway around the world—and back—un-refueled."

"How much payload?"

"Twenty-thousand pounds," George answered. He eyed Brian punching the calculator. "Ten tons," he said before Brian finished.

"OK, let's see what the gross weight is." He punched again.

"No need." George interrupted. "Your airplane has a gross weight of three hundred and seventy-five thousand pounds."

"That's—" Mike began.

"That's nearly as heavy as the Boeing Seven-Sixty-Seven," George said.

"How much thrust?" Mike asked.

"Rated thrust or installed thrust?"

"Installed," Mike said, impatient. "As it sits."

George took a deep breath. "Four hundred and four thousand pounds."

"What!" Mike and Brian chorused. "That's—"

"That's twenty-nine thousand pounds more thrust than you weigh—maximum weight, gross weight. The power's not there for high speed. It's there for acceleration and turning. There isn't a fighter in the world that can touch you, except at top speed, of course, and that's not very important for your mission."

"Speed is always important," Mike said.

"Not for this airplane," George responded.

"For any combat airplane."

"Not for this airplane."

Mike frowned. "Not for this airplane?"

George ignored the question. "You guys better close up or you'll catch flies."

Mike tapped an index finger on a CRT that displayed the engine instruments. "Every other jet I've flown had maximum engine temperatures of about seven hundred and eighty degrees. This one has a max temp of three thousand nine hundred degrees. Why?"

"Can't tell you that, either."

"But," Brian said, "steel melts at two thousand degrees, so it's not steel. Can't be titanium, either."

"What is it?" Mike asked.

"What's what?" George questioned.

Mike reached for George's sleeve again. "What's the engine made of?"

"Can't say," George said. "I'll tell you this. The engines in your airplane are about the size of hot-water heaters." He put his hand beneath Brian's chin and pushed up. "Like I said, you don't want to catch flies."

Different questions came together from Mike and Brian. George held up his hand. "Can't say any more, guys. Sorry."

"When?"

"On Day Forty-five."

"How many more times am I going to hear that one?" Brian said, disgusted.

"To find that out," answered George, "you have to wait until Day Forty-five." George rubbed his hands together. "Let's get started." He left the houseboat and sat at the console.

"Well, Mr. Mike," Brian said with resignation. "Until Day Forty-five gets here, you and I are little more than airline pilots. I want the blonde. You want the redhead, right?"

"Got a redhead," Mike responded.

"Oh, yeah. I forgot. Only one woman for ol' Michael." Brian's eyes saddened as a memory flashed by. "I wish—" His words trailed off.

"Say again?" Mike asked.

"Nothin'."

"Before Engine Start checklist," Mike commanded.

"Before Engine Start checklist, aye. Clear to start engines."

"Starting number one." Mike reached to the overhead console and pushed the first of four knobs. The knob glowed red. The engine RPM tachometer marked "1" climbed. When it reached 10%, Mike pushed the Number 1 throttle lever forward until it hit a slight resistance, called a detent. Fuel sprayed into the combustion chambers of the jet engine and resulted in a growl that rumbled in the airframe until the flame was well established. The knob popped out and the red light went off on its own, indicating the starter motor had automatically disengaged. The RPMs were at 18% and climbing and the growl was replaced by a muted whine of increasing frequency. Mike had selected the vertical display mode for his engine instruments. He smiled as the RPM and engine temperature climbed a scaled ladder. After peaking at 2,600 degrees, the engine temperature dropped back to 1,550 degrees as the RPMs stabilized. The engine was alive. Mike had to remind himself he was in a simulator. The WST mocked the pilots with its realism. "Starting number two."

After all four engines started, Mike called, "Before Taxi checklist."

Brian ran through a list displayed on one of his CRTs. Mike released the brakes and the cockpit moved. Incredible. The houseboat cockpit jostled as it rolled over the computer-duplicated taxiway and rocked with the paving imperfections and expansion joints. On the flat CRTs that simulated cockpit windows, they saw the buildings of Groom Lake Base, and beyond that, the expanse of Emigrant Valley. Stark beige mountains flanked the valley. The Pintwater Range was to the east. Shoshone Mountain and the Belted Range were to the west. George had set the WST up for a dusk flight. The sun fell behind Shoshone Mountain and sent streaks of red and orange across the valley to ignite the peaks of the Pintwaters with crimson caps that grew smaller as the sun dropped over the horizon.

The cockpit wrapped around them with black efficiency. It was studded with crisp colored numbers, switches, and buttons. Dry air-conditioned air blew from the edges of the instrument panel with a hollow sound that mellowed the whining of the engines. The classified parts of the checklist had been blanked out. For now, they were only to learn the basics. Knowledge of Rhombus' full combat capabilities would come on Day 45.

As they approached the runway, George's voice came over the intercom. "OK, you guys. To get you used to your rocket, I've set takeoff weight at maximum. That'll slow you down a bit. I want you to set your tachs at seventy-two percent for takeoff power. That'll give you about half thrust."

"Roger," Brian called.

Mike turned Rhombus onto the digital runway, an electronic duplicate of Groom Lake's Runway 14. The sun was a disappearing memory that crowned the Belted Range.

He pushed the throttles until the tachs reached 72%. He released the brakes. The engines shoved the airplane forward. The nose jumped up, then lowered as speed increased. Runway stripes streaked underneath and became a straight fuzzy blur.

At 170 knots, Brian called, "Rotate."

Mike eased back-pressure on the joystick and the runway disappeared.

"Gear up," Mike called. The call was a backup to the computer automatically raising the gear when Rhombus was ten feet above the runway.

"Gear up," Brian responded.

They climbed at 21,000 feet per minute with the nose 40 degrees high. Mike banked to the east. In the distance were the lights of Caliente and Panaca, Nevada. Beyond were the larger towns of St. George and Cedar City, Utah. The headlights of cars on lonely desert highways dotted the approaching darkness with pinpoint brilliance, like slow shooting stars. Las Vegas glowed in the south. A computer was inventing the lights from information scanned into its memory on some past date.

"It's so damned real," Brian said.

Broad grins crossed the pilots' faces. They were back in the air.

Meanwhile, at the console, George Koisumi pressed a button he called the Grin Eraser. He knew it would take about 10 seconds for Brian to notice the smoke that now wafted from his side console. George looked like a fourth-grade schoolboy who had just put a frog in Mary Sue's book bag.

The two aviators walked down the long hall that led away from the WST. Mike had learned something about Brian today. The man seemed to have a switch that turned a wisecracking view of life to absolute dedication, then back. He was a superb aviator—this first WST ride certainly showed that.

Mike wanted to praise him, but was afraid of coming across as condescending. Then it came to him. "I think we did pretty well, don't you." The word "we" felt right.

"Yeah. We did real good."

"Brian, you have, what, four thousand flying hours in the A-Six?"

"Yeah."

"It'd bother me to have that much time as pilot in command, then have an assignment like this—as a co-pilot."

"It does bother me."

"Why'd you take the job?"

"I wanted to do something significant."

"You don't call getting the Medal of Honor doing something significant?"

"OK, then. I love my country. What do you want me to say?"

"It's what I'm trying to say to you, Brian."

"Which is?"

"Which is that you graduated number one in your flight training class just like I did. You have as many flying hours as I do. As a man with the rank of Commander, you have to be the oldest co-pilot in the Navy." Mike searched for words. "It's just that you're so darned good, I feel bad about the whole thing."

Brian put his hand on Mike's shoulder as they walked. "Did I ever tell you about how I got the Medal of Honor?"

Mike knew how he got it. He'd read the official account. He'd also seen the scar on Brian's back where he got hit, but he wanted to hear it from him. "No, you never did."

"I found it in a dresser drawer in the bedroom of someone else's wife. I was under a great deal of stress, looking for anything at all to wear, so I could leave through a window in a timely manner."

Mike shook his head. Brian had thrown his switch.

1983, THURSDAY, 15 JUNE
2100 HOURS (9:00 PM)
GROOM LAKE BASE, NEVADA

They stood at the corner of the Quonset hut and waited. A hot breeze pushed curling lines of dust between the buildings. "Spooky," Brian said. "Ever seen an air station without flood lights? No lights of any kind?"

Mike looked across the ramp. The moon painted the concrete a dusty blue. Metal buildings stood around its edge. Beyond the buildings, Emigrant Valley stretched, a sheet of blue-black velvet running to ragged mountains. Somewhere nearby a metal door banged as the wind moved it back and forth on groaning hinges.

A door behind them closed.

"Hi, gents." It was Chris Patterakis. "Waiting for the bus?"

"Waiting here like you asked us to," Brian responded.

"Tomorrow's Day Forty-five," Patterakis said.

Mike and Brian nodded.

"I want you to see your airplane now. It's over there." Patterakis pointed across the ramp.

"Yessss!" Brian pumped his fist, the kid pouring out of him.

Mike grinned. His skin tingled. "Ah, man," he whispered.

They walked across the ramp toward the huge, distant, cube-shaped building. The concrete was still hot from the day and they felt its heat under their chins.

As they got closer, Mike saw that steel beams crisscrossed the top of the hangar. It reminded him of an abandoned bridge. The front of the hangar was in the moon's shadow, and it seemed to lean over them, threatening and defiant. The edges of the hangar's rusty roof reflected the pale light with a dull purple cast. Enormous metal doors with wire-reinforced windows covered the shadowed face and sat on steel wheels that rolled on metal tracks. A small personnel door was cut into one of the hangar doors. Patterakis turned the handle and pulled. Dry hinges protested. Patterakis stood to the side and motioned for Mike and Brian to enter.

Mike saw the dim interior of the hangar through the personnel door. He knew his airplane was inside. The hair on his arms stood up. He rubbed his hands together.

"Hot damn," Brian said.

"Well?" Patterakis questioned. "You going inside or not?"

They stepped through the door. It banged shut behind them. Mike scanned the broad expanse of the concrete floor and saw nothing, nothing but a vast, dim, empty hangar.

"Not funny, Skipper," Brian said. "Not funny at all."

"Be patient." Patterakis beckoned them to follow and walked to the right.

Brian shot Mike a disgusted look, careful not to let Patterakis see him. Mike shrugged. The hangar's gloom swallowed them. Metal ceiling beams jutted from the shadows. Patterakis walked toward a light that leaked a circle of pale light across a yellow and black electrical box and onto the gray floor. He opened the box. Inside was a panel that held a group of elevator buttons marked one through six. One glowed. He pressed six.

A klaxon sounded and lights illuminated the walls.

A red strobe light made the hangar look like an abandoned disco. "Brace yourselves," Patterakis called over the noise.

The floor shuddered as locks along its edges rolled back.

"Who-o-oa," Brian said.

The entire hangar floor sank. "It's an elevator!" The wall they stood by—the one that held the panel—was part of the elevator and descended with them. The men swayed with the floor as it dropped down a shaft that was hewn from solid rock. The elevator dropped by three underground hangar doors, one on each wall. Mike expected it to stop at the base of the doors. It didn't.

Patterakis shouted over the noise of the klaxon. "We can taxi a B-Fifty-Two into Hangar Eighteen and drop it to any of these floors you see us passing by. Then we can tow it into any one of the three doors per floor. Each door hides an underground hangar, except for one. That door covers a tunnel that goes to other parts of Groom Lake Base. This single shaft can hold more than fourteen large airplanes or several squadrons of fighters. We have Hangar Eighteen to ourselves, though."

Another floor went by.

Finally, five hundred feet below Groom Lake, the huge elevator clanged to a stop. The klaxon cut off.

Mike and Brian looked up. The red light still flashed, far away, and the rafters hid farther in the gloom. Twelve hangar doors, three to a floor, looked like huge metal grates on the side of a cliff. Mike and Brian's faces were frozen, their mouths open.

"Whatever you're thinking, hold that thought," Patterakis said. "You haven't seen anything. Yet."

The hangar doors covering each of the other three walls were closed.

Patterakis pressed a button. The elevator shaft rumbled as the doors on the far wall parted. "Let's go," he said as he strode off.

The large door parted farther as they walked, revealing nothing but blackness.

"My sense of humor is being tested," Brian quipped beneath his breath.

"Chill out, Brian," Mike said in a friendly way. "I know Chris. He's not playing with us. Personally, I need to hold onto something right now."

"A stiff drink comes to mind."

By the time they reached the other side, the door was wide open. The elevator lights far behind them cast their shadows on the dim floor.

Mike squinted for the glint of aluminum. There was nothing here.

"You know him, huh?" Brian asked.

Patterakis walked to the right. "Come on." His voice echoed in the giant room that had been cut into hard rock. They followed. As they approached the side wall, they saw another yellow and black box.

"Oh, the old yellow and black box trick." It was Brian.

Patterakis pushed up on a lever on the side of the box. Lights flashed on.

They winced at the brilliance, squinting across the concrete floor.

Again, they saw nothing.

"Uh oh. Someone stole our airplane," Brian quipped.

Patterakis pointed to a yellow square painted in the middle of the floor, about a hundred feet away. "Walk over to that square and stand on it," he commanded.

Brian whispered, intent. "Bet the damned thing's a trap door. He presses a button and we find our butts sitting in Death Valley. I told you to knock off those Greek jokes."

They reached the square and faced Patterakis. Mike called, "OK, Skipper. Now what?"

"Raise your arms," Patterakis said.

"He's going to shoot us."

"Do as the man says, Brian—and shut up."

Their knuckles banged into something just over their heads.

Mike jerked his hands away and looked up. All he saw was the cavern's ceiling and steel girders that spanned the dark hangar walls. Here and there were winches that rolled on the girders. Powerful lights beamed down between air ducts.

They raised their hands again.

"Glass?" Brian asked.

Mike opened his palms and pressed them against the transparent surface. It had a texture like vinyl, but it squeaked as he rubbed his hands over it. He glanced around to see where the glass—or whatever it was—ended. Nothing. He licked his thumb and rubbed it on the surface to cause a smear. The smear didn't take. He rapped on it with a knuckle. It was a metallic echo—not glass. "What the hell?" he whispered.

"Don't look at me," Brian said.

"Figured it out yet?" Patterakis called from the edge of the cave.

"Yeah," Brian whispered to Mike. "We're underneath a piece of glass. How hard could it be?"

"Say again?" Patterakis asked earnestly.

"Forget it," Brian whispered.

Mike dropped his arms to his side. "Skipper, what the hell's going on?"

Patterakis called, "Like the man on TV says, keep lookin' up." He pressed a button.

A quick, hard, tearing noise filled the hangar.

The glass sheet turned black. Its shadow wrapped around them.

"No-o-o-o!" Brian shouted at the immense black hood.

Mike jerked away. His heel caught. He toppled backwards—on his butt. He rolled to his hands and knees.

The massive black shape spread a hundred feet to each side.

Mike spun toward the hangar door and scampered to the edge of the shadow.

He was away from it.

He stood and faced it.

His heart pounded in his ears.

Brian ran into him, looking back.

He held onto Brian and kept him from falling. "What is it?"

Brian stepped back. "What the hell is this thing?" he demanded.

Mike was still. His mouth fell wider as his eyes moved up. "Oh, my," he breathed. He reached for Brian without looking at him. "C'mere." He missed.

He reached again and snagged Brian's sleeve. "Come here!" He tugged. "Look."

Their labored breathing stopped.

Silence.

"My God. Oh, my God." The words spread beneath the shadow.

An immense black object filled the hangar and floated seven feet above the floor. From the point just above them, sharp straight edges swept to each side at 45-degree angles. Mike bent at the waist and looked underneath. He estimated the object was about 200 feet across and about 75 feet long.

"What the hell is this!" Brian called.

Patterakis yelled back. "It's your airplane!"

"Airplane?!" Brian answered. "With all due respect, sir, this ain't no damned airplane!"

"Yes it is," Mike said, almost to himself. "Yes it is. This is the nose, and it's also where the wing begins. That's the wing's leading edge."

He bent at the waist. "Under here, Brian."

Brian remained standing, silent. Mike reached to his shoulder and pulled him down. "Look." Behind the wing's leading edge, sweeping curves widened to an almost-flat bottom. "The landing gear's up. There's the main-gear doors on either side— and up here—" He pointed. "See the edges of the nose-gear door?"

Brian nodded. "It looks like a manta ray. What the hell's it standing on?"

"Must hang from the ceiling."

Brian scanned the enormous machine. "But why didn't we see it before? I mean, where'd it come from?"

Mike rubbed his chin. "It must have lowered from the ceiling."

"That fast? It appeared out of nowhere. One second we're touching a piece of glass and the next, whammo! This thing appears."

Mike felt like a spectator at a magic show, trying to figure out how the appearance happened. "Oh, this is ridiculous," he said to himself. He called to Patterakis, "OK, Skipper. We give up. What's going on here?"

Patterakis walked across the floor with an object in his hand. His footfalls echoed between the concrete floor and the bottom of the airplane. He handed Mike what resembled a TV remote control. Many of its buttons were arrows that pointed in different directions. Along the left side were labels and beside each label was a button marked Off-On.

"What is it?" Mike asked. "What's this thing do?"

"You'll see. The maintenance guys will use it mostly. See the button marked Aurora?" Patterakis asked. "Watch your airplane and press the button."

Mike placed his finger on the button. He stared at the immense black airplane that spread its wings across the expanse of the cave. Would the airplane rise to hide behind doors in the ceiling? What was that glass surface? Where did it come from? Would it reappear?

The three men stood, faces upward.

Mike pressed the button.

The crackling sound echoed in the room, and the plane disappeared.

"Holy—" Mike's mouth fell open. "Where'd it go?"

"Nowhere," Patterakis said.

"Nowhere!?"

Patterakis pointed. "See? See the cables stretching down from the ceiling? See the hook at the bottom of each one?"

Three steel cables were attached to winches mounted on the rafters. They vibrated taut, like steel fishing lines hooked to an enormous weight. Except there was nothing on the hooks.

Patterakis pointed to another button. "Press that one." Mike pressed and hydraulic motors screeched. "Watch the cables."

The cables reeled down from the winches with their spiraling strands of shiny wire twisting like long screws. Their hooked ends dropped a ways, then stopped. The screaming hydraulic motors quit.

"Hold your hands in front of you," Patterakis coached. Mike held up his empty hand. Brian raised both of his. "Step forward—slow." Mike took two steps before he touched an edge that swept away to the right at a 45-degree angle. Brian took three steps before he stopped. Mike moved his fingers back and forth along the edge and felt the object widen as he reached over the top and the bottom of the edge. The surface squeaked as he touched it. He put the remote control on top of the edge, then stood back to see it floating in mid-air.

He gaped at Patterakis, his eyes wide. "No!"

"No!" Brian chorused.

"Keep your hands where they are, both of you, and press the Aurora button again," Patterakis commanded.

Mike retrieved the remote control. With his right hand touching the edge, he pressed Aurora.

Everything in front of him turned black.

"Jeez!" Brian jumped back.

This time, Mike stood his ground.

The glass he'd been touching was now black, and instead of being glass, it was the leading edge of the airplane wing they had touched before. He put the remote in his pocket and leaned onto the edge, hard. The airplane swung back a fraction, then returned.

"I'll be damned," he said.

"You gotta be kidding me," Brian added. "An invisible airplane? Oh, this is too, too much." He chuckled.

Mike grinned. He rubbed his hands along the wing until he reached the point of its nose. "I can't wait to get it airborne," he whispered.

"Hey, Mike," Brian said. "Can you see making an approach to a carrier with this thing? Half the crew would jump overboard."

Mike thought about the little show Patterakis had just put on. "Skipper, I don't know whether to hit you or hug you."

"One gets you in trouble," Patterakis responded. "The other gets us both in trouble." He waited. "Well?"

"Well what?"

Patterakis was like a parent who had just given his son his first bicycle, or the keys to a new car. "How do you feel?"

Mike regarded the sinister black airplane. Brian shrugged. They stood at the edge of a new world. In front of them was a machine beyond compare, or even reason, for that matter. A machine that would change everything. Joy worked its way out of both aviators as it replaced the adrenaline rush.

"You want to know how I really feel, Skipper?" Mike snickered. He leaned into Brian and put his hand on his shoulder.

Brian put his hand to his mouth.

"I feel like—"

Laughter burst through Brian's hand. It was contagious. Patterakis chuckled.

"Well, hell, Skipper—" Mike faced his airplane and held his arms open. "I feel like—Batma-a-a-n."

Guffaws exploded as Mike and Brian leaned against each other.

1983, Thursday, 15 June
2147 Hours (9:47 PM)
Groom Lake Base, Nevada

The three men walked away from Hangar 18, the moon at their backs. Brian walked backward a few steps. "Making sure it isn't following us."

"Listen," Patterakis said, "the maintenance guys see it tomorrow morning, as scheduled. I want you there. I'm holding a briefing afterwards, and I'll answer questions then. I know you'd like to go over things now, but today's been tough, so I'm turning in."

"Just one question?" Mike asked.

"An easy one."

Mike had a thousand questions about the invisible airplane. "What's with the hangar and the elevator."

"There are times when this base has a hundred airplanes and four thousand guys. Does it look that big to you?"

"No."

"That's because most of it's underground. All the hangars here have floors that are elevators. From time to time the tunnels are used for airplanes we don't want the Soviets to know about. Mostly, the Air Force uses them."

"What're the tunnels for?" Mike asked.

"The Ruskies watch this place from their spy satellites." Patterakis pointed up. "So when the Air Force wants to launch one of their secret fighters, they tow it underground to the end of the runway. When the satellite drops over the horizon, they raise it to the runway and take off."

Mike thought about the giant airplane that sat underground behind them. "I guess we don't have to worry about Soviet satellites seeing us, do we?"

"No."

1983, THURSDAY, 16 JUNE
1030 HOURS (10:30 AM)
GROOM LAKE BASE, NEVADA

The door of the briefing room burst open and a dusty sunbeam pierced its cool dim interior. The beam danced with the shadows of men walking through the door. Their chatter reverberated in the room, and their hands and arms moved with spirited animation. Someone threw a switch. Florescent bulbs flashed a cool light that pushed out the sunbeam.

The maintenance men had just seen the airplane for the first time. Patterakis had a hidden flare for show business, it seemed. While his men sat in folding chairs in Hangar 18, they didn't know that they were sitting beneath their airplane. Patterakis had walked to the podium and said, simply, "Gentlemen, your airplane has arrived." In an instant the men were in the shadow of the giant black bomber. The confusion that followed caused a ruckus as metal chairs fell over and men scrambled to escape. The adrenaline that had surged through the men had left its calling card, and excitement rolled into the briefing room with them as they moved forward to fill the front rows of seats first.

"Attention on deck," came the command from the rear. The men stood while their CO walked down the aisle and climbed the three steps to the small stage.

"As you were," Patterakis said as he took the podium. Several hundred thumps filled the room as theater-type seats lowered. Sobriety and wonder replaced the exhilaration of seeing such an unthinkable thing.

Patterakis began. "I apologize about the drama just a few minutes ago, but I thought it was the best way to introduce you to Rhombus." He paused. "Any of you get hurt?" There was no response. "I mean," he continued, "even the slightest injury?"

A single hand with a scraped palm went up. "It's OK, suh. It's just a scrape."

"I want you to see a corpsman as soon as you're dismissed. OK?"

"Aye, aye, suh," came the response, but before Patterakis could leave the subject the voice added, "Uh, Skippah? Since we are in a state of wa-ah, does this mean I get a Puhple Haht? " The room echoed with mild laughter.

The petty officer sitting to the wounded man's side hit him on the head with his Dixie Cup hat and said, "I apologize for my bunkmate, Skippah. He's a crackah from Georgia. If this little weenie scrape doesn't get him a Puhple Haht, what I do to him will." Laughter rolled again.

Patterakis smiled. His men were recovering from their shock, and the sense of confidence typical of a select group of people was taking form. "First of all, it's not a glass airplane. About five years ago, the United States Navy stumbled onto the secret of invisibility. As you all know, our submarines are coated with a substance designed to absorb sound waves, specifically SONAR pings. The problem with the stuff is that it wears off due to collision with marine life, docks, and the like. The Navy was splicing the genes of microbes together, hoping for a coating that would re-grow itself when damaged.

"They grew these things on a model submarine, put the submarine in a large tank, and hit it with SONAR. One test called for a microphone to be inside the sub. However, it was wet inside and they couldn't reach in to dry it completely, so this very lucky technician put the sub in a microwave to evaporate the water. That worked, but it also killed the microbes. The only thing that remained of the little critters was the crystal structure of their bodies. They thought, what the heck, we'll do the test anyway. They put the mic in the sub, put the sub in the tank, and turned on the mic. The mic short-circuited into the sub, and when the electricity flowed from the mic through the sub and into the water, the sub disappeared. They probably had a day like you're having right now." The room rumbled with men acknowledging their surprise.

"As it turns out, they didn't discover true invisibility. What they discovered was a biological coating whose crystalline structure, when energized with electricity, takes whatever light waves hit it and bends the light around the object so that each individual light wave exits on the same plane as it entered. When Rhombus was above your heads a few minutes ago, you didn't see the hangar ceiling through it, you saw the ceiling bent around it. In other words, you saw the lights above Rhombus projected from the bottom of the airplane. If anybody had been looking down from the ceiling catwalks, they would not have seen you through the airplane, but would have seen your image after it bent around the sides of it and manifested off the top. However, the results are the same as true invisibility.

"We call this coating and its technology Aurora. The Rhombus airframe is watertight, so it can be immersed in a liquid culture that allows the microbes to attach themselves to the skin of the airplane. After twenty-one hours of immersion, the airplane is removed from the culture, and the microbes die. It's then immersed in a molymer solution under a pressure of two atmospheres. In forty hours the molymer, which is a liquid plastic, has penetrated the dead microbe cells. The airframe is then removed from the solution and exposed to X-rays for three hours. The X-ray exposure changes the molecular structure of the molymer to create a polymer, which is a hard plastic. This plastic is of such clarity that if the oceans were made of it, you could see the bottom.

"It's nearly perfect. I say nearly because when Rhombus passes between the viewer and a high-contrast background, such as the night sky with stars, there is a slight distortion.

Keep in mind that the Aurora coating is very tough, and only the airplane's skin is covered.

"Thus, light that bends around Aurora can jump small gaps in the coating so it can move across landing-gear doors and access panels. When these microbes, or bugs as we call them, are subjected to different types of electrical stimuli, they do different things with light. Now for our next trick." Patterakis moved from the podium to stand in front of a small table.

"When the bugs are grown over an electronic grid, we have the ability to energize different parts of the grid, which will cause the bugs to do different things. Here." He stepped aside to reveal a three-by-three-foot piece of sheet metal that stood upright on top of a VCR. Behind the sheet metal was a four-by-four piece of plywood painted red-and-white checkerboard.

"Abracadabra," the CO said, then flipped a switch. The sheet metal mounted on the VCR disappeared, revealing the checkerboard behind it. "That's the invisibility part. Now watch this. You are paying attention, aren't you?" The men were so quiet, he thought perhaps they hadn't heard him. He tossed a remote control to one of the maintenance-division officers in the front row. "Here," he said. "Press PLAY."

The officer pressed a button. After a second, the sheet metal began projecting a VCR tape of an old Jimmy Stewart movie. Around the room, quiet remarks of disbelief mixed with excited surprise. The sheet metal had become a television screen. "You see, gents," Patterakis went on, "if you want, you can access a computer-graphics library and project whatever image you select on the skin of Rhombus. The airplane can become a MiG," he paused, "or it can become an airliner." No one spoke. Not a man moved while the movie's images stirred the sheet metal with streaks of color. "The Aurora coating includes a fine wire mesh between the airplane's skin and the bug coating. The airplane's computer manipulates the electrical field in the wire mesh, which, in turn, causes the bugs to either pass light through to make Rhombus invisible or causes the bugs to take on different colors and shades of gray to turn Rhombus into something else." He waited while his men watched. "Anybody got any questions?" His words drifted across the men and disappeared into the silence of the back of the room.

"OK. Then I'll start the questions," Patterakis said. "The first question I would ask myself is, if this Aurora coating covers the entire airplane, how do we see outside?" He scanned the room. Heads nodded. "The answer is," he paused, "we don't. Rhombus has no cockpit windows. Anybody care to guess how we handle this problem?"

Mike raised his hand, "Well, I'd guess that the inside of the cockpit is like the WST where the world is displayed on CRTs. This airplane must have cameras that see outside and display it on the inside."

"OK, you're getting there."

"But sir," came a voice, "you can't have CRT tubes mounted in a real airplane where the windows should be. The back of them would protrude outside the airplane."

Patterakis waited. He crossed his arms and tapped his toe.

"I know!" A hand waved. A short petty officer stood on his seat. "The sheet metal—I mean, if that piece of sheet metal can turn into a TV screen and show Jimmy Stewart—"

"Oh, yeah!" another man said. "He's got it."

Patterakis nodded to the short man. "Go ahead."

"Well, it's simple. You coat the inside of the cockpit where the windows are supposed to be with those bugs and turn the whole thing into a giant TV." Whistles came from here and there. The short petty officer took a bow. His nearby buddies pounded him with their Dixie cup hats. He sat down, a hero for the moment.

Patterakis continued, "The computer looks outside for us, and relays what it sees through a system called SID." He pushed a button. The piece of metal that had held the images of Jimmy Stewart changed to a slide that read SID—Synthetic Image Display. "Rhombus has sensors that see all around it. These sensors pick up visible light, infrared and ultra-violet light, radar waves, radio and TV waves, and all other radioactive waves. The computer converts what it sees into images that it puts on the SID so the pilots can see. It enhances the images with color, if necessary, so that no matter when Rhombus flies, no matter what the weather, the pilots can see the world as though it's noon and the skies are clear. They can also see the world as it really is, if they want, so they can enjoy things like the clouds and sunsets." Patterakis smiled. "People are like that, you know.

"Each of your two eyes sees things from a different perspective. That's what gives us depth perception or Three-D vision. Since each pilot sits in a different place, each sees the world from a different visual perspective. For example, when refueling in flight, the pilot sees the tanker above and to his right while the co-pilot sees it up and to his left. If the SID were just a thin CRT screen, there'd be no Three-D, and the pilots would see the tanker from the same perspective. Anybody hazard a guess how the SID handles this? Anybody? No?

"Rhombus has two pilots who have four eyeballs, so the trick is to give each of the four eyeballs a slightly different view of the world—same as in real life. You with me so far?" Nods. "The problem is that there is only one SID. So Rhombus' computer sends four different views to the SID, one for each eyeball in the cockpit. Each view is flashed on the screen thirty times a second for a total of a hundred and twenty flashes per second. The challenge is, how do you make sure that one eyeball sees only the flash meant for it?"

Patterakis walked to a table beside the podium. From beneath the table he retrieved two mannequin heads, each wearing a flight helmet with black visors extended to cover the eyes. "Watch this," he said as he pressed a button.

The left side of the visor on one helmet became clear and revealed the eye of one mannequin. He pressed again and the first eye was covered by black, while the second eye was revealed. The third and fourth presses revealed the eyes of the other mannequin in order. "So, when the SID flashes the image meant for eyeball number one, it blacks out eyeballs two, three, and four. When if flashes the image meant for eyeball two, it blacks out eyeballs one, three, and four. Get it? At thirty flashes a second for each eye, the pilots never notice it."

"But sir," came a question. "The computer would have to know exactly where each pilot's head is and which way he's looking."

"Correct. Earlier this month each pilot had his fillings replaced with gold." He looked at Mike and Brian. "Right, guys?" The two looked at each other, silent, now understanding why all their fillings had been replaced. "An X-ray of their noggins, including their fillings, was scanned into Rhombus' computer. Sensors in the cockpit tell the computer exactly where the fillings are, and based upon its skull maps, it knows exactly where their eyeballs are. Other sensors mounted in the visors read their retinas and tell the computer exactly where each eyeball is pointed, so it knows what image to flash on the SID for that particular eyeball."

A mixture of words peppered the room, words like wow, amazing, oh boy, and I ain't believin' this. Brian turned in his seat to the men behind him. "Wonder if that sucker can do this?" he said as he crossed his eyes.

Patterakis continued, "Each pilot can select any view he wants on the SID. One can look ahead while the other looks behind. The SID can zoom in or go wide-angle. Either of the pilots can look straight down, too.

"With the SID, it can always be noon, even during a midnight rainstorm. In any event, the pilots will never see outside the Rhombus cockpit. What they'll see is a display of what the computer sees. It'll look so natural to them, they'll forget that they're actually watching TV of the world around them.

"And it gets better," Patterakis continued as he walked back to the podium. "I've mentioned the computer several times. It's called the MPP. MPP stands for Massively Parallel Processor. Anybody out there know what the world's best MPP is?" No answer. "Each of you has one."

"The brain?" a tentative response came from the rear.

"Exactly—"

"Excuse me, sir. Not all of us have one of those." Laughter flowed with a few happy taunts.

"Exactly. The human brain is a massively parallel processor. Part of it is dedicated to speech, part to vision, part to hearing, thinking, memory, mathematics, and so forth. The different parts of the brain talk to each other through millions of circuits at the same time, rather than in a stream through a single circuit. If one part is damaged, other parts can learn how to carry the load. The MPP on Rhombus does the same thing. Part of it is dedicated to the SID, part to avionics, part to fuel management, air conditioning, threat management, and so forth. If one part is damaged, the others pitch in to make up for the loss. It's also fast, very fast." Patterakis pursed his lower lip. "Maybe I shouldn't tell you this, but—" He paused, reconsidering.

"But what the hell, right Skipper?" came a voice.

Patterakis grinned. "OK, don't take this seriously at all, but there's some talk among the computer guys that the MPP actually learns. There's even some speculation that with the proper programming changes, it might become self-aware." The room was quiet.

A voice was directed at Brian. "If that happens, I bet you'll think twice before crossing your eyes at it, huh Mr. Davis?"

The quiet shattered in another cascade of laughter.

"What if all the electrics fail and the MPP computer goes dead?"

"If all the electrics fail, Rhombus crashes. The shape of its body is optimized for the Aurora coating, and the shape is so unusual that Rhombus is highly unstable. Human beings simply cannot fly it. When the pilots move their joysticks, they do not move the control surfaces on the wings. Rather, the MPP reasons what the pilots want Rhombus to do and does it for them. Without the MPP, Rhombus is a lead boomerang.

"As in any airplane, Rhombus has several electrical busses to protect itself. Some are more protected than others. The most secure electrical system on Rhombus is the one that powers the MPP, as you might imagine."

"Why aren't all electric busses protected to the max?" a voice called out.

"Because if we did that, Rhombus would be so heavy it

wouldn't fly. You have to assign priorities when designing an airplane. That's why commercial airlines don't have eight engines. Eight is safer than four, right? You get the idea."

"Or like two condoms instead of one," came a quiet comment. After a moment of pondering that statement, everyone understood the tradeoffs given to all things when it comes to safety. Patterakis smiled while his men laughed.

Then the CO held up his hand. The laughter cut off.

"What about the engines?" Mike asked.

"Ah ha." He bent below the podium, then stood. He held an elegant china teacup close to the podium light as if to extinguish it. The cool fluorescent light changed color as it flowed right through the china and illuminated Patterakis' hands as though from a candle. He put the cup on the podium and crossed his arms. He waited.

After a few moments the most senior chief petty officer in the room said, "Ahhhhh. I get it." He flashed a smile at Patterakis. The chief didn't reveal what he had figured out. He wanted his younger petty officers to reason through the challenge.

One by one each man responded aloud as he understood what the teacup meant, but they all played the game and allowed each of the slower ones to mentally come aboard in his own good time. Eventually the room was filled with satisfied smiles, except one. Brian didn't get it. Every eye in the room was on him. Mike thrummed his fingers on the armrest in mock impatience. "Well?"

"Well, damned what?" Brian asked. After a few seconds of feeling the dubious honor of being the center of attention, he said, "The engine runs on tea. It runs on coffee. It's made by Noritake. How the hell should I know? Do I look like a mechanic?"

"You needn't offend us, sir," someone said from the back. The room erupted in laughter.

Patterakis raised his hand and the laughter died. He picked up the teacup and held it closer to the podium light. The light glowed through the thin material. "Beautiful, isn't it?" He moved the cup back and forth in the light. "If I were to fill this cup with steel ball bearings, I could melt them by putting a blow torch under it."

Brian smacked an open hand against his forehead. He took a deep breath and exhaled, "The engine is ceramic."

"Right-o, Brian," Mike said as he slapped him on the back.

"Ta-daaa," Brian sang, then joined the laughter.

Patterakis let his men have their fun for a moment, then once more held up his hand. "Rhombus' engines are made of ceramic. And because they're made of ceramic, they burn jet fuel at a far higher temperature than steel or titanium engines. So, we can get enormous power with little weight. The engines are, officially, CJ Ones, which stands for Ceramic, Jet, first generation. We call them CJs for short. They're about the size of hot-water heaters, yet they produce a hundred and one thousand pounds of thrust each. That's more than two times the thrust of a Seven-Forty-Seven engine."

Patterakis fumbled with some papers. "OK, let's get on with this. I'll hurry so we can walk over to Hangar Eighteen and you can inspect your airplane. You'll learn more details later. Since it's important that the enemy never discover Rhombus' location, it communicates by compressing information, then bursting it to a satellite network that transmits the information to our Command Information Center, CIC for short. This technique is called satellite bursting or SatBurst. Rhombus does not receive information this way because, frankly, when it's hidden, it's hidden from us, too, and there's no way to find it in order to focus a tight communication beam on it. This means that when Rhombus doesn't want to be found, communication is available only by messages rather than conversation, and the messages are one-way only.

"Let's go back to the SID for a moment. How many of you guys own radar detectors?" No hands raised. "Really," Patterakis said. Mike raised his first, followed by Brian, followed by a couple dozen or so. "Better. How many of you have seen a radar detector work?" All hands raised. "When a radar detector senses police radar, it warns you. You get a beep and a light. Rhombus has radar detectors, too, but when the MPP picks up radar, it can tell exactly where it's coming from and what kind of radar it is. Then it superimposes a red transparent image of the threat over the landscape on the SID. To make things better, Rhombus has a display called a TopDown. Think of the TopDown as a chessboard. Instead of red and black squares, the TopDown is a moving map of the terrain Rhombus is flying over. In addition to displaying threats on the SID, the MPP also puts them on the TopDown so the pilots can see things as if they were looking down from a space station."

Patterakis saw that most of the men understood. "OK, I'm flying along in Rhombus and the computer picks up a threat radar two hundred miles away. It knows that the radar can see Rhombus when it gets within two miles from any direction. Keep in mind the radar is turning, so its detection of Rhombus is four miles across. What I see in the SID is a transparent red sphere on the horizon that is four miles across. If the radar were coming from a radar airplane, the sphere would look like a red ball. Meanwhile, if I look on the TopDown, I see the sphere superimposed over a map."

He looked around the room. He had one more illustration to explain the SID and the TopDown. "Imagine that the windshield of your car is a SID. Now, imagine that a computer in your car could see police radar and display it on your car's SID as a visible beam, like a flashlight. That way you could either slow down before you entered the beam or steer around it."

"Ah, neat," came an involuntary comment from one of the younger men.

"Now imagine you had a TopDown display mounted in your car's console. At the same time you saw the police radar on the SID, you could see it on a display of the entire city on the TopDown—as if you were looking from above. That way you could take a different street to get around the radar long before you got to it."

"Whoa!" came another, louder, involuntary reply from the same young voice. The older petty officer next to him nudged him. Patterakis felt like they all understood now.

"A special missile has been developed for Rhombus. It's called the Fleshette. The Fleshette doesn't have an explosive warhead. Instead, it hits the target at eight times the speed of sound. The energy from the Fleshette's speed is what destroys the target. It's fired from Rhombus like a six-gun, believe it or not." Patterakis took a breath.

"The power of the CJ engines isn't there for high speed, but rather for high maneuverability. Because of its simple engine inlet design, Rhombus is limited to Mach one-point-six, or about eleven hundred miles per hour. However, Rhombus can make a thirteen-G turn. As you know, the best fighters can manage only nine Gs. Of course, when Rhombus is pulling thirteen Gs, a two-hundred-pound pilot weighs about twenty-six hundred pounds. To keep the pilots from passing out from the high Gs, Rhombus has reclining ejection seats. They start to recline when the airplane goes past four Gs. At thirteen Gs, the seats are almost flat. At some point during this reclining process, the pilots can't see their instruments, so the MPP computer displays basic flight information on the inside of their helmet visors."

Patterakis watched his men. They not only appreciated the magnitude of the more obvious Rhombus qualities, they were now appreciating the attention to the finer points. "Amazing, huh?" Patterakis said, himself caught up in the excitement of his young audience.

A hand shot up. "Sir, why did we spend all this money to make the airplane invisible when we could just fly at night, and nobody'd see it?"

The more experienced men in the room chuckled.

"Don't give him a tough time, guys. It's an honest question." Patterakis groped for the answer to something that was obvious to him, but he didn't want to belittle the sailor. "On average, half the day is dark and half is light. Therefore, being invisible means we've doubled the amount of time Rhombus can operate. That alone is an enormous gain in capability. Agreed?"

The young man nodded.

"Besides, there are only two days of the year when day equals night: the vernal equinox, which occurs on March twenty-second, and the autumnal equinox, on September twenty-second. In the Northern Hemisphere the day with the shortest period of light is December twenty-second when the North Pole is tilted away from the sun. The longest is June twenty-second when the North Pole is tilted toward the sun. On June twenty-second about eighty percent of the Soviet Union is in twenty-four-hour light, just like Alaska. Moscow itself only has about four hours of night on that date. Even the southernmost part of the Soviet Union is in darkness for only about eight hours, and the country has bases and missile silos where it's never night during the summer. You can see that for yourself on the big globe in the base library. OK?"

"Yes, sir. Thank you."

"Good. Real good." Patterakis regarded his men, a smile on his face. "Let's go." He said as he left the stage and walked up the aisle.

Patterakis led his men to the hangar on the other side of the ramp and stepped through the small personnel door. As the men stepped in, they fanned left and right in front of the massive matte-black airplane, respectful with their silence. Patterakis stood still, knowing that each man waited for a sign from him to approach the warplane. He gave none.

"Sir?" Mike asked, breaking the silence in the corner of the hangar.

Patterakis faced him. "I don't know what you're waiting for."

Mike shrugged. "What the hell, it's only an airplane."

He walked beneath the black expanse and peered into open access panels as would an airline pilot on his pre-flight inspection. The others followed and mingled with groups of technicians wearing white coats. Mike caught a toothy grin from a member of the white-coats. George Koisumi lifted a fist with an upward thumb. "Uh oh," Brian said, "Tlouble."

Patterakis' team crawled throughout and over the airplane, while the company tech reps gave answers that were previously secret. They reduced the giant airplane from an enigma to just another challenge.

After Mike did his walk-around, he stood in front of the giant black beast with his arms folded. "I don't know. What do you think?"

"I don't think it'll fly." Brian rubbed his chin.

"Then how'd it get here?"

"Osmosis."

"I don't think so."

"I keep wondering if we're on 'Candid Camera,'" Brian said.

"Strange how it looks with no cockpit windows."

"I noticed that."

"Who needs windows when you have the SID?"

"Curtains," Brian responded.

"Curtains?"

"Yeah, budget requirements. No windows means we don't have to buy curtains."

"Funny, Brian, funny. How would you describe the shape?"

"Well-l-l-l," Brian scratched his head and cocked it sideways as he scanned the unusual combination of sweeping curves and sharp straight edges. "It doesn't have a fuselage. It doesn't have a tail. I'd say it's a giant, black, apple turnover."

Mike squinted as he strained for the connection.

"Well, damn it," Brian said, "look at it—shaped like a triangle, more or less, and crimped along the back, and fat at the point of the triangle. That fat part is where the filling is. And guess what the filling is, compadre?" Brian asked, poking Mike in the side. "The filling is you and me."

Mike pondered the humor of being the filling in a giant black turnover. One of the things he loved about the military was its irreverent, dark humor. Dropping napalm was "making crispy critters." Firing cannon into the jungle was "tossing salad." Airplane factories gave their airplanes names like Phantom, Intruder, Thunderchief, Super Stratofortress, Corsair, and Galaxy. Warriors gave them names like Lead Sled, Sluf, Buff, Stoof, Scooter, and Fat Albert. While other professionals puffed the importance of their career fields, warriors dealt with their job by trivializing it—backing away from it. Perhaps it was the only way to deal with the cruel realities.

But what name would this beast be given? Turnover? Mike doubted it. Maybe no one would come up with a nickname that would stick to this airplane. It sat here, malevolent and sinister. If the universe had ever invented an icon for death, this was it. This airplane looked like it was coughed up from hell.

1983, Saturday, 20 August
0810 Hours (8:10 AM)
Las Vegas, Nevada

"Hey, Dad. Catch." Mike spun around with the morning paper in hand and focused on a baseball that flew in a gentle arc toward him. The ball smacked in his palm. There stood Scotty Christum, otherwise known by his father as Snooperman. His black cleats sunk into the grass under the mulberry tree, and his striped Little League uniform rose to his sharp chin. A big smile exposed teeth that were getting straighter with the help of a wire retainer. He had his dad's straight nose, but it was covered with his mom's freckles. Blue eyes flashed below the baseball cap that mashed red hair against his forehead and the top of his ears. He was eleven now.

"Hey, Dad. Catch," Scotty called again as he ran to Mike and jumped.

Mike stepped back, opened his arms, and braced himself. "Oooph!" Scotty thudded against him and flung his arms around Mike's neck. The paper bounced on the sidewalk. The ball bounced a time or two, then rolled to rest on the grass. Mike enveloped the boy and felt the brushy red hair against his cheek. He closed his eyes and enjoyed the feeling of his son held close. Moments like this were numbered as Scotty grew up.

Then, he remembered that he'd cautioned Scotty about

this very thing. He lowered his son to the ground, and pointed his finger at Scotty's nose. "Son, haven't I warned you about jumping up like that? If you hurt Dad's back, the Navy won't let me fly anymore." Mike was firm.

The boy looked down. "Oops. Sorry, Dad." His memory wasn't growing as fast as his body.

"Stop doing it."

"Sorry."

"No harm done this time, but try to remember, OK?"

"OK, Dad. I will."

It was so damned hard to see him grow up. He felt like he had just stolen a bit of Scotty's childhood. "Little fellers just passin' through," Mike's dad used to say, and Mike saw his responsibility as a father as making sure his children were ready for the trip through adulthood.

Mike smiled. "OK, Snooperman. Get your stuff ready."

Scotty had learned that when he heard "Scott," it was not good news. "Scotty" was pretty good. "Son" meant it was time for a lesson, but "Snooperman" meant everything was fine. "OK, Dad."

Mike saw Kachina framed in the doorway. Time had brought grace to her face. She held Lisa Marie, now eighteen months, on a cocked hip. "Hi, Button Nose," he called as he waved.

"Hi, Daa-ee."

Scotty raced by with his ball mitt. He pulled his red bike away from the trunk of the mulberry tree, its front wheel skidding on the grass. He threw a leg over the bar and rode to Mike. "Hey, Dad. When I get back from baseball camp, you wanna play video games?"

"Yeah. Sure. Loser buys pizza."

"Sir?" The bike skidded to a stop and the hopeful smile disappeared.

"You don't plan on losing, do you?"

"Heck, no." Then, taking a page out of his dad's child-training manual, "I just don't want to over—, uh, over-obligate myself."

Mike laughed. "I understand. I'll buy the pizza." Mike

placed his hands on the boy's shoulders. "Listen, you do your best today, OK?" He didn't wait for an answer. "Coach and your teammates are depending on you for that. I know its only practice, but you have to work just as hard as you work at the game. Got that?"

Scotty had heard the little speech before. "No sweat, Dad. I'm the little engine that can, remember?"

"The little engine that can." Words passed to Mike by his parents were now having an effect on his own children.

"See ya' later, Pop."

"Did you kiss your mother goodbye?"

"Yes, sir."

"Did you kiss your sister goodbye?"

"Ah, Dad. I gotta go."

Mike chuckled. "Adios, Mickey Mantle."

Scotty centered his rear on the seat and pushed down the walk.

"Wait!" Kachina called from the porch. Scotty stopped. "Your lunch!" She disappeared into the house while Mike walked to the porch. He reached up as she reappeared, holding a brown bag.

Mike took the bag. "Hey!" Scotty turned. "Catch."

The brown sack sailed through the air. Scotty's face was hopeful and concerned. Mike glanced at his wife, whose eyes were wide and white. Then he looked back at his son. Scotty was focused. A single arm reached up while the other steadied the bike. The bag slapped his small palm, then he pressed the bag against his chest. He was satisfied with himself, cocky. He and his dad exchanged grins. Kachina relaxed. "Bye, guys," he said, then pedaled down the sidewalk, his bike's front wheel wobbling as he picked up speed.

"Be careful!" Kachina called after him.

"Work hard!" Mike yelled.

Scotty waved over his shoulder.

"Michael," Kachina admonished, "that had a bag of potato chips in it."

"Oops." Mike didn't think it was a big deal, but he hadn't

put the lunch together, either. To him it was nothing but a sack lunch, but to her, he knew, it was a loving addition to Scotty's day, and therefore very important. "Sorry."

Kachina took in a deep breath while she shook her head.

A matronly woman wearing a blue dress with large white polka dots came up the walk. "Honey, Mrs. Robinson's here. You ready to ship off another crumb cruncher?"

Kachina kissed Lisa and put her down. The little girl descended the porch steps one at a time. Kachina cringed. Mike encouraged. When Lisa reached the sidewalk, she found her confidence and ran to her father with an uneven gait. Her blonde curls shimmered as she quick-stepped through the shafts of sunlight that filtered through the tree. Scotty was Kachina's child. Lisa was Mike's. She had his eyes, his face, and his attitude. In the old family photos, she looked like his mom at this age. He picked her up and gave her a squeeze.

"Bye, Da-ee." Lisa popped a kiss against Mike's cheek. He put her down. She stood for a moment with her mouth in an open smile. Mike had been trying to teach her to wink. He winked and waited. She squinted with both eyes, while her little button of a nose creased.

"Good enough," he said as he touched her nose.

She took Mrs. Robinson's hand.

"Bye, Sweetheart," Mike said as he watched his daughter walk away, holding the old woman's forefinger.

Mike walked to Kachina, who held out her slender arms. He took her by the waist and watched Lisa skip down the sidewalk. "I'm sorry about the lunch." One thing he knew about Kachina was that a sincere apology washed away all wrongs instantly. Well, most wrongs.

As the girl and the woman turned the corner, Mike and Kachina walked inside. The hallway was decorated with plaques and other mementos Mike had collected since commissioning in the Navy. He called it his "I Love Me" wall. On the wall was a plaque made of monkey pod that memorialized his 1972 tour at Yankee Station. Beyond that were plaques signed by squadron mates that spoke of five other cruises, each of which took him away from his family for an average of six months. There was a matted arrangement that included his commissioning certificate and Kachina's business degree.

At the end of the wall was a shadow box that held her collegiate swimming medals.

"I don't get it," he said as he walked into the kitchen.

"Don't get what?" she asked as she put bread into the toaster.

"How someone with skinny legs and big boobs can swim so well."

"My legs aren't skinny."

"Must be those big feet, then."

She spun around and put a tiny glob of margarine onto the tip of his nose.

He moved into her, grabbed her bottom, and lifted her to sit onto the counter with her legs spread to either side of him.

She wrapped her arms around his neck and her legs around his waist. With tiny licks, she removed the margarine from his nose, then kissed him full on the mouth. She felt him stiffen against her.

Then, she dropped an ice cube from the orange juice down the back of his housecoat.

He jumped and reached to his lower back. The cube hit the floor, then skittered beneath the refrigerator. "What did you do that for?"

"Next time you'll think before you call my feet big," she sniffed.

A shadow seemed to cross her face. The happiness that followed her everywhere left the room.

Mike saw her melancholy. "What?"

"Nothing."

He held his open hand on her cheek. "What, honey?"

"Nothing."

"You're biting your lips."

"So?"

"You always bite the inside of your lips when you want me to drag something out of you."

She looked up at him, a slight smile, but sad eyes. "It's just that … Umm. I know I shouldn't be—"

He lifted her housecoat. "OK. Enough of that. Wanna fool around?"

She shoved the housecoat back down. "No, I don't wanna fool around!"

"Then talk to me. Your choice."

"I'm not one of the kids, Michael. Don't give me the choices that you want."

He was a little sheepish now. "I didn't mean to do that."

She toyed with the fabric of his housecoat. "I know. You just want me to talk."

"Please?"

"It's this tour. This place."

"What about it?"

"Somehow, you're farther away than when you're on cruise. And I—I don't like the desert so much."

"You said you'd grown to like it."

"Oh, I do. This is a nice town, after all and the desert is beautiful."

"I don't understand."

"I think it's the wind."

Mike took a breath, looked at the ceiling for a moment, then studied her troubled eyes. "Kachina, what are you talking about?"

She tapped his chest with her forefinger. "It's in here, Michael. It's like a part of you is the desert wind—"

"Kachina—"

"Let me finish."

He nodded.

"There's something out there, where you go. And you bring it home with you. And what you bring home is—"

He didn't move.

Tears welled in her eyes. "What you bring home is—fear. And Michael, you're never afraid."

"I'm not afraid of—"

"Yes, you are!"

He was shaken by her conviction.

She was surprised, too. "I—I—Sorry. I didn't mean—"

"I know." He wrapped his arms around her. She hadn't felt like this—so small like this—not since they parted in Hawaii years ago.

She continued, "You're not scared for you. You never are. But this thing—I see it in your eyes when we're all around the table. I hear it when you talk to the children." She began to cry. "I know it's there. I can feel it—and I'm so frightened." Her shoulders shook as her tears turned into sobs.

"Kachina."

"Michael, you're not afraid for you. You're afraid for us!"

He breathed heavy through his mouth as he fought to keep control. He couldn't let her go and see him, confirm her suspicions, not about this. He tightened his hold on her. He raised his red eyes and looked out the kitchen window—out into the desert where the wind blew the tumbleweeds.

1983, SATURDAY, 27 AUGUST
1830 HOURS (6:30 PM)
GROOM LAKE BASE, NEVADA

This was their thirteenth flight in Rhombus. In spite of the risks of their profession, American warriors are not prone to superstition, although doing the thirteenth of anything does give one pause for thought. Perhaps in warfare the superstition of the thirteenth is also bad luck for your enemy, too. That would make it a wash.

Mike steered Rhombus toward the taxiway, while Brian attended to his co-pilot duties. The flight tonight was the first of a five-day evolution that would put Rhombus, its aviators, and its maintenance crew under maximum stress. Tonight, they would simulate an attack on the USS *Bunker Hill* as it steamed off the coast of San Diego. Tomorrow, they would fly a 15-hour mission to South America and back. The day after, they would stand on alert for a target that would remain secret until they were airborne. The exercise was to simulate warfare over an extended period of time. Whatever happened, they had to fly as much of the mission profile as they could.

The *Bunker Hill* was the most advanced ship in the world. A super-computer that saw the world through sophisticated radar controlled its weapon systems. It could see a bumblebee at ten miles. At one mile, it could shoot the bee down with a bullet fired from its Gattling gun. It would be at battle stations as Rhombus mock-attacked it from a 70,000-foot cruise. If everything worked as expected, the *Bunker Hill* would return to port tonight after a very boring time of seeing nothing.

Mike called for the Before Takeoff checklist as they approached the runway.

Brian pushed a button and the checklist appeared on one of the CRTs. He called the items. "Electrical systems, check. Flaps set to takeoff position. Stability augmentation, on. Autopilot, off. Spoilers, in. Thrust limiters set to two-point-five. Ejection seat pins, removed. Before Takeoff check complete."

"SatBurst that we're ready, Brian."

Brian typed on his keyboard, then pressed a button. The MPP compressed the message, then burst it in a nanosecond to the satellite net. The net burst it down to CIC. They sat at the end of the runway waiting for their take-off time. Rhombus idled.

"Scotty should be in the first inning right about now," Mike said as he looked toward Las Vegas.

"He bats third in the lineup," Brian responded. "You got a slugger there."

"Yeah, the little guy's pretty darned good, isn't he?"

"Sure is. I couldn't believe he got an in-the-park home run last Saturday. I didn't know what would blow out first, my ear or Kachina's voice."

"She does get into it, doesn't she?"

"How's she holding up on this assignment?" Brian asked.

"We leave at dawn on Monday morning from Nellis to

come up here and don't get back until Friday. All the while she thinks we're at Nellis."

"Yeah, but how's she holding up?"

"Yes. I mean, you have to believe something's not right when you're told your husband works ten miles away and can't come home on weeknights. When she asks, I just give her the same old line about flying A-Sevens with the Air Force—mission requirements and all that. She knows something's up, though. She's not stupid."

"Mike, you're not answering my question."

"I know."

"Sorry."

"Oh, we're OK. It's just that—it's tough."

After a pause, Mike added, "I wish this maximum flex exercise were taking place during the week. I don't like being away on the weekend."

"Well, things'll get back to normal next week. We're gonna be tired as hell when this is over, and I think the Skipper's gonna give us some leave," Brian said.

"Boy, that would be great." Mike eyed a jackrabbit crossing the runway ahead. "Keep moving, bunny. We don't want to run over you."

"Our takeoff window will open in sixty seconds."

Mike scanned the expanse of the valley and the mountains around it. "See here, Brian? See how the sun hits the mountains?"

"Mountains is mountains, I say."

Mike ignored him. "I took Kachina and the kids out in the desert north of Las Vegas this spring. You couldn't walk without stepping on a flower of some kind. This place looks like the moon until you get to know it."

Brian rolled his eyes.

"Gorgeous. Just gorgeous," Mike said to himself as he looked at the Pintwater Mountains.

Gorgeous. Just gorgeous, Brian mouthed.

"I think what I like most about it is—it's timeless. Like nothing has changed in a million years."

"Speaking of time," Brian said. "Five, four, three, two, one, go."

Mike eased the throttles and Rhombus moved toward the runway. The sun had just set, but its rays skimmed the tops of the mountains around the flat. The barren maroon-and-orange-tipped peaks seemed to move around the bomber as it turned its nose down the white stripes. Mike pushed the throttles forward, and he and Brian were treated to the work of thousands of engineers as the metal bird began its race to heaven.

When they reached their calculated takeoff airspeed, Brian called, "Rotate." Mike eased back on the joystick and Rhombus skied on the dry Nevada air. "Gear and flaps up," Mike called. Brian raised the appropriate levers.

Instead of pulling the nose higher, Mike pulled the throttles back and leveled off. "What's the matter?" Brian asked. "Heart can't take the climb anymore?"

"I thought you'd appreciate the view down here before we head for the cool blue."

"You and your views."

"You're a heathen, you know that?"

"I am a heathen, but you're a flake."

"Am not."

"Am too."

"Am not."

"Am too."

They were level at 7,500 feet. The powerful engines relaxed, their muted whine no more evident than a baby's breath, and the wind brushed by the bomber like a spring breeze. The sky was like a glass dome that bent the light from the setting sun in a grand arch over the landscape. In the west the dome was red where it touched the earth and, as it vaulted to the east, it turned from red to orange, to blue, and finally to black. The earth turned beneath them, and the blackness of night rushed from the east as the last ribbons of sunlight raced away to keep the falling sun from leaving them behind.

Mike pushed the throttles forward and pulled Rhombus'

nose 45 degrees up. The plane and its pilots left the earth behind, and the majestic Nevada mountains passed into irrelevance and seemed no higher than the expanse of the dry lake beds that lay at their feet. Mike rolled Rhombus to the right, and the war machine chased after the sun. It charged into the brilliant tangent of light that skipped past the earth's edge. Golden-red rays poured onto the bomber's bottom, wrapped around its giant body through the Aurora coating, then shot into space. Rhombus left no shadow in its passing.

The unknown was beauty, the horizon a mystery, and every tomorrow held a surprise. This was the intoxication of military flying.

Some months ago, long before this grand event took place, the turbine wheel of a CJ-1 engine was forged in a ceramic furnace. In spite of numerous and expensive safeguards, the furnace heated unevenly, giving the turbine wheel various strengths across its surface. That wheel had been installed in a CJ engine, and that engine had been mounted in Rhombus. As the two warriors and their airplane passed 60,000 feet, the ceramic turbine wheel of the number-one engine began to change shape, atom by atom, molecule by molecule.

When they reached 70,000 feet—about 13 miles above the earth—Mike leveled Rhombus and turned south. To their left America lay in darkness, even though brilliant sunlight streamed in from the right. Mike saw Interstates 10 and 8 cutting eastward through Southern California and Arizona, connecting the spots of light known below as San Bernardino, Phoenix, and Tucson. He banked to the right and saw the disk of the sun just above the curvature of the earth. The sun looked like the headlight of a train approaching from the darkness. Up here there were no blue sky and red sunsets.

Mike pulled back the throttles, flipped a switch on the center console that engaged the autopilot, and called, "Level-off and Cruise checklist." Brian pulled up the checklist, and a muted whine filled the cockpit as the warplane relaxed.

Whispering through the high heavens, a single machine made of man's genius flew higher than an eagle and was more ominous than a shark. Rhombus was fiction come alive. Like fire, it was, at the same time, man's greatest enemy and his greatest friend. And if any eagle could fly where Rhombus flew, the eagle would hear Rhombus' passing as the fire burned within it and pushed it over the curve of the earth. Nature had a million faces from the air. Each flight was a new adventure with the science of man pushing through skies that were never the same, their beauty defined by the passage of time.

The preliminary test routine had gone perfectly, so Mike and Brian were ahead of schedule and over the Pacific about 20 miles west of San Diego. In six minutes they would turn westward and head for the *Bunker Hill*. Mike looked to the northeast, back toward the Southern California coastline. The straight but fuzzy line called the terminator that separated night from day had rolled over San Diego about an hour ago. The full moon washed the earth in pale blue light. He turned in his seat to see back as far as he could. There, over his left shoulder, was a light mass that marked the edge of the Los Angeles metropolitan area. He looked along a thin lighted line he knew to be Interstate 5. Clumps of lights representing coastal towns clung to the line like pearls of various sizes to a strand. At the south end of the strand was the giant lighted pearl of San Diego.

On the north end of San Diego bay, sitting almost downtown, was Lindbergh Field, the city's airport. A spider web of gold and blue lights outlined its runways and taxiways. Across the bay from Lindbergh was another web of gold and blue lights where Mike had landed many times. It was Naval Air Station North Island. He rolled Rhombus to the left again, and saw the two runways on the air station described by intersecting double lines of white lights. One runway ran more or less parallel with the Coronado beach. The beach drew a crescent-shaped line by the coastal towns of Coronado and Imperial Beach and on to Tijuana, Mexico. He loved the area with its cool summer evenings and ocean breezes, and wondered what it must be like down there right now.

Mike turned his attention from the beauty outside to the

beauty inside. Sweeping from his left elbow across the cockpit and to Brian's right, CRTs glowed with quiet competence as they painted important information on their glass screens. Everything Rhombus did—where they were, how high they were, the level of their fuel, and a hundred other things—was monitored and displayed as charts, lines, circles, or numbers. Warm white light mixed with reds, greens, and blues. Switches stood this way and that, and the labels on switches glowed to show how they were positioned. Brian worked competently, his methodical movements softened by the glow.

Man does not really build machines, he only reorders nature into different forms. His reordering of nature to make one particular turbine wheel was not a high achievement. The turbine spun at more than 10,000 revolutions per minute, pushed into its rotational frenzy by flames shooting through its fan-shaped vanes. The fire had been less intense since Mike pulled back on the throttles. As a result, the temperature of the turbine dropped several hundred degrees. Like a rock cliff that heated and cooled, a crack developed in the wheel. It split a few millimeters, then exploded.

Ceramic pieces from one side of the turbine wheel shot away.

The lopsided wheel vibrated.

The engine hammered its mountings.

The compressor blades in the inlet wobbled and ground away the inside of the engine casing.

The imbalance shook Rhombus' insides.

Bits of hot ceramic and molten metal flew faster than bullets toward the fuel tanks.

They bounced off the titanium armor and sought the tailpipe as their only escape.

Outward into the night they flew, leaving a long streak of sparks behind, like the hand of God striking a bar of flint across the black wrought-iron sky.

Below, on the beach of Coronado, an old man held his grandson as he viewed the Pacific. The little boy raised a finger and pointed at the sparks that Rhombus trailed through the night sky. "Make a wish, Dappy," the little boy called. "Make a wish."

"What the hell?" Brian's voice flashed through the intercom.

The yellow Master Caution light flashed on.

Mike grabbed the controls and pressed a button on the joystick that turned the autopilot off.

Brian pressed the Master Caution light off. He scanned the engine instruments. In monotone he called,

"Number-one engine.

"Low RPM.

"Increasing temp.

"Low oil pressure.

"High vibration."

Mike retarded the throttles to lose energy in case he needed a rapid descent.

A warning light flashed on. The cockpit glared red.

"Number one's on fire," Brian called.

The CJ engines were buried deep inside Rhombus in tunnels that ran the length of the bomber through its fuel tanks. Number one was burning within inches of jet fuel—and they were 13 miles above the earth.

Mike pulled the engine's fire handle. Servos closed all fuel, hydraulic, and air lines to the engine.

He pressed a button above the handle. Foam shot out of a bottle in the front of the engine and flowed through the burning core. One thousand one, one thousand two, one thousand three, one thousand four, one thousand five.

The red light stayed on.

"Damn!" Mike pressed the button again. This time foam shot from a bottle mounted near the turbine section. One thousand one, one thousand two, one thousand three, one thousand four, one thousand five. The red light glowed.

"We're outta here." Mike slapped the joystick to the left. "Give me alternate airports, Brian."

The wounded warplane fell from the edge of space as it pitched its nose downward and streaked through the night sky for the safety of a runway.

Brian typed on his keyboard. The MPP scanned its memory for the best emergency runway. It had to be a runway at a military field with a Tango Team security detachment.

"Command steering to NAS North Island, Michael," Brian called.

Bars that looked like crosshairs appeared on Mike's attitude CRT. If Mike steered Rhombus to kept the bars centered, the MPP would guide them to the runway. If he selected autopilot, the MPP would fly the airplane for him.

Mike rolled upside down.

He pulled back pressure until the nose was straight down.

The altimeter moved, its numbers a blur.

Rhombus hurled toward the Pacific.

Airspeed climbed. Brian called it out. "Mach point nine-five.

"Mach one-point-zero.

"We're supersonic.

"Mach one-point-one.

"One-point-two.

"One-point-three.

"Max airspeed is one-point-six," Brian reminded.

Mike pulled back on the joystick until his dive changed from straight down to about 25 degrees down. His heading was northeast.

The airspeed climbed.

"Mach one-point-four.

"Mach one-point-five.

"Mach one-point-six! Maximum airspeed allowed!"

"Danger. Overspeed. Danger. Overspeed. Danger. Overspeed," the MPP shouted its metallic voice through the intercom.

"Mach one-point-seven," Brian called. He sat with his hands folded.

The red light pulsed through the cockpit: FIRE FIRE FIRE.

"Danger. Overspeed. Danger. Overspeed. Danger.

Overspeed."

Supersonic shock waves built inside the engine inlets and moved closer to the engines. If they touched the compressors, the engines would stall and probably destroy themselves.

"Mach one-point-eight."

FIRE FIRE FIRE.

A growl laced with dark danger filled the cockpit as the shock waves worked their way toward the engines while they banged against the sides of the intakes.

"Danger. Overspeed. Danger. Overspeed. Danger. Overspeed."

"Mach one-point-nine," Brian called. He glanced at Mike. Mike was impassive, as though he were sitting in a car waiting for a red light to change. Brian shook his head.

Mike scanned the instrument panel. The command steering bars were far from center. Rhombus was not where the MPP wanted it to be.

He adjusted his dive angle to hold an airspeed that kept the rumble in the airframe from changing—no louder, no softer. He was flying Rhombus by sound.

A loud bang knocked Brian's feet off the floor.

Mike forced his feet harder on the rudder pedals.

Another bang. "Damn," Brian said.

Tiny red flags popped up on number-two's instruments. Brian called, "Number two."

"RPMs falling.

"Temp going up.

"Seventeen hundred degrees—

"Eighteen hundred degrees—"

Another bang. Brian's fingers curled around the ejection handles. He continued his calls. "Number two EPR fluctuating.

"Nineteen hundred degrees.

"Two thousand degrees.

"We're losing two.

"Twenty-one hundred degrees."

"Danger. Overspeed. Danger. Overspeed. Danger.

Overspeed."

"Twenty-two hundred degrees."

"Danger. Overspeed. Danger. Overspeed. Danger. Overspeed."

The fire light winked off.

"Good," Mike grunted. He pulled hard on the joystick, but kept his throttles in position. He didn't want to risk having the other engines flame out.

Rhombus' nose rose until it climbed at a 45-degree angle.

"Mach one-point-six," Brian called.

Mike eased the throttles back.

"Mach one-point-five."

The growl stopped.

The MPP quit shouting its overspeed calls.

Upward they climbed as Rhombus bled off airspeed.

"Airspeed below Mach one," Brian's voice dropped in pitch.

The red flags on number-two's instruments retracted, and it restarted automatically.

Mike increased backpressure on the joystick until Rhombus went straight up, then over on its back.

Airspeed fell to 120 knots, the speed of a Cessna.

Rhombus swooped down the back of the loop and at the bottom of the loop it reached 465 knots.

The nose came up again until it was 45 degrees high. Mike held it there. He was using the loop and the climb to get rid of the energy that Rhombus gained in its dive.

The airspeed dropped to 250 knots.

Mike rolled Rhombus upside down again and pulled the nose 30 degrees down.

He rolled the airplane to the left until it was wings-level.

The crosshairs of the command steering bars centered. Mike had flown a convoluted course that intersected the course the MPP had set way back, and way up. The difference, though, was that the supersonic airflow through the number-one engine had blown the fire out. Fortunately, the overspeed hadn't hurt the other engines. "Did you enjoy the barbecue, Brian?" he asked.

Brian sat, his arms crossed. "Man," he said, "if we'd lost the other three engines, we'd be the world's heaviest glider right now."

"We had to risk it."

"I know."

Throughout Rhombus' gyration, the MPP had SatBurst data that was displayed on consoles in Groom Lake Base. "Uh oh," the petty officer said as information scrolled across his computer screen. "We have a problem with Shaman." He pressed a red button. Lights came on in the Pentagon, a building at NAS North Island, and in the White House.

"What's that noise?" Brian asked. The cockpit reverberated with a deep but muted rumble that came from everywhere. "Instruments are OK."

Mike pushed number-two's throttle forward. Its whine increased. He pulled the throttle back. He did the same for number three and number four. "It's not the engines." They scanned for a clue.

"I'll bet it's a harmonic in number-one's intake," Mike said. "Probably full of debris—air vibrating in there—like a big siren."

"Agree," Brian said.

Rhombus streaked toward San Diego through some of the heaviest air traffic in the world. The MPP picked the way around other airplanes. The SID displayed the world outside in Real Video mode. The San Diego area was a mass of lights surrounded by black.

"Go Standard Tactical Video," Mike called.

Brian pressed a button on the center console. Now it was bright as midday. Evening haze hugged the coastline, and ragged bits of it broke away and scudded inland.

"Go Clear Tactical Video," Mike called. Brian pressed another button. The haze disappeared. The MPP did its magic as it saw what the eye couldn't see and displayed the dark hazy world in midday brightness and color.

From the west Rhombus flew toward the Hotel del Coronado, its engines idle, spoilers out, and airspeed dropping. A half-mile from coastline, Mike rolled the big airplane into a sharp left turn. He retracted the spoilers and called for Brian to lower the landing gear. Three green lights in a triangle came on, indicating that the gear was down. He called for flaps. Rhombus pitched forward as the flaps extended. "Jeez, I can't believe this noise!" Brian shouted.

Mike almost called for Brian to pay close attention to the instruments. He knew that was already being done, so he kept silent.

Rhombus rolled out of the turn, headed for the runway. Their velocity dropped to approach speed and the screaming noise mellowed to a growl. Two rows of white lights lined each side of the concrete ribbon and opened for them like the arms of a guardian angel. Passing over the rolling surf, they descended into the mist.

Ahead, at the end of the runway, little red-and-white-checkerboard buildings came into view. Near the buildings was a Jeep Cherokee. Beside it a man was bent at the waist and looking in their direction. That guy's in for a surprise, Mike thought.

Green and red approach lights passed beneath them. Mike cut the throttles and raised Rhombus' nose in the landing flare. The wheels kissed the concrete runway with a protracted screech. It was so smooth Brian wasn't quite sure they'd touched down. He shook his head. "Damned amazing pilot."

"Say again?" Mike asked.

"I said my mother could've done better."

A small orange square flashed on the SID. It framed a Hummer sitting on one of the taxiways. Mike steered toward it and followed the vehicle into one of the large hangars. He braked to a stop inside the hangar on the signal of a sailor who held two flashlights. In seconds an unfamiliar voice came over the intercom. "OK, sir. You can shut the engines down now, but leave everything else on." Mike saw a sailor outside who wore a headset that was plugged into Rhombus' intercom system.

"Engine Shutdown checklist," he called to Brian.

As they went through the checklist, the three good engines dropped through several octaves of whining until they were silent. Mike guessed that the unfamiliar noise of ball bearings in a blender was what remained of number one. In a few seconds, only the electronic sounds of inverters and converters drifted through the intercom.

The two aviators descended the ladder to the ground, eager to see the damage to their airplane. Aurora was still on, so the ladder and landing gear appeared to rise into thin air, looking like a work of modern art. A chief petty officer approached them. "We have to keep it powered until we can obscure the hangar windows. Commander Christum, you and Commander Davis are wanted on the secure phone in that office over there," the chief nodded. "Door number two."

"But I wanted door number one," Brian said.

"Sir?"

Mike waved a hand. "Sorry, Chief. Nothing."

As they walked toward the office door, Mike put his arm around Brian's shoulders, "Well, Brian. We cheated death once again."

"Know what I like about flying this beast, Michael? Hours and hours of absolute boredom interrupted by brief moments of stark terror."

1983, Sunday, 28 August
0030 Hours (12:30 AM)
Naval Air Station North Island
Coronado, California

It had taken them more than four hours on the secure phone to brief Patterakis and a small team of engineers about the flight. That was the easy part. All the aviators had to do was to tell the technicians what had happened to a flying machine comprising several million parts, several million man-hours, and several billion dollars. Even when machines failed, there was predictability to them. When a CJ engine came apart, it just—came apart. It didn't make a decision to do so. It didn't complain, find fault, rationalize its behavior, or stake its territory. There was no such thing as machine politics. Dealing with human beings was something else, again.

Mike picked up a regular phone that sat beside an ashtray. He frowned and waved his hand at the smoke. "Brian, will you get out of here with that thing!"

"PMS," Brian grumbled as he added another butt to the growing mound. He walked out of the office and let the door slam shut. Mike's upper lip curled as he swiped a backhand at the ashtray. It fell into the metal spray-painted waste can with a thud. A small cloud of ashes rose over the can's edge.

He bowed his head and kneaded his forehead. Damn. Brian didn't deserve that. He leaned back in the creaky desk chair. His face was empty of expression as he stared across the small office. Light from the street came through a translucent glass window re-enforced with chicken wire. The chair creaked again as he stood and walked to the window to open it. Wisps of fog eased by the window and fresh air spilled in and rolled with the smoke. He lingered to breathe the scent of dune flowers that rode in on the current, then reached for the telephone. He pressed his home phone number and waited.

"Christum's residence," a young voice answered.

"Maggie, is that you?" Mike asked, surprised the phone was answered so late by Chris Patterakis' daughter.

"Ummm. Hi, Uncle Mike. I'm here because Scotty got hit at the ballpark, and I'm watching Lisa."

"What! Let me speak to Aunt Kachina."

"She's not here, Uncle Mike. She's at the hospital with Scotty. Here …" her voice trailed off as she reached for something. "Aunt Kachina gave me a number for you. She said to call as soon as you can. Do you have a pencil?"

Mike reached across the desk for a yellow pad and a black U.S. Government pen. "Go ahead." He wrote. When he finished he asked, "Is Lisa OK?"

"She's fine. She's asleep now, but she was scared for a while."

"Scared?"

"Well, Aunt Kachina was scared, and I think that rubbed off on Lisa because … Just a sec. I think it's her." The receiver rattled over the line.

"Da-ee?" It was Lisa's tiny raspy voice. "I scared."

He lowered his head to an open hand. He fought the urge to hang up and call the hospital. Lisa needed him. "Why are you scared, honey?"

"Cause Scotty's hurt."

"Do you love Scotty?" Mike asked.

"Yes, sir."

"Sometimes he can be a pain in the neck, huh?"

"Yeah, like when he tries to take my i-ceem."

"But he's funny when he tries to take your ice cream."

"He makes funny faces when he takes my i-ceem, but he not funny."

Mike relaxed a bit. "Is Dolly there?"

"Yes, sir." The phone rumbled for a few seconds as something soft rubbed across it. "She just said hi."

"Well, she told me something."

"She did?"

"Yes. She just told me she wasn't scared."

"She not?"

"No, she's not. She thinks Scotty will be fine."

"He is?"

"Yep. I'll tell you what. I have to leave now, but when I get to the BOQ, I'll call to make sure you're safe. OK?"

"Da-ee?"

"What, honey?"

"What's a BOQ?"

"It stands for Bachelor Officer Quarters." Mike grew impatient. He wanted to find out about Scotty, but one thing, one little person, at a time. "It's a place on base like a hotel. It's where I stay when I'm not home."

"Oh. You call me later?"

"Yeah, honey. I'll call you later."

Then, not a care in the world, "OK. Bye Da-ee. I wuv you."

"I love you, too."

"I go now. Bye." Mike winced at the noise. He and Kachina hadn't been successful in teaching Lisa not to throw the receiver to the floor when she was done. He pictured her blonde curls bouncing as she ran down the hall to her bedroom, clutching the blue-eyed doll with hair of red yarn.

The phone rustled. "You there?"

"Yes. Thanks for your help, Maggie. I'm going to call Aunt Kachina now."

"I'll be here all night, Uncle Mike. So don't worry about Lisa."

The long day pulled at him. "We have to check into the Coronado BOQ tonight, so I'll call as soon as I get there."

There was moment of silence on the other end. "Coronado BOQ? What're you doing there?"

"Oh, I'm sorry." Mike searched for an out. "It's been a long day, and I was just looking at a magazine that had pictures of Coronado in it." A lie.

"OK, Uncle Mike. I'll be here if you need me."

"Thanks, Maggie."

He moved to hang up. "Uncle Mike!" Maggie yelled.

"Yes?"

"Tell Daddy I love him."

"OK. I'll see him in a few minutes." Another lie.

Next, he called the hospital and asked for Kachina.

"Hello." Her fatigue oozed out of the phone, spread over him, dragged him down.

"Hi, sweetheart."

"Mike, where are you?" Her fatigue now had a tearful edge. "It's almost one in the morning."

"Where are you?" he asked, trying to change the subject.

"I'm at the nurse's station. Where are you?"

"I'm out here at Nellis, sweetheart."

"You sound like its long distance."

"You know. These circuits have been bad since we got here."

"I've been trying to reach you for hours. They said you were in a classified briefing. Scotty's hurt. He was hit on the head with a baseball."

"Is he OK?" Mike's military training forced him to the bottom line.

"He was playing ball when—"

"Is he OK?" Firmer this time.

"They're keeping him in the hospital overnight for observation. It was a pretty hard hit. They're sure he'll be fine."

"Well, that's—"

"Mike, I need you here. When will you be home?"

"I can't come home tonight. We have to fly early tomorrow." Another lie.

"Your son's in the hospital!"

"Sweetheart, you said the doctor said he was going to be OK, right? You know he's a tough kid." He coughed as worry tightened a knot in his chest.

"I don't care what I said. I need you here. And why are you coughing?"

"I dunno."

"It's your stress cough, isn't it, Michael?"

"Sweetheart …"

"When is this going to stop?"

"When is what going to stop?"

"When it's time for stitches, it's up to me. When its time to move, it's up to me. Our son's in the hospital and you—"

"I helped on the move to Las Vegas." He felt immature and stupid.

"Yeah," she said. "This time. And how many moves have we had, Michael?" She sniffed. "How many times?"

"Kachina," Mike cooed.

Her voice softened. "Oh, Michael. I know you can't help it. And I know I'm being emotional, but ple-e-ease, Michael. Please come home."

Tears welled in his eyes. His Kachina, his tower, rudder, uplifting wind, the woman who had stood against it all with graceful strength, needed his shoulder to lay her head on and cry her heart out.

"I can't, Kachina. I can't."

"I love you, Michael. You are my life." Then softly, "I have to go. Bye."

"Bye. I love—" A click interrupted.

Mike placed the receiver in the cradle.

"You OK?" came the voice from behind. It was Brian.

"You heard?" Mike asked.

"Yeah. Is Scotty OK?"

"They say so." He rapped a fingertip against the desk. "We gotta get home tomorrow. Come hell or high water, Chris Patterakis better get me home tomorrow. I'll walk if the airplane isn't fixed."

Brian put a beefy arm around Mike's shoulder.

"I'll give my life for my country, but the price my family pays weighs heavy on me, buddy. And my wife."

"She's doing fine, Mike."

"Brian, Kachina's never, ever, begged me for anything until now. I had to tell her no."

"Well, since I'm not married, I don't know those pressures, but there's one thing I know."

"What?"

"Men and women handle things differently. Just because Kachina's upset right now doesn't mean she doesn't understand, and it sure doesn't mean she can't handle it."

"I don't know."

"What was the last thing she said to you."

"Oh, hell. You know her. She told me I was her life."

"I rest my case." Brian paused. "Taxi's here."

"What makes you so darned smart about marriage, anyway?" Mike asked as he scooted the chair back.

"Easy. Since I'm no longer married, I'm not so close to it that I don't understand it."

Mike wasn't sure he understood that one, but in some convoluted way it sounded reasonable. "You're adding to my worries," he said.

"Why?"

"Because you're beginning to make sense to me."

"I see your point," Brian said. "That would be bad news

for both of us, wouldn't it?"

A chief met them outside the office. He was covered in oily soot. "It ain't too bad, sir." He looked down at himself. "In case you can't tell, I just crawled out of the engine bay."

"Well, damn," Brian said. "I was expecting an Al Jolsen tune."

The chief's teeth gleamed. "Sir, the harder I wash this face, the blacker it gets."

It was then that Brian noticed the chief's broad nose and kinky hair. He turned, well, white. "Ahh, hell, Chief. I didn't mean—"

"No big deal, sir." The chief held out a grimy hand. Brian reflexively took it. The chief shook real good and real long. Brian withdrew his hand, looked at it, then to Mike.

"You do this to me all the time," Mike said. "You get yourself into these things. You can get yourself out."

"I think I'll just—" Brian jutted a thumb at the men's head, "you know—go wash—you know—my hand. Hands!"

As Brian walked across the hangar, Mike smiled at the chief. The chief said, "Commander Davis is a good one, ain't he, sir?"

"He's the best, Chief." Mike made sure Brian was out of hearing range. "Do me a favor."

"Yes, sir."

"Act a little hurt around Commander Davis for a week." Mike winked. "That'll really get to him."

"You got it, sir." Then the chief turned to business. "The titanium armor casing held up OK. There's no damage to the airframe." He spit a few bits of metal into his hand. "The engine's toast, of course, but brought a new one with us. We'll have it replaced in about four hours. The other three engines look good. Give us five hours—six tops and you'll be ready to go. Then the rest of us'll pack up and get back home behind you."

"Chief, when you're one hour from being done, call us at the Coronado BOQ. I want to take off as soon as you're ready."

"Aye, aye, sir. Have a good night's sleep."

Mike met Brian as he emerged from the head. "Well?"

"Oh, man. I feel terrible."

"Good."

"I didn't hurt his feelings, did I?"

"He'll be fine in a week."

"A week! Oh, man. I feel terrible."

The two pilots walked past their invisible airplane and out of the hangar. Maintenance men pulled equipment from two C-141s that brought them from Groom Lake. The cool night air caressed the big jets with heavy veils of fog. The 141s had large graceful doors that opened at aft ends beneath jaunty tails with white lights at their tops. Their noses disappeared into the fog, and their navigation lights looked like red and green cotton balls glued to the tips of their long, high-mounted, droopy wings.

The base taxi moved through the fog toward the BOQ at Naval Amphibious Base, Coronado. "One of these days," said Brian, "I'm gonna pack underwear and a toothbrush in my helmet bag. Oh, the thought of brushing my teeth with a wash cloth is a joy that's hard to comprehend."

Mike didn't respond. He pondered the small neat homes they passed by and worried about Kachina and Scotty. Then, "What did you say?"

"Nothing."

Mike's worry tightened the knot in his chest and laid cords of sour putty in his stomach. "Brian," he said, his face curious. "What did you mean back in the office when you said you were no longer married?"

"I didn't say that."

"Yes you did."

"I didn't say that."

Mike looked back at the houses.

The car pulled up to the BOQ. "Thanks," they said to the driver as they stepped out. Cold, dark, thudding fatigue grew behind Mike's eyes. His armpits had a crunchy-sticky feeling that shouted for a shower. He walked along the sidewalk to the registration office and found no comfort in the heady scent of mock orange that mingled with the fog. He pushed open the aluminum-framed door and walked up to the desk. "Commanders Christum and Davis checking in."

Behind the counter a lovely Filipino woman welcomed them, had them fill out registration cards, gave them their keys, and directed them to the appropriate building in the BOQ complex. "Commander Christum," she said, then nodded to a corner of the lobby. "There's a man who wants to talk to you."

A master chief petty officer in khakis sat in the corner of the lobby beside a lamp that was turned off. He stood as Mike approached. "Sir," he said as he extended his hand, "I'm Master Chief Dick McIntyre. I need to talk with you, officially."

"Damn, Chief. Can't this wait until morning?"

"Afraid not, sir. Can we step outside?"

Mike looked at Brian and shrugged.

Chief McIntyre walked to a point on the lawn that was equally distant between two buildings. He said, "Sir, I'm a member of the Tango Team."

"Oh, brother," Mike responded.

"Sir, in your call to your family tonight, you told the girl who answered that you were checking into the Coronado BOQ."

"You heard my phone call!"

"We always do, sir. You know that."

"Is there a security violation in saying the wrong thing?" Anger took root in the ball of fatigue that grew behind his eyes.

Chief McIntrye stammered. "No—uh—no, sir. Technically not, but if the bad guys were also monitoring your phone call, they might suspect you're not at Nellis tonight. We just want to, uh, keep you out of trouble."

"Unbelievable," Mike said. Then in a challenging voice, "Is that all, Chief?"

"Yes, sir."

Mike glared at McIntyre for a moment, then walked toward Brian who waited at the corner of the building. Brian raised an eyebrow. The anger on Mike's face faded. He turned to see the chief disappearing into the fog. "Chief McIntyre!" he called.

McIntyre, seeing it was Mike, walked back. The two men met again and stood at arm's length.

"Chief McIntyre …" he began, searching for words with which to apologize.

The chief held up his hand. "Sir. It's OK. I know you've had a bad day." He paused. "I just want to say I'm honored to have met you, sir."

Mike regarded the chiseled face and the sandy hair. "Thank you, Chief." He held out his hand, "Likewise."

The chief shook his hand and saluted, and Mike returned the courtesy. Without saying anything more, McIntyre walked away and disappeared into the damp night.

Mike strode past Brian as he headed for the BOQ door. "I just hope this country of ours knows what the hell it's asking us to do."

Brian thought for a moment. "Probably not."

1983, SUNDAY, 28 AUGUST
0403 HOURS (4:03 AM)
IMPERIAL BEACH, CALIFORNIA

The tick-tock of the mantle clock settled in the living room of the small house in Imperial Beach, California. Faded orange and black Spanish-style furniture huddled on gold shag carpet. Framed photos of people who looked alike stood on a small dark table by the front door. The largest photo was a K-mart portrait of two blonde boys who sat in front of a blonde woman. A man, obviously proud of his family, stood beside her. He wore U.S. Navy dress blues with the stripes of a master chief. On his left breast were rows of colored ribbons that sat beneath the wings of a Navy SEAL. The man had a tight waist and powerful shoulders. He had sandy close-cropped hair and a chiseled face.

Pre-dawn light sifted through the sheers that covered the

door window. The shadow of a broad-shouldered man projected itself onto the sheers and grew larger than the man himself as he climbed the porch steps and reached for the doorknob. The careful rattling of a key clicked off the walls and was followed by the sound of the latch. The fragrance of the jasmine he'd planted at the edge of the porch the previous spring followed him through the door like the ghost of a faithful dog. He eased the door closed. Satisfied he hadn't awakened his family, Master Chief Dick McIntyre laid his keys on the table, then sat in his crushed-velour easy chair.

The clock ticked. He winced. Memories of the evening poured on him like an avalanche of bricks. He'd been so damned sure he could do what he had done tonight and not look back—have no regrets. His career was a blend of superb training coupled with total faith in his country and total loyalty to his superiors. He knew his assignment to the Tango Team was going to be tough, but he never imagined it would tear at his guts like this. He never imagined the remorse and sadness. Then, again, he had never killed an American before, and the American he killed last night was a naval officer—a member of his Navy.

His mind reeled at the vision of the dead officer in the Jeep Cherokee who was guilty of nothing more than sitting at the end of a runway. His mouth still tasted of the puke he wretched at the squadron building, while the washing machine in the corner hissed and bumped as it cleaned the bits of flesh and brains off his combat clothing. His lip curled as he thought of one of his team members monitoring Commander Christum's personal phone calls. He shook his head at the memory of telling the Rhombus pilot to be more careful. He hoped Christum's son was OK and knew how he'd feel if one of his boys were hurt.

The scenes of the evening repeated themselves via the VCR of McIntyre's mind, playing and rewinding, playing and rewinding, playing and rewinding. He lowered his head and placed his fists on his temples. He rocked back and forth with his eyes closed.

A shaft of light washed over the carpet from a door down the hall. Muffled footfalls from bare feet padded toward him. The woman in the portrait stopped at the door. Soft morning light showered her delicate features. "Hi," she said as she stood with her hands folded together against her tummy.

McIntyre looked at her, and words he needed to say piled against an invisible wall and stayed locked within. Her smile faded. She walked to her husband and knelt before him. She stroked his large hands and asked, "Did you have a bad night?"

McIntyre took three breaths, each more labored than the other. She placed her hand on his cheek as if her touch could erase his pain. He covered her hand with his own, then forced his eyelids together as though locking the gate on a monster within.

Often during their marriage, he had disappeared in powerful machines that carried him to parts unknown to do things he could not speak of and she could not dream of. Here, in his own living room, he was not a warrior but a loving husband and father who lowered his head to his wife's tender shoulder. She would never know why.

"Daddy?" came a worried voice from down the hall.

McIntyre eased his wife aside and walked into the kitchen. He splashed water on his face.

"Daddy?"

He lowered the paper towel to see his two sons framed in the doorway, the oldest standing behind his little brother. "Hi, guys," he said, forcing cheer between the cracks of his breaking voice. "What're you guys doing up?"

"Daddy, are you OK?" the smallest boy asked.

McIntyre pointed with both index fingers to his red eyes. He smiled and said, "You mean this? Oh, you guys know that my allergies act up sometimes, huh?"

"Yeah, Mark," the older boy said to his brother, relieved. "I told you Daddy was OK." The littlest boy frowned and faked a slap at his brother. He ran toward his dad and threw his arms around one leg. His older brother followed and grabbed the free leg. Both boys slid down McIntyre's creased khakis until their butts rested on his large feet.

"OK, guys. Back to bed," he said as he clumped down the hall with each boy anchored to the top of a foot. The boys held on.

The woman padded across the living room and turned the door lock until it set. She walked down the hall, following the laughter of the two boys and the gruff bear-like sounds of her husband. She'd make it all better. She'd hold him and care for him. He'd feel better after some sleep.

1983, WEDNESDAY, 31 AUGUST
THE WHITE HOUSE

"My God," the White House Chief of Staff said. He closed his eyes. "Oh, my dear God."

The Secretary of Defense sat on a chair in front of the desk, silent after telling the CoS the bad news. The CoS turned in his chair and gazed out the multi-paned window. Low dark clouds boiled across a gray sky. Large drops of rain slanted under the portico roof and hit the window with a sound more like a clump than a splash. A tall grandfather clock stood in the corner and rolled its soft mellow sound across the deep blue carpet. It chimed with rich tones as it marked 4:00 p.m. The CoS turned back to the SecDef and pointed a single finger at the clock. "I hate that thing."

The SecDef studied the beautiful chronograph, then looked at his friend. "You hate the clock?"

The CoS ignored the question and stared at the top of his desk. "When?"

"Saturday night," the SecDef said. He waited, patient, studied.

"Go ahead. Tell me about it," the CoS said.

"Rhombus was flying off the coast near San Diego. It was making a run on the *Bunker Hill*. One of the engines blew up. They landed at North Island. Problem is," the SecDef breathed heavily, "the Tango Team didn't have time to get security nailed down. An off-duty Naval Reserve officer saw it land. You know the rest."

"How many now? Fifteen?" the CoS asked.

"Sixteen."

"Sixteen! So far we've spent more than fifteen billion dollars on a weapon that hasn't killed a thing except sixteen Americans." He glared at the SecDef. "Is something wrong with this picture?"

"OK, damn it. You call someone in the Soviet Union and tell them what we have." The SecDef stood and waved his arms. "Let's just get this thing out of the way right now! Let everyone know! That way you and I no longer have to deal with it. All we have to do is push the buttons and head for the bunkers under the Greenbrier Hotel while everybody else in this country is turned to cinders. Let them all die while we have a clear conscience."

The CoS peered over his granny glasses and gave the barest of smiles.

"Hell," the SecDef said as he flopped back into the chair.

The CoS gave a no-problem wave and toyed with a paper clip. "You know what my favorite movie line is?"

"Pardon me?"

"Do you know what my favorite movie line is?"

"No."

"Do you remember the movie, *Oh God*? George Burns played God, and John Denver played this normal guy who God wanted—" He paused, searching his memory. "Well, God wanted some kind of earthly relationship with someone, and he chose this guy. Anyway, Denver wouldn't believe that God had appeared. Finally, after God did something that I can't recall, Denver believed. Do you know the first question he asked God?"

"No," the SecDef responded.

"What's the first question you'd ask God if He sat down here right now?"

The SecDef thought for a moment. "I guess I'd ask him

why He allows disease and war."

"Yep," the CoS responded, "and then you'd ask Him to give us a helping hand with this Rhombus mess."

"Yeah, I'd damn sure ask Him that."

"I think the answer would be the same He gave Denver in the movie," the CoS offered.

"And?"

"God said, 'I don't let all that stuff happen. You do.'" The CoS spun the paper clip on the tip of a pencil. "It's my favorite line. Since I've been in this job, I've thought a lot about what God has given mankind and how we've squandered it. Have you ever wondered if we could cure cancer if we put two billion into medical research instead of buying a single aircraft carrier?"

"Are you saying we shouldn't build a carrier?"

"No. What I'm saying is it's a shame we have to. I'm comfortable with America's values and morals. The Soviet Union is an evil empire. Hell, they've killed more than twenty million of their own people. They wouldn't bat an eye at killing us if they thought they could get away with it. No, we need carriers just like we need policemen, but it makes me sad that we need either one."

Both men listened to the clock for a while, absorbed in their private thoughts.

The CoS spoke, "We're doing the right thing. Aren't we." It wasn't a question.

The SecDef chewed on his bottom lip. "Nope, we're doing the only thing." He watched the darkening sky as he rocked back and forth in his chair. "I've sent Angela to stay with friends in Australia. I just—I just don't think we're going to survive this one. The Soviets will find out pretty soon, and when they do … Well, I figure she's safer somewhere in the Southern Hemisphere."

"Damn," the CoS said.

A cold dark rain crossed Pennsylvania Avenue.

The eye of time swept west from the White House. It flew beneath the storm clouds rising on the Potomac, up the Blue Ridge, and across the Alleghenies. It crossed the grain fields of the heartland, then over the Rockies and into the Great Basin. There it descended over the Grand Canyon, across Lake Mead, and into Las Vegas Valley. It stopped for a moment over a parcel of land shaded by ancient cottonwood trees that had been nourished by aquifers since the Civil War. As the sun peeked through the trees, it flashed a golden spark off a brass plaque mounted on the top of a casket.

Chasing the heaven-bound glint was a tiny flash the sun made as it struck the tear rolling over the cheek of a redheaded woman while she watched her once-vibrant son returned to the dust. Beside her, with his arm around her shoulders, was her husband in his Navy summer whites, lips set hard together as the muscles in his jaw twitched. Their young daughter's arms wrapped around her daddy's leg while she clutched a white hankie and her rag doll with the hair of red yarn. A Navy Commander with a small paunch knelt beside her.

Across from the family, on the other side of the coffin, was a silent group of boys in Little League uniforms. They'd seen it happen just the other night. The ball streaked off the bat. In the near distance, in the on-deck circle, Scotty Christum had just turned to his mom and sister sitting in the bleachers while he held the batting helmet, trying to adjust its strap. His red hair splashed as the ball pounded his skull. For several hours the doctors thought he'd be all right. Then, early the next morning, an artery broke, and Scotty died while he held his mom's hand.

A middle-aged man standing with the boys leaned down and spoke. They all turned and walked to the line of cars sitting at the edge of the grass.

Breaking her hold on her daddy's leg, Scotty's little sister walked toward the coffin. Her mother, Kachina, reached for her, but her father, Mike, tightened his hold on the woman. The girl stepped to the coffin and unfolded her arms from the small cloth doll. With two small dimpled hands, she held the doll in front of her, then kissed the cloth face. She placed the doll on the nearest coffin handle and straightened its little dress. Then she walked back to her parents.

Mike knelt down, and holding her tiny face in his hands said, "Honey, are you sure you want to leave Dolly here?"

"Don't be sad, Daddy," Lisa said. "Scotty will take care of her."

Mike Christum picked up Lisa and wrapped his arms around her. Together with Kachina they walked toward the black limousine. Young Scotty Christum, left fielder and future Top Gun, stepped into a different time as his family disappeared down the long drive and headed into the storm of fire and steel. He would take care of Dolly until he saw Lisa again.

1983, WEDNESDAY, 31 AUGUST
1736 HOURS (5:36 PM)
GROOM LAKE BASE, NEVADA

Chris Patterakis' Groom Lake office was several steps down in quality from the one he'd in Alameda. Like all the other offices here, this one had green walls rising from a green floor. Gray metal furniture and a single fluorescent ceiling light added to the flat ambience. Cold air blew from the air-conditioner, while a hot wind blew fine dust around the metal window frames and filled the office with a doleful moan that changed pitch and intensity as the speed of the wind changed. The CO sat with his arms folded and his attention on the speaker at the edge of the desk.

"Admiral," he said, "the Navy gave me complete authority to hire who I wanted. I chose Mike Christum, and I continue to support him."

"Well," the voice said, "I appreciate loyalty as much as the next man, but—"

"Sir," Patterakis interrupted, "this has more to do with capability than it has to do with loyalty. Christum is the best man for this job."

"Chris, I agree with you, except—"

Patterakis interrupted again, "Except he has a family?"

Patterakis heard the admiral's hand hit his desk. "Yes, damn it, except he has a family!"

"Are you telling me you want him replaced?"

"Look. We have a fifteen-billion-dollar airplane sitting out there instead of flying, and do you know why it's in the hangar? Because we only have two pilots for it, and one of them isn't on base. We've just missed the second flight in the max flex test."

"He's at his son's funeral, sir. Frankly, that's where I should be, too."

"I know damned well why he's not here, and don't insinuate that I don't understand a man's love for his family." The admiral's sharp voice, coming through the speaker, contrasted with the mellow moan of the wind.

"Admiral," Patterakis said. "I've known and respected you for years, but it's the White House and not us that has limited the program to one air crew. And you know what? I agree with them. It's a hell of a lot easier to train a new pilot if we need him than it is to keep the lid on this thing if we increase the number of air crews."

"That's not the issue, Chris, and you know it."

"I know, sir, but we considered many issues, and one was loss of time due to sickness and family matters—"

"It's not the lost time, Chris," the Admiral interrupted. "It's his state of mind. That thing out there is just too damned important to have pilots whose minds are off the planet when they should be in the cockpit."

"He'll be OK."

"I don't want him OK. I want him at his peak."

Anger flashed through Patterakis' voice. "Are you ordering me to replace him?"

"Damned right I am."

"No."

"What!"

"You'll have to fire me, too." Patterakis' ace-up-the-sleeve was one he had never played. He knew that no one, but no one, would challenge him if it meant drawing attention to Rhombus, and the replacement of the project's senior pilot, coupled with the loss of its commanding officer, would do so. Besides, he didn't have a chance of making admiral, anyway.

"Sir, I know you're responsible for funding this program, but I took this job because the Navy said I would have complete authority over operations. If that agreement is broken, there's no place for me here. If the Navy wants Christum fired, it'll have to find someone else to run the program."

Patterakis waited and listened to the smooth static that came over the line. The Admiral growled, "Let me put it this way: I'll have your butt unless you find someone else."

The gauntlet was thrown. Patterakis leaned toward the speaker. "You, sir, are not in my chain of command. I'm well aware of your responsibilities, but I was hired to run this show, and I'm going to run it as I see fit."

Fury seemed to drip from the speaker, like acid from the tines of a cold fork. "Good day, Captain Patterakis."

Patterakis typed a memo that summarized the conversation with the Admiral. He'd be getting a phone call from his immediate boss any time now, and he wanted to be as accurate as possible about the discussion. Leaning over the platen, he rolled the memo back, then rolled it forward as he read. After the last line, he slapped the return sideways to roll it down one more line and typed: "Took yet another giant step in pleasing my superiors and ensuring my continued advancement." He yanked the paper out of the typewriter, initialed it, opened a side drawer, and deposited it in a file labeled Memos for Record. The file was the thickest one he had.

He leaned back and sighed. A single man could be distraught over the death of a loved one, he rationalized. Still, nothing could be tougher than burying a child and leaving your wife to deal with her grief alone. He wondered whom he'd have chosen as the lead pilot if he could go back in time. Again, he knew it would have been Mike. Still, he worried. The truth was that billions of dollars and the safety of the entire planet rested primarily on one man, and that man was hurting.

"Damn." Patterakis reached for his cap and strode from his office. "I have an airplane to meet," he said to his yeoman. "I'll be back in fifteen minutes." The phone rang as he walked out the door.

Patterakis stood beside his staff car as the 727 pulled into the chocks. The hot wind blew grit through the air. Clouds of dust rolled across Emigrant Flat and obscured the mountains. As the airplane's turbines whined to silence, the stair in its rear extended to the ground. Christum and Davis descended on the stair, their uniforms flapping in the wind, their caps in their hands. Patterakis walked toward them and extended his hand to Mike. He studied Mike's face, how he carried himself, and the strength of his handshake. He looked for any body language that might reveal a man not in control of himself. The handshake melted into a hug between the two men. "I'm so sorry," Patterakis said.

"Thanks, Skipper." Mike walked alone toward the staff car while Patterakis shook Brian's hand.

Brian said to Patterakis, "So, Skipper, what's on your mind?"

"You know damned well what's on my mind."

The men stopped walking. Brian turned to Patterakis, his face serious. "Don't worry, Chris. He's OK. I'd fly to hell and back with him."

Patterakis exhaled between puffed cheeks. "Good, because that's exactly where you're headed."

1983, WEDNESDAY, 31 AUGUST
2010 HOURS (8:10 PM)
GROOM LAKE BASE, NEVADA

Brian flipped a wall switch that turned on a lamp in the living room of the BOQ suite. The concrete-block walls were painted with light-green high-gloss paint. Western-motif oak furniture sat on a dark green carpet. The suite had been home for them for the past four months, since they reported to Groom Lake Base. It had two bedrooms, an efficiency kitchen, and a living room. It was spotless, and its air hinted of apple-scented disinfectant.

"Hell of a briefing," Brian said as he dropped his briefcase beside the sofa.

Mike said nothing as he reached for the phone. He dialed and waited. "Damn."

He dialed again and waited. "Come on, Kachina. Answer the phone."

He dialed twice more, and each time waited a while for Kachina to answer.

Brian watched Mike stand with the phone in one hand, while the other hand kneaded his forehead. He could hear the ringing sound from the sofa, and its noise filled the living room with emptiness and sorrow—and desperation.

"You OK?" Brian asked as he kicked off his shoes, not wanting his worry to be obvious.

"Yeah, I'm OK," Mike responded. He sat down and stared at the carpet. "Well," he said as he looked up. "Where do you think we're going?"

"Diego Garcia," Brian responded, referring to a U.S. naval base almost exactly on the other side of the world from Groom Lake.

"The Indian Ocean, huh? I don't think so."

"Why not?"

"Because flying to the IO only flexes the airframe. It doesn't test the Aurora systems."

"Meaning?"

"Meaning that the only true test for Aurora is a flight over the Soviet Union," Mike responded.

"You can't believe they'd have us fly over the Soviet Union!"

"Don't be too sure."

Brian relaxed because he knew Mike was forcing himself to stay in the game—and better forced than not at all. Amazing, he thought. The man buries a child and six hours later has his head on where he's going and not where he's been. The events of the day ran through Brian's mind like pages of a photo album. The cemetery with its big trees that vaulted over Mike and his family. The small casket. Kachina, stately in her despair. Mike, with a curious mixture of strength and softness. Lisa's gift of her doll. The other boys. Mike's goodbye to his wife and daughter. The quiet flight back to Groom Lake. And what was it that Patterakis said? Something about headed for hell?

Mike fidgeted with his watch.

"I'm turning in," Brian said as he stood. He picked up his shoes. "If you need anything …"

"Yeah, I know, Brian. Thank you."

As Brian walked by, he put his hand on Mike's shoulder. "Better get some sleep. Tomorrow's a long day, and tomorrow may start tonight."

"Yeah. Sure. I will. Don't worry."

"'Night," Brian said through a fake yawn as he headed down the hall.

"'Night." Mike turned off the living-room lamp. He sat in the dark and let the past step through the doorway of his mind.

Push, sweetheart. Pu-u-u-u-u-ush. I can see its head. I can see its head! It's got red hair just like you. Pu-u-u-u-u-u-ush.

It's a boy! Sweetheart, it's a boy!

Come to Daddy. Come to Daddy. Can you walk like a big boy?

Oh, no! Stinky pants! Pee-you! Go see Mommy.

It is not. I changed him last time.

I love you a bushel and a peck, a bushel and a peck and a hug around the neck.

Fire twuck.

Shoo-shoo frain.

I Snooperman, huh, Daddy?

Snooperman, huh, Daddy?

Hey, Dad. Catch.

No sweat, Dad. I'm the little engine that can, remember?

The little engine that can, remember?

That can, remember?

Remember?

Remember?

Mike raised his eyes. Tears rolled down his cheeks and splashed on the combat ribbons and the golden wings and the white uniform. Just above a whisper and with a cracking voice, he said, "G'night, Snooperman."

Brian lay in his bed. His own eyes filled with tears as the sobs of his best friend filled the BOQ suite.

1983, Thursday, 31 August
2204 Hours (10:04 PM)
Groom Lake Base, Nevada

"Commander Christum! Commander Christum!" He jerked upright on the couch at the beating on the door. The phone was in his hand, and it was still ringing his home. He slammed the receiver down.

"Commander Christum!"

"Yeah, just a second." Mike staggered up and fell toward the door. He cracked it. "Yeah?"

The Shore Patrol petty officer at the door spurted out, "Sir! CIC has been trying to get hold of you, but your phone's been busy. You're alerted, sir, and you're about five minutes late."

"Thanks." Mike shut the door on him.

"Brian! We're late!" Mike ran down the hallway, stripping the white uniform he'd worn to the funeral. As he went by Brian's door, he pounded on it. "Brian!" he yelled. "It's going to be a long night, buddy. Let's go!"

He threw his whites in the corner. "Damn it, Kachina." He'd fallen asleep waiting for her to answer the phone. She hadn't. "Where the hell are you?"

There was a thud from the other bedroom. "Owww!"

Mike threw on his flight suit and boots, then headed for the john. He splashed cold water in his eyes, then raced down the hall. "Brian! Let's go!"

Brian's door flew open. He burst out hopping on one leg, with the other caught in his flight suit. He hopped down the hallway on one foot and tripped as he entered the living room. The lamp on the end table tumbled to the floor and shot electrical sparks across the carpet. "Son of a bitch!"

Mike helped him up. He was on his feet and running with Mike to the crew bus that waited by the curb. He held his boots in one hand and tried to zip his flight suit over his red and white boxer shorts with the other.

"Step on it," Mike commanded the driver.

As the crew bus careened on the base streets, Brian worked at getting dressed. Thumping sounds and swear words punctuated the effort as he flailed inside the bus. It reminded Mike of someone locked in a phone booth with a wasp.

Brian plopped into the seat across from Mike. "Ah, success!"

Mike grinned and shook his head. "You are without a doubt the world's most efficient method of turning hot dogs and beer into noise."

"Very funny."

They sprinted from the bus into the hangar where Rhombus sat in dim lighting. Maintenance people hurried around the airplane and pulled safety locks and covers from different parts of the airframe. Brian ran for the crew hatch and bounded up the ladder. Mike headed for the nose gear. He slapped a large red button mounted on the nose wheel strut. Rhombus came to life. Lights came on and hydraulic starter motors whined as they turned the CJ engines. Mike climbed the ladder, then pushed a button that retracted it and closed the crew hatch.

Brian was already in his seat, forcing on his helmet and pulling straps from the seat back and sides as he transformed from the clumsy clown on the bus to a supremely competent aviation warrior in the cockpit. As Mike strapped in, the bomber filled with whining sounds. Grunting coughs rumbled through the airframe as igniters lit the fuel and started the sustained explosion in the jet engines. The instrument panel blinked from every direction as the CRTs came to life. Gyros aligned themselves and other equipment went through self-test cycles. Engine instruments climbed steadily, showing increasing RPMs, temperatures, and pressures that indicated that the Alert Self-start cycle was successful.

After he fastened the last strap, Mike said over the intercom, "Pilot here."

"Co-pilot here," Brian responded.

"Call the Before Taxi checklist, Mr. Davis," Mike commanded.

"Aurora on," Brian called.

Maintenance people watched the massive black shape ripple, then disappear into thin air. Only the landing gear was visible.

The hangar doors rolled aside. Large ducts that channeled outside air in for the engines and took the exhaust gases out moved away from the airplane and retracted into the rafters.

"Clearance lasers on." Tiny lasers in the wingtips flashed red dots on the concrete so the pilots and the maintenance men would know where the wingtips were. When the hangar doors rolled past the red dots on the floor, Brian called, "Doors clear."

Rhombus moved.

Mike pulled the throttles back as the warplane cleared the hangar. "Check six o'clock."

Brian hit a button on his joystick. The SID displayed the world to the rear of the bomber to Brian at the same time it displayed the world ahead for Mike. "We're clear. Switching to front view."

Mike advanced the throttles and brought Rhombus to a 60-knot taxi speed. Brian set the SID to give him a telephoto display of the taxiway ahead. "Taxiway clear." Brian read the checklist, to which both he and Mike responded where appropriate. At the end of the taxiway, Mike braked Rhombus for the turn onto the runway. As the nose of the big crystal bird aligned itself with the white stripes, Mike shoved the throttles full forward.

The CJ engines spooled to 104% RPM.

Acceleration plastered the pilots into their seatbacks.

Within a few seconds, Rhombus' nose pointed to the sky. They flew straight up while accelerating through 280 knots in an airplane that weighed as much as a civilian jumbo jet.

The CJ engines screamed at the Nevada night.

Several miles away a vigil was underway, as it had been for years. On one edge of the Groom Lake Base range was a graded area beside a dirt road. People scrambled out of pickup trucks, RVs, camping trailers, and tents. They reached for their binoculars and turned them toward the thunder that climbed into the night.

"See anything?"

They waited as they watched.

"I think I see something!" came a voice from the edge of the group.

"What is it?"

"Sorry. It was just a star. I thought I saw it move back and forth." The thunder became a rolling rumble that faded to the northwest.

At 41,000 feet, Mike eased back on the throttles and lowered Rhombus' nose. He flipped a switch to engage the autopilot and threw another marked Mach Climb, then pressed a button on the throttles that gave Rhombus control of its own engines.

As the airplane split the air at 63,250 feet, Brian pulled a manila envelope from a map case. "Interested?"

Mike mimed the opening of an envelope. Brian placed the unopened envelope against the forehead of his helmet. "The Soviet Union," he said dramatically. He pulled a string that broke a seal. He blew into the envelope and with two fingers extracted a single sheet of paper. "Voila! Or is it viola? No matter." He waved the paper to open its folds. He held it under a B-4 map light he had maneuvered from his right. "Oh Jeez. Oh damn."

Mike drummed his fingers on the throttles. "Are … you going … to San … Fran … cisco?" he sang in a monotone, trying humor to wash away the grief that now mingled with an exhausted aching feeling.

Brian opened his face shield and turned to him. The cockpit lighting illuminated his wide eyes.

"Well?" Mike asked.

"You're right, Michael. We're headed for the Soviet Union."

"I knew it."

Brian read the flight order, summarizing its contents as he did. "We fly to geographical coordinates fifty-five North, one seventy-seven West, where we rendezvous with a tanker at thirty-one thousand feet to top off our fuel. From there we fly at our discretion between thirty-five and forty-five thousand feet. We are to simulate dropping a bomb on the Petropavlovsk naval base. After the drop, we select RTB—Return To Base, don'tcha know—and let the MPP fly us back home. We fly the entire profile sub-sonic unless we need the speed for escape.

"Hmm. Now, this is curious. The MPP is programmed to flare at the end of the runway and hold an altitude of twenty feet as long as it can." Brian's eyes moved down the page. "They're not satisfied with the performance data they have on how our bird here flies in ground effect, so the MPP is to keep us just above the runway until it quits flying and drops us." Brian turned the paper over. "Says here that they expect ground effect to reduce the drag by thirty-four percent, which should carry us about two thousand feet farther down the runway than normal."

"Well," said Mike, "since our wingspan is a hundred and eighty feet, ground effect will be ninety feet or below." Mike was fascinated with the realm of flight known as ground effect. When a flying machine's altitude is half its wingspan or less, drag is reduced quite a bit, and it doesn't matter whether it's a jumbo jet or a humming bird.

"Magic," Brian said as he waved a white letter-sized envelope in Mike's direction. Mike reached for the envelope that was addressed to both of them in Chris Patterakis' handwriting.

Gents,

Are you having fun yet? Did you remember your pass-
ports? Your flowered hats?

This is our first probe of Soviet defenses with Rhom-
bus. There are no cyanide pills, so don't look for them.
The only purpose of this flight is to prove that Rhombus
works as advertised. In order to prove your presence over
Petropavlovsk, the MPP will SatBurst your ID code at
the moment you simulate your weapons drop.

Also, I hope you don't mind the firm landing. The
MPP is programmed to flare 20 feet above the runway
and hold that altitude until you run out of flying speed.
We'll be picking up your telemetry, and we'll find out pre-
cisely when you enter ground effect and how much it ex-
tends your time in the air.

When you have understood your flight orders, signal
so by sending your ID by SatBurst.

Cheers,
Chris

Mike handed the letter to Brian. "I understand. Do you understand?"

"I understand," Brian responded.

Brian reached to the center console and lifted a red-colored guard that covered a button. He pressed the button and a microwave burst a thousandth of a second long streaked from the top of Rhombus to a satellite. The satellite relayed the burst to a receiver located on a peak several miles outside Groom Lake Base. Patterakis sat in front of a computer display and watched the Shaman ID appear on the screen next to a blue symbol. The symbol now crossed the Pacific coast near Reedsport, Oregon, and headed for the Aleutian Islands. A monitor in the basement of the White House showed the same thing.

◆ ◆ ◆

"You know," Brian said. "For the past three hours I've been thinking."

"Amazing."

"What?"

"Thinking."

Brian ignored him. "What's more boring than watching grass grow?" He didn't wait for an answer. "Flying at thirty-five thousand feet over the North Pacific is one. Flying at thirty-five thousand and one feet over the North Pacific is another. Even worse is flying at thirty-five thousand and two feet over the North Pacific."

Mike and Brian were at 65,000 feet. Brian hummed "One Hundred Bottles of Beer on the Wall." At least he did until Mike punched his shoulder. Then he said, "Are we there yet? Are we there yet?" Mike punched him again.

The solar winds ebbed and allowed Brian to tune in short-wave broadcasts. The aviators had listened to the news on the BBC, diatribes against the United States on Radio Amsterdam, and Calling Africa on the Voice of America. They'd tuned through Radio Australia, which broadcasted a single verse of "Waltzing Matilda" over, and over, and over again. They were now listening to ham radio operators around the world using their radios to talk to each other about their radios.

Mike watched the ocean and clouds roll by beneath them. It still amazed him, this SID thing. Here it was, the middle of the night, and he was watching the clouds as though it were midday. He couldn't sleep, even though Brian encouraged him. Within him a battle raged, fatigue on one side and apprehension on the other. Both grew stronger by the minute, an arms race between physical and emotional well-being. Dear God. Please let her be OK. Please. Someday, maybe, he could tell Kachina why he hadn't been there when Scotty died and why he couldn't be there now.

Mike thought about the machine he was in, where he was,

and where he was headed. He and Brian hadn't fired a shot, but they were in a war that was as real as the day that Danno died. It was very remote, but shooting could begin in a few hours if the Soviets saw them over Petropavlovsk or, worse, if they crashed on Soviet soil.

He imagined what an air assault on the Soviet Union would be like. F-111s and B-52s would hug the earth, while their pilots fought to avoid more than 10,000 radars in the Soviet Union. Those airplanes would punish their crews with rides akin to speeding desert dune buggies. Once radar picked them up, MiGs would vector for the kill. Onward they would push, toward Moscow, toward Minsk, toward Stalingrad, their numbers diminishing as they flew. The prey of the American bombers would be the cities and defense sites of the Soviet Union. But these American bombers would be the prey of Soviet fighters. Men in the bombers would die as cannon shells ripped holes in their airplanes, as air-to-air missiles tore them apart, and as their airplanes cartwheeled down, leaving streams of fire in their passing. The crews that weren't eliminated would make it to their targets knowing that their families had already been scraped off the face of the earth and sent skyward as particles of dust in the rolling mushroom clouds. Yet, they would lower their eye patches and press on through the nuclear hurricane. Rhombus crews wouldn't need eye patches because the magic of the SID would protect them from the nuclear flashes. For all the others, the final stages of attack would have one pilot wearing two patches and the other a single patch—one good eye flying the airplane. When a flash burst ahead, it would sear the unprotected eye. The pilot would remove the patch from the good eye and fly on, until the next flash, after which there was nothing more he could do. The second pilot would raise a patch, and if another bomb went off ahead, he'd use his one good eye and pray it was enough: Blind men sent on a mission by other blind men who now hid in air-conditioned bunkers beneath the Urals and the Appalachians. Few bomber pilots believed they would survive a successful attack. Ejection over friendly territory was the best they could hope for. Some would drop their bombs and follow them into the caldron, American kamikazes driven not by their adoration of an emperor, but by the desperate thought of flying home to nothing. What would survival bring them? Their land would be scorched and the fabric of their society, from the Pilgrims to the present, would be erased, and they would die long cancerous deaths. The greatest fear of American bomber crews was what lay beyond the target. Their nightmare did not involve dying over the Soviet Union, but surviving.

Mike hoped that if he and Brian were discovered tonight, he would be back home with Kachina before the warheads fell on America. Las Vegas would die because the Soviets would throw several warheads at Nellis, but at least he and his family would face the holocaust together.

Where is she?

The possible doom of the future turned to an unfamiliar emotion that settled within him as a ripping apprehension. What would he do if he knew the bombs were on the way and he couldn't find Kachina and Lisa? How terrible for them to die apart. He had just lived that experience, and his feeling for it was beyond hatred.

It was a paradoxical truth that the taller America stood, the less likely it was she would have to fight. But Rhombus reached beyond this truth. Its very existence, because it so profoundly threatened the Soviet Union, guaranteed World War III. The Soviet Union had only two ways to handle the problem given it by Rhombus: Strike before America used it, or turn itself inside out politically. The latter was not likely.

"I'm so bored I could kill my grandma," Brian said out of the blue, breaking the silence.

"I'm so bored I could go to war."

"You think that's bad? I'm so bored I could join the Navy."

"Hmm. You think that's bad, I'm so bored I could enjoy your jokes."

They watched the sea roll by beneath them, trying to think of something to talk about.

"Hey, Brian?" Mike asked. "What's the most southern state?"

"Texas."

"No."

"Florida."

"No."

"Is this a joke?"

"Hawaii."

Brian ran a finger on an aeronautical chart. "Really keen, jelly bean. You're right. Got any more of those?"

"OK, Brian. What's the most northern state?"

"Alaska."

"Right."

"Awriiiiight." Brian balled his right hand into a fist and pulled it back against his side in a victory display.

"Now," Mike continued, "what's the most western state?"

"I'll bet you think I'm going to say California, but I'm going to say Hawaii."

"No. Alaska."

"What?"

"Look at your map."

"Damn, you're right," Brian said as he saw how far the Aleutian Island chain stretched across the North Pacific.

"OK, Brian. This is a toughie. Ready?"

Brian hunkered down. "Yes."

"What's the most eastern state?"

"Maine!"

"No."

"OK. I give up."

"Alaska."

"Alaska? But it's the most western state," Brian protested.

"Yeah, but it also sits across the one-hundred-and-eighty-degree meridian, which puts part of it in the Eastern Hemisphere. That makes Alaska the most western and the most eastern state at the same time."

"W-o-o-ow," Brian said, mocking a ten-year-old boy secretly watching a friend's teenage sister take a bath.

Silence fell over them again as each searched for ways to break the monotony. "How's your mother?" Mike asked.

"OK. Arthritis is pretty bad. I'm having someone clean her house once a week. She's having more and more problems getting around." Brian paused. "She's not going to a nursing home, Mike. I couldn't live with myself. She never put me in day care—I'm not putting her in nursing care."

"You know, Brian, sometimes that's what's best. I mean, if your mother gets to a point where she can't fend for herself …"

"As long as I have a nickel, she lives at home if she wants, even if I have to hire a full-time nurse."

"Is she still in Phoenix?"

"Yep. Still perkin' along in Phoenix. I'm going down there on the next leave. House needs some work, and I gotta tend to some business for her. Brad—I told you about my boy, Brad, huh?"

Mike nodded. "About a million times."

"Oh, yeah. He's gonna help. Shouldn't take too long."

"You're a good son, Brian Davis," Mike said as he reached across the console and squeezed Brian's arm.

Brian shrugged. "You'd do the same thing."

The miles rolled by as each man poked around in his own memory. Brian seemed to have settled into melancholy. "I miss Susan."

"Who?" asked Mike.

"I miss Susan. Susan was my wife and my boy's mom. We got married in high school. She died when Brad was eight. Mom helped me raise him. When I went on cruise, I'd ship him off to Granny's—kinda like summer camp."

"How come you never talk about Susan?"

"She was—" Brian's voice cracked. He punched his microphone off and turned away.

The United States fell farther behind, while Rhombus headed for the Soviet Union through the blackness at the edge of space.

THE NORTH PACIFIC
55 DEGREES NORTH, 177 DEGREES WEST

Brian pulled the keyboard from beneath the instrument panel and started typing. "The MPP will notify us in about a minute that the tanker's at two hundred miles," he said to Mike. He waited then called, "Ten-nine-eight-seven-six-five-four-three-two-one-ding."

"Bong, bong, bong," came over the intercom.

"I'm getting pretty good at outguessing the sucker, huh?"

The CRT in the center of Brian's panel switched to TopDown mode. At the edge of the TopDown, over the curved line that represented the 200-mile range, a purple symbol representing a tanker appeared. At the same time an identical symbol appeared on the SID, marking the point in space where they would see the tanker if it were close enough.

"I like the color purple," Brian said.

Mike pushed a button on the autopilot. "Refueling profile."

"Roger," Brian replied. "You're not going to fly it?"

"No. Too tired. You want to?"

"Nope."

The MPP performed a billion calculations a second as it made its observation of the tanker's track, airspeed, and altitude, then planned Rhombus' descent and approach so that hookup would occur as soon as possible. The airplanes would not communicate, for to do so would reveal that another airplane was near the tanker. The Soviets had been watching the tanker on radar since it arrived on station a half-hour ago. However, it was not flying a classic refueling pattern that would alert the Russians to its purpose. It was flying a pattern that was typical of the spy missions flown by EC-135s.

Mike and Brian watched with fascination as the MPP retarded the throttles and began a descent.

"Let's see what you are," Brian said as he pushed a button on the SID control. The world they were watching expanded. The friendly, purple, airborne symbol stayed at the same point on the SID, while numbers in the corner changed to show the degree of magnification. After a few seconds the tanker appeared behind the symbol until it filled the SID. "Ah. Big surprise. A tanker, a KC-One-Thirty-Five, a flying gas tank. What's it doing way down there at thirty-one thousand feet?" Brian sang, "You can trust your car to the men who wear the star. The bright red Texaco sta-a-a-a-r." Then to Mike, "Why do I have this urge for an RC Cola and a bag of pork rinds?"

"Roger that," Mike responded. "I could use a Pepsi and a bag of peanuts."

"Ugh."

"Bring the SID back to scale," Mike ordered.

"Wilco," Brian said, following Mike's cue to tone down the humor. The SID zoomed back to the normal view. The TopDown display showed no other bogies in the immediate area, but it did show the presence of four civilian airliners and a US Air Force C-141 flying an airborne highway that spanned the North Pacific between Alaska and Japan and skirted the Soviet coast off Kamchatka.

Brian pointed to the TopDown. "Look at the six-hundred-mile ring," he said, referring to a thin line that represented what the MPP saw 600 miles away. "It looks like we have a Soviet airliner up here. It's headed for Soviet airspace, but the MPP put a 'friendly' symbol on it, and it says it has General Electric engines." Brian studied the TopDown closer. "We got normal Soviet fighter traffic, too. The MPP has painted them as 'hostile' as it should. Strange. A friendly airliner wouldn't be headed for Soviet airspace, and Soviet airplanes don't have GE engines. I think our big boy here has a glitch. I'll write it up when we get back."

Rhombus had been cruising at Mach .96, which is 96% of the speed of sound. The MPP was slowing them to Mach .71, the planned tanker-hook-up speed. It was somewhat slower than that used for fighters, but Rhombus pushed a large bow wave ahead of it that became bigger at higher airspeeds. If it flew beneath the tanker at high speed, the bow wave would lift the tanker's tail and make the hookup dangerous.

Mike and Brian saw the tanker traveling opposite their direction of flight about ten miles ahead and about two miles to the left. It began a shallow left turn. "This always amazes me," Mike said.

"Me too!"

The tanker's belly exposed itself as it turned in front of them, crossing from their left. The MPP had already computed the precise moment when the tanker would be straight and level, and it approached the tanker so that it would be within hookup range at that moment. At about a mile from hookup, Rhombus slipped just below the tanker's altitude. While Mike and Brian witnessed the results of technology's pinnacle, the tanker crew saw nothing but the darkness of night. Their orders told them they would be refueling a B-52.

Following the standard procedure for refueling, Brian called, "B-Fifty-Two on Aurora Pixel Grid."

"Confirm B-Fifty-Two on the APG," Mike responded.

Brian typed. The MPP sent the appropriate electrical impulses to the electronic grid that was beneath the Aurora coating. The coating responded by displaying a B-52 on Rhombus' skin.

Before the tanker rolled level, Rhombus began its close approach from behind and below. The MPP would take visual cues from the tanker and fly into position. Since the refueling port was behind the cockpit, Mike and Brian would be looking at the mid-section of the tanker, while the tanker's tail extended above them. "Refueling port open," Brian called.

Just as the tanker rolled level, the MPP placed Rhombus in precise position. "Refueling—On Station" blinked on the SID.

"Damnedest pilot I ever saw," the Air Force staff sergeant said to himself as he watched from his perch in the tail of the KC-135. He moved his joystick to fly the boom into position. Once there, he moved another control that stabbed the telescoping tip of the boom into the B-52's refueling port. As soon as the boom sealed with the port, fuel flowed at about three tons a minute.

Brian looked at the belly of the KC-135 just above them. He scanned the horizon and the sea below. "You know, it's easy to forget that he can't see us."

"Pardon?" Mike asked.

"Well," Brian said, "here we are looking at the world around us and the airplane above us as though it's midday, and all those guys in the tanker can see is darkness. And that boom operator, he thinks he's looking down on a B-Fifty-Two. I have to remind myself that the reality you and I fly with is not the reality everyone else flies with."

"Yeah. I know. Sometimes I worry about a collision. Even though I know the MPP'll keep us away from other airplanes, my instincts make me worry that friendly pilots can't see us, either. Go to Normal Video on the SID."

The SID turned black except for a string of lights that marked the underside of the KC-135 above. "Well, it is dark outside," Brian admitted.

"Now," Mike said as he looked at the night, "don't you think there's something reassuring about seeing the world as it really is? Night is night. Day is day."

"Sometimes."

"Sometimes?"

"Well, there's times when it's good seeing the world as it is, like at sunset and sunrise, or when the sky is filled with clouds and enough blue sky to fly between them. Times like that."

Mike folded his hands in his lap as he looked at the 135's formation lights. "What are your favorite times for letting the SID turn night into day?"

"Two times, mostly."

"Like?"

"Like when we're penetrating the Soviet Union is one."

"And the other?" Both pilots cocked their heads and pondered the tanker lights just feet above them.

"Well, like when I'm five feet away from a flying gas tank doing five hundred miles per hour over the North Pacific."

Mike scanned the SID from far right to far left. Only the

string of formation lights on the bottom of the tanker illuminated the darkness. "I think you're right."

"Roger that. Going back to Tactical Video." In a flash the world in the SID came alive with daylight color. "Ahhhhhhh."

When Rhombus' tanks topped off, the MPP moved it down and back, breaking the connection with the KC-135. The refueling port snapped closed. As the boom operator saw the B-52 slide back into the darkness, he retracted the boom. He would have something to talk about when he got back to base. He had just witnessed a rendezvous and formation so perfect it could not be imagined.

"Mission Profile," Mike called.

"Roger," Brian responded. He typed a command. Rhombus rolled to the right and the throttles moved forward as the nose pitched up. "Aurora Pixel Grid off," Brian called. The B-52 displayed on the skin blinked off and the giant airplane disappeared. Once again Rhombus climbed.

They settled into a westerly heading at an airliner altitude of 41,000 feet. Mike had an eerie feeling. They were getting ready to fly into the most heavily defended airspace in the world and they were doing it as leisurely as a Delta Airlines dinner flight. He watched the coast of Russia getting closer on the TopDown and thought, Surely it can't be this easy.

"Bong. Bong. Bong."

"Threat Mode" flashed on the SID.

"Go Threat," Mike commanded.

"Roger."

Over the horizon the tops of red transparent spheres appeared on the SID. On the TopDown these spheres were displayed as colored wheels laying flat. The spheres and their corresponding wheels represented Soviet radars. While Rhombus was invisible, it could still be seen on radar at very short distances. These red spheres and wheels represented the distances at which Rhombus could be seen by the individual radars. If Rhombus stayed clear of them, the Soviets would never see it. At the edge of the TopDown, a red X indicated the target.

"Here's traffic," Brian said.

Symbols representing other aircraft appeared on the SID and the TopDown. Red symbols marked Soviet airplanes, blue represented friendlies, and yellow were unknown. The MPP and its sensors had numerous ways to determine the bad guys and the good guys. Part of it was that friendlies broadcast a special radar code. The MPP could also see the infrared pulses of airplane exhaust. Each type of engine had a unique exhaust pattern, and the MPP knew them all. Problem was, sometimes a friendly and a hostile nation flew the same type of airplane. "Looks like we have someone getting closer," Brian said.

"Where?"

"Well, he's over here about twenty-five miles, but he's converging with us," Brian responded. "Look at Track Fifty-Seven."

Mike pressed a button on his console until he saw "Track 57" on a corner of the SID. "What is it?" he asked.

"It's the same guy we saw a ways back that I thought was a Soviet airliner. Remember? The one the MPP said had GE engines? I'm going to zoom in on him." Brian put his SID on telephoto. The airplane filled the SID. "It's a Seven-Forty-Seven, and it looks like a civilian. I can't pick up the markings. Looks like the MPP was right; it is a friendly. Why the hell is a civilian Seven-Forty-Seven headed into Soviet airspace?" Brian typed. "Mike, I've asked the MPP to compute a flight path for the airliner. It's headed for Petropavlovsk, too, so we should cross paths just as we reach the target."

"We're checkin' this out." Mike disengaged the autopilot and turned Rhombus to the right. He pushed the throttles and set up a course that would place them near the 747. As good as Mike was, his intercept would not be as precise as the MPP's, but then again, the MPP was not as flexible as a good pilot.

Brian switched the SID to normal zoom. As the distance between the 747 and Rhombus closed, the 747 grew larger and larger on the SID. Meanwhile, the coast of Russia approached.

"It's Korean," Brian said.

"Korean?"

"Yeah. A Korean Airlines 747."

"What the—!" Mike maneuvered Rhombus to the left and behind the airliner. The windows along the Boeing's sides showed the dim warm lighting in the cabin. Flight attendants moved about. They retrieved blankets and pillows from storage bins and gave them to passengers. Other passengers hustled around, going back and forth to rest rooms and stopping to talk. Mike moved Rhombus behind and below the big airplane so that he could see the white navigation lights shining rearward from the tips of the enormous horizontal stabilizer. Strobes on the top and bottom of the airplane flashed red. Lights on the wingtips glowed red on the left and green on the right. The 747 was outside the range of radars located in Alaska and Japan, but it was certainly within range of Soviet radar. The MPP picked up a radar transponder signal from the 747. A transponder responded to radar sweeps to make an airplane appear larger on radarscopes. With its transponder on, this airplane shouted its presence.

"Bong. Bong. Bong."

"We're in Soviet airspace," Brian called.

"Yeah, well, so are they," Mike answered, nodding at the big Boeing. "Brian, why don't you turn on the radio scan. Set it on HF, VHF, and UHF. That covers all the radios he's carrying, plus those of the Soviet Air Force. Record everything, including the SID displays."

"Roger."

"Also, lay in a new attack heading from this point. I want to tag this guy for a while. Let's drop back a thousand feet and hold that position."

Mike selected the autopilot again, and Rhombus dropped back. He and Brian watched the 747 fly deeper into Soviet airspace, while its lights flashed and its transponder made it visible on any radarscope that looked in its direction.

"Mike, we got fighters off the ground!"

"Yeah. I see 'em," Mike said as the red symbols popped up on the TopDown.

"I'm going to monitor UHF for a sec."

"OK," Mike responded.

Brian came back on intercom. "Mike, I don't have to understand Russian to know there's hot chatter over Soviet tactical frequencies."

The MPP flew Rhombus toward the weapons release point. They would be there in two minutes. The 747 held the same course.

The two red symbols moved toward them on the TopDown. "Fighters at six o'clock," Brian called. "Two miles and closing."

"Look here." Brian typed. In a flash the noses of two Russian fighters replaced the view of the 747's rear. The TopDown showed the fighters closing on the big airplane with Rhombus between them. "Going back to front view," Brian called. "I ain't believin' this."

"I'm watching the Seven-Forty-Seven. Keep your calls coming, Brian."

"Roger. Fighters closing from behind. I'm sure they're onto the Seven-Forty-Seven and not us, but who can tell."

"Off autopilot," Mike called. He rolled Rhombus into a sharp turn to the right. They streaked away from the airliner at a 45-degree angle.

"They're after the Seven-Forty-Seven," Brian called.

Mike snapped Rhombus back to the left. "Heading for the weapons release point."

"That'll take us behind the Seven-Forty-Seven," Brian called.

"Don't have a choice. We'll be OK unless the fighters do something stupid."

Mike flew Rhombus at the 747. The giant airplane got larger in the SID as the weapons release timer counted down: 11, 10, 9, 8—

The row of windows became visible along the side of the airliner.

7, 6, 5—

The white lights at the tips of the horizontal stabilizer flashed.

4, 3—

Mike moved the joystick. The giant warplane banked hard to the right and took a position just behind and below the 747.

2, 1. "Bong."

Weapons Away flashed red across the SID as the MPP simulated the bomb drop. The Shaman ID was SatBurst to a satellite just dropping over the south horizon. The ID appeared on a screen at Groom Lake, superimposed over Petropavlovsk.

"Lock-on Alert" flashed across the SID.

"The Soviets are painting the Seven-Forty-Seven with fire-control radar!" Brian called. "They're going to launch missiles!"

Mike snapped Rhombus to the left, yanked back on the joystick, and jammed the throttles forward.

The G-meter climbed as the bank got steeper.

Five Gs. The ejection seats reclined.

Six Gs—

Seven Gs—

Eight, nine, ten, eleven, twelve Gs!

The seats were flat. The pilots strained to breathe against the crushing pressure on their chests. Skin on their faces pulled at the corners of their eyes and mouths. Mike watched the inside of his visor where the MPP showed him his airspeed, heading, and altitude.

"O-o-oh, man," Brian grunted from the right.

At 12 Gs Rhombus weighed almost 5,000,000 pounds. The CJ engines howled as they pushed the incredible mass around the tight turn.

The wind crashed into the warplane's bottom and rushed over its top where the enormous energy of the turn tore the air apart with a ripping sound that tangled with the howling of the CJs. The ripping wind formed a cloud over the back of the bomber that followed it in the frenzied turn.

As Rhombus turned, the fighters flew by.

The compass spun.

When Rhombus reached its original heading, Mike rolled out of the turn. The howling and ripping stopped. The ejection seats shot upright and forced the pilots against their shoulder straps. Mike pulled the throttles back.

The intercom hummed. Air-conditioned air poured from the cockpit vents with a hollow sound. The wind swished over the warplane's smooth skin. CRTs displayed their colored circles and lines. It was calm inside.

Outside was another matter.

By turning in a complete circle, Rhombus was now behind the fighters.

A wisp of smoke swept past.

"They launched!" Brian called.

The orange glow of a missile motor spiraled erratically around a point and became smaller as it sped toward the 747.

A second spot of orange appeared below the fighter wing and followed the first toward the passenger airplane.

The first missile flew into the 747's number three engine, the one closest to the right side of the cabin.

"Good God!—" Brian exclaimed.

Mike tugged on the joystick to get Rhombus above the explosion.

The missile warhead hit the 747's spinning turbine blades. Hot gases burst out and tore at the engine and its casing. Pieces of metal flew upward like bullets and shot holes through the wing and the fuel tanks.

The Soviet fighters broke hard right to avoid the debris.

The shock wave hit Rhombus from below. The warplane lurched.

Chunks of metal sped from the 747's disintegrating engine toward the right side of its fuselage. The chunks hit the side of the airliner and ripped its skin into scimitar-shaped shards that curved inward. Pushed by the force of the explosion and the 500-mile-per-hour wind, the scimitars tore away to the inside and whirled through the cabin. Their razor edges hissed while they sliced through skin and internal organs. They sent streams of blood from their tips in swirling spirals that painted red stripes on the cabin walls.

Before the pain registered, the second missile hit the same engine.

The butchering began again.

Mike kept Rhombus in position as debris shot by beneath. The second shock wave battered them anew.

Fire streamed from the 747 engine like a neon ribbon. The engine swung left and right on the pylon in ever-widening arcs. Finally, it snapped away in two large pieces that shot toward the tail. One piece flew into the right horizontal stabilizer. It sheared away its tip and the white navigation light.

The other—the large fan section in the front of the engine—spiraled over the top of the airplane and slammed into the base of the vertical stabilizer. It pounded into the large metal beam that ran from the fuselage to the tail's tip. The 500-mile-per-hour gale pushed the fan up the front of the beam. It ripped away the metal skin, then spun away at the top, leaving only a tall jagged metal finger that protruded upwards from the top rear of the fuselage.

Mike winced as the fan flew by just below Rhombus' nose. Damn! Should have been higher.

"Whew," Brian breathed.

Mike increased the altitude.

Like a giant animal unaware of its fate, the 747 flew straight and level.

Brian sat forward in his seat, intent and curious. "This is like watching a movie."

"Where're the fighters?" Mike called as he kept his attention on the debris still flinging by beneath them.

Brian studied the TopDown. "They're headed back to base. They're not sticking around to confirm their kill."

"They're day fighters directed by radar. There'll be no question about a kill when this thing hits the ground."

The scene ahead had a dream-like quality. The Boeing looked strange with two engines on its left wing and one on the right. Half the right stabilizer was gone and a jagged beam jutted up at its rear where the graceful tail used to be. The ribbon of flame followed the airliner like a bright red strip of crepe paper being pulled through the air at the end of a child's stick.

"Oh, no. No. No. No. Please, no," Brian pleaded.

The airliner's right wing dropped. At the same time, the airliner's control surfaces moved as its pilot fought to keep the airplane level. He had no rudder to help. The spinning fan had taken that away.

Farther and farther the Boeing rolled. "Sweet Jesus, help them," Brian said.

In his mind, Mike could hear the calls of the pilots as they fought for control. He could hear the screaming in the cabin, see the couples grasping hands, feel the children clutching. The father in him wanted to help, to rescue, to cry. The warrior in him flew his airplane well back of the 747. The two airplanes rolled together as the great invisible warbird followed the huge aluminum airliner in what might have been a slow and majestic airborne mating ritual.

Over the 747 rolled while its nose fell.

Upside down now—

"Hey," said Brian. "He's bringing it around."

The airliner continued its roll and began to right itself.

Its pilot pulled at the controls to stop the dive.

The long wings bent upward, forming a huge crescent that strained to haul the heavy body out of its dive.

Wing rivets popped and sheet metal tore.

Access panels ripped away.

Wing flaps fluttered as they yanked themselves off their rails.

The debris shot past Rhombus in a flashing metallic river of airplane parts.

And then the scene was peaceful again. The airliner was straight and level. The fire under the right wing blinked off. Mike and Brian sat in wide-eyed amazement that the big airplane was still in the sky. It had lost 31,000 feet of altitude and now held steady at 10,000 feet.

"I am flat stunned," Brian said.

"This just isn't happening," Mike replied.

"I'll tell you," Brian said, "that big mother has one hell of a good pilot. And what is that?" Brian zoomed in with the SID. The trailing edges of the wings were no longer straight. The missing flaps left huge notches as though giant dogs with square jaws had bitten the wings. Sticking out of the notches were rails on which the flaps used to ride to move up and down during landing and takeoff. Misty streams of jet fuel flowed from the wing. The airliner looked like a flying junkyard as it made its way over the Poloustrov Kamchatka and headed for the sea.

"We're sticking with him."

"You're sure?" Brian reminded. "We're supposed to stay with the mission profile as briefed."

"We're sticking with him."

Brian nodded, "Good."

Mike eased closer to the 747, still wary of flying debris. Here they were, two of the finest airplanes of their kind in the world, American iron—one undetectable and the other seemingly indestructible.

Mike continued to move Rhombus a little closer and to the right. As he did, his mouth dropped.

"See that?" Mike asked.

"Yeah."

The explosions had ripped away a huge section of skin. Much of the right side of the fuselage was open to the night and the screaming wind. Plastic cups, pieces of cloth, and bits of paper swirled around inside the airplane, then flew out, into the sky. People struggled to keep their oxygen masks on as the biting hurricane rushed in, spun around, then left. A few turned around to look behind. They'd stare until the carnage behind them registered, then their eyes would open wide as their hands flew to their mouths. Some puked between their fingers, and long strands of vomit twirled in the wind.

Mike and Brian were silent. The two airplanes flew onward. The coast of the Kamchatka fell behind. They were flying southwest over the Sea of Okhotsk. Ahead lay the Sakhalin Islands, and beyond that …

Beyond that lay the Soviet Union again.

"This guy doesn't know where he is, Mike," Brian said. "He's lost as hell."

Then the Boeing started a gradual turn to the left. After a while the airplane stabilized on a new heading.

"Where's he going?" Mike asked.

"Just a sec," Brian said as he pulled out his navigation chart and drew a line with his finger from where they were to where they were headed. "He's figured out where he is, and he's heading for Misawa."

"Where's that?"

"It's a U.S. Air Force base on Hokkaido." Brian put his chart back in its case and studied the TopDown. Petropavlovsk was out of the range he had set in previously. He pressed a button to expand the range. "Just a sec, Mike. Just a sec," he said. "Goin' off intercom to monitor UHF."

Mike's skin tingled. Brian was excited, and Mike didn't like the sound of it.

The intercom clicked. "I'm back on, and we have problems. Look." Brian pressed a button that displayed the TopDown on one of the CRTs in front of Mike. "They've scrambled two more fighters, and they're comin' our way."

Mike glanced at the TopDown. The MPP displayed the 747 as a blue symbol in front of them. Two red symbols were behind, 250 miles and gaining fast. He looked at the people in the airliner. Most had dark Asian hair. Some had long hair, and some had bald spots. Their heads jolted as the wind tore at them and shook them like rag dolls.

"Look," Brian said. "See that?"

"Where?"

"On the floor, crawling on the floor." He pointed.

A flight attendant inched down an aisle. The wind slammed her against the metal seat frames. She motioned for calm to each row as she passed by. She stopped at one row and reached for a child and pulled his seatbelt tighter. She worked her way toward the rear, where the carnage was. She crawled into the area where the wind was most brutal. It ripped at her as she held onto the leg of one seat while she reached for the next. Hand over hand, she pulled herself along. A gust lifted her body. She grabbed a seat and held on with both hands. She lowered her head between her outstretched arms as her blouse and skirt ripped away, flew through the hole, and streaked by Rhombus.

"Oh, please," Brian begged. "Please let it be over."

The wind had stripped her of the authority of her uniform and the dignity of her clothing, yet the small Korean woman raised her head and looked to the rear. She forced her feet into a seat leg and moved again, using the legs like a ladder.

"Please don't do this, lady," Brian pleaded. "Please don't do this."

She crawled over torn metal, while streaks of blood from her hands and feet flew away in a red mist. Her bra and panties turned crimson.

Mike's face hardened.

Hand over hand she inched along until she disappeared into the rear of the cabin. Mike moved Rhombus forward and looked back to see her. She'd disappeared.

"Can you see her?" Brian asked. "Can you?"

"No, I think she made it."

"Oh, man," Brian said, his voice cracking.

Mike moved Rhombus back. He considered the airplane he was in. Rhombus whirred away and offered him all the technology he could ask for at his fingertips. Even the clothing he and Brian wore prepared them for the unexpected. But these folks—these folks nearby—all they expected out of the night was a movie and a peaceful snooze. All they wanted to do now was to land somewhere, anywhere. But the wolves would not leave them alone. Predators approached from behind at supersonic speed intent on the death of the innocents, intent on hiding what they had done. "How much time until they get here?" Mike asked.

"About twenty minutes," Brian said.

Mike groped for a solution. He had no weapons. He

couldn't reveal their presence in order to decoy the fighters. What he wouldn't give right now for an F-14. He wouldn't even use his missiles. He'd toy with the cowards—maneuver the marvelous fighter behind them while they fought to escape, then take his time to rip each of them apart with cannon fire. He gritted his teeth.

Brian broke Mike's thoughts. "What's that? Hydraulic fluid coming from the tail?"

A light red fluid poured out of the rear of the 747 and dispersed behind the airliner as a pink mist. "It is!"

"When he runs out, he's a goner."

An idea burst into Mike's brain. Guard! Civilian guard frequency!

"Brian," Mike called, "set the VHF to guard frequency."

"You sure?"

"Just do it!" Mike ordered. "And set the power to minimum."

Brian touched a finger to a knob on the center console. He set the radio to a frequency of 121.5. He turned another knob that adjusted the radio's power. "Done."

Mike pressed the radio button on his throttle lever. "Korean Airlines 747 enroute to Misawa. Korean Airlines 747 enroute to Misawa. You have been fired upon by Soviet fighters. Damage to your aircraft is extensive. You are losing hydraulic fluid rapidly. Repeat, you are losing hydraulic fluid rapidly. You must ditch immediately. Repeat, you must ditch immediately."

Mike watched for a sign that his radio call had been picked up by the 747 crew.

"You going to tell them about the fighters?" Brian asked.

"Only if I have to."

They waited. The red symbols got closer. Just as Mike pressed the radio button to make another radio call, the Boeing's nose dropped.

"He heard us," Brian said.

It was a game of time now. The fighters would shoot again when they arrived. The only hope for the 747 was to ditch before it either ran out of hydraulic fluid or was shot down. Brian called out their altitude and their distance from the fighters.

"Nine thousand feet. Soviet fighters at one hundred twenty miles," Brian called.

"Eight thousand feet. One hundred and two miles."

"Seven thousand feet. Eighty-four miles."

Rhombus trailed the 747 like a mother deer that followed her fawn as it bled to death after a wolf's attack. The wolves were coming back.

"Oh, no." Mike muttered.

The pink mist stopped.

The airliner had just lost its most precious fluid.

It was time to die.

The 747's nose swung to the right, a giant airborne bus skidding down an ice-covered highway.

Mike slammed the throttles back and opened the spoilers to keep Rhombus from overrunning the Boeing.

Too little. Too late!

The airliner filled the SID.

"Damn!"

Mike closed the spoilers and jerked Rhombus' nose up. The bomber climbed. He slapped the joystick to the left.

Rhombus barrel-rolled, a single corkscrew movement around the Boeing's flight path that chewed up energy and time and kept the warplane behind the Boeing.

The airliner came back into view on the SID.

"What next?" Brian asked.

The airplane's right side was visible as its nose swung farther.

The right wing dropped, slow but definite. Then, as the left wing rose and bit harder into the wind, the 747 snapped over.

Mike slapped the joystick to the right, yanked the throttles back, and opened the spoilers to stay behind.

Farther the giant rolled.

Upside down.

Past upside down.

Then right side up again.

Then over again—faster.

Mounting pins, designed to hold the big engines against thrusting and vertical forces, broke as the sideways forces built.

The number-one engine flew off and spiraled at a distance, flying formation with the airliner.

The number-four engine flew off.

Wing panels broke away and scattered like drops of water from a shaking dog.

Landing-gear locks broke.

The wheels dropped into the airstream. The tires exploded, and streams of black rubber tore away.

Mike rolled Rhombus with the 747.

The ocean rushed up at them.

At the bottom of the second spiral, the airliner skimmed the whitecaps.

Its enormous nose rose. Straight up … a wounded angel reaching for home.

At 3,000 feet above the water, its climb stopped. It hung there for a second, its giant wings useless, one engine roaring.

The airliner seemed to cry as it toppled on its back, toward the sea. Upside down the giant angel fell, spread-eagle, while its remaining engine spun it around like a leaf from an autumn tree.

It hit the water.

A cloud of spray erupted.

The spray cleared and revealed the airliner on its back, still in one piece, at the bottom of a shallow trough. The edges of the trough formed a circular white-capped wave that paused, then rushed inward from all sides. The wave closed over the airliner and shot up, a spout that looked like a blue-white hand reaching from a grave. At the end of its reach, the hand dispersed into drops that sprinkled over the sea like spring rain.

The two Soviet fighters zoomed by and turned away.

Mike held a shallow orbit over the area where the Boeing had disappeared. He and Brian stared as the water erased all evidence, as though to say it was time for life to move on. After two orbits Mike said, "RTB, Brian."

"Yeah," Brian replied. He typed. Both pilots settled in their seats as the MPP took control. The invisible warplane reached for the stars and turned eastward—home. Rhombus climbed into the dawn as it flew away from the cold sea and the clothing and toys that rose from the bottom.

They were at 70,000 feet. The SID compensated for the brilliance of the sun on the eastern horizon.

"Dim it some more," Mike said.

"Roger."

The MPP was flying them home, managing their fuel supply, regulating the cockpit temperature, and SatBursting their location through the satellite net. It had everything under control.

"I feel like I should say something."

"Me, too."

"Got it all recorded?"

"Rog."

"SID, too?"

"Yes."

"Let's …" Mike paused. "Let's get some sleep."

"OK."

"I'll do the checklist. See you in a few hours."

"OK."

Mike pulled up a checklist on one of his CRTs. He satisfied himself that the MPP was doing what it was supposed to do. One final look around the cockpit and he'd relax, too.

Brian was already gone. He'd pulled his metal dental tool out of a pocket, but that's as far as he got. Mike lifted the tool from his hand and slipped it back into Brian's pocket. He pressed a toggle switch on Brian's seat and watched it recline.

He reclined his own seat. He thought of his son. The horror of watching several hundred die was not as painful as burying one freckle-faced boy. Where is Kachina? Sleep came so fast he didn't know it.

WEST COAST AIR DEFENSE IDENTIFICATION ZONE (ADIZ)
UNITED STATES OF AMERICA

A chime sounded. Brian reached out as though searching for his snooze button. He shook his head. "Hey, Michael," he called as he shook Mike's right arm. Mike didn't move. Shaking harder this time, Brian called again, "Hey! Wake up! We're punching through the ADIZ. It's time to go to work."

Mike's head shot back, and his eyes opened wide, confused. He looked down to investigate why his chest felt so cool. It was drool. "Yuk."

"What a slob," Brian remarked. "Kachina is more woman than I thought."

Kachina, he thought. Then the screaming images of the 747 returned, like the sun seared on the retina. As much pain that lay in the waters behind, it paled to his own grief, his own desperation. Scotty.

"I hate these long missions," Mike said, trying to break the grip of all the hands reaching to him from the grave. He loosened his lap belt and raised his rear off the seat. "My butt itches, my head itches, this helmet hurts my ears, I got crud in the corners of my eyes and drool on my chest. Ain't this a crock?"

"I'll call room service for you," Brian responded.

"Sarcasm. Why is it only funny when I do it? Clear me off intercom. You have the airplane."

"I have the airplane," Brian responded.

Mike unfastened his helmet strap and pulled the plastic contraption off his head. He lay it in his lap and stretched. He massaged his ears and scratched his head. He pulled a tube from the side console and urinated in it. He retrieved a Mylar pouch and extracted a pre-moistened towel. "Ahhhhhhhhhhh."

"Here," Brian said over the noise of the cockpit. He held a bag of water.

Mike extracted a tube from the bag and drank. He handed it back to Brian and put his helmet back on. "Pilot, here."

"Roger."

"I got the airplane. Your turn."

"Roger. You got the airplane."

Brian relieved himself and drank as the MPP flew Rhombus in a gradual descent. They were crossing the Sierra Nevada south of Lake Tahoe. Groom Lake Base lay ahead.

There, a man named Holtz lay prone in a ravine a hundred yards off the runway. He gloated at those less intelligent than he, which meant, in his mind, everyone. He thought his plan was brilliant, its sinister aspects hidden behind the skirts of its innocence. When he was caught, he'd just play dumb. This was going to be the easiest money he had ever made. He sneered as he lay on the ground and doodled in the sand. "Fools. Damned military fools."

Two years ago Holtz retired from a firm that protected high-level corporate executives. Like a number of people in the security business, he rode a fine edge that separated the legal from the illegal. He was fascinated with the contest between the science of evasion and escape and the science of detection and capture. He scoffed at the idiots who camped out on the fringe of the base range in their campers. They were amateurs who were trying to prove that the United States government flew alien flying saucers from Groom Lake Base, cowards who wanted to learn a secret without sacrificing for it, and, worse, idiots who wouldn't get rewarded for it.

During his career in private security, Holtz had met an FBI agent who told him that because of Nellis AFB, the Nevada Test Site, and Groom Lake, Las Vegas had more Soviet KGB agents than anyplace this side of Moscow. It made sense to him. After retirement, he moved to Las Vegas and started rumors at local bars that he worked at Groom Lake. It had taken only three days to snare a KGB agent. Holtz snickered,

"Damned guy's cover is an undertaker. Jeez."

Holtz was careful to build a reputation as one of those who made a hobby of sitting vigil at the edge of the Groom Lake security frontier, hoping to see a flying saucer. "Goofies," he called them. The difference between him and them was that his KGB contact would pay big money for good information.

His plan had been to work himself to the runway from the edge of the security perimeter, moving at night. He carried only enough water and high-energy food bars for a one-way trip. He planned to stake out the runway for a day, then deliberately get caught. Hell, he thought. With my security background, the worst that'll happen will be a night in jail. Those flakes who crash the gates on the nuke testing range only get a fine. If he saw something, he'd make some money. If he didn't, his standing with the goofies would be enhanced. Hell, just to say he was there would be enough to make this worth it.

It had taken him three days to cover the distance from his pickup parked at the security perimeter. Patience had paid off. Here he was, right in the heart of the world's most secret place. He'd been here since dawn.

Nothing rewarding had happened so far, except for something that took off last night and climbed straight up. The desert wind whistled through the bushes and blew grit in his face. He spit, brushed the grit away, and swore. He leveled his binoculars at a peak to the west.

Mike and Brian flew over Boundary Peak as Rhombus descended into Nevada. The desert seemed hospitable compared to where they had just been. Scenes of fire and flying metal still flashed through their minds. They hadn't talked about it.

About a mile from the base the MPP extended the flaps, but kept the landing gear up so as not to reveal Rhombus' presence to radar. The computer lowered the landing gear just as Rhombus crossed the runway threshold. The airplane flared and held at 20 feet above the concrete, as planned. It was in ground effect and moved over the runway like a ski on smooth water. When it passed its normal landing point, the airspeed was 45 knots higher than normal. As the airspeed dropped, the airplane's nose rose to compensate for the loss of lift. Finally, not even ground effect could keep it up. Just as the airframe shuddered, the MPP lowered the nose, then flared just before the wheels touched down. Rhombus was 2,000 feet past its normal landing spot.

♦ ♦ ♦

"What the hell is that!
"What the hell *is* that?"
Holtz saw large wheels appear out of thin air and fly past. After holding a constant altitude, the wheels dropped to the runway in a burst of blue smoke.
Holtz blinked. "Damn, an invisible airplane. Damn!"
He stood.
He watched the wheels stop and turn onto a taxiway.
He noted the airplane's strange exhaust sound, a muted hissing rumble.
It was time to be captured. By next week he would have his new truck. Truck, hell, the Russians would kill for this.
He froze.
Adrenaline poured through him.
He dropped to the ground.
If the Russians would kill for this, the Americans would, too! "What the hell am I doing?"
He bit his lip as he watched the giant wheels disappear behind a mound of creosote bushes that crested a hummock.
"What the hell am I doing!" he cried into the dirt. "They aren't going to let me get away with seeing this! Gotta get outta here!" He scurried away from the runway. "Gotta get outta here!"
Holtz wasn't a soldier. He was a cop. His career was in a world of Barettas, Uzis, and armored limos. Now he was in a world of M-16s, attack helicopters, Specter gunships, cluster

bombs, B-52s, and—and invisible airplanes! Holtz was in the show now. This was the major league in the game of death, and he didn't like it one bit.

Mike stopped Rhombus in front of the hangar and waited for a ground crewman to plug in the intercom. "Good afternoon, sirs."

"Afternoon," Brian responded.

"We've got you on external power. You can shut down now. We'll tow you into the hangar." A light on the overhead console confirmed the external power connection. The pilots went through the Engine Shutdown checklist.

Holtz came to a shallow gully in a full run and jumped from its rim. Instead of landing on the other side, he landed on the edge and fell back as he dragged dirt with him. Unhurt, he scampered out of the gully. He turned to see if anyone followed. Nobody. He ran. The buildings of Groom Lake Base sank farther and farther into the shimmering heat of the dry lake in Emigrant Valley.

An hour after Rhombus landed, the recordings of the events over Petropavlovsk were transferred to standard audio and video cassettes. The cassettes were sealed in a briefcase and handcuffed to a Lt. JG's wrist. The JG boarded a small business jet in Air Force markings and headed east to Langley, Virginia, where people in a fifth-level basement would interpret the tapes and pass the information along to the White House.

Holtz whimpered. He tried to keep his eyes on a peak in the distance, but he didn't seem to be getting any closer. The climbing desert sun evaporated the sweat from his desert camouflage fatigues. The fabric crackled as dried salt flaked off. His blood thickened as the sun and the wind stole water from his body. His fingernails were split, and his fingers bled after digging in dry washes for water. He staggered. He tried to rub the headache away with fingers that left streaks of red in his hair. He looked into distance and swore, but the words came around his swollen tongue as if spoken through a gag. "'Odd 'ammit. Sum bishes."

He dragged his right foot and left gouges in the dust. His arms swung back and forth like dead weights.

Holtz grabbed his chest. His eyes focused for the first time in hours. He pitched forward, and his body hit the ground, dust puffing away. His open mouth hit a rock. Tooth splinters scattered. "'Odd 'ammit." His body convulsed, then went still.

The desert whistled through a nearby bush and blew wisps of grit into Holtz' face. A fly buzzed in an ever-tightening orbit and landed on his open eye.

"I think it's over," one man said as they looked at the dead man on the television screen. "The KGB keeps sending 'em, and they all die the same way."

The other man stood. "I'll take care of this one."

"I hate this job," the first said as he glanced at the screen again.

"I don't. Lousy KGB traitors."

In a few months, or maybe a few years, someone would find another John Doe buried in a shallow desert grave. The Nye County Sheriff would log it as another victim of the mob days and would note the time of death as "probably in the 1950s or 1960s." It was as much a part of life in Nevada as the ringing of a slot machine.

1983, Thursday, 1 September
1710 Hours (5:10 PM)
Nellis Air Force Base
Las Vegas, Nevada

The 727 descended into Las Vegas Valley through air swept clean by an earlier weather front. The city spread across the valley floor. High-rise hotel towers stood at its center. Mike looked in the direction of his home. He carried within him a marbled mixture of powerful emotions that swirled together like drops of bile in sweet fudge. The gamut of emotion spanned from Scotty's death to the 30 days of leave Patterakis had just declared. It was time that he and Kachina needed. Kachina hadn't answered the calls he'd made from Groom Lake this afternoon.

The 727 stopped on the ramp at Nellis. "I'll be at Mom's next week, but from then on, who knows," Brian said, cutting into Mike's thoughts. "A month off. It's been so long since I had leave, I don't know what to do." Brian looked at his friend. "Any luck with Kachina?" He already knew the answer.

"No." Tension showed in the corners of Mike's mouth and eyes. "I'm worried, Brian."

"Everything'll work out." He put his hand on Mike's shoulder for a moment, then stood in the aisle.

"Yeah," Mike muttered. He wanted to scream at the crew to hurry and open the door so he could run out and call Kachina again. He remembered her face as he told her he had to leave after Scotty's funeral. The mystery of her emotionless stare tore at him.

As he left the 727, he stomped through the rippling heat. Brian worked to keep up.

"Got a quarter?" Mike asked.

"Yeah. Here." A coin tumbled through the air.

Mike caught it and put it in a pay phone. He dialed, got nothing, hung up, pocketed the coin, and headed for the parking lot.

"I'll call," Brian said over the roof of his car, clearly worried.

No response. Brian shrugged.

Mike drove out of the base and headed west, into the sun, screaming under his breath at those who drove slower.

The old Cougar GT left small tornadoes in the desert dust off the side of the highway to Las Vegas. It squalled in the street corners and squealed when each light turned from red to green.

Home. He pressed the remote control and thrummed on the steering wheel as the door rose. His stomach churned and he fought the urge to hit something—anything.

He couldn't wait for the door to open enough to get the car in the garage. He ripped the house keys off the key chain in the ignition. The Cougar sat running, it's door open, as he ducked under the rising garage door.

Kachina's car was gone!

He fumbled for the door key and shoved the door open.

He stopped. The emptiness of the house overwhelmed him. He looked across the kitchen and the living room toward the bedrooms. A memory of Scotty's trilling laughter echoed from the back of the house. This is what it was like for Kachina to come home after the funeral, Mike thought.

He leaned against the kitchen counter and looked into the family room. Where are they? Where the hell are they?

The air-conditioner cycled off. The silence in the house roared in grief-stricken anger and threw loving memories against the walls. Through the open jaws of the quiet, a hot wind blew at Mike with questions of why. Why weren't you here when Scotty died? Why weren't you here when she needed you most? Why are you never here? Why can't you have a job like everyone else? What is so wrong with you that you hear the lure of the sky and the call of the country over the pleas of your family? Why can't you understand the weeping of your wife? Why can't you see that your daughter's gift of her beloved Dolly to her dead brother was her cry for comfort?

Mike tore the khaki hat from his head. His arm arched sideways as he flung it across the room. It tumbled toward the coffee table—toward a glass vase with a dead rose. It tackled the vase near its rim and the vase and the cap tumbled together. Dry rose petals flew away, and slimy green water spilled across the table and the light pink envelope.

Mike stared at the envelope. Its soft color and straight edges burned into his consciousness and flung everything else aside. "Damn," he said as he tore paper towels off a roll. He ran to the table and slapped the wad against the water around the envelope. Damn! He picked the envelope up by a corner, opened it, and extracted the pages. They were dry. He unfolded them.

Dearest Michael,

I can't live like this. I love you, but going on isn't possible. I cannot live with what I feel. I have so much pain and so much bitterness.

In our years together I have moved our home, cared for my children, paid the bills, mowed the lawn, and worried about the car's mechanic being honest with me. I have slept many nights without you.

I could understand your not being here for Scotty when you were on cruise, but I cannot understand how you can be stationed so close, yet we only see you on the weekends. How, dearest Michael (I cannot write this without crying), how could you not be here to hold your son's hand while his little life left him? How could you just leave after we buried him? Where are you? What is out there?

Mike cringed.

So many times I have said goodbye, not knowing if I would ever see you again. Not knowing if my children would have a father. I have lain awake worried about you. And when you could, you have always been here for me. I know that.

But this time you were not here at my darkest time. I have tried not to complain about your duty, but my heart is breaking now. It breaks for my own weakness as much as it does for yours. But my son has just died. My pearl child is gone. I am bitter, and I am angry. I sit here with my precious Lisa Marie and realize I cannot properly care for her while I feel this way.

I have to go. Forgive me.

Kachina

Crayon scrawls marked the letter beneath Kachina's signature. Even though attacked by overwhelming grief and anger, Kachina had taken time for Lisa to write I love you to her Daddy. He couldn't help smiling, a little.

The letter dropped to Mike's lap, and he closed his eyes. The letter at face value was bad enough. But the undertones were ominous, and bitterness bled through. She called Scotty and Lisa her children, not theirs.

He picked up the phone. "No, she wouldn't go there." He put it back. "Where?" He paced. Kachina's parents were dead. She had no close relatives. Even in her grief, she wouldn't burden their military friends with a marital problem. Her best friends lived in Florida. No, she wouldn't go there. Where would she go for support? Mike froze. No. Why not? Don't women go home to mom when they leave their husbands? My mom is the only mother she's ever had. Oooh, that would be tough for her to do, but—Kachina would go where he would find her.

He reached for the phone and dialed. A voice on the other end answered, "Christum's residence."

"Hi, Mom. Is there somebody there I know?"

"Oh, Suzy. Wait a second. I left it by the other phone. Can I call you right back? Are you at home?"

Mike picked up the code. "Yes." He hung up the phone and relaxed a bit. In a moment it rang. Mike tore the receiver away. "Mom?"

"Mom? I always knew we were close but—"

"Not now, Brian." Mike slammed the phone down. Brian would be OK. He'd call back. He waited. He stood. He paced.

He walked into the kitchen and poured a glass of water. The phone rang. The half-full glass thumped in the sink. He yanked the wall phone from its cradle. Silence—then, "Hi, son. It's Mom." Mike breathed again. "Kachina's here, son, but she doesn't want you to know it."

Mike closed his eyes, lowered his head, and sighed. He took a deep breath, then spoke. "Where else would she go, Mom? You're the only parent she has."

"I don't know what to do, Mikey. She sure is a hurt girl, and Lisa is a bewildered little thing. Kachina begged me not to tell you she was here, but I couldn't do that."

"I know, Mom."

"What should I do?"

"Treat her like she's your daughter."

"She is my daughter. I love her as much as I do you and Scotty."

"Mom," Mike said, relaxed, "she realizes I'd know where to find her, so she can't blame you for telling me. Tell her we talked. Just be honest with her and give her all the love you can. I'll catch the first flight out tonight. I should be there tomorrow."

"What about your Navy job?"

"Navy job." He grinned. Mom never quite understood military life. "The CO—uh, my boss has given us thirty days of—vacation."

"Oh, thank goodness. Shh! I gotta go!" she whispered. The line went dead.

It was a few minutes after midnight. He sat in a near-empty Delta 1011 as it climbed into the night sky on its way to Atlanta. There he'd connect to another flight and be home in the afternoon. He felt old.

He watched the dark landscape below move by. With every minute that passed, he was seven miles closer to home. Falling away behind him, in the middle of a barren flat surrounded by stark mountains, a collection of buildings stood in the darkness. Inside one of those buildings sat a large black airplane. Behind the airplane, a single mercury-vapor bulb poured blue-green light across the funeral-colored machine. For the next thirty days it would sit here. No electrons would bring warmth to its circuits. No hydraulic fluid would flow to its control surfaces. No rushing wind would flow around it. No fire would burn in its engines.

But it would wait.

1983, FRIDAY, 9 SEPTEMBER
HINTON, WEST VIRGINIA

The river was in the shadow of the ridges that lined each side of the gorge. Cooking smells wafted through the neighborhood. Mike sat here as he had every day at this time since returning home the week before. Behind him was Cousin Jimmy's house, and up the street was his boyhood home, where Kachina and Lisa were staying. He plucked a daisy and tore off the petals. One by one he threw them into the moving water. They made a long string of tiny white dots as they bobbed up and down on the current.

He was staying with his cousin because Kachina needed—what was it?—space? Where did they come up with all these new concepts? His telephone calls were rebuffed by Kachina who would say, "I can't see you just yet, Michael." Well, at least there's promise in the word "yet." At least she knows I'm here and that I'm trying. Still, it's been a week! Another daisy petal hit the water.

"Hey, Mikey." A stout hand clapped his shoulder.

"Oh, hi, Jimmy."

Jimmy sat down beside Mike. Neither man spoke as Jimmy watched the river, and Mike pulled up more of his cousin's flowers and flung pieces of them into the current.

"Woman problems can drive a man crazy." Jimmy spoke

in the thick slow brogue of southern West Virginia. Like blue-grass music, the dialect was passed down from Irish and Scots who had settled here after the Civil War. "Yes, sir. Woman problems can make a man absent-minded."

"Absent-minded?"

"Yep."

"How do you figure?"

Jimmy changed the subject. "Mikey, ever think of movin' back here?"

"Every day."

"What'd you leave for in the first place?"

"Things to do." Mike was home now, and he reverted to the short uncomplicated answers of mountain folk.

"Like what?"

"Fly. See things. Fight."

"You never liked fightin' as a kid."

"Nope."

"Ran from every one of 'em, as I recall."

"Yep."

"Plumb strange."

"Yep." Mike nudged his cousin. "You ever think about leaving?"

"Nope."

"Why not?"

"And do what? Work somewhere else so I could dream about movin' back? I barber when I want, drive a school bus three hours a day, and guide rafters down that river. You ever do anything that much fun?"

Mike thought of sunsets over the Indian Ocean, mornings on the Pacific, the majesty of exploring the clouds, the joy of serving a cause above one's self with people you respect, and the technological marvel of flying—especially Rhombus. "Yep, a time or two."

"Ever think about bein' a gardener if you come back?"

"No. Why?"

Jimmy put a stripped daisy stem between his teeth. "Oh. Just a thought."

Mike flicked another petal.

Jimmy stood, brushed the dirt off his backside, and patted Mike on the back. "Suzie'll have dinner soon."

"I appreciate you letting me stay here."

"As long as you need to, Mikey." He took off his baseball cap and swatted. "Damn bug."

Mike flipped another daisy petal into the river.

"Uh, Mikey?" Jimmy put his cap back on.

"Yeah?"

"It's none of my business or nuthin', but you know, I was thinkin'."

"What?"

Jimmy put his hand on Mike's shoulder. "Everybody in the clan hears that you're the best fighter in the Navy."

"Some say."

"Shot at?"

"Yep."

"Kill people?"

Mike flipped a petal with his thumb. "Yes."

"Well, I was wonderin', when're you gonna start fightin' again?"

"Next war."

"What do you fight for?"

"What I love."

"Like I say, none of my business," Jimmy clapped Mike once on the back, "but it looks to me like you best get crackin', boy."

It was the same kitchen table where Mike had eaten all his meals for eighteen years. Scott smiled at the sight of his brother's wife and little girl as they raised their heads from the grace he had just said. To his left sat Mom, who was always a bubbling ball of irreverent fun. Scott was happy Mom had asked him over, but he felt strange to be sitting here with Kachina and Lisa, while Mike was just down the street at Jimmy's. He came over because he didn't know what else to do.

His mind rolled back to a day some fifteen years before. It was 1967. "Don't worry, Mom," Mike said as he backed into the street. "I'll drive safe." Scott was only fifteen, but he felt a mixture of panic and pride at the thought of his big brother being a Navy fighter pilot. Mike waved once more to them as he disappeared down the tree-covered street and turned toward the highway. Scott ran across the street and down the edge of the riverbank. He caught his toe on something and fell to the edge of the water in a long painless tumble. He got to his feet and peered beneath the branching sycamore trees to see the flat concrete bridge that spanned the river downstream. He knew that in a minute or so Mike would drive across the bridge and pick up Route 20 to head south. There he was! Scott saw the black Cougar as it moved across the bridge. It stopped. Mike's door opened, and he walked toward the near rail of the bridge. Scott saw him wave and yell something.

Scott whispered to himself, "Something, something, little brother. Something, something—at Christmas!"

Scott's face screwed up as he concentrated. "Oh, I get it!"

He cupped his hands around his mouth and yelled, his voice breaking, "See you, too, big brother. See ya' at Christmas!" Scott jumped up and down and waved his arms. Mike waved once more, then got back in the Cougar. The car disappeared in the trees on the other side of the river as it headed away. Scott sat down on the bank and threw pebbles into the water. He knew Mike was heading into what he thought was a great adventure. For Scott, however, he had just waved his big brother off to war. Mike would want him to be brave, not to cry. He tried.

"Enough is enough, Kachina." The booming voice rolled across the table and pulled Scott from his daydream. There he stood, his big brother, Mike, and boy, was he mad. "Hot damn," Scott said to himself. "Now I feel like eating." The screen door banged shut behind Mike.

"Da-ee, Da-ee!" Lisa yelled, her face joyful, her feet pounding the high chair. "Da-ee, Da-ee!"

Mike's anger flew away, and he bent at the waist to kiss his daughter. She put her arms around his neck. She let go, and Mike smiled, unaware of the red Jell-O that streaked his cheek. Lisa said to everyone at the table, "My Da-ee's home. My Da-ee's home." She put a tiny spoon into a pile of corn and held it up, spilling all the kernels but one. "Da-ee, want some corn?"

Mike nibbled the one surviving kernel from the spoon and rubbed his stomach while he puffed out his cheeks, "Hmmmmmm. Good. Lisa's corn is goooooooood."

Lisa turned her attention back to her dinner and dug her spoon into a small mound of mashed potatoes. "My Da-ee's home," she said for nobody's benefit but her own. To her, the world was suddenly very normal.

Kachina gaped at Lisa, astonished. In all her own grief and bitterness, she'd forgotten that Lisa had not only lost her brother, but, for a while, also her father. Kachina didn't know if she could forgive Mike, but she wouldn't cause a scene here—not at this table.

He caught her eye. They looked at each other, the only sound in the room being the munching of a small mouthful of corn. He gave her a gentle smile and nodded outside.

Kachina dabbed her lips with the napkin and laid it on the table beside her plate. She rose from her chair. Mike opened the screen door for her. Mike touched Lisa on the nose and blew Mom a kiss. He lifted his mother's car keys from the hook beside the door. "May I?" His mother nodded, silent.

He pointed his finger at Scott and shot him with a mock pistol. Then he was gone. Mom looked at Scott with a question on her face. Scott shrugged, "It's a guy thing, Mom."

As they walked down the driveway, they heard a small voice come from the kitchen. "Da-ee's home, Unca Scott. My Da-ee's home."

They drove without speaking up a single-lane country road that climbed out of the New River Gorge. Topping a hill, Mike turned down an old logging road. Wildflowers swayed to the side and bent under the car as it passed. Hickory, poplar, maple, oak, and ash trees leaned over them like the arching walls of a cathedral. After a few hundred feet, the cathedral of trees opened into a meadow of tall grass. The meadow was dotted with Queen Anne's lace, sweet pea, trillium, and a dozen other types of wildflower. A mist stretched on the meadow and fireflies rose through it and disappeared in the dusky sky.

Mike stopped the car and came around to open the door for Kachina. They walked toward the center of the meadow, a wonderland of color, scent, and tiny green flashes. When they stopped, she turned to see that trees surrounded the meadow on three sides. A beautiful maple tree stood alone at one edge, and the open side of the meadow fell away to a dimming view of the gorge. A thousand feet below, the waters of the river rushed to the sea, just as they had for millions of years.

Mike reached for her hand. She pulled away.

"This is it," he said, holding out his arms.

"This is what?"

"This is the meadow we want to build our house on."

She looked over each shoulder. "It's nice."

"It's better than nice. Great battles took place here, and rocket ships left for the stars. I've wanted to show you this for years. I finally got permission from the owner."

Kachina waited.

"It belongs to a man named Arvel Neely."

Kachina looked past him.

"Mr. Neely is a barber during the week and preaches on the weekends." He looked off, uncomfortable. "He's a Primitive Baptist elder. Ever heard of Primitive Baptists?"

"No."

"He's owned this meadow since before I was born. It was my favorite place when I was growing up." He pointed to a slight rise. "There," he said, "is where the pioneers were surrounded by Indians." He pointed to another place at the edge of the tree line. "And that's where Jimmy and I attacked from. We were in the Cavalry, you know?" He grinned. "It was an epic battle that happened many times. Jimmy, Scott, and Rusty were my most trusted friends."

"Who's Rusty?"

"Rusty was my horse, of course."

"I see."

"As I grew up, this meadow became different things to me." He looked past her at the soft landscape. "During high school I'd wonder who I was going to marry. I dreamed of bringing her here."

"Well, there's no time like the present, I guess."

"Sometimes I'd come up here on moonless nights and spread a blanket and look at the stars. I got to know the stars, too."

"Yes, I know you did."

Mike pointed. "The bright one there is Pallas, and that one's Altair. In a month or two Orion will rise in the winter sky and—"

"I know, Michael. I know." She lowered her tone. "But that's not why we're here, is it?"

He sighed. "Kachina, I have something to tell you." He looked over each shoulder. When he looked back, his face was intense, worried. "We're not here because it's beautiful or because I want to talk about the stars. I … uh … well …" His thoughts rolled back to sea and the sleek ships that moved like gray ghosts through a morning sky's downy horizon. He pictured the faces of brave men, youthful faces with hearts of pride and trust in each other. Mike's thoughts raced among the images in his mind. Brian—Brian, loyal and trusting, and strong. I owe Brian. And Patterakis? Would he ever, in the worst circumstances, tell his wife what I'm going to tell Kachina?

"What is it, Michael?"

"Well," Mike began. "I … uh … I …" Mike looked through her at places and things and people she could not imagine. He reached deep within himself to do what he knew he had to do. I gotta tell her. It's the only way to take her pain away. Of course, she'd never tell. Who would hear us out here in the middle of the field? It'll hurt nobody, and then she'll understand. It's what's right. It's the right thing to do.

"What?"

In sickness and in health, 'til death do us part.

That I will support and defend the Constitution of the United States.

His heart swirled with conflicting vows and battling loyalties.

"Hey, Dad. Catch."

"We're at the brink. You and I are either going to bring down the Soviet Union or we are going to provoke World War Three."

I can't let 'em down. Can't do it. Just can't do it.

"I … love you."

"What." It was not a question.

"I love you."

"Oh, dear God, Michael Christum." She fought for words. She fought to say something, anything that would express how she felt. "Our son died and you weren't there. Our son was buried, and you left. You abandoned me! You abandoned Lisa! I … I …" She brought both fists to the side of her head and drove them at his chest. He staggered back. Kachina stepped into him and beat her fists against him. Her tears wet his shirt as she pressed her face against his chest. Muffled cries of "Why?" poured out. Suddenly, she opened her fists and held her palms against his chest. Rolling sobs retched from her as she pushed away.

Mike wrapped his arms around her. Kachina leaned back against his hold. Her head fell back, and she cried, her face turned upward. Her pain flew on the wings of her whimpering and moved through the meadow and shattered its peace. Mike pulled her to him, her head against his chest. Like a small child who had cried too long, her sobs turned into ragged breaths. Her strength melted away, and Mike tightened his hold on her. They sank to the ground together.

As he sat on the damp earth, he held his wife and listened as her breathing returned to normal.

She was quiet for a while and Mike relaxed for the first time in days. He had her back. She opened her eyes and sniffed. "And?"

"And what?"

Her eyes squinted under angry eyebrows. "You love me and what else?"

Mike had brought her here to tell her about Rhombus. He couldn't do it, and now he didn't have a plan. He fought for something to say. "That's all," he said.

"After all that's happened, all you can think of to tell me is that you love me?"

"I'm sorry, too," he added.

She watched the fireflies rise from the meadow. She smiled while she imagined three little boys riding make-believe po- nies from its edge to save the pioneers. "When I was in first grade, I came home excited about a boy." She smiled. "I told Momma that he made my heart feel funny." She chuckled. "Momma said that my heart was fluttering because it was filled with love. My Sunday school teacher told us that the more love we had in our hearts, the easier it would be to fly to heaven." She plucked a daisy, then touched a finger to its golden center. "So I figured that the fluttering in my heart was caused by angel wings, and I also figured that the more people I loved, the more angels there would be in my heart and the easier it would be to fly to heaven."

Mike grinned.

"Oh, sure," she said. "I get this from a guy who was in a cavalry made up of three boys and an imaginary horse named Rusty."

The grin collapsed.

"So, you see, Michael, when I was a little girl I believed I would be carried to heaven on fluttering angel wings." Tears trickled over her cheeks. Mike brushed at them. She sniffed. "It's what I have to hold to when you're gone, Michael. It's why I know my son's in heaven. I loved him so much." She snuggled against him. He held her as his own tear-filled eyes reflected the soft light.

After she quieted a bit, he asked, "Do you know that I love you?"

"Yes."

"Do you believe that I loved Scotty?" he asked.

"Oh, there's no doubt of that."

"Then, what else is there to understand, Kachina?"

He felt the stab of her small fist in his chest, and he heard her rising voice ask, "Why couldn't you be there when I needed you most? That's what else there is to understand."

"Damn it, honey," he said, his own voice rising in frustration. "How do you know?"

"How do I know what?"

"How do you know I wasn't where you needed me most?"

"Would you please stop talking in riddles? All I know is that you weren't there."

"Where?"

"Oh, damn, Mike. On top of everything, you're playing mind games with me."

"Kachina. Where was I when our son died?"

"You weren't with me or with him. That's all I know."

He felt as though a long glass sliver was sliding through him. He stroked her hair while he watched the moon rise above the grass. "Yeah, but wherever I was, how do you know it wasn't where you needed me most?"

Kachina broke from his hug. "What!"

"I was somewhere on the planet when Scotty died, and I had to go somewhere after his funeral. You know how much I love you and the children. Did you ever think that being away hurt me as much as it did you? No, let me answer that. You didn't. Not once did you consider that I had no choice. Could it be, Kachina, that the world is about to catch fire, and I have to help stop it? Could it be that"—he changed his voice to an intense whisper—"that I'm tired of being scared for you?"

Mike felt the hair on the back of his neck stand up. What he was saying had him standing with his toes over the edge of the cliff, and small pebbles were rolling from beneath his feet into the abyss. He stared at her, trying to pound the words into her head one by one. "You. Have. To. Trust. Me!" He held her face between his hands. He stared needles into her eyes. "Trust me, Kachina."

Kachina's face took on a mixture of astonishment and understanding. She raised her hand to her open mouth. "Ohhh," she said as she pulled away. "Ohhh."

Mike put a finger to her lips to stop her from saying anything else. She stared at him, wide-eyed.

Then in a voice below a whisper, "I did the best I could, baby. I did the best I could."

She stood and brushed leaves off her clothing. She walked away, toward the edge of the meadow that fell off into the gorge. The tall grass made swishing sounds against her clothes. Mike got to his feet and walked after her. He touched her arm, but she stormed away without looking back. "Damn it, stop! Come back here." He grabbed her, spun her around, and pulled her to him.

She bounced against his chest, her eyes sparking. "How many times in all these years have I waved goodbye to you?" she asked.

"Too many."

"How many times have I watched you take off to God-knows-where in a tiny aluminum tube that has wings and fire coming out the back?"

"Too many."

She bit her lip. "How many times have we made love?"

"Too many."

"Not enough, you mean." She raised an eyebrow over a softening face.

"Yes, not enough, that's what I meant."

"Better answer." She took his hands into hers. "How many children do we have?"

"Two," he squeaked. "Two." He raised his face. "Oh, God," he cried loud enough so his words wouldn't be choked off. "I miss him so much."

She held her husband's hands and thought of all they'd done. These hands had flown airplanes faster than sound; pulled a trigger that caused someone to die; touched her with gentle loving kindness; and held their children with paternal pride and loving warmth. These hands did not belong to a man who'd leave her unless there were good reason. What good reason was it this time? Where would these hands go next? What other trigger would they pull? What other machine would they fly into harm's way? Guilt enveloped her. *He is, after all, a warrior, and there must be many, many things he can't share with me. Oh, I've been so stupid. God only knows what he's been doing at Nellis, God and Chris and Brian.* She put her slender arms around his neck and felt his strong arms slide around her waist. The night wrapped them, while the crickets sang.

Holding hands, they walked back to the car, their eyes puffy and red, their hearts sad but at peace. He opened the door for her.

The car turned in the meadow and moved toward the arching trees. From the edge of the meadow, a solitary figure crouched and watched as the fog turned their taillights into red smudges. Chief Dick McIntyre stood and removed his black-knit face cover. He slung the parabolic microphone over his shoulder and jogged after them, but far enough behind so that they couldn't see or hear him. Just after the car turned onto the paved country road, McIntyre emerged from the path and sprinted down the road in the other direction. Within a few seconds he approached a beige Chevy Caprice, partially hidden by a large poplar tree. He pulled the door open and threw the microphone and recorder into the back seat. He slid onto the front seat beside his partner. He was silent with creases between his eyes.

"You OK?" the partner asked.

"I almost wasn't," McIntyre said.

"What does that mean?"

McIntyre exhaled a long breath. "For a second there, I almost messed my pants. I thought he was going to tell her."

"Do you think there's a risk of that?"

"Nope," McIntyre said as he tugged on the door handle, "and I'd bet my life on it. Let's go."

The rear wheels spun on the grassy berm and left long streaks of bare earth. The tires chirped when they hit the pavement. The Chevy's taillights disappeared down the country road.

1983, Saturday, 10 September
Hinton, West Virginia

"Oh, for goodness sake, Mike. The Chicken Hut is just down the road." Kachina rose from the kitchen table with its red-and-white-checked tablecloth. His mother sat at the table, a smile on her face. Mike had stayed here with Kachina last night, and they were themselves again.

"I don't want you and Lisa to go alone," Mike said. He stood under the doorway arch.

"Lisa and I are going to have dinner, then come right back. We'll be fine. You stay here with Scott. You haven't seen much of each other in a while. Do you want to come, Mom?"

Mike nodded encouragement to his mother, but some mysterious woman-to-woman communication took place between her and Kachina. "No, sweetheart. I have too much to do for the church circle meeting." Mike gave up.

Kachina brushed at Mike's cheek. "Listen, big boy," she said, "when you're on the carrier for six months at a time, who do you think runs this family operation, anyway?" He opened his mouth, but she placed a finger on his lips. "Every day I take care of the cuts and the bruises, and squabbles at school, and the broken car, and the bedtime stories, and at the end of that day I sit down and write you a letter." She held her hand to his mouth again, "Ah-ah. Don't interrupt me until I'm through."

She continued, "And those letters tell you, in the gentlest way I know, about our problems and how I've solved them. Can you think of a single letter you've received that complains, or moans, or gripes, or whines over the problems we have at home?" He started to answer. She held a finger against his mouth again. "No, you haven't. Do you know why I handle things myself?" He was quiet this time. "I do it because all I want you to worry about is your safety. It's here, Michael," she said pointing a finger at her heart, "that I do what I can to keep you alive."

She moved her hands to hold either side of his shirt pleat and stepped closer. "The only way I can live with the danger you're always in is to accept my own risks and try to lift some of the burden from you. It's how I do my part. You don't let your fears stand in your way. I don't either. Lisa and I are going out on our own." She grinned with mock victory. She tiptoed to place a kiss on his neck, then bent toward Lisa. "Come on, baby," she said with a slight groan as she picked Lisa up. "Give Daddy a kiss."

Lisa leaned away from her mom with her arms outstretched. She put her arms around his neck, grunted as she squeezed, and placed a loud smack against his cheek. He kissed her nose. "OK, OK. I give up."

Kachina threw her heavy purse over her shoulder. "See ya' in a little while." She held Lisa backward on her shoulder. Lisa stretched out a single hand and opened and closed it in a goodbye to her father, who stood behind the screen door.

"Bye, Da-ee," she said.

He watched Kachina bundle Lisa into her car seat. Then, she got into the driver's seat. He stood watching long after the Malibu disappeared at the end of the block.

Mike returned to the house and settled down in the living room with his brother. Humor came easily to Scott. He sounded like Jimmy; his accent rolled and gave color to everything he said. He was slimmer than Mike, with a sharp angular face and lanky limbs. Mike saw Mom's gentle manner in him. For an hour they talked brother stuff, guy stuff. They told old stories and old lies in a wondrous rush of good feeling. Mom sat in the kitchen with her file of church materials on the table. Once in a while Mike looked into the kitchen at her small but rounding frame and the green eyes that sparkled beneath wavy silver-lavender hair. He loved these two people. He was proud to have named Scotty after his brother. He looked out the window, into the distance, and wondered if Scotty would have been an adventurer like him, or someone like Scott, the owner of a body shop in an aging town, his life a daily thanks-to-God for the beauty and peace that flowed around him.

The phone rang. Scott answered. "Hey, Mike. It's Kachina. Want her to bring something?"

"Yeah, three-piece chicken dinner."

"Hey, Mom. Want anything?"

"No. I'm fine. I have some carrots and celery."

He whispered to Mike, "Mom wants fried chicken, but she doesn't want to admit it." He winked. "She thinks she's on a diet."

"Kachina. Two three-piece chicken dinners and a two-piece. OK?" He looked at Mike. "Anything else?"

"Yes. Tell her to drive carefully."

"Kachina—" He looked at Mike. "Oops. She's gone."

"Figures."

Scott put the phone back on the hook. He intertwined his fingers, looked down for a moment, then at his brother. "Mike, I never got to see Scotty much. Feel like telling me about him?"

Mike didn't want to talk about Scotty. The pain was deep, and his emotions were just below the surface. He swallowed hard to keep his composure.

Scott held up a hand. "You don't have to if you don't—"

"He was a … good kid. He liked baseball." Mike looked at Scott. "Like you. He was always tinkering with things …" Mike grinned a bit. "Like you."

Part of the pain of losing Scotty was the unknown. What kind of man would he have been when he grew up? It became clear to him as the two men talked. Mike pondered his brother's animated way of talking, the openhearted goodness, and the quirky humor. As they talked about Scotty, Mike grew to know that he named his son after the right man. Mike looked at Scott, and he saw not just his brother, but his son. For the first time in days, he had the luxury of a genuine smile.

"They should be back by now."

"Sometimes the Chicken Hut gets busy," Scott said.

"Just the same, I'm gonna call." Mike read the restaurant's phone number off the pad beside the kitchen phone. The voice on the other end said the redheaded woman and the blonde girl had left a half-hour ago. Mike pulled Scott's keys off the shelf. He tossed them across the living room. "Let's go," he said. "They should be here."

"Scott still drives a little fast. Good," Mike thought as his brother headed down Route 20, then across the bridge to town. On the other side they saw a State Police cruiser parked on the grass. Its red lights flashed into the wisps of fog rising from the river. Farther down the road they pulled over as a fire truck sped by.

"Hurry," Mike said.

"Huh?"

"Hurry!" Scott understood and sped toward town. They wheeled into the restaurant's parking lot. Mom's Chevy was gone. "Head back to the bridge!" Mike ordered.

"They probably took the old road back to the house," Scott said to ease Mike's growing apprehension. Mike said nothing.

When they reached the bridge, they saw that other emergency vehicles had joined the trooper's cruiser. "Pull over," Mike ordered. Scott was seeing the side of Mike he didn't know, the military side, the officer side, the take-charge side. Scott pulled over. Mike got out.

"You keep looking for Kachina and Lisa," he ordered through the open door. "As soon as you find them, come back here and get me." He slammed the door and sprinted at the side of the road toward the flashing lights.

Scott turned back onto the blacktop. He hoped he would find Kachina and Lisa at home, hoped they had taken the old road. His car sped past the sprinting Mike.

"What's happening, trooper?" Mike asked as he approached a state policeman at the scene.

The trooper was dressed in a forest-green uniform and Smokey Bear hat. He considered telling Mike to move on, but saw his worry. "Got a car in the river," he said, pointing at the edge of the riverbank marked by deep fresh tire ruts. "Diver's gettin' ready to jump in now." Mike saw two faint taillights about ten feet under. Bubbles rose to the surface, then ran downriver with the current.

A man stood with a group of firemen by the bank. Water dripped from him, and his chest heaved. "I seen it happen. I seen it." The man pointed to the other side of the highway where a white-tailed deer lay in a growing pool of blood. Its long legs kicked the air. "Deer over there jumped in front of the car." The man took several quick breaths. "Car hit it and skidded in the river. I jumped in, but the current carried me down river 'fore I could reach 'em. I tried, man. I tried. Three times I tried." A paramedic threw a blanket over his shoulders.

Mike jerked at the splash of the diver hitting the water as he held the end of the wrecker's tow cable. The diver entered upstream, and pulses of bubbles broke on the surface as the current swept by. His body was a ghostly image as he obscured the taillights while hooking up the cable. He surfaced and pulled the air hose out of his mouth. "OK. Bring 'er up."

The winch strained.

The greasy cable strands twisted as they eased out of the water.

The taillights rose.

The black water swirled, and the men who stood by the bank were silent.

Mike bounced from one foot to the other. He wrung his hands. In all the carrier launches, night landings, flak, bullets, dead and dying friends, and Purple Hearts, he had never felt the cold bite of panic before. He turned away and clenched his fists. He turned back. Hurry, hurry, hurry, hurry, hurry. The winch strained.

He wanted this rescue done his way—the military way. He wanted to reach for his emergency radio and call for the magic of close air support and rescue helicopters. He wanted his people here—his guys. He wanted SEALs jumping into the water from a huge helicopter. He wanted the helicopter to reach into the water with a big hook and pull the car out. He wanted the vehicle to be a Jeep, or a Hummer, or a tank—anything but a car. He wanted to jump into the river and make everything OK. He felt pressure on his shoulder that startled him.

It was Scott. "Couldn't find 'em, brother."

"Oh, God," he pleaded. "Please, no."

HURRY! HURRY! HURRY! Mike's brain screamed as he watched the car's taillights come closer and closer through the black water. Finally, the rear of a white Malibu broke the surface and the black water turned to white riffles as they swirled around a license plate that read, "MOM C."

Scott's hand tightened on Mike's shoulder. "It's Mom's car."

Mike's mouth fell open in a silent scream. His throat convulsed.

The wrecker's engine sighed to an idle as a fireman swung a hammer at the window to relieve the pressure of the water inside. Water gushed onto the grass and down the bank.

"Oh, God," Mike said just above a whisper. Scott threw his arms around his brother's shoulders from behind.

The fireman yanked at the door handle. The door burst open as water inside cascaded out. Mike stooped, and saw …

There, in the gloom, a tiny arm flew out as if reaching after the water that rushed away.

Ring around the rosy, a pocket full of posies. Ashes. Ashes. We all fall down.

A fireman shone a light into the car.

Lisa's head lay to the side on her right shoulder. The river had straightened her blonde curls and they lay across her arm, lifeless, like thin strands of wet straw.

Twinkle twinkle little star, how I wonder what you are. Up above the world so high, like a diamond in the sky. Twinkle—twinkle—twinkle … The laughing bouncy music of Mike's life was ground to rubble. Ash-es. Ash-es. All—fall—down.

The fireman lowered his light. Kachina's dress was pasted to her body. She lay face down across the seat. Her delicate hands grasped the buckle of Lisa's car seat.

"Be damned," someone spoke. "She tried to save her baby."

Kachina moved!

Mike reached toward the car.

Kachina's right hand pulled away from the buckle, and she rolled away from the seat and onto her back. Her hair was plastered to her face in sweeping red swirls. Mike bolted from Scott. "That's my wife and daughter!" he yelled as he pushed past the firemen. He skidded on the wet grass until his shins hit the doorsill. He reached through the flashlight beam and saw the shadow of his own hand on Kachina's hair-covered face. As though she lay sleeping in their bed, he reached out to brush the strands away from her eyes. She was so cold. With a finger he lifted her hair away. The only midnight-blue eyes he had ever seen stared through their dead child.

Nevermore—

nevermore—

nevermore.

"Could she swim, sir?" a young fireman asked.

"Yes," Mike squeaked.

Awe fell across the scene as men who thought they had seen it all pondered the courage of a woman who fought in the darkness to save her child from the rising black water. The young fireman turned away. He leaned against a sycamore tree and cried.

"Sir, you'll have to move," the trooper said gently just as Scott reached for Mike. Bustling paramedics carried metal cases toward the car. Scott pulled Mike back, and little by little the cold porcelain faces of his beautiful girls disappeared behind a flurry of yellow uniforms that reflected the red beams of emergency lights zinging around and around into the night.

◆ ◆ ◆

Scott's car pulled onto the grass of the riverbank next to the bridge. Its tires squished in the damp soil. Mike looked out the windshield at the scene painted by the headlights. Just a few hours earlier, this quiet place beside the highway had pulsed with the fury of an emergency. It was now nothing more than a grassy area marred by tire ruts and broken saplings. Sycamore trees leaned over the river, praying with their heads bowed against the water. All the people who had been here with their yellow uniforms and loud vehicles were now dry and warm in their homes, telling loved ones about the woman and the child who died in the river tonight. Aunt Ruth was with Mom, and Mike had signed all the forms that certified the identities of two lovely children of God named Kachina and Lisa Marie Christum.

"Leave me here," Mike said.

"Mike. No."

Mike squeezed his brother's arm. "I won't do anything stupid. I need to be alone. I'll walk home."

"You sure?" Scott asked.

"Yeah. I'm sure." He got out of the car. Scott drove away. He walked to the edge of the bank and stared at the gloom. The New River's waters rolled and churned, while wisps of fog rose in tiny lazy tornadoes. He slipped down the bank and stumbled into a large log. He stepped over it, then sat down and faced the river. He bowed his head and prayed with the sycamore trees. And he listened. He listened for the sound of fluttering angel wings.

Scott drove across the bridge and pulled onto a gravel turnaround. He walked back across the bridge, careful that Mike wouldn't see him. He climbed the bank on the other side of the road from the river. As he climbed, he turned several times, trying to see his brother. With a small sigh Scott's face registered his relief as he got a glimpse of Mike sitting down by the river. He plopped down into the damp forest soil.

As the seconds passed into minutes, then into hours, Scott watched his brother's quiet form. Mike had lost his wife and children, but he still had family who loved him, and they loved him in a way that never needed recognition or acknowledgment. Mike would never know it, but his little brother, Scott, sat with him all night.

1983, WEDNESDAY, 14 SEPTEMBER
HINTON, WEST VIRGINIA

Scott stood by his car on the gravel drive that drew a curving line around the knolls of the hilly terrain. Clumps of flowers and stands of trees stood like members of separate families staring at one another across the expanse of trimmed grass. On the most prominent knoll stood a large statue of Jesus with arms outstretched. Cold rain dripped from its metal robes. Jesus gazed across the grass at the bronze grave markers that lay flush with the ground, some with flowers beside them.

Brian Davis leaned against the grill of Scott's car. His breath puffed past the collar of his overcoat and lost itself in the cold drizzle. "I should have put money on this."

"On what?" Scott asked.

"That today would be like this." Brian felt the motor's heat rise past him in gentle currents.

"Yep," Scott agreed. His hands were jammed in the pockets of his sheepskin jacket, and his eyes were fixed hard on the gravel road.

"The only things missing from this scene are an iron fence and a hoot owl," Brian said, "and a black cat."

The two men watched Mike in the distance. Sheets of rain slanted in the wind and folded around him as he stood next to the fresh earthen mounds. Cold drops ran from his dark hair and down the back of his neck as he prayed. He thrust his hands deep in his coat pockets, then turned from the graves and walked toward his brother and his co-pilot through the thickening rolling fog and worsening deluge.

Scott said to Brian, "I'm glad you're here. I'm glad you're here to take him back."

Brian raised his face upward and allowed the rain to fall full against it. He placed his hand on Scott's shoulder. "Scott," he said, then paused to collect his thoughts. "Scott, Mike is your big brother, not mine. He was your childhood playmate and protector, not mine. He has shared his life with you in ways I can't imagine, because I don't have a brother." He watched Mike walk from the distance. "Not one I grew up with, anyway. But I'm not here to take Mike back. I'm here out of respect for him and his family—for Kachina and Lisa, for you and your mom, and all the others."

Scott looked at him. "What in the world're you sayin'?"

Brian thought a moment. "Hell, I don't know." He gave up on trying to put Scott at ease. "Being philosophical, I guess. Forget it."

"I ain't forgetin' it," Scott said in a matter-of-fact way. "You're tellin' me I don't need to worry about my brother."

"Well," Brian dragged a finger across his forehead and flicked the water off, "you say what you're thinking, don't you?"

"Brian, there's a reason two of you fly together. Am I right 'bout that?

"Yeah. So?"

"Because it takes the two of you to get there—and back. Right?"

Brian nodded for a moment, then, "Yeah. Right."

"Somethin' else I know. You're a Medal of Honor winner. Mike told me."

Brian groped for a quip, then gave up. "Yes. I am."

"Those men you saved. They didn't make it back without you, did they?"

"No, they didn't."

"See what I'm askin' here, Brian?"

Brian sucked a tsk while he nodded. "Yep. Think I do."

They both stared at the gravel. "Brian," Scott said, "promise you'll look after my brother."

Brian grinned, then struck a soft punch at Scott's shoulder. "You got it. I promise I'll look after him for you."

Scott smiled and elbowed back. "You're a good man, ya' know that?"

An hour later Scott stood at the riverbank in front of his mother's home. He watched the rain splash on water. The bridge seemed more distant than usual, its straight lines softened by the mist. The car with Mike and Brian sped across the bridge, a dark ghost moving ahead of its own shower, wet leaves swirling behind.

Once again he stood on the bank and watched his big brother go to his mysterious world of challenge and danger. Only ... only this time the challenge wasn't a happy horizon to be explored. Scott waved to the car that disappeared behind the wet curtain. This time there was no response.

1983, Tuesday, 27 September
LaMadre Avenue
Las Vegas, Nevada

The air that blew into the open car window was tinged with the warm currents of a leftover summer. Brian thrummed his fingers on the steering wheel as he drove. He strained to see if a car was in the driveway, way down the street, at 1322 LaMadre. He had flown from West Virginia via Phoenix to see his mother and just landed at Las Vegas. Mike wasn't answering his phone—hadn't all week.

Brian pulled into the driveway, turned off the engine, and looked around. The lawn was dry and brown, and the leaves of the shrubbery were curled with drought distress. The sprinkler-valve box at the edge of the sidewalk was open and beside it lay a screwdriver, a memento of an unfinished job.

He noticed something familiar leaning against the mulberry tree. He bit his lip. As he walked toward the tree, his feet crunched on the dry grass and scrapped at the yellow leaves that were scattered about.

He stopped at the tree and closed his eyes. "Oh, man. This is too much."

Brian winced as he put his hand on Scotty's red bicycle.

He wheeled the bike to a place beside the front door. Something on the sidewalk caught his eye. He reached down, picked up a pink toy purse, and held the little thing in the palm of his hand. "Oh damn." Tears welled in his eyes as he looped the purse's straps over the bike's handlebars. He turned away from the front door, looked at the street, and breathed hard to regain his composure. Ghosts lived here now.

The front door was open a bit when he knocked. "Mike!" No answer. He called louder. "Mike!" The door swung open. He stepped in.

It was dark and quiet—and empty. The carpet was dimpled where the furniture used to sit. The hallway wall was bare with nail holes in it where pictures used to hang. "Hey, Mike." His voice echoed as he headed toward the bedrooms.

At the end of the hall was the master bedroom. There, sitting on a box with his back to the door, was his friend, wearing a white T-shirt and blue cutoffs. He was staring at a delicate gold chain that was threaded through the eyelet attached to a single pearl he held in his palm. Brian cleared his throat. Mike stiffened and spun around. When he saw Brian, he relaxed. "You're lucky I didn't shoot you."

"Thank you very much," Brian said in a half-hearted Elvis voice. He looked around the room, which was also empty except for a dozen or so packed boxes and three open suitcases.

Mike put the necklace in a ring box, then packed it in an open suitcase that lay on the floor.

"Want some help?"

"With what?"

Brian poked a thumb over his shoulder. "Sprinklers, for one thing."

"What's wrong with the sprinklers?"

"They're off."

"Oh, yeah. I started to fix them, but forgot …"

"Forgot about a week ago, did you?"

Mike put a few more things into the suitcase. "Excuse me. What did you say?"

"I said—" He shook his head and turned. "Never mind."

"Where you going?"

Brian was firm. "Never mind." He walked down the hall, through the kitchen, and into the garage. He looked at the sprinkler controller.

"The rain switch's on." He flipped the switch, then pressed the "Cycle On" button. He heard clicking, then hissing outside the garage. The sprinklers were running. He opened the garage door, walked outside, put the cover back on the valve box, retrieved the screwdriver, laid it on top of the hot-water tank, then hit the button to close the garage door as he walked back into the house.

"Mike—"

"I can't do it."

"Can't do what?"

"Fly. I can't ever fly again."

Brian sat down on the bed beside him, crossed him arms, looked at him, then waited.

Mike stared at the floor. "Please." He patted Brian's hand. "Just go."

Brian opened his mouth to speak, but the words wouldn't come. Then, "OK." He left.

He sat behind the wheel and watched the water spray over part of the lawn. After ten minutes or so, the spray stopped, then began again as the sprinkler control shut down one valve, then opened another to water a different part of the lawn.

The sun touched the horizon and the gentle pink radiance reminded him of the beautiful redhead who used to live here. The one who always met him with a hug, a wonderful kiss on the cheek, a glass of wine, then stuffed him with all the lasagna he could hold. The one who fretted because he didn't have a good woman in his life. The one who never forgot a thing—never forgot a birthday card to his mother or his son or him, never forgot a Tupperware container full of chocolate-chip cookies delivered by Mike every Monday morning on the 727 to Groom Lake. There was only one other woman he had ever known like Kachina, and now both were …

He snapped away from his thoughts and watched the sprinkler shower dance with the sunlight. He grinned a bit when he noticed the rainbow it made. The colored arch spanned from one side of the lawn to—to the red bike with the toy purse that dangled from the handlebars.

"I just can't handle this!" he groaned as he dropped his face into his open hands. He raised his head and took a peek between his fingers. The rainbow still ended at the bike and the purse.

"Damn." He got out of the car, slammed the door, and stormed back into the house.

"How can you understand, Brian?"

Brian sat across from him on another box. He leaned toward Mike, intense. "What is it I don't understand?"

"This—this thing that's happened to me."

"And just what makes you think you're so unique in the suffering department, bud?"

"You haven't lost—"

"What? What haven't I lost?"

"You … you …" Mike's eyes widened with remembering that Brian never talked about Susan. "Brian," he said as he looked at his friend. "I'm sorry. I didn't mean …"

"Yes, you are sorry, hot shot." Brian lowered his tone. "And I'll tell you why." He leaned further toward Mike. "You are absolutely the best pilot I have ever known—anybody has ever known. And, you happen to be just about the finest man I've ever met. And your family—I'd give my right arm to have people like your mom, Scott, Jimmy, and the others. Do you have any idea how special your life is just because you have them?"

"Yeah, I think—"

"You don't know all the pain there is to know, Mike." He softened. "You just don't know."

The men looked at each other.

Brian softened even more. "Mike, how many times have I been over here and watched you help your kids grow up—especially Scotty?"

"I—"

"Was that thing about the little engine who could a snow job?"

Mike stiffened. "Hell, no. It wasn't a snow job."

"You meant it, then?"

"Damn right I meant it!"

"Then how would you explain to Scotty that his dad didn't have the courage to follow the lessons he taught his son?"

1983, Sunday, 2 October
2037 Hours (8:37 PM)
Groom Lake Base, Nevada

A light at the rear of the massive black warplane threw its shadow on the huge door. The desert wind with its raspy moan was elsewhere tonight, and a distant faint ticking sound bounced around as the cavernous building contracted with the falling evening temperature.

A booming clang chased the ticking sound into hiding as the steel personnel door slammed against its metal frame. The sound of footsteps ricocheted off concrete and steel. Mike walked in the light that shone beneath his airplane. He stopped at Rhombus' nose. His eyes took in the unusual combination of sensual sweeping curves and sharp straight edges. In a strange way he felt the presence of the black warplane as one might feel something alive, something that watched from the dark.

It would be easy to see Rhombus as romantic and whimsical and sinister all at the same time. But the fact was, it was here for the same reason he was. If it could think, if it had feelings, surely it would be happiest playing in God's sky among the clouds and the sunsets. Surely, if given a choice, it would prefer to carry joyous children through the wonders of the heavens rather than bombs into the jaws of death. But it had no mind. It had no emotion. It had no love of him, nor of the sky. It was the key to the end of the Cold War, but without its pilot, it was a hulking pile of organized junk.

This airplane was now his life—at least for the time being, he knew. He looked at the machine as though it had eyes, and as though it had ears he said, "You have no heart, and I wish I didn't." Sorrow washed his face. "Which of us is less human?"

He walked away.

Rhombus sat alone as the ticking returned. If the big black warbird could dream, it would dream of chasing the silvered wind along while leaving the sky full of trails marked with the laughter of children.

1983, Sunday, 2 October
2104 Hours (9:04 PM)
Groom Lake Base, Nevada

Mike entered his BOQ suite carrying two large suitcases. The oak furniture was still there, and so was the smell of disinfectant. He went outside and reappeared carrying another suitcase and a briefcase. Mike moved into his new home.

1983, Saturday, 31 December
2304 Hours (11:04 PM)
Groom Lake Base, Nevada

"Know what you need to do?" Brian asked as he reached for the potato chip bag on the coffee table. "You need to get out of here." He crunched the chip to oblivion and chased it down with a beer as he watched New Year Eve revelers on the TV.

Mike shook his head and continued reading his tactics manual.

Brian changed channels. "Hey! You hear me?" he called without looking away from the TV.

"Yeah, I heard ya'."

Brian lowered the volume. "And?"

"And, I got away from here yesterday."

Brian flipped back to the original channel. "We flew yesterday."

"Right. Yesterday I went to Pensacola and back. So did you."

Brian chomped more chips. "You know what I mean."

"Yeah, I know what you mean."

The partygoers blew their horns and danced in the street.

Brian turned off the TV.

"The silence is deafening," Mike said, still looking at his manual.

"I'm not going to turn it back on."

"I can't take the quiet. The least you can do is start eating again."

Brian leapt from the couch and yanked the manual from Mike's hands.

"Hey!" Mike yelled.

"What?" Brian asked.

"Are we married?"

"No."

"Then quit nagging me."

Brian put the manual back in Mike's open hands. He

plopped back on the couch. "It's not that I want you to get out of here so much as I want to get out."

Mike motioned, "There's the door."

Brian mumbled something about sitting in a BOQ room on New Year's Eve.

"What?" Mike asked.

"Nothing." Brian picked up the remote and turned on the TV again. The lighted ball dropped. "Happy New Year!" he called.

Mike dropped the manual to his lap. He looked at his crumb-covered friend, nodded his head, and smiled. "Brian—thanks."

Brian shrugged. He turned the TV off and cleared away the empty chip bag and the bottle. He opened a drawer and pulled out a pile of AAA travel books, maps, and photos and dumped it all on the coffee table. As he shuffled through the pile, he said, "We pick up another bomber at the factory day after tomorrow. What's this, number seven?"

"Yeah. That gives us our machine, one flyable spare, and five in storage down in the caves."

"I love being part of this," Brian said.

"Me too."

"You should. It's your whole life."

"Are you nagging again?"

"Yeah, I am. You haven't been off this base since—since we got back from West Virginia. Why don't you come to Phoenix with me the next time I go?"

Mike noticed Brian's concerned expression, then ignored it. He flipped the page and moved the plastic bookmark. A verse on the bookmark caught his eye:

> *Yea, though I walk through the valley of the shadow*
> *of death,*
>   *I fear no evil:*
>   *For thou are with me—*

He dropped the manual to his lap. Mike watched Brian shuffle through the mound of books and maps. Worry was a corrosive thing, and Mike realized how selfish he was to allow Brian to worry about him. Was he, himself, afraid of the outside world—the valley of the shadow of death? Was he brave enough to venture out only when he was surrounded by a machine that saw things through its impersonal sensors and displays? He'd been thinking only of himself, of his own grief, and what he had to do to get through each day. Not once since his family died had he thought of Brian's needs. Brian had lost his wife, too, and still refused to talk about her. He knew Brian wrestled with finances to find the money for his mother's care and his son's education. Mike had offered money, and he probed about Brian's wife a time or two, but those gestures didn't add up to friendship. Friendship was something you showed every day, as Brian had done for him. Shame swept over him and coated him with a feeling of unworthiness that soaked through his skin and made him frown at the taste of who he was.

"Your mouth's open," Brian said.

"Huh? Oh. You're right. OK, I'll go," Mike said as he regained his composure.

"Go where?" Brian asked, his attention on the coffee table.

"Go to Phoenix with you. I'd love to meet your mom and son."

Brian stopped messing with the maps. "Good."

Mike and Brian flew Rhombus at least twice a week. Because of the warplane's long range, the United States became their backyard. On one mission they flew low over Las Vegas, then jetted north along U.S. 93, through Lake Valley and beside the Ruby Mountains. They flashed across the border into Idaho, where they dodged the mountains around Sun Valley before streaking west across eastern Oregon toward the Cascade Range. Flying just above the treetops, they climbed the sloping green sides of the old volcano that held Crater Lake, crested its rim, then zoomed down toward the lake before they shot up the other side and headed down and west, toward the Pacific.

A hard left bank where Oregon met the ocean had them heading over the pounding surf beside buttes that rose from the water like the fins of giant stone whales. Down the California coast the whispering thunder rolled behind them as they banked left again and sped beneath the Golden Gate Bridge, then over San Francisco Bay, past the patchwork of farms around Modesto that rose into the vaulting beauty of Yosemite. They looked up at Yosemite's grand granite cliffs as they blasted by. Down the sheer eastern scarp of the Sierra Nevada they went as the greens turned to browns. They turned south and skied the air over Owens Valley before turning east and heading for Death Valley. Cresting the Panamint Range, Rhombus dove for the floor of Death Valley, then up and over the Funeral Mountains and across the flats of the Amargosa Desert. Then, home. The 3,000-mile trip had taken six hours.

After each low-level mission, Brian added to his log the names of every major geographic landmark they'd flown by. Over the months the list grew: Yellowstone, Jackson Hole, Atlanta, New York City, the Great Lakes, Everglades, Mississippi, Hudson River, Fort Sumter, Padre Island, Mount Rushmore, Badlands, Fort Peck Lake, and a thousand other places. They had little time to enjoy the beauty as they flew. There was just too much to do in Rhombus, and, of course, they were going like hell.

Still, at the end of each mission and the debriefing that followed, Mike and Brian would sit in their living room and reminisce about what they'd seen. Brian's private library of AAA maps and travel brochures grew and they'd use it to reinvent their mission as if they had just taken it on motorcycles. They planned to buy Harleys after the Rhombus project was over and tour the land beneath the sky they knew so well. They were convinced they had seen more of America than any two men who ever lived, but they wanted to see it at a slower pace— and they wanted to touch it. Brian put it best when he said, "Remember all the times we flew down the Oregon coast and saw the patches of blackberries growing on the mountainsides? I want to taste them."

They often talked of laying on their backs in one of the patches above the crashing waves. They would eat the berries, watch the sunset, feel the ocean mist, and talk of whimsical memories that brushed by on soft wings. Mike would sing:

Blackberry pie, blackberry pie.
I come from the sky to eat blackberry pie.

The little ditty had become their anthem for—someday, when this was all over. And just maybe, Mike thought, maybe while we're laying in that blackberry patch, Brian will talk about Susan.

1985
KOKOPELLI

1985, Thursday, 28 February
1900 Hours (7:00 PM)
Groom Lake Base, Nevada

Low black clouds moved through the night from the northwest, across Kawich Valley, over the Belted Range, then through Emigrant Valley. One after another they came, thick curtains with crashing liquid hems. Chris Patterakis stood in the doorway of his office building at the edge of the ramp and watched Hangar 18 through the moving waterfall. Its large doors rumbled open and allowed a widening shaft of intense light to hit the concrete where it was swallowed by the marching clouds. Rhombus' song of whispering thunder forced its way through the roar of the rain. Patterakis smiled at the majestic scene and pulled his collar up to protect himself from the droplets that bounced off the concrete. Metal beams in the hangar curved as the light reflected from them swept through Rhombus' Aurora coating and around the massive airplane. The curved lines wavered as the thunder swelled. Rhombus moved.

Patterakis watched the rain fall on the invisible warplane and reveal the huge manta-ray shape. The torrent pounded its top and poured in small airborne rivers to its edges. The rivers broke into waterfalls that fell to the concrete, where they framed a glassy sheet of tranquil water that was shaped like the airplane. Huge tires rolled through the sheet, leaving wakes that widened to the rear. The exhaust of the four CJ engines picked up huge amounts of rain and shot it rearward in a level spray. Steam rose from the spray and dissipated into the gloom. As Rhombus taxied away, the rain curtains closed behind it, and its song faded.

Patterakis peered into the gloom as rain dropped at the doorway, spattering his cuffs and shoes. After a minute or so the doors to Hangar 18 eased together and squeezed away the last light. Patterakis backed into the office building and pulled the door closed. Groom Lake Base hunkered down against the storm, while its child of wonder headed away.

"I feel like I'm in a submarine," Brian said as he attended his co-pilot duties and glanced outside. "Couldn't be a better night for seeing the ol' hometown, I say. I guess they'll be lining the streets to watch us fly by."

Ever since Mike touched his first airplane, he'd dreamed of this mission. He was going to fly over his hometown at low altitude. It was the dream of every military pilot to fly above childhood friends to show them that no matter what they had done in life, no matter how successful they were, none but he had command of the sky—none but he could put out his hand and touch the face of God. The problem was that Mike didn't fly an airplane that sparkled in the sun as it soared above his friends and family and blasted them with roaring fury. Mike flew a ghost, an aberration that left no tracks in its passing. The only people in Hinton who would know he was there would be Brian and himself—and his girls, who lay in the cemetery overlooking the New River Gorge. Mike shook away the thoughts of the day he had buried them there 18 months ago. He shook away the vision of his freckle-faced boy.

In the right seat Brian programmed the MPP computer

for the mission, which was to be "Hi-low-hi" profile with an MPP-coupled rough ride. For the layman, that meant they would be at high altitude for approach cruise, low altitude for attack, and high altitude for the return cruise, and that the MPP would be flying Rhombus for the attack phase of the flight. They planned a cruise at 60,000 feet; then, over Indiana, they would dive to low level and fly east until reaching the New River Gorge. They'd fly up the gorge in a mock attack on the Bluestone Dam, located at the edge of Hinton. Mike had grown up in a house that sat in the shadow of the dam. The concrete monolith was a part of his life. Tonight it was to play the role of a target. It would not be the first time it was a target. When he was a boy, he'd flown numerous missions against the dam with the air force that was fueled by his imagination. He wondered how the dam survived his childhood.

The SID flashed. "Will you quit playing with that thing?" Mike said to Brian as they neared the runway. "You'd think that after almost two years you'd be used to it by now." Mike shook his head and Brian ignored him. He was entranced by the SID as it displayed the murky torrent-filled blackness that swallowed the taxiway and its blue lights; followed by the same scene that looked like night without the rain; followed by the same scene that looked like the brightest clearest day; followed by a wide-angle view of the flat; followed by a magnified view of the runway threshold; followed by the cycle repeating itself time after time.

Rhombus turned onto the runway. The CJs screamed and the big machine leapt forward. As it tore through increasing amounts of rain, the water flowed along its skin and took on greater definition. When it passed 100 knots, Rhombus looked like a bullet streaking through an aquarium.

The massive airplane lifted its nose. Spirals of air rolled off its wingtips, horizontal tornadoes that followed Rhombus from the water-pounded runway. The bomber flew heavenward as it punched through a turbulent air mass that covered North America and continued headlong into the night, above the weather and beneath a starlit sky. Tonight's low-level target run would simulate a failure of the SID to see through the weather. Whatever a normal airplane would see, Mike and Brian would see. However, infrared and radar data would be displayed on the TopDown as the MPP flew the mission.

Over the Mississippi, Brian downloaded the latest weather satellite map. "Damn, look at that," he said as the map appeared on one of the CRTs. Another swirl of clouds, 800 miles across, painted itself across eastern America and dropped huge snowflakes in sweeping bands onto the land below. A timer in front of Brian counted down to zero. "Here we go," he called.

The Altitude Hold switch flipped off, and the throttles snapped back.

Rhombus nosed over.

Mike and Brian pitched against the shoulder straps.

Down, down, they slid like a metal ball in a greased tube. At 30,000 feet they dove into the swirling cloud mass.

"Twenty-thousand feet," Brian called. The atmosphere grew denser. The cockpit sounded like it was running through a car wash.

"Ten thousand feet."

They hit turbulent air.

"Five thousand feet."

Maps and manuals rattled in metal compartments.

"Two thousand feet," Brian called.

"Hang on!"

The clouds broke open.

A farm filled the SID and got larger as Rhombus bore down, headed toward the center of the earth.

A pasture of snow-covered grass filled the SID.

Brian stiffened. "Damned thing better work!"

Rhombus jerked up. Their butts slammed down. They grunted as Rhombus pulled five-Gs like a car at the bottom of a roller coaster.

They leveled off at 200 feet above the earth. The siren song of the CJs mixed with the rush of the air as Rhombus skimmed over the rolling landscape and the frozen farms.

Brian relaxed. "Kinda like opening the curtains to see a truck coming through the window, huh?"

Mike didn't answer.

At the west bank of the Ohio, Rhombus dove to the water. The river was dotted with chunks of ice that moved together like a parade of white cars on a wide black street. They crossed the river, then popped up on the east bank as they entered Kentucky south of Louisville. Onward they jetted into the snowstorm.

"Here comes the Big Sandy River," Brian said.

Giant hammers pounded them as Rhombus hugged the craggy terrain south of Huntington, West Virginia. "W-w-w-welcome to W-w-w-west Virginia," Brian said. "I c-c-can't wait until we d-drop to fifty f-f-f-f-feet."

"You ain't s-seen n-n-nothin' yet," Mike responded through coughs caused by the rough ride.

"I've never f-f-flown over your fair state before. Such nice weather, t-t-too."

They bore a long ragged hole through the darkness and snow. Periodically, they flew over small towns whose lights illuminated the snowflakes that formed long white streamers, which Rhombus split apart as it passed.

"B-beckley off the right beam," Brian called as they passed abeam the small city. "New River G-g-gorge just ahead."

A dark line on the TopDown representing the gorge moved downward. When it touched the symbol that depicted Rhombus, the warplane's nose pitched forward into the black gash.

"Oh, man." Brian drew a breath. "Here we go again."

Rhombus rolled right.

It flew a diagonal course down the 1,000-foot wall.

At the bottom of the gorge, it pulled four-Gs for a split second, then leveled over the black river at 50 feet. The riverbed didn't rise and fall as the terrain had, so the vertical ride was fairly smooth, but Rhombus banked sharply left and right as it snaked up the crooked gorge.

"Unbelievable!" Brian said whenever the airplane threw them at stone walls on either side of the river, then rescued them at the last split second.

Mike chewed the inside of his mouth.

The bomber jerked up. "Sandstone Falls," Mike called. "Target just ahead."

"Roger. Auto-drop on."

"Roger."

Rhombus whistled up the river and tunneled a serpentine path in the falling snow.

It banked around a bend.

Hinton zoomed by on the left.

"Weapons Release" flashed in red on the SID.

Their heads bobbed down as Rhombus jerked up.

It leaped over the dam and leveled off over the placid freezing waters of Bluestone Lake.

A woman with silver lavender-tinted hair paused while she swept her porch steps of fresh snow. She turned to an unfamiliar thundering sound that rolled up the river and over the dam. There, bathed in a single light that reached up the face of the concrete wall, two spirals of snow lay swirling beside each other. The swirls dropped down the face of the dam and rustled the branches of the bare trees on the riverbank. The woman's face was expressionless as she looked at the sight. She climbed the porch steps while she held the metal handrail and thanked God that the United States Navy would never let her Mike fly on a night such as this.

Onward through the snow, Mike and Brian flew as their wake swirled behind them. On the skis of electrons they slalomed through the shallowing gorge. They jetted through the pass where the New River cut through East River Mountain, then rushed into Shenandoah Valley toward Roanoke. As the Blue Ridge sped at them, Rhombus pitched up and reached for the stars that lay beyond the tumbling murk. Higher and higher the bomber shot, a shooting star in reverse. When they reached 25,000 feet, Mike pressed a button that disconnected the autopilot. He pulled Rhombus over on its back until it climbed west, then rolled until the wings were level and the nose was high. In a flash they burst from the thick boiling clouds into a star-jeweled sky.

"We did good," said Brian.

"Yes, we did."

"Remind me to clean my pants out when we get home." He laughed at his own joke. Mike didn't respond. Brian knew that Mike's mind was behind them, standing in the snow beside the graves on the knoll that overlooked the river.

Farther and farther the graves fell behind as Rhombus sped west through the high dark sky. Mike wanted to roll the airplane over and travel the black gorge again because the challenge of it all kept the sorrow away—the wonder of the technological magic filled the empty night. The miracle of this grand machine with its titanium, steel, plastic, rubber, glass, and fire filled only a part of the heart that many times had been filled to overflowing with only a small warm smile and a tender loving hug. He looked ahead, into the black, and prayed he could forget. Then he prayed he wouldn't.

1985, MONDAY, 18 NOVEMBER
1146 HOURS (11:46 AM)
37,000 FEET, 300 MILES EAST OF MOSCOW
RUSSIA

The Soviet Premier sat in the overstuffed chair on the left side of the big Tupolev airliner as it sped at 37,000 feet from Moscow to Geneva, Switzerland. It was 100 miles out of Moscow and heading southwest. The low sun streamed through the cabin window and interfered with his reading, but he welcomed the warmth. He removed his glasses and rested his arms on the table. He closed his eyes and relaxed as he sponged the rays that were born just eight minutes ago in the nuclear reactor called the sun.

He liked hitting the road. He mused at the phrase. It was one he had heard so many times when briefed by his intelligent officers about the United States. He recalled the political cartoons in American newspapers that would show American presidents and their staff leaving Washington on diplomatic travels when the domestic political situation in America became uncomfortable. "Hitting the road," they called it. The Premier wondered if Americans took anything very seriously. He found it hard to believe that a people who could make a sport out of throwing cow pies and racing lawn mowers would want to conquer the world. The edges of his mouth turned up.

In Geneva he would meet the American President for the second time. He liked him, and better yet, he grew more trustful of him. He didn't like it when the President called his country the Evil Empire, but there was no doubting that's what the President believed. He felt at ease with someone who spoke his mind. One always knew where such a person stood. Far better a person to tell you what he thought than to tell you what he thought you wanted to hear. He could do business with the President.

The light that streamed through the cabin window blinked off. The Premier frowned a little, then opened his eyes to see what had taken the warmth away. He was sitting in the shadow of a MiG-25 that was holding a position just off and above the tip of the left wing. Excited conversation came from behind him. He frowned as he wondered what the MiG was doing there.

"Sir?" There was a delicate prod at his right elbow. His air force aide knelt beside him. "I am alarmed. That airplane should not be there."

"It is one of ours, is it not, Vitalie?" the Premier asked.

"Well, yes, sir. But it does not answer on the assigned frequencies. Where could it be flying from?"

"Vitalie," the Premier looked over the glasses he had just put back on, "do not come to me for answers. I do not believe this is something we would have planned without your knowledge."

The shadow moved off the aide's face. He looked out the window and frowned. The Premier looked to see what was happening. The aide rushed to another window to see the MiG increase its altitude and disappear above the airliner. Some of the staff moved to the right side of the cabin and strained to find it. Nothing.

Excited chatter again filled the Tupolev's cabin.

"Here! It's coming back this way!"

People moved back to the left side of the cabin to see the edge of a large black disk flying above the Tupolev. A few feet away someone talked over the intercom to the cockpit. The Premier strained to see as much of the disk as he could. The object inched down, revealing more of itself as it did. They could see that a portion of the disk was painted a flesh color and that a curved black line ran from one side of the flesh color to the other. As the disk moved farther down they saw— they saw—eyes? Large eyes!

The disk moved farther down until they saw two smaller black disks mounted side by side on top the large disk.

"It's Mickey Mouse!" someone yelled.

"What's a Mickey Mouse?" someone else wondered.

Just as the Tupolev's pilot moved the control wheel to take evasive action, Mickey Mouse blinked off.

1985, Thursday, 21 November
1715 Hours (5:15 PM)
Geneva, Switzerland

The President was worried about the talks with the Soviets this week. One bright spot was the new Soviet Premier. He liked him. His gut feeling was that he could trust the man. The President sat in a high-backed chair in his suite on the top floor of an old Swiss hotel. The chair faced a fireplace that filled the room and its French Provincial furniture with peace. A large Persian rug covered the hardwood floor to within about a foot of the pastel blue walls. He looked through the small panes of the French doors to see rain spattering on the balcony. The deepening gray of the world outside seemed miles away from the warm room.

He got up, opened the balcony door, and held his arm out to catch a drop or two of the pelting liquid. He pondered the rainwater in his hand. A hundred years from now, a thousand years from now, whether this hotel still stands or not, drops like this will fall on this spot. The President moved his hand until the drops reflected the fire. The water he held could have evaporated from the Mississippi, or the Volga, or any of the world's oceans. Who knows how many of God's creatures, back over millions of years, had found sustenance in the very water he was holding. How many times had this moisture been part of a baby's breath or the memory of a man's kiss on a woman's cheek? Had it been used to cool white-hot steel or ever gurgled out of a schoolyard water fountain? Did it ever pass through the reactor coolers of the USS *Nimitz* or had it ever been on a tissue used to wipe a speck of dust from a child's eye? How many times had it been the tear of a woman holding a flag in her lap beside a grave at Arlington or Leningrad? As it evaporated from his hand, he wondered what its next destination would be.

He picked up the bulky ornate telephone from the table beside the chair. "Dave," the President spoke, "get me the Premier. I would like to meet with him now if it's convenient for him. Nobody else in the meeting. Just him and me ... and the interpreters, of course." The President replaced the receiver.

The phone rang. "Sir," Dave said, "the Premier is on the phone. He called before I could call his people."

"Hmm," the President said as he nodded. The line clicked. "Mr. Premier," the President acknowledged.

He heard a gruff but sunny voice. "Say, how about them Redskins!"

The President shook his head and blinked. "Mr. Premier?"

"Yes. It is I."

"Well, I'll be darned." The President chuckled, then snickered, then laughed. The tension of worrying about a private overture to the Premier washed away. "Why didn't you tell me you could speak English?"

"Why didn't you ask?" the Premier retorted.

"Because I don't know enough Russian to ask." The easy laughter was not just a joy in how it felt, but in the promise it held.

"Mr. Premier," the President asked. "What do you drink?"

"Vodka. You cannot drink the water in the Soviet Union. What do you drink?"

"Well," the President paused, "water—because you can't drink the vodka in the United States."

"I think we should drink vodka and water," the Premier allowed.

"I'll bring the water," the President said.

"You have …" The Premier searched for the right term, "… a deal."

"Mr. Premier, I'm going to propose something."

"Yes?"

"Do you have dinner plans?"

"Yes, but I can change them."

"Come on over for vodkas and dinner."

"I think you have another deal."

"I think I can get my people to agree with the idea," the President said.

"I know I can get my people to agree with it." Both men laughed again.

"Well, I'd like to meet with you alone, but I know you have people you must bring. I have those, too. I'll have the hotel set up dinner for them in the suite next door. Of course, they can't have any vodka."

"Of course not," the Premier responded with a smile in his voice. Both men had just handled the issue of what to do with their respective military aides who carried valises filled with codebooks and communication devices. These items carried the "red buttons" that the American and Soviet leaders would use to launch a nuclear war against each another's country.

"When will I see you, Mr. Premier?"

"In an hour?" the Premier responded, continuing to reduce the formality of the relationship another notch.

"That would be great. We'll order a pizza or something."

"A what?"

"A pizza," the President responded. "A classic American dish."

"Piss-a it is," the Premier responded.

The President started to correct the Premier's pronunciation, but thought better of it. "See you in an hour."

"Super-duper," the Premier responded. "I'll be hitting the road soon." The President chuckled as he held the receiver, then put it on the cradle.

"Dave?" the President called as he motioned with a forefinger to the aide who was standing by the door. "You heard what the plans are. Keep it small." Just as the aide turned to carry out his orders, the President said, "Oh, one more thing. Don't let word get to the Italians that I called pizza a classic American dish." The aide's expression was blank. The President tried to pry a smile from him with a wink. It didn't work. Finally, giving up, he said, "Thanks, Dave." The aide left the room.

An hour later there was a knock. The President walked across the living room and opened the door to see the Soviet Premier standing before him with a beaming smile and an extended arm holding a bottle of Russian vodka.

"How did I do?" the Premier asked.

"Good. Real good," the President said. He turned to a lamp table just inside the door. He then extended his arms to reveal two glasses of ice water. "How did I do?"

The Premier grinned and took one of the glasses. "I must have your recipe for this ice." The small crowd of Russian and American security agents in the hall relaxed.

The President motioned and the Premier entered the suite.

The President leaned forward into the hall and spoke to

all, "You boys relax. Dave, here, will take care of you," he said slapping his aide on the back. Grins grew all around, except for Dave. The President raised his glass to the men in the hall as he shut the door. Approaching the Premier, he held up his glass and said, "Well?"

The Premier hesitated. "Oh." He unscrewed the cap on the bottle of vodka and added a splash to each glass.

"Cheers," the President said.

"Cheers."

"Seat?" The President motioned. They sat across from each other at a small mahogany dining table. The fireplace flickered, adding to the growing warmth. "Where's your football?"

"My what?" the Premier responded.

"We call it the 'football,'" the President said. "I want to introduce you to someone. He's a nice enough guy, but I hate having him around." The Premier's face was a question. The President picked up the phone, "Send Colonel Rhodes in, please."

Almost immediately, a U.S. Air Force colonel entered carrying an armored briefcase. "Mr. Premier, I'd like you to meet Colonel Lloyd Rhodes."

The Premier eyed the colonel, who stood ramrod straight in his dress blue uniform. His African features added an air of dignity and strength to his stature.

"Colonel Rhodes' nickname is 'Smooth,'" the President said. "How long have you been following me around, Smooth?" he asked.

"A year, sir." Rhodes grinned, proud.

"A year. Boy, time flies. Mr. Premier, you're looking at a future general here. Isn't that right, Smooth?"

Colonel Rhodes smiled behind a ruddy blush, "That's up to you, sir."

The President waved his hand. "No, it isn't. It's up to you." He asked the Premier, "Do you have a football carrier?"

"Ah," the Premier exclaimed. "Yes, I do have a football."

"Who carries yours?"

"Colonel Sergei Volonovich," the Premier responded with

bravado.

"You're proud of him—the way you say his name."

"I am proud of him, but I like to say his name. Ser-gei Vo-lon-o-vich. It has a nice Russian ring, no?"

"No. I mean, yes. May I ask him to come in?"

The Premier's smile broadened. "Yes."

The President picked up the phone. "Would you ask Colonel—" He looked at the Premier. "Volonovich?"

The Premier nodded.

"Ask Colonel Volonovich to come in."

A tall Russian army officer entered and stood at attention. "Smooth, would you stand by Sergei here?" the President asked. Rhodes did as instructed. Both officers stood at attention, each holding his briefcase.

"Am I doing OK?" the President asked. The Premier nodded. "Smooth," the President said, "open the football and put it in front of the Premier."

Rhodes frowned, confused. "Sir?"

The President was deliberate. "Open your case and put it in front of the Premier."

Colonel Rhodes set his case on the table. He opened the lock with keys he retrieved from a bracelet on his wrist. The latch shot back with a clack. He opened the lid, paused with a glance at the President, then spun the case so its contents faced the Premier.

"Colonel Volonovich," the Premier called.

Volonovich put his case on the table, opened it, and spun it toward the President. He back-paced to stand by Rhodes. The uniformed warriors eyed each other while they stood at attention.

The two leaders considered the event for a moment. Squinting over the raised lid, the President asked, "Mr. Premier, may we dismiss these two gentlemen?"

"Indeed," the Premier said. Each man asked his colonel to step into the hall. As the two officers left the room, the Premier whispered, "Sergei is a nice man, but I hate having him around. I wonder," he winked, "how wide are the eyes in the hall right now?" He closed the case with the American launch codes.

The President did the same with the case that held the Soviet codes. For a moment, he looked at the ordinary aluminum briefcase with its nicked black-plastic handle and the scratches on its sides. It could have been just another briefcase shoved beneath the seat of an airliner, tossed in the back of a taxi, jostled by a bellman who hustled it to a room, or smeared by a child's dripping ice cream cone. As it was, it carried within it the codes to kill 250 million American people.

The President pressed a forefinger on the case. "This pretty much—" his voice cracked, "—says it all, doesn't it?"

"Indeed, Mr. President. Indeed."

The men put the cases beside each other at the end of the table. Then, they looked at each other, their faces brightening to smiles.

"So," the President said, rubbing his hands together in delight. "How about that pizza?"

"Not 'piss-a'?"

"No, not 'piss-a.'"

"I don't eat much pizza," said the President

"Why not? It's very good," the Premier responded.

"It keeps me up at night."

They sat on a couch with their shoes off and their feet toasting in the firelight. They talked of indigestion, family, sports, hobbies, and other inane things that reminded them both of their humanity. The footballs sat on the other side of the room.

The President interrupted the small talk. "What would happen if you folks discovered a technology that gave you the ability to strike the United States with impunity?"

"Why would we want to do that?" the Premier asked.

"Discover the ultimate weapon?"

"No, why would we want to strike your country with impunity? I'll tell you, if we ever invaded your country, what would we do with it? If you couldn't win in Vietnam and we can't win in Afghanistan, how could we take over each other's country?" He leaned toward the President. "And your citizens are much better armed than are ours." He leaned back. "No, Mr. President, where we are now is because of distrust and blunders."

"You know," the President said, "I've never had a doubt that I could use Colonel Rhodes' football."

"Nor I Colonel Volonovich's," said the Premier.

"Let's say something happened," the President searched for words. "Say both Colonel Rhodes and Colonel Volonovich came through that door right now, handed each of us our footballs, then told us that one of my country's missiles had been accidentally fired at Moscow. Would you use yours?"

"Perhaps. It is our job to prepare for such a thing," the Premier said.

"Then you would press your buttons before I could convince you that we had fired accidentally?" the President asked.

"Yes. Such a thing is what we must expect from each other."

"Then, when I saw that you had launched your missiles, I'd have to launch a full strike," the President said, half a statement and half a question.

"Yes," the Premier responded. He bit his lower lip.

"Now, let's say that you and I have both used our footballs, and Colonels Rhodes and Volonovich have handed each of us a pistol," the President said. "Would you shoot me?"

"Of course not."

"I couldn't shoot you, either." The President swirled the ice around. "Why is it that you and I would find it easy to kill the other's people and impossible to kill each other?"

The flapping of the fire quieted while the rain continued. The President walked to the fireplace. He moved the screen back and fed the fire with several pieces of wood.

"The President of the United States feeds his own fire," the Premier said as the President walked back, smacking his hands together.

The President sat down and picked up his glass. He twirled the ice again. "I want to talk about nukes."

"Pardon?" the Premier asked.

"Nukes. I want to get rid of the nukes... All of them."

The Premier puckered his lips, then, "If that decision were yours and mine alone, we could shake hands now and be done with the, uh, nukes. It is not so easy. You have your hawks, and I have mine. You have your naive ones, and I have mine."

"Are we questioning trust here?" the President asked.

"Between us? No. We are talking about ..." he thought for a moment. "We are talking about momentum, and—precedence, and history."

"What would your generals say if they discovered that we were building a weapon that could destroy you without any risk to ourselves?"

"Well, they would try to convince me that our only defense was to launch a surprise nuclear attack against you and destroy it."

"Would you?"

The Premier rubbed his chin. "Sitting here right now, I don't know. But surrounded by my military chiefs?" He shrugged. "I think probably."

"What if ..." the President collected his thoughts and changed course slightly. "What would your generals think if they knew we've had such a weapon for several years, but haven't used it?"

"Yes," the Premier said. "And, as you say, I wasn't born on the pumpkin truck yesterday."

The President smiled at the jumbled metaphor. "Well, what if?"

"They would wonder why you had not used it."

"Would they expect us to use it?" the President asked.

"Yes, of course. Wouldn't you? If the—how do you say—if the shoe was on the other foot?"

The President shook his head and frowned. "I mean, if we had such a weapon and had not used it, wouldn't that show good faith? At least?"

The Premier sighed. "There is a point to this, isn't there?"

The President squeezed his hands together and held them to his chest, bowed his head, and closed his eyes. He barely rocked, back and forth. "We have …" He brought his clenched hands to his mouth.

"Mr. President. Are you—"

"It is called," the President gritted his teeth behind tight lips, "Rhombus!"

"I don't—"

The President held up his hand, then opened his eyes. "We have an airplane that even we can't imagine. There is no way you can stop it." He looked through the French doors, at the rain. "Nor us for that matter."

"My friend, it would come as no surprise to you that we, uh, have our sources in your country. I think we know of all your secret airplanes."

The President ignored him. "We've had it for several years." He looked at the Premier. "It is not a fighter. It is a bomber … a big bomber."

The Premier grinned slightly and raised his eyebrows. "We have ten thousand radars in my country."

"Your radar cannot see it."

"We have three thousand interceptor planes," the Premier parried.

"They cannot see it."

The Premier snorted, blowing a little of his drink out his nose and into his palm. The President handed him a napkin and patted him on the back. After coughing a few times and regaining his composure, the Premier smiled, "An invisible airplane? Excuse me," he coughed through a growing smile, "but is this one of your famous jokes?"

The President, now fully relaxed, said, "Not only is Rhombus invisible when it wants to be, it has a computer that can make it appear as something it's not."

The Premier grinned. "I think you are—how do you put it—pulling my leg." He winked.

"Give me one minute to make my point. OK?"

"OK." The Premier smiled and raised an eyebrow. "I love 'OK,' by the way."

The President rubbed his tongue against the inside of his mouth while he pondered the Premier's attitude. He nodded, then began. "We have a bomber your radar cannot see, one your eyes cannot see. Our Rhombus bomber can fly anywhere in the world undetected. If we strike anything, all anybody knows is that something just blew up. There is no trace of the bomber's passing. We've even designed missiles that leave no evidence of themselves in an explosion. And," he made a slight pause for effect, "the Rhombus fleet can carry enough of these missiles to destroy your command and control so you cannot fire your ICBMs."

"That would be a nice trick." The Premier was still smiling.

"It sure would be." The President lowered his head and looked at the Premier through his eyebrows. "Especially if it became a MiG-twenty-five and flew formation with the Soviet Premier's airplane just after it took off from Moscow on Monday." He paused. "Especially, if it became," he raised an eyebrow, "Mickey Mouse."

The Premier's glass thudded against the carpeted floor, stood for a second, then tipped over.

The fireplace played melody while the grandfather clock beat rhythm. The President stoked the fire again. Orange sparks raced up the flue, and new flames danced among the embers. He placed the stoker back in its holder as the clock chimed ten. Reaching down to retrieve the glass from the carpet, he said, "Mr. Premier?"

"*Da?*"

"May I fix you another?"

"*Nyet,*" the Premier interrupted. He stared at the fire.

The President waited.

The Premier tugged his gaze away from the flames. "Tell

me, if you were me, what would you be asking right now?"

"For a further explanation," the President responded.

"Yes, please." The Premier motioned for the President to continue.

"We started working on the technology in the late nineteen-seventies. We began building it a few years later. Originally, it was to be only invisible to radar. We figured with that technology alone, we would force you to spend about a trillion dollars to develop a defense against it. When we stumbled across invisibility, we knew there would be nothing you could do to defend yourselves. It first flew in nineteen-eighty-two."

The President fidgeted a bit, uncomfortable with the detail he was providing.

"We have only one crew flying a single airplane and a backup. All the other bombers are being placed in storage. The reason for this, Mr. Premier, is that we have been scared you would discover its existence. We are afraid because we know, at this point, your only defense against it is to strike us first. Do you remember what happened on September first, nineteen-eighty-three?" He didn't wait for an answer. "That was the day your folks shot down the Korean airliner. You'll also remember how stunned you were that we had audiotapes of your pilots shooting it down. Well, a satellite didn't make those tapes. The Rhombus bomber made them. It was flying a practice mission over Petropavlovsk."

"What!" the Premier jerked upright. Then, his features softened and he relaxed back into the chair.

"By coincidence the crew witnessed and taped the entire incident—and I don't mean just audiotape."

"You have pictures?"

"Videotape."

The Premier dropped his head and exhaled a long breath.

"This will be painful." The President picked up a remote control that was beside the telephone and pressed a button. The TV came alive with a rear view of a 747, then a front view of two Soviet fighters. The next scene was of both the 747 and the fighters from the rear. Radio calls in Russian accompanied the view. The Premier had heard the radio calls before. The entire world had. The tape played on. It ended with a shot of the ocean swallowing the airliner.

The President picked up the Russian football and placed it on the Premier's lap. "Here," he said. "Here is your only defense against Rhombus. And my only defense against you is my case sitting over there. It's not really pizza that keeps me awake at night." The President sat down. "Offhand, I'd say we are in a hell of a mess, and I figure it's up to you and me to take care of it."

The Premier took his football off his lap and placed it on the floor. He frowned. "Uncertainty," he said, "is a terrible thing. For too long we have been eaten away by our mutual distrust, by being uncertain of each other's motives. Your motives are clear to me, now. It is obvious that had you wanted to destroy our country, you could have done so by using your Rhombus fleet instead of storing it."

"We mean you no harm."

"I have been waiting for this, what I would do if told you had invented what has been called the Doomsday Machine. I imagined that I would be sitting behind my desk after being told and having my general staff demand a launch against you. I could never have dreamed that I would be told this way." He eyed the President. "I think you are a brilliant man. You knew the problem was too big, too big for big decisions made by big governments. You knew it could only be solved by you and me and our trust in each other—as men."

The Premier scratched the side of his nose and smiled. "This is like those western novels you are fond of." He raised a finger. "I read one of your novels once. There were two cowboy families at war over water, as I recall. The two men who headed the warring families sought shelter from a storm and found themselves in the same cave. As a result of being forced together, they discovered themselves not so different." The Premier gave a wry smile. "You remember that one, also?"

"Yes, I remember that one." The President grinned.

"Do you know what our biggest problem is now, Mr. President? Our biggest problem is in how to reveal your Rhombus to my central committee and my military." He sighed and looked away as he put his glass on the table, then he leaned forward, his hands on his knees. "Mr. President, my country is very secretive. We must think of a way to display your bomber's might to my leadership, but we must do so in a way that the Soviet Union cannot hide it from the world. We also must find a way that does not humiliate us. We have farther to go than the distance we have already covered."

The men stood. Each grasped the other's hand. "Let's set aside some time tomorrow to discuss this," the President said.

"Definitely so."

They made firm eye contact. They both knew the same thing—that even though they had grown up on different continents and in different cultures, they now had more in common than any two men who had ever lived.

"I enjoyed the—the—pizza," the Premier said.

"Thanks for coming over. Next time," the President winked, "Texas barbecue."

Each man put a tentative hand on the other's shoulder. Their personal warmth conflicted with formality. "Oh, hell," the President said as he threw his arms around the Premier.

"*Da, da, da,*" the Premier said as he hugged the President. "I see you tomorrow."

The President opened the door. Those in the hall stood. In the doorway, the Premier grabbed the President's hand. "Oh, I forgot to ask. Why, the other day, in the air, Mickey Mouse?"

"I think we can attribute that to an expressive co-pilot." The President winked.

"I am afraid that such a co-pilot would be hanged in my country."

"Well," the President nodded and smiled.

As the Premier stepped through the doorway, the President noticed his counterpart was empty-handed. "Wait a second," the President said. He stepped back into the living room and reappeared. He held a metal briefcase. "You forgot your football."

The President considered the open mouths in the hallway. Pointing to the case that was now in the Premier's hand, he said, "I couldn't get that one to work." He waved to the Premier and closed the door on the astonished faces. He smiled and listened to the Premier's bellowing laughter come through the closed door as he headed down the hall.

1986
WAR DRUMS

1986, TUESDAY, 4 MARCH
1421 HOURS (2:21 PM)
THE KREMLIN

The Premier sat in his leather chair, his back to his desk, and watched the snow fall outside his office window. The window was tall. It ran from just above the radiator to the high ceiling and was lined on each side by dark red drapes. A lighter shade of red wallpaper covered the walls. A mural of Lenin, standing in his greatcoat and looking into the distance, dominated one wall. A mahogany desk dominated everything else. Once in a while the radiator banged. The Premier's hands were pressed together in a peak on which he rested his chin. For several minutes he sat, motionless, speechless, keeping General Riga waiting. The chief of the Soviet military sat, staring at the back of the Premier's chair. A large manila folder lay on the desk, open and illuminated by a brass lamp.

"Are you sure?" the Premier asked, his voice bouncing off the window. "Are you absolutely sure?"

"Yes, I am sure, Comrade Premier," the General replied.

"Who knows of this?"

"As you instructed. Only one other man I trust," the general replied. "General Markov."

"The two of you came to this conclusion, then?" the Premier asked.

"Yes, Comrade Premier."

"You can think of no other way."

"No, Comrade Premier."

"How many people will die, do you figure, General Riga?"

"We do not know."

"We do not know," the Premier repeated.

The Premier turned in his chair to face General Riga. "Your briefing has been very thorough. It is a brilliant idea, but you understand why I cannot bring myself to congratulate you on your conclusion."

"I understand, Comrade Premier."

"The Americans have invented a horrible weapon, Comrade General. I do not know how they kept it from us until the President told me about it."

"We all can be thankful they did, Comrade Premier," the general replied.

"Yes, but …" the Premier paused. "How do you keep such a secret without killing people?"

"You do not. Even here we could not keep such a secret from the Americans without executions. They surely could not," the general said.

"The American President assures me they have killed no one," the Premier responded.

"That is impossible," the general said emphatically. "Do you believe the President?"

"Yes, Comrade General, I do. After all, he shared with me his country's greatest secret, did he not? Such a man does not lie."

"Then," the general replied, "he does not know."

The Premier rubbed his forehead. "Have you studied Churchill?"

"Winston Churchill, Comrade Premier?"

"Yes. I do not need to tell you, Comrade General, that the British cracked the German Enigma Code in World War II. Prior to the great German air raid on Coventry, the British intercepted message traffic on their stolen Enigma that revealed when the Germans would strike."

"Yes, Comrade Premier, I remember. I admire Churchill. I even met him once."

The Premier continued, "Churchill faced a terrible decision. If he alerted Coventry and evacuated its people, the Germans would realize the British had the Enigma. If he did nothing, the Germans would not suspect that Enigma had been compromised and the Allies could use the information to their benefit over the course of the war. The result was that people died in Coventry during the air raid."

"Yes, Comrade Premier. Such decisions have been faced many times."

"He chose not to alert Coventry. He sacrificed Coventry for the greater good of England."

"Yes."

"Comrade General, I think I am now sitting across the desk from one of the bravest men in Russian history. I have asked you for an impossible answer."

"Comrade Premier," the general said, deflecting the discussion, "you and I and a few others are dedicated to change our country. There are many people in my command who will turn on us if we fail to prove what we know in a very convincing manner. Just prior to the Rhombus penetration of our airspace, I will inform my staff of what is to take place. I will give them the hour that the target is to be attacked. We will turn every available resource to stopping the bomber. If it gets through and hits the target, we will continue to hunt it down and kill it. If it succeeds and gets away, it will be a very shocking event."

"It is the only alternative I see to a nuclear war with the United States," the Premier said. "If our party system learns of the existence of the Rhombus through normal intelligence channels, pressure will grow to strike the United States with everything we have. If the Rhombus attack takes place and the bomber fails to get out of the Soviet Union, I also see war. Our only hope is for the Rhombus to succeed, but the Rhombus can only prove itself invincible if it survives the strongest possible defense. Are you sure about the target you have chosen? Can't we find another?"

"The target has to be deep enough in our territory to provide a maximum challenge to the Rhombus," the general responded.

"Yes, but … This?"

"Because, Comrade Premier, the attack must result in a minimal loss of life, and it must, at the same time, be of such magnitude that it is impossible for us to keep it from the world." General Riga added, "I do not need to tell you, Comrade Premier, that we have been very good about keeping the world from knowing about massive losses of life that have occurred because of our technological failures."

"To be sure, General Riga," the Premier responded, tapping a pen on the leather desk inlay. "To be sure."

The Premier opened his center desk drawer and retrieved a sheet of stationery. Placing it in front of him, he wrote. While he waited, the general fidgeted a bit and admired the memorabilia on the office walls. "Comrade General, pick a date," the Premier said, plucking the general out of his interest in the walls.

"A date for what, Comrade Premier?"

"A date for the attack."

"The Saturday before the May Day celebration."

The Premier circled the date on his calendar. "That's April twenty-sixth."

"Yes, Comrade Premier, I know. It is my wedding anniversary, as well."

"I think this year you should buy lots of flowers. Pick a time."

"Comrade Premier, we are not familiar with operational matters involving the Rhombus." The hairs on his neck stood. "I suggest you let the Americans pick the time."

"Agreed," the Premier said as he returned to his writing. The general studied the mementos again.

When the Premier quit writing, he folded several sheets of stationery, slid them in a folder, and sealed the folder in a manila envelope. "I assume you have someone you trust to hand-carry this to the American President?"

"Yes, Comrade Premier."

The Premier stood. The general stood. "Here," the Premier said, "this must arrive at the White House without delay."

The general closed his eyes and shuddered as he took the envelope. He saluted and disappeared through the office door.

The Premier looked down from his window at the black Zil limousine that drove General Riga away through the March snow. The die was cast. There was no turning back. He hoped that he—that his country—would live to see next year's March snows. As the Zil moved through the Kremlin gate, he thought of something the President had written in a letter. How did it go? You are the master of the unspoken word and the slave of the spoken word. He thought about the folder that lay beside the General on the car seat. He did, indeed, feel like a slave to what he had just written.

1986, WEDNESDAY, 24 APRIL
0809 HOURS (8:09 AM)
GROOM LAKE BASE, NEVADA

"You guys want a challenge?" Chris Patterakis asked.

The manila folder hit the briefing-room table and caused the ashes from Brian's cigarettes to swirl out of the glass ashtray. Brian dragged his forearm across the table to clean it. Mike leafed through his emergency-procedures manual.

"What-cha got, Skipper?" Brian asked.

"This might be your last long flight in Rhombus, boys," Patterakis said.

"Where to?"

Patterakis ignored the question. He opened the folder and retrieved a letter. "This is the only copy of this letter," he said as he slid it across the table to Mike.

"What's the matter?" Brian asked. "Afraid I'll spill something on it?"

"The thought occurred to me."

Brian faked being stabbed in the heart. Mike unfolded the letter. "The President thought you should read that," Patterakis said.

"The President?" Mike asked.

"Of the United States," Patterakis said, without humor.

Mike read the letter in silence, then slid each sheet across the table to Brian. After passing the last sheet, he watched Brian.

When Brian finished reading, he exhaled and shook his head. He stared at the center of the table for a moment, then, as if breaking a trance, he pressed a finger on the letter and asked, "Can I make a copy of that? You know, for my wall."

Patterakis pointed behind them. "Did you notice them?" Mike and Brian turned. Standing in the doorway was a Marine captain with a drawn sidearm. Behind him were two other Marines with M-16s. "He's standing back because he's not supposed to know what's in here. What he's supposed to do is shoot if one of us pockets any of this or heads to a copy machine. Otherwise, he'll wait for us to finish, then body-search us. When all that's done, he'll watch, while I burn everything in a special canister. I'll be naked while I do this, of course, as will you. Then he'll take the canister back to Washington. There, it'll be tested to make sure the chemical composition of the ashes is what it's supposed to be. If it isn't, they come back to interview us," he raised at eyebrow at Brian, "in a cell, under a spotlight, if you get my drift."

Brian smiled at Chris. "You know, Skipper, I'm amazed at how convincing you can be on the subject of home decorating." He scratched his head. "You're exactly right. I got enough stuff on my wall."

Mike picked at the edge of a manila folder. "Did this come from the Premier, too?"

"Yep, sure did," Patterakis responded as he opened the folder. "Let's get started. You boys leave in two days."

"Where to? Honestly, this time," Brian asked.

"Soviet Union. Just like the letter says," responded Patterakis.

"Just my luck," Brian said. "And I was beginning to like Groom Lake." He looked over his shoulder at the Marines.

It took the better part of a half-hour to study the documents.

"Well?" Patterakis leaned back. "Anybody going to say anything?"

"What's the target?" Brian asked.

"Well, you saw the pictures." Patterakis pointed to the package.

"It looks like a small factory, but nothing in here says what it is."

"Fact is, they didn't tell us," Patterakis said.

"Why?"

"I don't know, Brian. All you guys have to do is put a hole," he tapped the tip of his pen on part of the building, "right here. The MPP will be programmed to lead you to it. Just do it—and fly through the entire Soviet Air Force, of course."

"Oh yeah. I almost forgot that part," Brian quipped.

"We'll have a full intelligence package developed by the end of the day—satellite photos and the whole nine yards. You have some mission planning to do, but I think you're ready for this. What do you think?" Patterakis asked.

"We've had two years to study the planet," Brian said. "We could take off right now and fly to the area without a problem. We just need to come up to speed on target information and get the latest weather."

Mike's eyes were on the table, his mind elsewhere. "Mike?" Patterakis pried. "Mike?"

"Oh, sorry," Mike said as he looked up.

"You OK with this?"

Flinty determination replaced the glazed-over look in Mike's eyes. "I was born for this mission. This is it," Mike said quietly. "This is really it."

Brian spoke. "It's safe to say, I suppose, that all our eggs are in one basket?"

"Yeah," Patterakis responded. "It's safe to say that."

"That's an understatement," Mike said. "I never worried about losing a war before. I always believed Uncle Sam would win whether I came back or not. My thoughts were to kill the enemy and make it back with my wingmen, make it back to …" a shadow seemed to pass over Mike's face, "… to our families."

Patterakis and Brian lowered their eyes.

"Fact is, Skipper," Mike continued, "I believe Brian and I will make it back, but I'm not sure Dallas or L.A. will be here. I'm not sure you'll be here."

1986, Thursday, 25 April
1400 Hours (2:00 PM)
Groom Lake Base, Nevada

The day before, a mild gust of air brushed in from the Pacific and crested San Francisco's Telegraph Hill. It skimmed the ranches and farms of the San Joaquin and climbed over the snow-crowned Sierra Nevada before sweeping down through Inyo National Forest. After splitting around Boundary Peak, it rustled the cactus and wildflowers of Emigrant Valley and picked up the sweet smells of sage and mesquite. The gust whistled through the razor wire, then tumbled across the concrete parking apron. It crested the steel hangar and twisted into a tiny tornado as it crossed the lip of a large metal grate before being yanked into a dark tunnel. The air entered the CJ engines where spinning compressor blades chopped it, squeezed it, then mixed it with jet fuel. A split second later it entered a chamber of flame where it was transformed into heat, carbon dioxide, and water vapor, then shot through another set of spinning blades before being directed up and out the roof of the hangar. There, the gust blasted skyward in a shimmering heated pillar and dispersed into the sky to continue its journey across the land called America.

A klaxon sounded as huge hangar doors rolled apart. The large silver-colored ducts that had fed Rhombus air and took its exhaust away now moved up and away from the massive black shape. An instant later, the airplane winked into ether. Rhombus moved. The clock started.

MISSION TIME—00 HOURS: 00 MINUTES

Large tires rolled beneath an illusion as the invisible machine and its two pilots moved down the sun-hammered taxiway. Desert songbirds swirled around the great warbird, swooping to catch the insects that flew up to escape the advancing sound. A mourning dove flew headlong into the airplane and fell to the pavement, its body flung away by the torrid exhaust. At the end of the taxiway, Rhombus turned right and lined up on the long rock-colored runway, which disappeared into the luster that lay on the desert floor. The powerful machine accelerated, its thunder betraying the might that lurked inside its sheer appearance. When it reached flying speed, it pitched into the sapphire sky.

Rhombus toyed with the edge of space and turned due north. As it flew, it flirted with the border that separated Idaho from Oregon and Washington. Onward it pressed above places in Canada with melodious names like Kaslo, Yoho, Fort Vermilion, and Rae. High over the Northwest Territories it flew, over the Queen Elizabeth Islands, then the Arctic Ocean. Below, beneath the ice, the continental shelf fell away to underwater features like Canada Basin, Makarov Basin, and Fram Basin. There, just to the north of Lomonosov Ridge, under

12,000 feet of ice and water, was the North Pole. At the North Pole, Mike, Brian, and their airplane were about 3,500 miles from home. Behind, due south, was Groom Lake. Ahead, due south, was Murmansk. They had 2,500 miles to go.

Southward they sped, across the Barents Plain, over North East Land and Spitsbergen, and over the Svalbard and the Murmansk rise. Falling behind were places with names like Boca Raton, New Orleans, Santa Barbara, and Des Moines. Ahead were places with names like Moscow, Stalingrad, Omsk, and Minsk.

Mike looked at the sea and thought of how each person on the planet used it, and was responsible for it. At the beginning of last winter, his mother had taken down a hummingbird feeder from an old poplar tree. She'd poured the sugar water over the rocks that jutted into the river. The sweet liquid flowed down the New, Kanawha, Ohio, and Mississippi, then into the Gulf of Mexico, where it soaked up the sun as it moved through the Florida Straits, then northward. The British Isles were as far north as parts of Alaska, but the Florida warmth in moving water kept the isles green. Farther northeast the stream coursed, around the north coast of the Scandinavian Peninsula and then to Murmansk, where it kept the Arctic ice pack at bay with what was left of its heat. There, it sank to the bottom of the sea and began flowing along the sea floor back from where it came—back to the southern shores of the United States to pick up more sunshine, then return to Russia.

How unique we humans are, Mike thought as he watched the ice slip by below. We're tied together by the flow of the earth, yet separated by our passions. Ahead and below, in the drift of the sea, nature sent to Russia the warm water from Mom's hummingbird feeder, while up here, in the great spaces of the sky, man sent Mom's son on the wings of death.

For the first time in his life, Mike associated south with cold—deep and dangerous cold. But he found a strange warm peace as he headed into the dark forbidding lower heaven that covered the Soviet Union. The danger ahead replaced the emptiness behind. Danger was a comforting friend that soothed the sights and sounds of personal agony and the reminder of life's most profound accounting rule: The deeper the love, the more the reward and the greater the loss. When the sky turned to fear, her midnight-blue eyes no longer winked from the edge of each cloud, the autumn fields of the heartland quit being the color of her skin, and the pinks and reds of sunsets didn't remind him of her soft and spirited manner. When the engines whined, they replaced the sounds of a cracking base-ball bat. When his finger pushed a button, it was no longer the teasing finger pressed to the tip of a little girl's nose. The rush of air outside scoured away the nightmare of tiny feet kicking at the rising water while a shrill voice screamed, "Momeee! Momeee!" as the black water covered the windshield and poured around the doors. The growing pinch of straps, the smell of plastic, and the images glaring from CRTs replaced the smiles, giggles, challenges, and rewards of bringing chil-dren into the world and growing with them. Over the hori-zon, the Soviet Union rushed at him. He wanted it.

They slouched in their seats. Dark circles grew around their eyes. They don't sleep last night. Warriors usually didn't sleep the night before battle.

Rhombus carried within her bomb bay twelve Fleshette missiles that were mounted on a rotary launcher. When the trigger was pressed either by the pilot or MPP, the bomb bay doors opened, the launcher extended far enough into the air stream to expose just one missile, the missile fired, and the doors closed. The whole process took just a quarter of a sec-ond. The speed at which the process worked was critical, be-cause Rhombus lost much of its radar stealth and part of its invisibility while the doors were open. Fleshettes flew to their targets at more than 5,000 miles per hour. These particular Fleshettes were armed with a dense non-explosive tip that was designed to tear holes in thick hardened concrete, thereby leav-ing the structure vulnerable for a follow-on attack.

Mike and Brian were going in light. They were not refueling prior to penetration. The target was about 6,000 miles from Groom Lake, so Rhombus had enough fuel to get there and back with enough remaining to fly to Atlanta.

"Bong. Bong. Bong."

"Go Threat," Mike called.

"Roger. Going Threat," Brian responded as he typed.

Rhombus came to full alert.

The SID displayed a horizon over which red threat spheres rose higher and larger. Corresponding wheels appeared on the TopDown.

A more direct route would have taken them over the Scandinavian peninsula, but to steer clear of any diplomatic problems in case of a problem, they'd planned a route that made landfall at Murmansk. The MPP flew Rhombus while Mike and Brian monitored progress and the threats.

The SID flashed red.

"Whoa! Where did that come from?"

Rhombus banked into a screaming right turn to avoid the sphere.

"They have ships out here on coastal picket duty! Instant-on radar, too."

They skirted the edge of a red sphere. Pierce the sphere, and the Soviets would see them.

Lower they went—almost vertical. Down, down, beside the red dome.

The CJs were at idle, the airspeed at Mach .95.

The blue-black ocean took on greater definition as they shot for the safety of the water.

Rhombus jerked up. Mike and Brian grunted.

They leveled off at 100 feet above the sea, just beyond the edge of the sphere. They sped toward the coast. Red symbols dotted the SID, each superimposed over a fighter that Rhombus sensed, but too distant for its pilots to see. The same symbols were arranged on the TopDown, superimposed on a map of the earth surrounding them. "Jeez," Brian said. "Do you think they're expecting us? This gives me the creeps."

"But look at the flight patterns." Mike pointed at the SID. "Nobody's being vectored toward our path. They don't know where we are."

"Still."

The CJ engines, at one-third power, shoved Rhombus over the white caps at 650 miles per hour. The Soviet coastline grew larger by the minute, then by the second. The coast blasted past in a blur of blue, then beige, then green.

"Feet dry," Brian called.

Below, on a small fishing boat in a small inlet, two men stopped hauling their net when they heard a strange whispering thunder pass just above them. They looked up—to see nothing.

In the SID and on the TopDown, threat spheres grew all around. To Mike, they seemed like the heads of angry gods that rose from the earth to smite the tiny speck he flew over the vast Soviet countryside. Here and there, fighters of all types executed tactical patterns at various altitudes. Helicopters cruised below 5,000 feet as their pilots strained to see a fleeting shadow, hoping to get a lucky shot and with it the Order of Lenin. "They have everything they own out hunting for us," Brian said.

If Rhombus were a B-52, the threat spheres would be far larger and, in fact would overlap. There would be no way of getting through this without being seen. Of course, if they were a B-52, they would be one of several hundred airplanes penetrating the Soviet Union, and the Russian defenses would be spread out.

"It seems like the Ruskies have concentrated their defenses along our expected flight path," Mike said. "What we see near the target will be interesting."

"I reckon."

Rhombus bounded over the Russian tundra as it threaded its way through the gaps in the threat spheres. In a few minutes, every sphere they could see was behind them. "We should have smooth sailing until we get inside the Ukraine," Mike said.

"Why doesn't that comfort me?" Brian responded.

Mike glanced out the side of the SID. "Strange. It looks a lot like Minnesota. I'll bet these are nice people."

"Good thing there aren't any mountain views," Brian mumbled.

"Say again?" Mike responded.

"Nothin'."

Southward they flew with the eastern border of Finland off to their right and the waters of the Beloye More to their left. A hundred thousand lakes flashed from the flat lowlands of the Karelia as they flew from Murmansk to Leningrad. Past Leningrad, they entered the Republic of Belarus. The threat sensors were quiet, but Rhombus flew like whistling death along the countryside of the Soviet Union as it rushed deeper and deeper into the jaws of the monster.

MISSION TIME—7 HOURS: 4 MINUTES
THE KREMLIN

"May I speak openly, Comrade Premier?" came the voice over the speaker phone on the Soviet Premier's desk.

"Yes, General Riga. You may. I have Minister Rudavich here with me."

"Good day, Comrade Minister Rudavich," General Riga greeted.

"Good day, Comrade General."

Without preliminary remarks the general said, "We saw nothing, Comrade Premier."

"Nothing?"

"Forgive me, Comrade General," the minister spoke up. "The Premier has not told me how you planned for this." He looked at the Premier. "Do you mind?"

"Certainly not."

"Please. Give me a brief background, Comrade General," the minister spoke. "I know you are busy."

"Well," the general said, "all the Premier and the American President have given us is what the target is and when the attack will occur. I have relayed that information to my general staff, and the reaction from them was good. There is agreement that should the target blow up, we will have proof that the Americans indeed have a weapon we cannot defend ourselves against. They also believe that should the Americans have such a weapon, they have shown good faith in that they have not used it. We all regret, comrades, that the mutual distrust we have with the Americans has brought us to this, but without such a dramatic display, it will be very difficult to break that distrust."

"Agreed," the minister replied.

"Comrades," General Riga continued, "we are throwing every possible resource against this Rhombus bomber, keeping in mind that we still have to maintain our normal defenses. Forgive me, Comrade Premier, but we must not let our guard down." The general became defensive. "How do I put this, comrades? Just in case this Rhombus attack is a diversionary attack."

"You are doing your job correctly," the Premier assured.

Emboldened by the Premier's support, the general continued. "We know nothing about this Rhombus except that we cannot see it or pick it up on radar. We concentrated air defenses at our perimeter where its most likely penetration point should have been."

"What do you mean, 'should have been'?" the minister asked.

"Well, Comrade Minister," Riga replied, "if it is to hit the target on time, it is already in our country." A soft hiss from the speaker was the only sound in the office.

The general broke their contemplation. "We believe we saw him on radar north of Murmansk when the cruiser Borshov used its instant-on radar and something skirted the edge of his scopes for a few seconds, but we are not sure. We launched our forces around Murmansk, but there were no more contacts." The general paused and waited for a response. He got none. "I don't need to tell you, Comrade Premier, that even though there is understanding of why this is taking place, our pride wants us to defeat this airplane."

"Yes, Comrade General," the Premier responded. "I feel the same."

The minister spoke. "Comrade General, how would you describe your defensive forces around the target?"

"We have encircled the area with radar planes and fighters. They are patrolling from one hundred to two hundred miles away from the target," the general said. "Closer in, our forces are massive. I don't know how a bird, or even an insect, could get through. If this Rhombus is successful, the Americans are more advanced than I ever dreamed."

The Premier and the Minister nodded.

"Comrade Premier," the general said, "we have been good friends for many years. I must tell you that what we are doing saddens me. It has been a very difficult time. We have people who would launch our missiles at America right now if given a chance. I must also say that you, the minister, and I will not survive if the Rhombus bomber does not succeed." The general waited for a moment. Then, "With your permission I must go, comrades. If there is a Rhombus, he is in our country and should be entering our internal defense area shortly."

"Thank you, Comrade General," said the Premier.

"Thank you, Comrade Premier. Good day, Comrade Minister."

The Premier broke the connection.

The minister swallowed hard. "You know, Comrade Premier, if this Rhombus bomber does not succeed, you and I will be under interrogation within twenty-four hours. How can you be so sure it will work?"

"Because," responded the Premier, "someone I trust is involved."

"Is this someone a friend of the Soviet Union?"

"No, he is not. But I believe what he says."

MISSION TIME—10 HOURS: 37 MINUTES
THE DNEIPER LOWLANDS, THE SOVIET UNION

"Flight's been a walk in the park since Murmansk," Brian said. For more than two hours they'd been flying low over rolling countryside that was covered with the yellow-green of spring. The MPP checked all airplane systems several hundred times a second, so Brian played with the SID while Mike watched. He zoomed it back and forth in each quadrant of the sky, looking for fighters, farms, and couples fooling around beneath the trees. "Damn," he said, "the only things carrying on around out here are cows and pigs."

"Are you spying on people again?" Mike asked.

"No, at least not until I see someone. I want some good video shots to take back to the guys."

"I don't think their idea of a good shot is a babushka straddling a pig farmer."

"You forget we're talking about American sailors here, Christum. You know our motto, 'If she doesn't meet your standards, lower 'em.'"

"Oh, right. *Those* sailors." Mike chuckled. "Well, maybe in Russia the animals do it outside and the people do it in the barns."

"O-o-o-o," Brian said as he fiddled with the SID controls. "Good idea!"

Mike bowed his head and moaned.

Their target lay near the Dneiper River in an obscure city in the northern Ukraine. Mike had been watching the Dneiper as a line on the TopDown. They had followed the river from its headwaters in the Valday Hills, southwest of Moscow. Now they skirted the eastern end of Pripjat Marshes.

"Oops, what's this?" Brian asked. The tops of transparent red threat spheres rose over the southern horizon. In the center of each sphere was a radar attached to an airplane or helicopter that wanted to kill them. As they flew, the spheres rose higher.

"Holy hell," Brian said. "Holy hell."

Mike and Brian's feeling of invincibility wilted like a piece of lettuce on a hot sidewalk. In all their test and tactics flights against U.S. Air Force fighters flying out of Nellis, nothing had prepared them for this. So many threat spheres rose that there was no room between them.

"Look at that!" Brian exclaimed. "They've surrounded the target with a large circular holding pattern that is, oh, about ten miles across. The target is in the center of that circle. It looks like no airplane is more than a mile from the other. Just a sec." Brian looked closer at the TopDown. "They're shuttling airplanes in and out of the holding pattern from the Anotov field at Kiev. What're we gonna do now, coach?"

Beneath them the Belarus countryside blasted past in a rush of blurry green. Ahead, in the SID, the threat spheres grew larger as Rhombus closed the distance by about 900 feet every second.

"Mike?" Brian queried.

The fatigue that grew behind Mike's eyes flashed away. It had all been so easy up to now. They had knifed through every defense the U.S. armed services could throw at them. They had flown into the airspace over Petropavlovsk as easy as an airline dinner flight over Kansas City. They had flown just above the earth over the entire United States and nobody but nobody had seen them. On this flight they were to hit their target and reverse course to fly out. A flight with daunting consequences to be sure, but one that required little more forethought than the Pittsburgh Steelers would have before a game against Miss Mary's Boys School. They had flitted around the threats over Murmansk like a chimney swift dodging rooftops. They had relaxed as they enjoyed the landscape, while Brian played with the SID to break the boredom. Now, ahead, the Soviet Union had thrown up a radar wall so dense that they couldn't see through it. What lay ahead made their missions over Hanoi look easy. The magic of Rhombus had vastly reduced the range of each radar, but the Soviets had responded to the threat by putting everything they could into the air. Stalin had a theory on quantity. He said that quantity had its own quality. The best that America had to offer was now head to head with the most that Russia had to offer. The playing field was even, and Mike and Brian were deep in the enemy's homeland.

"Mike?" Brian called.

Mike swallowed. He studied the massive red wall ahead. "What is it we get paid to do?"

Brian jerked toward Mike. "Huh?"

"What is it we get paid to do?"

"Fly," Brian said—half an answer, half a question.

"And that's what we're going to do. Remember your Vietnam days?"

"Yeah."

"We're going to make this fifteen billion dollar crate fly like the fighter it is. It's time to go to work. We're through being systems managers. In order to get through that," Mike nodded toward the spheres, "we're going to have to be pilots, United States Naval Aviators." He pointed ahead. "We'll have to pull them away from the target—do an end run to make them think we're going after something else. If things open up, we'll make a run at the target. I don't know any other way. You?"

Brian grinned. "Ready when you are."

Mike jerked the throttles back. The airspeed fell to 400 knots, or Mach .6. He advanced the throttles to hold the new airspeed. "Turn on the transponder to very low power and give them a squawk. We'll let them know we're here and see what happens."

Brian rolled the transponder power knob to low and pressed the button. The transponder sent a signal to every radar that swept past, placing on each screen an elongated dot that looked to each Soviet radar operator like Rhombus was larger than it was.

"Watch the threat spheres," Mike called. In a flash each sphere grew many times its former area. All encompassed Rhombus in their red glow, meaning that Rhombus was now within the radar range of each one.

"Picking up lots of new comm traffic on the radio," Brian said. "I think we woke some people up."

"Transponder off," Mike ordered. The spheres returned to their smaller size. A mile or two went by. "I want you to turn the transponder on until you see their airplanes move in our direction, then turn it off. When you see them turning back, turn it on. I want 'em to chase us, but not too close. Make 'em think we have an electrical problem."

"Rog," Brian said as he pressed the transponder button. "OK, Michael. There's movement!" The spheres in the holding pattern closest to Rhombus moved closer. The TopDown showed the circular holding pattern bulge toward them as the Soviets began concentrating forces along what they believed to be the attack corridor.

"Turn it off," Mike commanded. "Tell me what you see."

"Threat spheres are back to normal size again, but there are spaces between them."

Mike rolled Rhombus into a left turn and headed east. "Squawk 'em again."

Brian pressed the transponder button. "OK. The bulge is moving toward us."

"Squawk off."

"Roger."

"We're going to take advantage of Soviet paranoia."

"Say again?" Brian responded.

"OK, if this were a real shootin' war, what target would we be attacking in this area?"

"The Anotov aircraft factory at Kiev."

"Right."

"We'll swing well to the east of the Dneiper, then south, then head toward Kiev from the east. I want you to manipulate the transponder so they think we have a problem. We have to convince them we're headed for Kiev. When a hole opens in the defense circle around the target, we'll go for it. Perhaps you should display a B-Fifty-Two on the pixel grid."

Brian pondered the idea. "If we display a B-Fifty-Two, they may think we're part of a larger force. That could cause

World War Three if the Soviets think they have been duped."

"Hmm. That's right. Keep those good ideas coming."

"I've been playing around in the visual lab, and I scanned into the MPP an image of one of the Star Wars movie models I've been working on."

"You scanned in an X-Wing fighter!"

"Not exactly."

Mike let Brian's response pass. "Damn," he said. "I can't believe you and I are making decisions on what may or may not cause World War Three."

"Somebody's got to do it. Why not us?"

"Why not, indeed, Mr. Davis. Engage."

Brian selected from a list of airplanes in the MPP's electronic library. He pressed a button. "Pixel Grid in Display Mode," he called.

The invisible Rhombus flashed and became something else. Mike smiled at how it must look to a farmer on the ground as a fighter from space zoomed across the earth. Brian smiled because he knew that what the farmer saw was the Millennium Falcon, Han Solo's dirty, beat-up, and lopsided space freighter.

"Hi ho. Hi ho. It's off to work we go." Mike shoved the throttles. The CJs shot Rhombus forward. "I just love our office, don't you, Mr. Davis?"

In ten seconds flat, Rhombus' huge mass streaked 250 knots per hour faster. She was doing 640 knots at Mach .98.

As they blasted east, Brian pulsed the squawk button. "Here they come!"

Threat spheres bulged from the circle toward them, this time from the eastern side of the circle.

Fighters that had been part of the defensive circle pursued them. They streaked over the Central Russian Upland and skirted the southern edge of Smolensk and Lokodnya.

"Over the Oga River," Brian called.

Mike snapped Rhombus into a right bank, then he rolled out heading due south.

Bolkhov and Orel shot by in a blur. Kursk lay ahead.

"Remember what the Strategic Air Command did when they bombed Hanoi in nineteen-seventy-one?" Mike asked.

"Yeah," Brian responded. "Used predictable checkpoints for their bombing runs. Showed no flexibility. Typical. Killed a bunch of their crews."

"With luck, the Soviets'll think we learned nothing from it."

"Over Kursk," Brian called.

Mike yanked the joystick. Rhombus rolled right. Southwest they went, toward Kiev.

"Careful what you wish for. You may get it," Brian called. "The eastern quadrant of the circle's in pursuit, off to our right. The southern quadrant is moving toward Kiev to intercept us."

"See the Anotov factory yet?"

"Just a sec." Brian maneuvered a small button to place a target symbol over the factory in his CRT. "There you go, Michael."

Mike rolled into a right bank so that the nose pointed at the factory. It was still 150 miles away, but they would reach it in less than 15 minutes.

"Should I quit cycling the transponder?" Brian asked.

"No."

"I need more fingers."

Onward they rushed, 200 feet above the hills, toward Kiev.

To the right, Soviet fighters five miles away maneuvered behind them, rabid dogs after the sprinting gazelle, dozens of men hunting the two.

Brian pressed the transponder button on, off, on, off.

Soviet radar operators tapped their scopes. "There it is! No, over here! Now it's over there!" They barked commands to the fighters. "It's to your right. No, left. It turned west."

Meanwhile, a few hog and grain farmers in the Soviet republic of the Ukraine watched the Millennium Falcon as it streaked over their fields and disappeared over a tree line.

"Getting intermittent tones!" Brian called. "Fire-control radar trying to lock on. Missile launch coming!"

"Stop squawking when you get fire control. When it loses lock, squawk again."

"Roger. My finger's tired."

100 miles, 90 miles, 80 miles … down the numbers rolled.

Ahead, threat spheres filled the screen as fighters rushed at them.

70 miles—60 miles—50 miles …

"Missiles!" Brian called. "Heat seekers in the air! Six o'clock. Two of 'em."

40 miles …

"Pixel grid off," Mike called.

"Roger." The space freighter winked off. Rhombus became a ghost again.

"Hang on," Mike called.

He slammed the throttles back. Hot roaring exhaust became a trickle of warm air.

Electronic heat-seeking brains in the missiles broke lock. Their electronic eyes rolled—searched for their missing prey. The eyes locked again. The missiles turned toward the heat. Long white trails sped at the ghost.

"Hang on!" Brian called. "Heat seekers at our six o'clock. Heading our way. Close—very close!"

Mike dare not turn Rhombus away. He'd need power to turn, and that meant heat from the exhausts. Nothing to do now but hope the tactic worked.

Brian switched his SID to rear mode.

He saw the missiles head-on, dark dots in the middle of cotton balls of smoke that grew as they got closer.

Closer.

And closer. Brian saw the missiles' fins flitting back and forth as they made flight corrections. Their exhaust smoke filled the SID.

A roar to the right. Another roar to the right.

Brian flipped the SID to the front.

Bright streaks to the right!

Two smoke trails—

Flying by—

Fins moving back and forth as the missiles bore in on the sun reflected off a silo.

Two thousand feet ahead the top of the silo burst. Flame sent aluminum panels spinning away. Building stones pelted the ground with small bursts of dust as Rhombus flashed by.

Held breaths now returned.

Hearts slowed.

"What the hell! SAMs!" Brian called.

"Kiev missile defenses." Mike slammed the throttles ahead. Distance—gotta put distance between us and the missiles—need distance.

Rhombus shot ahead.

"Getting a solid tone," Brian called. "SAMs behind."

The airspeed jumped. Mach 1.

Mach 1.1.

Mach 1.2.

1.3.

1.4.

934 knots per hour!

The SAMs rose from the ground and climbed above Rhombus. They nosed over, left smoky arches in the sky, and dove for them.

"Two SAMs—closing—two thousand knots."

Can't outrun 'em. What to do? "Cobra!" Mike yelled.

Brian grabbed his armrests.

Mike pushed a button on the joystick. He yanked the joystick back.

The nose snapped straight up, so fast that Rhombus quit flying.

The entire bottom of the warplane became an airbrake, a giant metal platter going flatways through the sky, a parachute on a dragster, 14-Gs in an instant.

The ejection seats slammed back. "Ouch!"

Mike released the back pressure. Only blue sky filled the SID. "Nose ninety degrees up," Brian called.

"We're in Cobra!" Mike called.

"Ah, hell—" Brian said. "Altitude two hundred feet above

the ground and holding," he called.

"Holding.

"Holding.

"Holding."

Airspeed dropped 100 knots per second.

"Airspeed seven hundred knots. Six hundred. Five hundred. Four hundred. Three hundred.

"Altitude holding."

Rhombus flew level with the earth at 200 feet, its nose pointed straight up.

The wind screamed as it tore around the warplane's sides. Wildlife and farm animals panicked and fled the noise.

"SAMs, twelve o'clock, five thousand feet behind. Our airspeed is two hundred knots," Brian called.

Airspeed fell.

"SAMs, three thousand feet. We're at one hundred seventy knots.

"Two thousand feet. One hundred forty-five knots."

"One thousand feet. One hundred twenty-five knots."

Rhombus whistled through the sky.

Mike hoped 125 knots would be slow enough for the SAMs to break lock.

Four loud bangs pounded the airplane.

The CRTs jumped. "SAMs just went by," Brian called. "That's their sonic booms.

"Altitude falling.

"Airspeed sixty knots."

Brian looked at the TopDown. Red symbols zoomed past the symbol of Rhombus in the middle of the display. He looked at the SID. Fighters shot by, dark, blurred streaks. "The whole Soviet Air Force just went by," he said.

"Airspeed zero," Brian started his cockpit calls again.

"Airspeed zero!"

The huge airplane hung in the sky.

It pointed straight up.

It fell—slow at first—backwards.

"Altitude one hundred ninety feet and falling."

Brian curled his hands around the ejection handles. He looked to his left, waiting for the signal.

Mike jammed the joystick full forward. "Give me calls, Brian." Brian let go the handles and scanned the CRTs. "Sliding back," he called.

"Altitude one hundred fifty feet—

"Sliding back.

"Nose still ninety degrees up."

The CJs screamed. Glossy transparent pillars of hot gases shot from the bomber's rear and flattened on the meadow. Grass blasted flat in all directions.

"We got airspeed."

Rhombus clawed for its life.

"One hundred sixty feet—

"Ten knots. We got airspeed—

"One hundred seventy feet—

"One hundred eighty feet—

"Forty—fifty—sixty knots."

The CJs screeched at the ground.

"Two hundred feet! We're climbing.

"Two hundred twenty feet.

"Eighty knots."

The control surfaces on the wings were useless. There was no air flowing over the bomber for them to bite into.

"We're falling on our back. We're going over."

Mike slammed the joystick forward. Don't fall, don't fall, don't let it end like this.

Rhombus still climbed while if fell backwards, a rocket out of control.

"One hundred twenty knots, five hundred feet."

"Still falling back."

Rhombus tumbled over.

They were pointed at the ground, upside down and 500 feet above it.

Mike and Brian hung in their shoulder harnesses.

Bits of dirt and other debris fell from the floor and pelted the cockpit ceiling.

Mike slammed the joystick to the left.

"Airspeed accelerating rapidly.

"One hundred eighty knots—

"One ninety—

"Two hundred—

"Rolling left."

Thank God.

"Rolling left.

"Nose still falling.

"Two hundred twenty knots."

The nose was 45 degrees down.

The wings were 45 degrees to the earth.

The SID was filled with a meadow that rushed at them.

Mike had the joystick full left and full back.

Rhombus leaped forward and down, rolling left as it dove.

The wind over the wings increased.

The full-up control surfaces dug into the air. They pushed down on the rear of the airplane to pivot the nose up.

The wings leveled.

They still headed down.

They saw small bushes and stock-animal trails in the SID. Cattle scattered away from the coming thunder. In the near distance, a tree line moved toward them.

"Nose coming up—

"Up.

"Up.

"Wings level."

But the bomber still sank toward the earth, even with its nose rising.

"We're in a high-speed stall!"

Rhombus shook.

Trees sped at them.

Brian winced, wondered how dying would feel.

Mike was doing all he could do. We're not going to make it. "Prepare to eject!" he called.

Then the hand of God reached beneath them. They hit ground effect 90 feet above the earth. The sinking stopped.

The giant airplane skimmed over the pasture.

The tree line rushed at them.

Brian stiffened. His fingers dug into his palms, buttocks pressed together, eyes wide.

Rhombus heaved skyward.

The tops of the large pines swept beneath its wings.

Just like always, the magical airplane toyed at the edge of death and suddenly—everything was so normal.

They were 1,500 feet above the earth. "Boy, I think I sucked my seat cushion into my rectum," Brian said.

"Check for bogies," Mike called.

This guy's soooo damned good, Brian thought. I don't know whether to kiss him or kick him.

Brian studied the TopDown. "Hell, Mike. Everything that was following us is now ahead of us."

"Is the target open?"

"Damn sure is. The entire southern half of the circle is a shambles. The wave of airplanes that was behind is now trying to keep from hitting the ones that are waiting for us over Kiev. Things are a general mess for the Ruskies."

"Give me command steering for the target."

"You got it."

Mike got his bearing to the target and saw that most of the Soviet defense forces around the target were at low-level. He shoved the throttles full forward. Rhombus climbed again. Up and to the northwest they flew. They skirted the northeastern edge of Kiev and swept by the Anotov factory. At 15,000 feet they leveled off. "Soviets have no idea where we are," Brian said as he studied his CRTs. He typed. A target symbol flashed on the SID, superimposed on a concrete building in the distance. On the TopDown, the symbol rested on a spot across the Dneiper River at the confluence of the Pripjat and Uzh rivers. The target was beside the river.

Mike rolled Rhombus upside down.

He jerked the throttles back and pulled Rhombus' nose down.

Straight down the target lay in the center of the SID. Mike

pressed the arming button on his throttle, then squeezed the trigger on his joystick. Within a half-second, two Fleshettes were on their way.

The missiles screamed 8,000 feet in one second and disappeared into the steel and concrete structure beside the water.

Mike rolled Rhombus to the north. He pulled out of the dive and leveled off 200 feet above the ground.

Brian looked at his CRTs. "The defense ring is a shambles. We'll pick our way out easy."

Mike looked at the SID. He agreed.

"Going to rear view," Brian called. He watched the building by the river get smaller as Rhombus sped northward along the Dneiper. "It looks like a small factory," Brian said. "It's got high-tension electrical wires leading to it. I hope we hit it."

"We hit it."

"I know we hit it. So where's the explosion?"

"Maybe it wasn't supposed to explode."

"I don't get it," Brian said. "A target deep in the Soviet Union—cause enough damage so that the Ruskies can't keep it a secret. The damn thing's still there. Beats me."

"Let's get out of here," Mike commanded. "We'll pick our way through the remainder of the circle, then we'll climb to sixty thou or so and head back just the way we came in. Just like we planned."

"Rog," Brian said, his mind still working the puzzle of the building.

Ahead, two threat spheres remained. An open space formed a triangle between them and the earth. Mike maneuvered Rhombus between the two spheres and the ground. "We'll get well clear before we start our climb."

In a minute the spheres passed to the side. Mike eased the throttles forward and the nose up. They were leaving the danger behind.

Brian retrieved a water bag and passed it to Mike. He drank from his own. "Know what?" he asked.

"What?"

"When we get back, let's talk the Skipper into another

thirty-day stand-down. We'll rent the Harleys and head for the Oregon coast."

"OK," Mike said.

Brian stretched and put his hands behind his helmet. "I don't care where we stay. I don't care if it rains or shines. I don't care how long it takes us to get there and get back. I just want one sunset over the coast. Just one sunset where we can lay on a hill, munch on blackberries, and—"

The world flashed white. Then black.

MISSION TIME—11 HOURS: 38 MINUTES
THE DNEIPER HIGHLANDS, THE SOVIET UNION

He lay on his side and she lay with her nude body snuggled against him. His arms were wrapped around her; his hands cupped her breasts. He buried his face into her red hair and kissed the curve of the neck that smelled so sweet. The bulge of her buttocks pressed warm and firm against his groin and squeezed him. She rubbed her calves against his shins as his toes played with the soles of her feet. He dozed, half in and half out of consciousness. Her warmth lay on him like a soft comforter. This was heaven, and he lay, lingering for hours among its clouds.

But where was the music coming from? What kind was it? Louder and louder the strain rolled across the clouds—at first pleasant, then louder as it began to scratch at his nerve endings with tiny bits of sandpaper. The soft warm breeze got colder, causing her to snuggle closer. The chill in her body grew into small shivers. The comforter blew off, and the wind howled in the spaces between their bodies.

"Mike," a voice wheezed from far away.

The music shouted in his ears, carried in by the force of the cold gale. Large drops of cold water spattered against the edges of the open window, shattering into tiny showers that burst upon them.

She became colder than the wind and harder than the driving rain.

Was the noise music, or was it the shattering gale that whistled through the screen door? And what was that thumping sound? Thump, thump, thump, thump, thump. The cold wet wind, the piercing siren—both grabbed at his neck while they wrenched her from his arms.

"Mike. Wake up," the voice came again, its words gurgled through chilled water.

Where is she? I want her back. Don't take her away again!

The seat bit through his clothing. The nylon straps dug into his chest and kept his loose body from folding forward. His head bobbed up and down on his chest. It hurt.

The wind, the wind. Where is it coming from?

His right arm moved out and down, searching for her, and hit metal and plastic. The wind tugged at his glove.

"Mike, wake up."

He fought to hold his head still.

He blinked, hard.

The world spun, streaking his vision with black and white and blue and red.

Black with white letters.

Color CRT screens.

Switches everywhere … and red.

Red everywhere, streaking on the merry-go-round of his swirling vision. Red splatters. Swirling steaks of red.

Oh, my head hurts.

His vision focused and refocused like a projector in an old movie house.

His view of the cockpit was like a crumpled photo being smoothed out on a table.

Blood streamed across his instrument panel, thrown by an invisible bucket from the right side of the cockpit.

It rained blood!

Fly the airplane. Fly the airplane. His training grabbed him, shook him, and told him no matter what, fly the airplane. No matter what was burning, or falling off, or blowing up—no matter what! Fly the airplane!

Mental fog swirled. He slashed away at it. The CRTs moved in and out of focus. Airspeed—430 knots. Altitude—5,100 feet. Attitude—level and a slight descent.

He reached for the joystick. Missed. Shook his head. Reached again. The joystick was stiff, as though someone else had control of the airplane.

"I got it." The voice wheezed through the intercom.

Time? Three minutes had gone by since he passed out.

Heading? North. Rhombus was steady on a north heading.

Fly the airplane. Ahead, in the SID, the Dneiper Highlands rolled beneath.

He pressed the autopilot switch.

It wouldn't hold. He pressed again.

"It doesn't work," the voice gurgled. "I already tried it."

Headache. He put his hand to the side of his helmet. Something had bashed it in, but he didn't feel any blood flowing down his neck.

He flipped his oxygen controller to 100% and sucked in the pure dry gas as his chest heaved.

Like a child's top falling over, Mike's vision bobbled and reversed course, then came to rest.

The cockpit was a shambles—blood, strips of metal, bits of plastic and glass. Brian's instrument panel no longer existed. In its place was a jagged hole, larger than a basketball. Dim light came through. Something had torn through Rhombus' skin. Wind rushed in, a siren carrying the scent of hot electrical wires. Mike looked toward Brian, toward the thumping sound.

"Oh, Brian," he reached out. "Oh, Brian." Brian's left shoulder was ripped open. His right seat strap held him erect. His left strap was shredded and buried in the bloody mass of his wound. The mass pulsed with his heartbeat and squirted blood into the wind. His collarbone stuck out, and so did an empty socket where his arm used to be.

With his sleeve Mike wiped at the blood drops spattering his visor. He reached for his friend.

"No," the voice said.

"Brian, I've got to stop the blee—"

"No." The single word stood on its own, its meaning pure, unclouded by inflection.

"But I've got to stop the—"

"No, Mike. I'm done."

Brian's chest heaved and his chin thrust out. He coughed. Blood sprayed around the seal between his face and the oxygen mask. It blew forward through the exhalation valve. "Let me fly, Michael." Brian's voice rattled. "Let me fly."

"Dear God, Brian. I can't—"

Rhombus hit a pocket of turbulence. Brian cried out. His hand clenched his joystick. His breath was ragged as he forced it out and in. The shock let go, and the pain poured in. Mike heard his teeth grind over the intercom.

"Brian?" No answer. Brian sat like an old Roman statue, impassive, intense, shattered, the remnants of something once great, once alive, and resolved to its fate.

"Damn." Mike reached into his side console, pulled out a canvas roll, and opened it on his thigh. He slipped out a device that looked like a tiny toothpaste tube attached to a hypodermic needle, morphine in the tube. He twisted the cover from the needle and reached for Brian.

"No," the voice rattled. Mike paused. Brian continued, "I flew her while you were out. I saved her when you couldn't. I—I want to fly her—when it matters—while it counts." He turned to Mike. "Just—let me fly."

"You got the airplane, Brian. This will let you fly it farther." He jammed the needle into Brian's thigh through his flight suit and squeezed the tube. He looked at his instruments. Brian had Rhombus headed north. Altitude was 4,200 feet and descending. They were in great jeopardy because the hole in the airplane must have damaged Aurora. If so, every foot above the earth made it easier for the enemy to find them. The safest thing to do was to force Rhombus into a dive and scream into the safety of the low sky. Mike yanked away his apprehension. "OK, buddy. You gotta get us back down."

"I can't—the throttles," the voice gurgled.

Mike winced. Brian's left arm—the arm that normally worked the throttles—was gone. "Rog, I'll work the engines. You call for power."

"Engines back to thirty percent," Brian called.

"Roger, engines coming back. Tachs stable at thirty percent."

Rhombus' nose dropped, and the land eased up toward them.

"You feeling better, Brian?"

"The pain's going away, but I don't have a buzz."

"You won't. When morphine's chasing pain, it won't give you a buzz."

"Then what's the point?"

"Hell if I know, Brian. Hell if I know."

"I'll hold one thousand feet above the ground," Brian said, then ordered, "set the throttles to hold four hundred twenty-five knots." He coughed. "I'd take her down to two hundred feet, but that'd make you nervous."

"No it wouldn't," Mike lied.

"Liar." He sucked in a big breath. "How about I do a loop, then?"

"That would make me nervous. Two thousand above," Mike called as they passed 2,000 feet above the ground.

"Roger, two thousand above." Brian trimmed to reduce their descent, and Mike added power to hold airspeed.

"One thousand five hundred above," Mike called.

"Roger, one thousand five hundred …" Brian's voice faded off.

"One thousand five hundred above," Mike coached.

"One thousand five hundred above," Brian returned. He trimmed Rhombus again and leveled at 1,000 feet above the ground.

Mike added power. "Heading is dead on three hundred sixty degrees. We're headed north."

"Roger," Brian answered. "Keep—" He coughed. Blood sprayed. "Keep those calls coming, Mike." He laughed once, then coughed again.

Mike responded, "Altitude good. Heading good. Oops, airspeed a little low. My fault." He eased the throttles forward.

The SID went awash in red. "We're in a threat sphere!" Mike called. "Got to get her lower."

"Roger," Brian said. "Starting—starting—" he coughed, "down."

Rhombus stayed level. "Down, buddy," Mike reminded as he pulled the throttles back.

Rhombus nosed over. At 750 feet above the ground the threat sphere disappeared. Brian kept the nose down. Mike called, "Five hundred above.

"Four hundred above.

"Three hundred above.

"There's two hundred. Level off."

"One fifty, Brian. One hundred fifty feet above the ground."

"One hundred feet above." Tree tops rushed by.

Mike tensed, his butt raised off his seat.

Rhombus jerked up, climbed to 200 feet, and leveled off. Mike relaxed.

"Scare you?" the voice gurgled.

"Yes."

"Why didn't you take the controls away from me?"

"I trust you."

"Even now?"

"Especially now."

"You want the airplane back?" the voice asked.

"No."

"Sure?"

"Yes."

The breath rattled a time or two more.

"You have the airplane," the voice whispered.

"No. I don't want it."

"You have to—" Brian winced.

"For God's sake, Brian. You fly. I want you to fly. Take us home, Brian. I want you to take us home." Mike looked at his friend. The bloody mass no longer pulsed. Blood no longer squirted. It ebbed like ketchup from a bottle.

The voice gurgled, "You know what to tell my boy and my mom—and—and—" A grin. "Tell—tell Scott that I kept my promise."

Mike didn't ask.

"Go home, Michael. Go home and eat the blackberries." Brian lifted his hand from the joystick and gave a feeble wave. "Co-pilot checking off intercom."

"Roger," Mike said as he reached for the controls. "I have the airplane. The co-pilot's—" his voice cracked. "The co-pilot's cleared off intercom."

Brian bowed his head.

A sigh rushed through the intercom.

A lone sob followed.

Mission Time—11 hours: 48 minutes
The Dneiper Highlands, The Soviet Union

He stared, numb. The back of his brain, the subconscious primal part, moved his hands and guided his airplane over the countryside. A city rolled toward him from the far horizon. Like an unreadable scribble on the margin of a calendar, it poked at his mind and begged for interpretation.

An unrealistic world pulsed. The cockpit seemed to throb. The airplane's sounds were far away. The city moved closer, demanding attention. Inch by inch, Mike's world as it was crept back into his reality.

The hole in Brian's instrument panel still screamed—and there was that thumping sound. He pried his eyes off the land-scape like a parent dividing his attention between the road and a noisy child in the back seat. He looked back. Brian's severed arm was in its sleeve, which was still attached to the rest of the flight suit. It flailed in the wind and hit the map case. Thump, thump, thump.

Mike grabbed the arm, then lifted Brian's seat belt and tucked enough of the torn sleeve beneath it to secure it in place.

He reached across his visor with his left forearm and pulled it back across its Lexan surface. His Nomex flight suit cleaned off enough of Brian's drying blood so that he could see his instruments. He'd give it a better going-over later.

He considered his options, took a deep breath, and let it out in a long slow blow. Decisions rolled at him with the green hills. Each second of delay in making them reduced his options.

A red sphere filled the SID.

Threat Alert flashed in red.

He had let his altitude climb to 1,100 feet.

He dove for the ground.

The screaming from the hole got louder as he hurled his machine toward the safety of the earth.

At 750 feet above the ground, the sphere disappeared. He pulled Rhombus into level flight at 200 feet above the ground.

Got to stay as close as possible to the ground. Got to stay down here until I'm out of the Soviet Union.

The city of Vitsyebsk grew larger in the SID. If he continued due north, he would retrace his route back to Groom Lake. By turning left about 30 degrees now, he would fly the more direct Great Circle route and save about a thousand miles. Doing that would force him to fly over the Baltic, the Gulf of Bothnia, then Sweden and Norway. If the Swedes and the Norwegians see me, they'll think I'm Soviet and maybe shoot. Got to head due north to get out. Blast by Murmansk, then head out over the Barents Sea. Been there. Done that. Do it again.

Mike felt more secure as the seconds ticked by without another sphere appearing. No doubt that radar got a return from me, but with luck, only a sweep or two. Maybe its operator didn't see the blip on his screen.

Minutes passed.

He figured that Rhombus' airframe was still sound. While the air stream was blowing by at 425 knots, it was not entering the cockpit at that speed. Except for the hole, Rhombus was airtight, and for air to come in, it had to have a way out. Still, some wind blew in and out and pushed streaks of thickening blood around. He reached above and flipped a switch on the cockpit pressurization panel to manual, then rotated a knob to increase the air pressure in the cockpit. His ears popped. The wind stopped. Good. The screaming continued, though. *I can't hear myself think.*

Rhombus climbed to 550 feet while Mike's attention was on the pressure problem. A threat sphere popped up on the horizon. He pushed the nose down again. The sphere grew smaller and blinked off. *If I climb, I die. Nobody to blame but me.*

He looked back at the hole in the instrument panel. He couldn't see the hole in the skin, just the light coming in through Brian's panel. He didn't know what shape Aurora was in. Mike knew from computer studies that when Rhombus was holed or lost a skin panel, it was less invisible over the entire airplane—like a flying mirage. But how the whole airplane looked depended on the size and shape of the hole. He had to figure out a way to know for sure.

There was no question the damage made Rhombus more visible to radar. He guessed his radar cross-section was about equal to that of a small Cessna. Normally, such a radar return would be ignored, but this Cessna was doing 425 knots. That wouldn't be ignored. He had to stay low. The SID would still warn him, so that didn't seem to be a major problem.

Rhombus skimmed at a constant altitude over the rolling terrain. Mike's mind was still focused on survival, the primal instinct casting all other considerations aside. He switched the SID to look in all directions for interceptors. He could stay on side, rear, and overhead views for only a second, because without the autopilot, he had to see ahead to fly the giant machine. The earth below was only seconds away.

He flew over farms and he wondered what, if anything, the farmers saw overhead. Just off the right of the nose, a large lake appeared on the other side of a low ridge. It passed off to the side, then moved behind as Mike skirted its bank.

Wait a sec!

Mike rolled Rhombus into a shallow left turn. He turned away from the lake, then back toward it. There it was, ahead, blue and smooth and big.

The shore rolled under the nose.

He flipped a switch that changed the buttons on his joystick from weapons controls to SID controls. He pressed a button and the SID filled with trees 500 feet below and zooming by at 425 knots. Mike looked straight down. He checked his CRTs to make sure he wasn't losing altitude. Trees flashed behind—and there she was, Rhombus reflected in the water.

The news wasn't great, but it wasn't awful, either. Where nothing should have been was now the shape of the giant machine, its color a translucent gray. Rhombus looked like the glass in a bathroom window.

He pressed another button. There, in the water, was the Millennium Falcon, but it was indistinct and unreal.

One by one Mike was answering his survival questions. He could be seen by radar if he didn't hug the earth, and he was visible if someone or something got close enough. He went back to front view on the SID and turned left to head north once again.

A smell nagged him.

Next survival question: What was the hole like? He'd looked, but he couldn't see it when he was over the lake. But what might happen if the air forced itself under the airplane's skin and tore a bigger hole? He decided not to go faster. He would hold as close to 425 knots as he could. Without looking at his charts, he figured he was about 15 hours from Groom Lake at the slower airspeed. He frowned from the shrieking noise of the wind rushing by the hole.

Now, what still works in here? The autopilot's shot—tried that. Have to hand fly it all the way. Jeez, I'm tired. Figured Brian and I would trade off naps on the way back. Been up, let's see—he looked at the clock—forty hours with only a cat nap or two. Fifteen hours to go. Fifty-five hours total. Staying awake will probably be my biggest problem.

That smell. Electrical? Something is hot, burning even.
He looked at each CRT. Normal. Normal. Normal.
Oh, no! A red line flashed across his heading indicator.
The MPP automatically switched to the backup.
A red line flashed across it, too.
The last backup.
Another red line.

He tapped the CRT, an old habit. His heading gyros were out! He leaned to his right and looked up to a point at the top center of the SID. There was the magnetic compass. Regardless of how exotic an airplane was, they all had a magnetic compass as a backup. In all his years of flying, he'd never had to use it.

The big problem with using a magnetic compass is that the magnetic North Pole and the true North Pole are not located at the same spot. It's easy to correct for this problem at lower latitudes, but it's a gigantic problem near the poles. As he flew for the North Pole, he would pass magnetic north to his left. While Rhombus computers automatically dealt with this, Mike would have to compensate manually. There would come a time when to fly true north, he would have to take a southerly heading on his compass. It was something he and Brian had trained for, though.

Gas. Can I make it home? Can't land anywhere else and give the secret away. Next landing will either be at Groom Lake or nowhere. No options. I have to climb to save gas once I'm out of the Soviet Union. Don't know if I can make Groom Lake. Don't know how much more gas it'll take to fly at a lower altitude. Don't know how much drag the hole adds. He looked over to Brian's console to check the fuel. He noted the amount remaining and pressed the stopwatch. I'll fly for ten minutes and see how much gas I'm using.

The MPP was still on-line, so his fuel would be managed for him. From the flight over, he had a pretty good idea of what the winds were. Right now, the priority was to get out of the Soviet Union. Stalingrad was just off the nose.

He wanted TopDown information, but only the co-pilot

could get that. He reached across to Brian's keyboard. It was still in one piece. With his forefinger he type a code that asked for TopDown information. No response. He typed again. No response. Damn! He slapped the keyboard and looked back at the SID.

Rhombus had rolled into a right turn and was 25 degrees off heading. "Damn!" He'd let the airplane get away from him. Disgusted, he slapped the joystick. Rhombus snapped into left bank. Mike heard a thump on his right. Still angry, he snapped Rhombus out of the turn when he was back on his original heading.

What the hell!

Like the arm of a metronome, Brian's body swayed one way, then the other, as Mike rolled Rhombus left and right. Brian's body slipped through his torn left shoulder strap and crashed across him. Blood dumped on his lap. Burgundy clots slid over his thighs and the edge of his seat and plopped on the metal floor. Red blood seeped through his flight suit, flowed down his crotch, and pooled between his butt cheeks. He made no attempt to pull his friend's body away.

He stroked Brian's back as if to comfort him. He twisted at small strands of his hair that showed beneath the back of the helmet. He rubbed the beaded chain that held his dog tags and fingered the gold chain his son Brad had given him last Christmas for good luck. He flew for long minutes, impervious to any outside threat, uncaring about life and death, unmoved by the past and unflinching about the future. He flew while he comforted his friend's dead body. Dreams of sunsets and blackberry patches fell away and buried themselves among the green forests and mirrored lakes of western Russia.

He patted the back of Brian's helmet. "Sorry, buddy. I'll be more careful. I promise." He pushed Brian back into his seat. Blood dropped in globs on the center console and the floor.

Mike pulled Rhombus up to gain a little altitude. While cross-checking his compass to make sure the airplane stayed on course, he adjusted Brian's straps until he was sure the body would stay upright. He pulled on Brian's hand so he could secure the damaged arm under the seat strap.

It slid out of the sleeve and Mike's tugging pulled it onto his lap.

He stared, mouth open. Brian's arm lay in his lap—the arm that held the coffee mug, the one Brian put around Mike's shoulder at the funerals. He considered the arm's pale color and blood-smeared hair. The chill of death came from it. Frustration and horror covered Mike's face. He looked around for a place to put it. He didn't know what to do with it.

"Christ Jeeeesuuuuus! What have you dooooone!" His scream forced its way out of the rubber oxygen mask where it competed with the screeching wind. His head spun and a veil of blackness descended.

He threw the arm to the right.

His stomach rolled.

He groped for the connector that held his mask in place.

His blood-slicked gloves slipped on the release.

He was too late.

His insides gushed up and into the mask.

The vomit squirted around the mask's edges and through the exhalation valve onto his chest. Yellow bits of bile and food hit the CRTs and slid down their glass faces, leaving slimy trails.

He choked.

Can't breathe!

His eyes opened wide as his bloody gloves slipped on the mask connector. He held his breath to keep from drowning on the yellow pool in his mask while his stomach rolled and forced its way up again.

The clasp clicked.

The mask burst away.

A chunky spray ejected from his mouth.

His lungs gasped for air while his stomach turned inside out.

Bulging eyes through a scarlet face tried to see to fly as he convulsed and shot his insides everywhere.

Vomit turned down his windpipe, cut his breath off.

Can't breathe!

The world dimmed. Got to fight—fight.

He locked both hands together, formed a fist, hit himself below the ribcage.

Vomit shot from his windpipe.

Heaving coughs and gasps for air fought each other.

Narrow dark vision became brighter. Focus—focus—keep flying—keep your head up—keep flying.

Breaths came in ragged raspy rushes.

Coughs poured out in heaving belching sprays.

It took a minute or two until the last of the liquid erupted from his lungs and his breathing mellowed to deep inhalations.

His shoulders fell with exhaustion. The stench of puke now mixed with the smell of blood.

He wiped his mouth and face with his sleeve.

He'd climbed a little, so he reduced his altitude back to a couple hundred feet above the ground.

He gagged on the fetid air. But—

He lived.

♦ ♦ ♦

"Sir. Sir? Captain Patterakis, you awake?"

Patterakis raised his head from the console in the CIC to see the large display on the wall in front of him. It comprised three giant TV screens. The left screen was blank, the center screen displayed a map of the earth, and the one on the right displayed the portion of the earth in the vicinity of Murmansk. "Yeah. It's OK. How long I been out?"

"Not long, sir," the chief responded. "Only about an hour, but we have a problem."

"What is it?" Patterakis asked, the web of deep sleep tearing away.

"We didn't get our scheduled SatBurst," the chief responded.

"When was the last one?" Patterakis asked.

"You saw it, sir. The one we got when we hit the target." Patterakis reached for a stale glass of water. "What do we do now, Captain?" the chief asked.

Patterakis pondered the bottom of the glass and rolled it so that a single drop raced in a circle. "We wait. Notify the White House."

It had been two hours since he hit the target. A sickly ache injected itself into his body. Long steel pins punched through the marrow of his bones. Flying a couple hundred feet above the ground at 425 knots rode a razor-fine line. Every second, every single second, required his full attention. Too high and he might be picked up by radar. Too low, and, well, too low is too low. What he'd been doing for two hours was the equivalent of a car driver placing his right wheels on the white line at the side of a curvy highway and never, ever, allowing the tires to leave it. The dull heat of fatigue built behind his eyes, and dehydration added an ever-sharpening bang to the back of the brain.

He'd been sitting in the same seat for hours. Brian's blood caked on his lap and in his crotch. Mike couldn't clean the blood from the control switches, because his priority had been flying. He didn't know what effect the blood would have on the switches until he needed them. He had wanted to poke around the cockpit, try to figure out what blasted the hole in his airplane, but he didn't dare. Right now, life involved a specific order of priorities and strict adherence to following it. Investigation wasn't a priority.

Murmansk lay off the nose and beyond it the Barents Sea. In the SID Mike saw threat spheres, but they were dispersed. A sphere appeared off the coast. Probably the same ship that almost saw us coming in.

Murmansk fell away to the right and with it the tundra of the northern Russian coast. Farther and farther the coast fell behind and on the radar CRT it showed as a jagged horizontal line with islands here and there. The line crossed the 10-mile range mark, and then, in a few seconds it passed 12 miles. He was out of the Soviet Union.

He eased the throttles forward. The nose rose. He climbed to 15,000 feet. He no longer needed to keep the wheels on the white line. Leveling off, he pulled the throttles back and relaxed. He rubbed the knots in his shoulder muscles and squeezed the back of his neck. He rolled his head around and tried to stretch his legs. On the radar CRT he watched the northern coast of Norway to the west.

I'll take a great circle route from this point back to Groom Lake—clear the Norway coast, then make a shallow left turn until my heading is 30 degrees west of true north. He fingered a line on the map from where he was to somewhere close to Montana. If I can get back to the States—piece of cake once I'm there. His finger retraced the line. Let's see. Longyearbyen is ahead at the southern tip of the Svalsbard, then across Greenland and Baffin Island, Hudson Bay, and Manitoba. Then, Montanahhhhh. Still got ol' SID here, so I can see where I'm going. He made another attempt at realigning the direction gyros. Damn.

"Gas? Gas!" He leaned across Brian to check the fuel panel. He had about 80,000 pounds left, and the engines were using about 10,000 pounds per hour at this altitude. Not enough to make Groom Lake. The low altitude and the drag caused by the hole were having an effect. He'd better climb. Oh, hell. Got to put the mask back on. Mike looked at his mask. Chunks of half-digested food and drying streaks of bile coated the inside. He put it to his face while he held his breath. He looked down to his oxygen panel and inhaled. He gagged, but nothing came up. The oxygen-flow meter didn't blink. The mask's valve was stuck. He looked across the cockpit at Brian, whose mask dangled from the side of his helmet. Mike reached around him and unlatched the far clasp. He tugged on the mask, the accordion hose stretching like a phone cord. He pulled until he thought the hose would tear. The quick-connect popped, shot across the cockpit in front of Mike's face, and smacked hard against the SID display at his side. He disconnected his own mask and stowed it in an empty map case. He connected Brian's mask. It worked, and it didn't smell so bad.

Rhombus bounced. It bounced again.

He typed on Brian's keyboard to select Video on the SID. The sky was nothing but gray. He was in clouds. He heard a roar.

A torrent of rainwater poured through the hole in Brian's instrument panel.

It sprayed the right instrument console and circuit-breaker panel. It hit Brian's body and blasted blood off his helmet.

Don't have time or fuel to work my way around this squall. Got to go through it.

He pressed the throttles forward and pulled the nose up. He passed 20,000 feet, Still, the rain came in. At 22,000 feet it stopped. He leveled off.

The squall had been a light one, so light, in fact, that the MPP did not trigger an alarm that it was ahead. But flying through a light rain at 425 knots put hundreds of thousands of gallons of water over Rhombus, and hundreds through the hole. The cockpit had been designed to handle some water, but this had been a deluge. An inch of rainwater sloshed on the cockpit floor. Lazy twists of blood swirled with bits of flesh as the liquid disappeared.

The water was gone. Where? He knew where.

A rush of adrenaline pushed the fatigue away.

He waited.

The hole screeched.

He looked across the array of multicolored CRT displays.

The SID washed the cockpit with light blue light.

Then it happened.

The lights went out.

The CRTs blinked and turned black.

The SID flashed, narrowed to a horizontal lighted band, then shrunk to a white dot that blinked off.

The darkness was total.

The devastation was complete.

Mike sat in the dark. No fear. No pain. No hope. Death lay ahead, a dark stranger selling the drug of infinity, beckoning him to the world of painless silence. Whatever the stranger promised, it was better than this, better than the loneliness, better than telling himself that God had a purpose in taking Kachina and his children. Better than breathing the air that contained the stench of Brian's insides. Better than the rolling waves of nausea and pounding fatigue. Better than anything. Death was the ultimate drug, the greatest high, the most fulfilling pleasure. It was within reach. Pull the throttles back and just sit here and wait. Won't even see it coming. Airplane'll dive into the water, and it'll be over. Everything. The pain, the responsibility, the secret—everything. He tightened his hand around the joystick and reached for the throttles. He pulled them back. The CJs spooled down and Rhombus descended. Five minutes until it happens? Ten minutes? It doesn't matter. Eject? And do what? Hang in the parachute straps while Rhombus disappears down in the distance? Hear the thump when it hits the water? Land in the freezing ocean, have it shock me wide-awake so I can enjoy the pleasure of dying while my blood turns to slush? Oh, you bet. When Rhombus hit the water, the metal in front of him would tear him to shreds before it registered in his brain. He wouldn't even see it. Maybe he could go to sleep on the way down.

He looked to his right as his eyes adjusted. Weak Arctic light eased through the hole and dropped dim blue shadows in the corner of the cockpit like a tired old fluorescent light in a New York alley.

His head dropped. Sleep came on rushing tiptoes, and it carried a grab-bag of warm memories and fitful dreams.

Dad. Dad is out there in the river. Out in the riffles spincasting for bass, wearing a baseball cap with lures stuck in it. It's late afternoon and the sun is setting on the crest of the gorge, casting a growing shadow across the sparkles on the water. Damselflies circle in the sunlight like a shimmering doily rolled into a vertical cylinder.

My Daddy. I love my Daddy, Jimmy. He makes me behave. He doesn't let me give up.

My Dad is an amazing man, Kachina. The day he went to college, he had twenty dollars in his pocket, and the only clothing to his name was the old hand-me-down suit he was wearing. He walked twenty-eight miles that day from his home in the little town of Sandstone. He worked every day to put himself through school. He got up every morning at four a.m., stoked the boarding-house furnace, then cooked and served breakfast. The day he graduated he caught the train to go to war.

Dad died holding my hand, Mom. It was so sudden, I didn't have time to come get you. He loved you more than anything else in the world. The last thing he said was, "Take care of your mom, and tell her I love her." He was in so much pain, Mom. It was time.

Isn't that pretty? Grandpa's church sitting among the trees, the sound of singing flowing out its windows.

Amazing Grace, how sweet the sound that save a wretch like me.
I once was lost, but now I'm found. Blind but now I see.

"I'm sorry, Mrs. Christum. You son and Brian Davis were killed on a mission yesterday."

Brian's mother rocking in the living room as she cried and prayed they would find her son.

Mom sitting on the couch, crying, asking God why he hadn't taken her instead.

Lying in my bed with the soft air coming through the window and my arms wrapped around Beanie Bear. Sleepy. Mom helping me remember the words.

Now I lay me down to sleep,
I pray the Lord my soul to keep,
If I should die before I wake,
I pray the Lord my soul to take.

Something nagged at his newfound peace. It pulled at him, a small ritual, forgivable if forgotten but important, like an untied shoelace.

A flash of adrenaline pulled him back for one last thing. His mother had taught him to pray before he went to sleep. He always had, but he almost forgot this time. His lips barely moved. Almighty God, I ask your forgiveness for the wrongs I have done, and I pray the world is better for my passing. I hope I have pleased you. In the name—

The adrenaline was spent. Mike collapsed against his shoulder straps.

1986

REDEMPTION

Chug, chug, chug.

Chug, chug, chug.

When God spoke, it was never like the old movies. Few had seen flaming bushes, heard a voice from a mountain, or saw the sea part. To the believer, God sometimes spoke through the voices of others and sometimes through the world around them. Sometimes He spoke from the past.

Chug, chug, chug.

He stared into the haze of his dream, the captain of a tired old boat finding his way through a Louisiana fog.

"'Chug, chug, chug,' the little engine said. 'I know I can. I know I can. I know I can.'" The young woman's voice rolled through the dream haze, confidant and loving. He remembered the voice.

"Mom?" he questioned the fog.

"Up, up, up the mountain the engine went, pulling all the cars with all the toys. Chug, chug, chug, until, at last, they reached the top of the mountain. 'Hooray,' the toys shouted as the little engine went down the other side. 'Christmas will come this year for all the girls and boys, because the little engine wouldn't give up.' As the little engine went down the other side of the mountain, he thought it wasn't so hard after all. He chugged, and he chugged, 'I knew I could, I knew I could, I knew I could.' And all the toys shouted, 'We knew you could, too.'"

A whooshing sound came off the starboard beam. He turned the boat toward it. The fog glowed at first, far above the jungle canopy on the horizon. The glow grew more intense as though a flare dropped through it, ever faster. It wasn't a flare. It was an airplane. An A-7. Mike watched the flaming jet bore a hole through the haze while the sound it made became silence, a silence rendered gallant by Danno Riley, who refused his fate and fought for life until the airplane crashed into the jungle in the distance.

The sound of a beating heart pulsed and sent circling waves away from the sides of the boat. Familiar perfume wafted across the water and spun with the lazy miniature tornadoes that rose from the surface. "It's here, Michael," she said, "that I do what I can to keep you alive."

"Be damned," someone spoke. "She tried to save her baby."

The little engine roared from Mike's childhood bedside while memories of Danno, Brian, and Kachina reached for him. Like unwanted lessons and nasty-tasting medicine, his memory tore at his resolve to die, tore at his selfish commitment and his disregard of all he loved and respected.

"No-o-o-o-o-o," he screamed at the dank cockpit. "No-o-o-o-o-o-o-o!"

"Go home, Michael. Go home and eat the blackberries."

"I want my family back! I deserve to have them back."

"Be damned. She tried to save her baby."

"Don't do this to me, God. Please don't do this to me. I miss them so much, and I'm so tired. Please take me back."

"Be damned. She tried to save her baby."

"Oh, God."

"You know what to tell my boy and my mom—and—and—tell your brother I kept my promise. Go home, Michael. Go home and eat the blackberries."

He tore the helmet off his head and slammed it into his lap. He slapped at his own face. Tears rolled. White knuckles clenched the armrests. He threw his head back and screamed, "No-o-o-o-o-o-o-o-o-o-o-o-o-o!"

The warplane glided downward in the Arctic sky, toward the sea, its idled engines whining, its skin glimmering in the low sun. From the hole in its nose came the siren wind and the anguish of its lonely pilot. It wasn't his time, and those he loved were showing the way.

His breath came in heaving gulps. A tooth chipped under grinding teeth. He eased the joystick back and put the throttles in a position to give him a shallow climb. His breathing slowed to irregular huffs as he fought to control himself.

Rhombus climbed away from the sea. Mike's bloodshot eyes looked at his brave friend who had smiled through it all and died with honor. Brian had carried him through the tough time. He patted Brian's leg. "I'll get you home, buddy. I'll get you home."

A yellow light pierced the darkness.

"Oh, no."

It was the Master Caution light. He pressed on the light to extinguish it. It called his attention to a series of lights on his side console. Each light showed the failure of a separate electrical system. Only two were not lit, meaning only two systems worked. They were MPP Computer and Isolated AC. He smiled. Thank you, God. At least something works. He pushed the throttles a little more to increase his climb.

More light flashed on. It was from the two B-4 map lights on either side of the cockpit. Rhombus was fixing herself. "C'mon. C'mon. C'mon," Mike chanted with his eyes closed. "Dear God. Please turn the SID back on. Please turn the SID back on. Please?" He opened one eye just a crack. He winced, then opened both eyes. The SID was black. He was still in an airplane he couldn't see out of.

He checked his compass. He was headed in the right direction and the compass wasn't changing. That meant he flew a straight course and that the wings were level. The noise from the wind hurt his ears. He put his helmet back on. Better.

He had to climb as high as he could to preserve fuel, but he had no altimeter. Couldn't go too high or he'd pass out. Too low and he'd hit something—probably the Rockies. What to do? What? What? What? He refastened his mask. Wait! That's it! Pressure breathing! At 31,000 feet the pressure of the atmosphere falls below that of the gases in the human body, so the blood gases rush out, even if the pilot is on pure oxygen. Pressurizing the cabin normally solves this problem. Because of the hole, Rhombus had no cabin pressure, so the oxygen system had to apply it by forcing the gas into the lungs and forcing the pilot to exhale. It was perhaps the most tiring thing a human being can do, because it made a person conscious of every breath, and every breath was a labored one—like asthma in reverse. Mike reasoned that he would climb to a point where the pressure breathing started, then play with the throttles to hold an altitude where the pressure would be barely evident. That would put him near 31,000 and would be high enough to get over anything.

Altitude problem solved.

He reached behind and to the left of his seat. Feeling a metal door, he opened it and extracted a large loose-leaf binder. His eyes were compensating for the weak light in the cockpit. He opened the binder to the Electrical section and pulled a finger down the page until it came to "Bus, Electrical, Isolated AC."

As he studied, he glanced at his magnetic compass. Its numerals glowed like an old luminous watch. After a few minutes, Mike figured out what components still worked. Aurora was OK, so he was partially invisible, as he saw over that lake in Russia. Big deal, he would gladly trade it for the SID. The MPP was still on line. Good. All engines and hydraulic systems were still working. He had no airspeed indicator, and no altimeter. He had no fuel indicator. He had no radios. He had cabin heat. He had the needle-ball instrument.

The needle-ball was a basic flight instrument, just like the magnetic compass. The needle moved left and right to show Mike when he was turning. The ball was mounted in a tube filled with oil that was curved up, like a smile. If the ball was at the center of the smile, the airplane would be in coordinated flight. If it was to either side of the smile, he would be either skidding or slipping through the sky. He had to keep the ball centered.

He could get by without his airspeed indicator. He had more than 2,000 flying hours in Rhombus and knew what throttle setting produced what airspeed at different altitudes. He didn't have engine instruments, but he knew the sound of the CJs. He had always set his throttles by sound, anyway, so he wasn't too worried about airspeed. He also knew the feel of his airplane at different airspeeds. Landing would be a big problem. It was where airspeed was most critical. Too fast and he would overshoot the landing. Too slow and he would stall. Stalling was not a problem. When Rhombus came close to a stall, a shudder filled the airframe. All he had to do was to nudge those wonderful little CJ engines, and airspeed increased quickly.

He checked his compass.

Shoot, I got this thing down to only three problems: How do I know where I am? Do I have enough fuel to get to where I want to go? How do I see the runway? I got the situation pretty well in hand. Yeah. Lost, blind, and running out of gas—no sweat!

He checked his compass.

He replaced the flight manual and opened another case. After running a thumb along the top of a series of navigational charts, he pulled one out and replaced the others.

He checked his compass.

He figured he was an hour past Murmansk and over Spitsbergen, the major city on a group of islands about 500 miles north of Norway. He unfolded the chart. Reaching in the case once more, he retrieved a metal and plastic device, a navigational computer that worked like a slide rule. He used its straight edge to draw a line from Spitsbergen to Groom Lake.

He checked his compass.

From the angle the line intersected the chart's north-south lines, he knew what true heading he needed to take. From that, he used his chart to determine what magnetic heading he needed to take.

He checked his compass and rolled right about five degrees to set up on his computed heading. He reset the stopwatch to zero, then pressed start. He should be home in 8.4 hours.

Gas? Well, there was either enough or there wasn't. Hopefully, by being near 30,000 feet, he'd extended his range enough to make Groom Lake. If he ran out, he would do the best he could to steer toward an uninhabited area, then he would command eject both himself and Brian. He would use the survival radios and the locator beacons to summon help.

He checked his compass.

Wait a minute! We do have radios, Brian. I can use the survival radios in the survival packs under our ejection seats. Problem is, will I disarm the seats if I try to get to them? We got time to think about that one. Lots of time.

He pulled out the water bag and drank nearly all of it, which wasn't enough. He needed to save a few ounces for something he had to do. Besides, there was still water in Brian's bag, plus the extra bag they carried beside Brian's seat.

There were 3,600 miles to go, and each went by like drops from a slow leak. He imagined someone locking him in a dark closet with a bucket that held 3,600 drops of water, and that he was given an eye dropper and told the door would be unlocked after he bailed the bucket out with the dropper only one drop every 10 seconds or so. One drop down, three thousand five hundred ninety-nine to go. Another drop down, three thousand five hundred ninety-eight to go. As the miles rolled by, each seemed longer than the one before it. The long pins still bore holes in his bone marrow, the hot pressure thudded behind his eyes, his heart beat a hammer in the back of his head, the blood in his lap crackled, his eyes invented things to see in the dim cockpit, the dry cotton of thirst clogged his throat, and the screaming siren from the hole slashed at his hearing. Mike settled into his seat and tried to make himself as comfortable as possible. Home was three thousand five hundred and ninety-five drops of water away.

He checked his compass.

MISSION TIME—17 HOURS: 27 MINUTES
NORTHWEST TERRITORIES (APPROXIMATELY)
CANADA

Things are going just perfect. Really. My ears don't hurt anymore. That's probably because they're ruined.

Mike's breath was a white cloud in the near freezing cockpit. Several hours ago, he'd turned the cockpit heat down to stay awake. It was working. He shivered, sometimes violently.

It was five hours ago that he pressed the start button on his stopwatch over Spitsbergen—or at least over where he thought was Spitsbergen. He continuously checked his heading on the compass. There was little else to do. He'd trimmed Rhombus to fly at an altitude that barely caused his oxygen regulator to force oxygen into his lungs. He set the throttles to give him the sound pitch from the engines he wanted. Somehow he could hear their lower whine through the shrieking of the hole. He hoped he'd compensated enough for the drag so that his airspeed was close to 425 knots per hour. From what he remembered of the winds on the trip over, he used an old manual computer to figure what heading he had to take to correct for winds. He also calculated his speed over the ground. During the times he used the device, he'd turn the heat up so his shivering would stop and he could use his hands. He worked it quickly, because as the warm air bathed his body, he'd nod off.

At least every 15 minutes, he checked his navigational charts to determine the difference between true course and magnetic course. He also had to correct his heading for the crosswind. It was like anchoring a boat in the middle of the Mississippi, then jumping in at the shore and swimming to it with his eyes closed. Before jumping into the water, he had to determine which direction he had to swim to correct for the flow, then he had to estimate how long it would take him to get there. This form of navigation was called "dead reckoning." Lindbergh had used it to cross the Atlantic. Mike was using it to cross the Arctic.

Mike thought of Lindbergh's flight. Mike had four engines to Lindbergh's one, but he'd gladly trade three of them for a window. There would come a time, he knew, that he'd trade all four engines for a window. No matter how much money you spend on an airplane, things can happen to it that make it no more capable than the Wright Flyer. Most of the technology that surrounded him was dead.

MISSION TIME—21 HOURS: 17 MINUTES
1117 HOURS (11:17 AM), GROOM LAKE TIME

Mike had reduced his altitude to what he figured was 25,000 feet. Now he could remove his oxygen mask for a short time without risking unconsciousness. The damned thing was killing him, and his lungs ached from the pressure breathing. He squeezed the connector that latched the mask to his helmet. As the mask pulled away, it tugged at his skin and revealed the deep creases it had made where it sealed itself to his face. Pulling the mask away delivered a sensation so wondrous, it forced all the other points of irritation out of reality, but then, Mike took in a partial breath and the thick stench of the cockpit poured down his windpipe like rancid molasses, stopping his breath midstream. He clenched his teeth and forced his tongue against the roof of his mouth as he fought the retching that pressed up from his stomach. He jammed the mask back on and looked around. The cockpit was filled with a gooey mixture of body parts, blood, and vomit all ripened with rainwater. He relaxed as he took long pulls on the oxygen. The mask's irritation was better than the smell. His was a world of lesser evils.

He looked at the needle-ball indicator. It was steady. He arched his back and stretched. As his muscles lengthened, he brought his arms back. His left hand scraped against the SID panel to his left side. His right hand hit … Oh, God!

He tensed and squinted to his right.

In the very dim light he saw his right fist buried in Brian's mangled body.

He breathed hard as he sat, looking ahead, unmoving.

He pulled his fist away. It was cold and wet, and dripped snotty strands of blood.

He wiped the hand under his left armpit.

He closed his eyes and sucked on the oxygen. He rocked back and forth in his seat, while faint begging words beat through his mask to be swallowed by the noise from the hole. Gradually, the rocking stopped, as did the begging. He opened his eyes and hoped to see the beauty of the sky and drew strength from it as he had done so many times before. The dead SID reflected a portrait of him painted by the faint light and held in front of him by technology reduced to a black mirror. There he was, blood-speckled helmet, oxygen mask, and red eyes sunk into black sockets—a smudge of a man sitting in hell.

He opened a small metal door mounted in his side console and retrieved a foot-long red-cloth streamer attached to a three-inch-long device shaped like a T. He inserted the long part into a hole drilled in his ejection seat. His ejection seat was now on safety—it couldn't be fired. He lifted a small lever in his lap to unfasten his seat belt. He maneuvered the belts and shoulder straps to the side of the ejection seat and pushed the seat back, away from the controls. While keeping his eye on the needle-ball to make sure Rhombus stayed level, he took off his left flight boot and his long cotton sock, then put the boot back on. He then started to breathe hard, hyperventilating on the pure oxygen. When dizziness began to overtake him, he held his breath, then unsnapped his oxygen mask and removed his helmet. He looked at the dried blood splattered across the visor. It had to be clean for what was to come.

He retrieved his water bag and dribbled a stream on the visor, then rubbed at the goo with his sock. Still holding his breath, he repeated the procedure several times until his body's demand for oxygen overtook him.

He put the helmet back on and fastened his mask. He breathed hard, like a swimmer under the water too long. He saw small smudges on the visor and wiped at each with the sock until it was clear. He flung the sock over his shoulder.

He hyperventilated on the oxygen again, removed his mask, then rose up in his seat. His flight suit crackled as the dried blood in the fabric fractured. As he straightened out, the crust in his crotch yanked out his pubic hairs—on a normal day a major event, like a dripping faucet on a quiet night, but now only an incremental increase in consuming misery, like a dripping faucet in a flooding house.

He reached behind Brian's seat and pulled the tip of the second plastic water bag. The flaccid vessel had dripped its entire contents through holes caused by the shrapnel of Brian's bursting instrument panel. He groped for the extra water bag, eyes wide. Oh, no. The shrapnel got it, too. His thirst seemed immediately worse.

Now comes the hard part. If I'm gonna see outside this thing, there's only one chance I have. I have to fly it from Brian's seat. He lowered his visor and stretched across Brian to open a metal door in the co-pilot's side console. From the console he retrieved another ejection seat T pin. He safetied Brian's seat and released Brian's seat belt. He reached between his co-pilot's legs and pulled a small lever sideways to push the seat back so he could move Brian's body.

The seat shot back against the rail stops.

Mike spilled forward, over Brian, head down into his lap. He hit Brian's joystick.

Rhombus slammed to the right and threw him against the left side of the cockpit.

He landed across his seat. Pain shot through his kidneys and turned his vision into white flashes.

Rhombus rolled faster.

Brian's body lifted out of its seat.

Mike fought to stay conscious.

Through his clearing vision, he saw Brian's shattered body just as it hit him full force.

He reached around Brian for something to hold on to.

He grabbed his joystick, a mistake.

Rhombus rolled back left. The G fell to zero as the airplane nosed over.

Their bodies lifted to the ceiling.

Mike's hands flailed.

He grabbed one of the handles on the overhead console, then shoved at Brian's body.

It flew back across the cockpit and landed behind the co-pilot's seat.

He groped for his headrest and pulled himself into the seat. He latched his seatbelt and grabbed the joystick and the throttles.

He had no idea what Rhombus was doing.

He looked at his needle-ball instrument. The ball was centered. That was good, but the needle was off to the right. That told him he was turning right, a boat in a whirlpool. If he banked one way or the other until the needle centered, it would mean he was no longer turning. Then, if he was right side up, pulling the joystick would raise the nose skyward. If he was upside down, pulling the joystick would throw him into a steeper dive—fifty-fifty odds.

He rolled to the left.

A beam flashed from the right side of the cockpit.

His eyes stabbed at it.

Sunlight!

It was glorious, beautiful, miraculous sunlight!

The beam blasted through the hole and hit Brian's seat. Rhombus' nose was pointed at the sun! His nose was up!

He looked at the needle-ball. The needle was centered. "Hot damn!"

He sucked his tongue against the roof of his mouth. He knew from experience that when he did this, the soft tissue in the back of his mouth moved slightly because of the lower air pressure when he was above 4,000 feet above sea level. It didn't move! He was below 4,000 feet! If he was in high country, he was in serious trouble.

Climb!

He jammed the throttles forward. He was climbing.

At light weight, Rhombus climbed at more than 75,000 feet per minute. In just a few seconds he'd be above any mountain in the world.

He pulled the throttles back and pushed forward on the joystick. The sunbeam traveled a small distance across the cockpit and went away. Good. The needle-ball was steady. He listened for the pitch of the CJs. They sounded about right for level flight.

He did some mild cause-and-effect maneuvering while watching the needle-ball and listening to the intensity of the shrieking hole. As he changed airspeed, the shriek rose or lowered in pitch. The pitch was steady, and he was no longer turning, so Mike was satisfied Rhombus was in stable, straight, and level flight.

Gee, I feel good all of a sudden. This is neat. He put his hands in front of him and wiggled his fingers. Why do I have blue fingernails? I've seen them like this before. Where? Where? Altitude chamber! I'm hypoxic!

The high altitude sucked the oxygen from Mike's body in a painless stream that left bliss as its calling card.

The edges of his vision darkened.

He fumbled with the oxygen mask and forced it onto his face. He didn't get the blast of oxygen.

He looked down at his oxygen regulator. The white flow indicator didn't move. He flung the switches back and forth. No flow. He had to get to Brian's oxygen quick or he'd die.

He yanked his oxygen hose from the regulator.

He moved across the cockpit, threw himself into Brian's seat.

He stabbed his oxygen hose at the receptacle in Brian's oxygen regulator.

He missed.

Tried again.

Missed.

The edges of his vision pressed in, a narrowing tunnel.

He held the hose on the regulator and scooted it around, trying to find the right angle where the hose would slip into the receptacle.

One more try.

Just—

one—

more—

try.

The tip of the hose moved around the rim of the receptacle like a basketball slowly circling the hoop after a last-second shot.

Slower—

Slower—

Except for a tiny part in the very center, Mike's vision was gone.

Slower—

He crumbled forward. The metal hose connector scraped across the receptacle—then clicked into place.

The mask puffed against his face as it filled the soft rubber seal with pressurized oxygen. His world reintroduced itself as his vision expanded. The noise came back, the pinpricks in his crotch returned, the sewer-like cockpit filled his view.

He tightened the mask against his face and had to force his breath out. He was above 31,000 feet. The screaming wind dropped in pitch. Airspeed dropped. Mike reached for the seat lever between his legs and pulled it to the side. He grabbed a handle on the instrument panel and pulled himself forward.

He peered through the shambles of the instrument panel and saw that the angels had moved a curtain back to show heaven's light. Through the twisted metal and shattered glass he saw the most beautiful sight he'd ever seen.

Blue sky.

He grabbed the controls. Rhombus ran low on airspeed and its nose dropped. Mike saw another beautiful sight. Earth. Green earth. Glorious green earth. A green and brown horizon now moved from the bottom of the hole until it squeezed the sky out at the top. Mike eased the throttles forward so that the nose wouldn't fall too fast. He lowered the seat as much as he could and trimmed Rhombus so that the horizon stabilized near the top of the hole. Rhombus was in a shallow descent and airspeed was increasing. The screaming started again.

He held his hand toward the hole. Amazing. Almost no air coming through, yet it's going by outside at more than 400 miles per hour.

He smiled as he looked at the wonderful world below. The needle-ball on this side of the cockpit was destroyed, but being able to see out was better. Can't lose sight of the horizon or I'm dead meat.

He shifted his attention to the damage. The instruments on the right side were shattered. Square bits of safety glass were everywhere, all covered with Brian's flesh and blood, looking like diced red peppers and strings of meat smothered with ketchup. The hole in the instrument panel was about a foot across. He leaned forward. Whatever hit them entered the airplane dead on, and the air stream had rolled the skin back. The wound in the skin was about two feet high and six feet wide.

Mike glanced at the magnetic compass. Keeping on course was easier now because he could pick out a point on the horizon and fly to it, rather than checking the compass so often.

He pulled out a small flashlight from a pocket on his upper left sleeve. He shone it at the rubble behind the instrument panel. Torn metal bent toward him. Broken and blackened wire bundles twisted and looped. What the hell did this?

He jerked.

In placing his concentration on the hole, he'd let Rhombus' nose fall. He couldn't see the horizon.

He nudged the joystick. It wasn't so bad. The horizon was

close, but the shock of being in trouble again jarred him wide awake. What a great plan. If I almost die every half-hour or so, I'll stay awake.

The horizon appeared again at the top of the hole. He was banked to the left. He corrected and found his navigational spot on the horizon.

He was making more and more mistakes. His brain felt like it had been shot full of Novocain. He swore at the ever-growing mental numbness.

He aimed his flashlight into the hole again. His eyes darted between the scenery outside and the jumbled mass behind the instrument panel. What caused this? The search was impossible because he couldn't take his concentration off the scenery for too long, couldn't adjust his eyes to the darkness, couldn't focus.

He turned off his flashlight and jammed it back into the pocket.

Now, where the hell am I?

Nothing was familiar. Where, where, where?

He shook his head at the numbness, a dog shaking water from his ears. Damn. He pressed his eyelids together, then opened them wide—repeatedly. He slapped his thighs. Stay awake—awake—awake—too close to let go—too—

His head nodded, then jerked back.

I can't—I gotta—

His head dropped. His chin hit his chest.

Like a splash of cold water, fear wrenched him awake. His skin tingled. The feeling was familiar.

He watched the earth roll by below as the tingling faded.

Gotta do it. I know I can. I know I can.

He turned the temperature down. The chill splashed over him. His hands shivered like an old man with palsy.

He grinned, then broke into laughter. Silly, stupid, pointless, humorless, his laughter rolled out. "A fifteen billion dollar Armageddon machine, and right now I'd give my left nut for a Piper Cub. What am I saying? I'd give both nuts for a Piper Cub." Tears rolled down his cheeks. Mike made the mental swing beyond pain. Long-distance runners called it passing through the wall.

The rolling good-time giddiness was his worst enemy, because it would carry him to hell while making him look forward to the trip. It would take him on a roller coaster ride whose last dive ended at the bottom of a cliff.

"What!" He leaned forward. "I know that. I know that. It's … it's …" He pointed a feeble shaking finger.

He'd flown over it a dozen times—at least a dozen.

It was a blue lopsided arrowhead buried in the green carpet of landscape that rolled by beneath him.

"Oh, God. What is it?" he pleaded.

Laughter changed to anger, then to hair-pulling frustration. "I know what that is! I know what that is! Lake—Lake—No. Fort something! Fort—Fort—Fort—Fort Peck Lake! Yessssssssss! Hello America!" Tears welled. America opened her arms.

He was over Larslan, Montana. He turned Rhombus more to the west and pointed the nose toward the town of Grass Range. As the little town passed beneath him, Mike wagged his wings to a friend who grew up there. What was his name? Shoot. I flew with him off the carrier. He died before Danno did, I think. No, he got out of the Navy and died while flying his biplane.

Mike giggled. A biplane, what a great idea. He reached overhead and reduced the cockpit pressure. Wind poured through the hole. It was like flying a biplane, except he couldn't see much. Where's my white scarf?

Continuing to the southwest, Mike passed over the crested beauty of Yellowstone and followed US 20 to Pocatello. The wind blew around him. Deep creases formed at the side of his red eyes as his head bobbed to some internal tune. "Dum de dum dum. Dum de dum dum."

"Heh, heh, heh, heh." Smiling at the wind blowing by, he stayed on his southwesterly heading and skirted the northern edge of the Great Salt Desert as he sped toward Wells, Nevada. "Ah, Nevada. Nevadahhhhhhh!" He reached behind his seat and patted his friend. "We're almost home, Brian. We're almost home. Hang in there."

The ease with which he'd been able to reach Brian set off a small alarm. I forgot to strap in! He retrieved the lap belt. He reached behind his head for the shoulder straps. One came forward intact. The other was nothing but an 18-inch shred, bloodied and severed by the same force that had torn into Brian's chest. Mike threw both shoulder straps back over the seat. He fastened his lap belt. If he had to eject without shoulder straps, he would die as he left the airplane. There would be no way out of this one if Rhombus ran out of gas. He'd go down with it. Besides, he couldn't leave Brian behind—not now.

The happy stupor poured a thick, sweet, codeine-laced coffee that soothed as it kept him awake. "Dum de dum dum. Dum de dum dum." One eye squinted as he imagined the Grim Reaper looking at him through the hole. "Screw you. I am the king." The wind of America blew by his face, and he felt like Captain Eddie Rickenbacker and Captain James T. Kirk rolled into one.

Over Ruby Valley and the Humboldt National Forest, he and Rhombus flew, his imaginary white scarf blowing in the breeze like a flag in a stiff gale. Ahead was US 50, which ran across central Nevada and drew a black east-west line through beautiful brown emptiness. The Loneliest Road in America looked pretty good.

Normally, when taking this route, Mike would start his descent over Eureka. But Eureka was behind him, and Mike was singing. Those magnificent men in their flying machines, they go uppity up up, they go downity down down. They take all the ladies and steal all the scenes, dum de dumdity dum dum—

An emotional pendulum had swung a wide arc from misery to capriciousness.

Rhombus sped toward the horizon with its pilot blissful, unaware of a damned thing, except the wind in his face and the joy it brought—unaware that oblivion was gaining on him.

The pendulum swung again. As though shot, Mike struggled at the edge. The wall his mind had built was being torn down by the accumulated wretchedness, a crumbling earthen dike against the raging river. The death, the dehydration, the fatigue, the pain—it all crashed against the falling wall of fortitude. He shook his head and cried for the little train that knew he could.

"I know I can—I know I can—I know I can," came his mother's voice through thickening fog, getting weaker with each word.

"I am the king. The king I am."

The sharp pain in the back of his head ran away with the fog and swirled with memories of his past, memories numbed by the anesthetic of impossibility. Like a deer, still alive as its belly is being torn open by wolves, Mike sat, eyes glazed, and felt no pain as death gnawed away.

Those magnificent men—in their flying machines—

The landscape quit moving.

They go upity up up, they go—when they steal—all the ladies—and all the scenes.

His eyelids closed.

His head dropped to his chest.

MISSION TIME—22 HOURS: 30 MINUTES

The airplane skidded right. His body, not secured by shoulder straps, fell across the center console. A toggle switch on number-two UHF radio slid beneath his left eyelid and scratched the white part of his eyeball.

He jerked up, clamped his hand against the left side of his face. I know I can—I know I can—I know I can. His memory flashed Danno Riley's A-7 as it fell with flames streaming from its boiling cockpit. He shook his head and fought to focus on the desert that swept beneath the hole. "I'm not giving up, Danno. Damned if I'm giving up!"

"Ouch. My eye!" Pain finally blasted the fuzzy mental cloud away. Through the hole he saw the horizon at an angle. He moved the joystick to roll Rhombus level.

The airplane didn't feel right.

Didn't sound right.

Rhombus skidded.

He kicked in left rudder, which brought the nose back on heading.

Listen.

Listen.

The whining engines sung to him, talked to him.

He moved the left throttles forward, then back. Rhombus' nose swung right, then left. He moved the right throttles. Nothing.

He pressed the restart buttons on the right engines.

Nothing.

He pressed the buttons again and hoped for the rumble as the flames ignited.

Nothing.

He looked at the fuel panel. "Damn!" Engines 3 and 4 had sucked the right tanks dry. The left tanks hardly registered. Rhombus was running out of gas. The Grim Reaper smiled through the hole as he swung his scythe back and forth, closer.

Mike winced as he opened his left eye. The eyelid fluttered as he tried to open it. He was above Ralston Valley, within 50 miles of Groom Lake—too close for a long descent and experiment with the controls. He slammed the throttles to idle and lowered the nose. Rhombus dove. If engines 1 and 2 quit, he'd dead-stick it on the desert floor. He owed that to Danno—and to Brian. If Rhombus survived a crash landing, the boys from Groom Lake could cover it with something and truck it home.

Ahead, through the hole, Emigrant Valley spread against the hot earth like a beige griddle. In the middle of the flat was the white smudge of Groom Lake Base. As he went down, the air coming through the hole got warmer. He unsnapped the clasp, and the mask fell away.

The loss of engines 3 and 4 created drag, but helped him lose altitude. His worry about being too high faded. He saw the runway and turned right, then left, so that he was lined up with it. For a while the maneuver forced him to lose sight of the base, but he was familiar with this territory, so he knew where he was as he streaked toward the desert.

He had to gauge his speed by the progress he made over the ground and by the feel of the airplane. Since he had only a small area to see through, which afforded him no peripheral vision of the outside, feel was about all he had. He had to shoot directly for the runway. Gas was precious. He left eye was swelling, but he was able to keep it open—mostly.

After diving for 40 miles, he saw the runway stripes. He was two miles out and around 3,500 feet above the ground. He fell from the sky about four times steeper than an airliner. Still, he believed his airspeed was about right. He lowered the flap handle. Hydraulic motors whined. Rhombus pitched down from the drag of the flaps dropping into the airstream.

He pushed the throttles to keep the airspeed from dropping too fast. He was a mile from the runway. He lowered the gear handle. He heard the sound of the landing-gear locks rolling back, then the sound of the hydraulic system forcing the gear into the airstream. Since the lights on the landing-gear panel were powered by an emergency battery, all three glowed red, showing the landing gear was unlocked and on the way down.

He had a half-mile to go, and he could make out the texture in the runway.

Two landing gear lights turned green, indicating the main gear was down and locked.

The runway filled more and more of the hole as Rhombus flew toward it. I think I'm too fast. Damn airplane doesn't feel the same with this hole in the side. Too fast. No. No. Maybe I'm OK.

Mike glanced at his landing-gear panel.

The nose gear was red.

"Come on, damn it!" he yelled. He leaned forward and hit the red light with the fleshy part of his fist, "Come on!"

The light stayed on. Hitting the light forced him off course a bit. He sat back and settled on the controls again. It wouldn't be the first time an airplane landed gear up. It wasn't his biggest problem, not by a long shot.

The screaming air lowered its pitch and became more subdued as airspeed dropped.

The whine from the engines on the left side sighed into silence. Rhombus was out of fuel.

The nose swung left.

Mike kicked right rudder. Dried blood yanked hair out by the roots.

He pushed the nose down to keep his airspeed up. The runway disappeared at the top of the hole.

The uneven desert, with its hummocks and sagebrush rushed at him.

He raised the flaps back up to reduce the drag.

Like a soldier diving for the safety of a foxhole, he dove for ground effect. It had saved him half a day ago over the pasture east of Kiev. Maybe, just maybe.

The sandy floor of the valley raised its gritty fist to kill him.

He calculated when to pull back on the joystick to level off before he hit the ground, but lower than 90 feet above it. It was a small target for an enormous airplane with no power and only a tiny damned hole to see out of.

If he pulled too soon, his drag would stay high and Rhombus would stall, then dig a scorched shallow grave short of the runway. If he pulled too late, Rhombus would take him beneath the flat's sandy soil in a headlong rush to oblivion. Trying to gauge when to pull the nose up was like a skydiver having to open his chute no higher than nine stories above the earth while he peeped through a small hole in a blindfold.

Now! He pulled. The nose rose. Not enough! Not enough! Ohhhhhhhh! He pressed his feet against the pedals like a passenger in a car that was skidding out of control. Too steep!

"Oh God!" A scream. "Oh, God," a prayer. "Please."

And then there was blue.

Blue sky filled the hole.

Rhombus' nose was above the horizon.

Mike had nailed it, and the warbird's great bulk swept over the earth on a giant rolling pillow of air.

The will to live blasted through him. He was awake like he had never been awake before, and his mind moved like a videotape running at fast forward with its zipping images and its chipmunk voices.

He eased forward on the joystick. The nose dropped. Rhombus must not climb out of ground effect.

In a flash, the blue disappeared and the fuzzy dots of rushing creosote bushes sitting on the crowns of hummocks brushed by the hole only 50 feet below.

The runway threshold lay in the distance, centered in the hole. As it grew larger, Rhombus' airspeed fell, and so did lift. Mike eased back on the joystick to raise the nose and keep the lift.

He lowered the flaps a notch.

Slower still.

More back pressure. Another notch of flaps.

Slower. More flaps. More back pressure.

Slower. Flaps. Back pressure.

Full flaps now. The runway was close, a quarter-mile at the most. One more drop in the bucket, just one more.

The joystick vibrated. Rhombus was near a stall.

Then he heard the sound and felt the shudder in his feet. The air over Rhombus' back separated from the airplane. Thousands of small eddies of air rapped on the skin and gave a pleasing vibration.

Slower.

The eddies grew larger and turned into thumping shattering tornadoes that pounded the warplane's back.

Nose up. More shuddering.

Rhombus was stalling.

After taking off from this place and flying halfway around the planet and back, it'd had enough. The airplane was out of airspeed.

Rhombus shook, the death throe of a giant beast just short of safety.

"Damn you!" Mike shouted at his airplane. "Damn you! We didn't come this far to quit! Damned if you're giving up on me."

When Rhombus entered a full stall, the bomber and its pilot would nose into a ravine and somersault in a swirling mass of metal and flesh.

Mike eased the joystick forward. Better to land on the ground than to nose into it.

They hit the ground.

Thunder boomed.

His head pitched forward.

The wind flew out of his mouth and nostrils and spewed saliva and mucus.

Rhombus hit the ground again. Thunder.

He lurched forward.

His chest folded against his thighs.

His breath exploded out of him.

His upper body bounced off his thighs and jerked his head back. Blood squirted from his mouth and nose in thick strings.

Thunder.

His head slammed against the seatback.

Eyes wide, he fought for breath.

Blood turned in the airstream and flew back.

Through his feet, through his seat, and through the air itself, his airplane shook with blows from a giant jackhammer.

The tires ripped off.

Massive belts of rubber and steel spun from the wheels and flailed the airplane's bottom. They flew away and hit the desert in large puffs of desert dust and sand.

Rhombus bounded over ravine-cut terrain at more than 150 miles per hour.

Mike fought the joystick to keep the nose up, to keep from digging in.

Rhombus shrieked as the earth tore away strips of metal.

Pieces of Brian's body flew off the floor, hit the overhead

console, and ricocheted around like wet red dough flung from an open blender.

Maps and charts flew out of their storage cases and filled the chaotic gloom with fluttering white flashes.

Rhombus blasted across the tops of desert hummocks, skipping from one to the other like a flat stone hurled over the water.

Its tires gone, Rhombus' metal wheels ripped gouges in the hummocks and left exploding clouds of dust behind.

Stay down, Brian! Please stay down!

He fought to keep the nose from digging in.

Then—

Mike had the joystick full back. That's it. That's all there is. There was nothing more he could do. Where and how Rhombus' nose fell was up to it alone.

The shattering thunder stopped.

Concrete with herringbone stripes rushed by beneath.

They were on the runway overrun.

The ride felt almost serene as Rhombus rolled over the concrete on its magnesium wheels. A continuous scraping ring filled the cockpit, sounding like a manhole cover sliding down the interstate.

The airplane jolted over the red and green lights that marked the beginning of the runway.

Red and green glass exploded.

The herringbone pattern sped past.

The cockpit flashed as Rhombus rolled over the broad white centerline stripes that reflected the sunlight through the hole.

The nose dropped—fast. It crashed to the concrete runway.

The abrasive surface ground at the warplane's nose.

Sparks poured through the hole, a dazzling horizontal geyser that split as it hit Mike and flowed around him.

Slivers of metal tore at his helmet, visor, and mask. They shredded the knees of his flight suit and stripped bits of skin from his hands.

Only one more thing to do now.

His arm reached through the sparkling stream and threw the switch labeled "Main." Rhombus went to sleep as it rolled down the long runway.

Mike folded his hands in his lap. He'd brought his airplane and his friend home. He collapsed while the river of sparks flowed around him, knowing that Mom and Dad, and Danno and Brian, and his beloved Kachina would approve of what he had done today.

SATURDAY, 26 APRIL
1302 HOURS (1:02 PM)
MISSION TIME—23 HOURS: 0 MINUTES
GROOM LAKE BASE, NEVADA

Through the cloud of a receding stupor, Mike heard the voices come through the hole. "Sirs! Commander Christum! Commander Davis! You OK?" Then, "They don't answer. Blow the hatches!"

The cockpit filled with daylight as the hatch over his head blew away. Another explosion blew the other hatch off. The acrid odor of explosive cord rushed in with the smoke. Mike sat, too stunned to be grateful, too exhausted to be anguished. Through the clearing smoke, the outline of someone's head appeared in the hatch opening. It cast a smeary shadow along a fuzzy shaft of sunlight.

"You OK, sir?" The petty officer fought to see in the dark.

"More or less," Mike said. The wind still rang in his ears and blood dripped from his mouth. "How long have I been here?"

"About three minutes, sir. Captain Patterakis said we should wait for you, so we've been out here beside the runway for about four hours. We saw you coming when you hit the ground off the end of the runway. It was kind of hard to—" The young man's eyes had adjusted to the darkness inside the cockpit.

"Dear Mother of God." He saw the rumpled bloody pile

of Brian Davis behind the ejection seats. He looked at Commander Christum with his gashed helmet, shattered visor, and blood pouring from his knees, hands, and face. The fresh blood added a new red layer over the dark clotted blood that was everywhere. The cockpit was like a small dank slaughterhouse. The smell of raw meat and vomit mixed with the sharp metallic smell of fresh blood. The petty officer gagged as he tasted the smells in the air.

Mike raised what was left of his visor. Pieces of it fell away. He squinted at the petty officer through the beam of smoky sunlight. "As you can see," he said in a voice that rolled like gravel out of a wooden barrel, "I've had a bad day."

"I'm getting you out of here, sir." Two powerful hands reached down for him. Mike gave a small grateful smile and passed out again.

The giant bomber sat with its nose down on the runway. Its black skin soaked up the desert sun and smoke drifted away from its landing gear. A yellow fire truck sprayed foam that piled up beneath Rhombus in frothy mounds. A dozen emergency vehicles surrounded the airplane with red strobes that flashed pitiful shots of light into the brilliant sky. An ambulance sped away.

Two medical corpsmen worked on the top of the warplane. They tugged a black plastic body bag through one of the hatch openings. They slid the bag over the side and into the waiting hands of two other corpsmen, who carried it to a second ambulance. The second ambulance was in no hurry.

A sailor emerged from the top of the warplane through one of the hatches and lowered himself to the concrete. He ran to the edge of the runway and fell to his knees. An older man, wearing the uniform of a chief petty officer, knelt at his side, patted his back, and gave him his handkerchief.

MISSION TIME—23 HOURS: 2 MINUTES
GOTTLAND ISLAND, SWEDEN

The invisible whispering thunder had come and gone less than 12 hours ago. The thin smoke that Brian saw coming from the target lifted into the sky and swept northwest as it spread a wider and wider path. It carried its ash across Belarus, Lithuania, and Latvia, before heading across the Baltic Sea. Part of the cloud swept ashore at Gottland Island and into an atmospheric collector mounted on a stone building on the edge of the town of Burgsvik.

The technician had been on the phone for several minutes trying to convince his superiors in Stockholm of his findings. He sat at a metal desk that was lit by a single lamp. It was the only light in a dark room that was filled with electronic equipment. "Yes. I am sure. There can be no doubt," he said into the phone. "The pattern of the winds and the composition of the ash make it certain that it came from only one place. Where? The northern Ukraine, as I said. What city? Ahhh, just a moment."

He bent over a map that sat on the desk. He touched his finger on a dot that marked Kiev. He moved his finger up the Dneiper River where he found another dot that represented a small town located at the confluence of the Pripjat and Uzh rivers. "The radiation is coming from an old graphite reactor located in the town of—I can't pronounce it, but it's spelled C-H-E-R-N-O-B-Y-L."

1986, TUESDAY, 26 JULY
1011 HOURS (10:11 AM)
HANGAR 18, GROOM LAKE BASE

Rhombus sat one cavern below Hangar 18. Nineteen identical airplanes were stored in the lower caves where they swung on steel cables. Over the past three months, Mike and Patterakis had flown them in from a secret location, and the maintenance crews had mummified each one. Airplanes worth billions of dollars slept as they swayed in imperceptible harmony with the Earth as it sped through the Cosmos.

Rhombus was the last to be stored, because repairs had taken so long. When he got word his airplane was fixed and about to be mothballed, he walked to Hangar 18 for the last time. He stood in front of his warbird as it sat there on its landing gear. Sailors in white jumpsuits walked across its back and attached the steel cables. Others pulled carts holding containers of plastic spray and snaked high-pressure hoses beneath the airplane. One petty officer noticed him standing there, oblivious to all that was happening. The man in the jumpsuit waved to the others and pointed. They all quit what they were doing and stood, silent.

Mike opened a paper bag and withdrew a can of red spray paint and a roll of masking tape. He knelt in front of the nose gear. He tore off a length of the tape and wrapped it around the nose strut just above the shiny cylinder that moves up and down with the wheel.

One man looked at another, questioning. The other shrugged.

Mike wrapped another length of tape around the collar just above the first. He shook the can of paint. The ball in the can echoed in the quiet cavern. Mike sprayed the area between the two lengths of tape, circling the nose gear as he did. He stood with his hand against the gear for a moment, then carefully pulled the masking tape away. A thin red stripe remained.

He opened his shirt pocket and pulled out a plastic label that read, "Do Not Remove Red Line—Tech Order 1072-363-304-63." He peeled the label away from its backing and pressed it on the red line.

It was an old ritual of his. He'd done this on the A-7 he flew off the *Kitty Hawk*. Several years later he spotted the airplane sitting at a small airfield near Battle Mountain, Nevada. The Navy had donated it to some local businessmen who planned to put it in an air museum beside Interstate 80. His old airplane sat there with a bird's nest in its intake and a thin red line around its nose gear strut, silently sharing war stories with a nearby F-4.

Painting the red line was as far as Mike would go to tease military bureaucracy. Everyone who would ever work on Rhombus—whenever that might be—would see the obvious red line, but nobody would ever trace the genesis of the fake Tech Order number. Nobody would ever take the responsibility of removing the line, either. After all, even though they would never figure out what 1072-363-304-63 was, they also could never prove it shouldn't be there. In a bureaucracy, that was the surest way of guaranteeing the future of anything.

The technicians watched, curious. Mike leaned against the nose-gear strut and put his forehead to the cold metal. He closed his eyes.

A sailor whispered, "What's he doing?" The chief beside him held up his hand.

"Adios, my good and faithful friend," Mike said to Rhombus. He touched his airplane. "Adios."

He turned away and walked toward the staircase that spiraled up to the ground floor of the hangar. The cavern echoed a scuffing ring each time his foot hit a metal tread. One man clapped his gloved hands to the beat of Mike's steps. Another joined him, then another. Thumping applause drowned out the sound of his movement up the staircase. "Way to go, Commander Mike!" came a shout. "Way to go!"

A technician pressed a button, and screeching hydraulic motors joined the ovation. Steel cables strained. The steel door at the top of the staircase banged shut. Rhombus rose from the floor—as if to follow.

1986, TUESDAY, 29 JULY
1614 HOURS (4:14 PM)
THE OREGON COAST

The dampness in the soil seeped through the seat of his pants and made his jockey shorts feel like part of his skin. He stood, stretched, and tugged at the back of his trousers. The shorts pulled away from his behind like a Post-it note. He rubbed his backside and sat again. The rolling ocean pounded on the cliff below, soft thuds that mixed with the roar of the spray that shot straight up. A lone storm on the far horizon blocked out the late-afternoon sun and became the dark ragged center of an airborne flower whose petals were made of sunbeams. He wiped the mist from his sunglasses with a hanky and flipped up the collar of his nylon windbreaker. The faces of those he'd lost over the years flowed around him in a melancholy stream of memories. He prayed for them, and he prayed for himself. He was lonely, yet at the same time he was fulfilled. The ocean, the storm, the communion with his Maker were all out of touch to his fingers, but they gave him strength because they touched his soul.

Mike had always reached for his dreams, but Brian reminded him to deal with life as it was, not as it should be. He now knew he was more than a married man without his wife, a father without his children, a friend who had lost friends. He was a human being, a tiny speck in God's great pocket, but no less important than anything else. Memories existed to enlighten and to show the way. They were there to be cherished for either the joy of having them or the lessons they imparted, or both. Memories could either destroy or create, which was one's own choice. One had to move on.

Three days earlier, he'd retired from the Navy over Chris Patterakis' strong objections and bought the Harley that sat on the bluff behind him. He looked back to see the deepening pink of the sky reflected in its chrome. It was a pretty machine, a throwback to the '30s. Its engine vibrated. He had to wear earplugs to protect his hearing from its noise, and its four-speed transmission fought every effort to change gears, only surrendering to each push of his toe with a clunk. The Harley was so different from Rhombus, which had moved with technical beauty like a symphony of parts that described great sweeps in the sky. Rhombus now hung with the others, in the caves beneath the Nevada desert.

What a time, he thought of the last few years as he watched

the sun descend beneath the cloud and touch the ocean. He plucked a blackberry from one of the bushes. Purple juice rolled down his fingers. It tasted sweet, and it made him smile.

Blackberry pie, blackberry pie.
I come from the sky to eat blackberry pie.

He walked up the bluff to the Harley and removed a single leather saddlebag, then walked back down. He opened the bag.

"Brian Davis," he said looking inside, "we always dreamed of coming here, so here we are, and here you shall always be. I'll be back to watch the sunset, smell the ocean, and eat the blackberries. I leave all that's here in your good hands, and give you back to Susan."

He reached out over the cliff, turned the bag on its side, and watched the ashes of his friend's body spill out and away. A breeze blew against the cascade and sent it flying back, spreading the ashes around the blackberry patch and over Mike. He brushed at himself. "Jeez, Brian. A pain in the butt to the very end."

The Harley thumped south, away from the blackberry patch and down the Oregon coast. He headed toward a rendezvous with Kachina, Scotty, and Lisa. They were all going home.

1988

PHOENIX

1988, Saturday, 19 November
High Meadow
New River Gorge, West Virginia

The lush green mantle of the Appalachian summer was gone. October had exploded with color, which ran away in early November leaving the craggy countryside with gray trees. Mike walked along the path of the high meadow. His boots crunched on the frost. To his right, the meadow fell away over the mountain's rounded crest to reveal the black line of the New River pounding through the ancient gorge on its way to the sea. Mike knew that over the coming months the black water would become part of the Gulf Stream as it headed for Murmansk to keep the winter ice pack at bay. He'd bought this meadow from old Arvel Neely two years earlier, after his retirement. It was the patch of land where he and Kachina came to terms with the death of their son. Behind him, getting smaller with every step, stood the small home he had built. Smoke from the chimney of his wood-burning heater curled into the crisp November morning.

He walked to the edge of the meadow, its boundary defined by a beautiful sugar maple tree whose bare branches seemed to be lifted in prayer to the coming winter sky. Mike stood beneath the tree with his head bowed and the fingers of his scarred hands locked together. He pondered the three white marble crosses that stood watch. He knelt and picked up twigs that had fallen across the graves since yesterday. He walked to the edge of the meadow and dropped the twigs on the ground.

He and Kachina had dreamed of building a home on the high meadow. They had shared the dream with Scotty and would have shared it with Lisa when she was old enough to understand. They'd talked of grandchildren at Christmastime and of riding snowmobiles into the woods to pick the perfect tree. They looked forward to the coming springtimes and the joys of sharing the same town with extended family.

This edge of the frost-crunched meadow was as close as they would ever come to having the dream come true. He'd moved Scotty from Las Vegas and his girls from the cemetery on the other side of the gorge. They were home now.

He walked back to the house, retracing his footsteps, dark oval prints in the white frost. In the distance, on the other side of the field, a car came into the meadow from the path through the woods. He didn't recognize it. He picked up his pace. The car reached the front of the house at the same time Mike approached from the side. Momentarily, the porch blocked Mike's view of the car, but he heard the sound of its motor dying and its door closing. He rounded the edge of the porch, then stopped with hands at his side when he recognized the driver. Chris Patterakis stood with a collar turned up against the cold. His breath turned to wisps of frozen fog that disappeared over his shoulders. He lifted an arm and pointed an index finger at Mike. "Uncle Sam wants you."

"Uncle Sam can get lost!" Mike responded, pointing back. "And when are you going to get a warm coat?"

"It's the Californian in me."

"Well, the Californian in you will freeze if we don't get it inside."

Mike and his old warrior friend threw jacket-covered arms around each other. Hollow thumps from their backslapping filled the chill. "Come in. Come in." Mike slapped Chris on the back. "I've never had a Navy Captain in my home before."

"You're not likely to, either."

"You finally retired? I'll be," said Mike, his arm on Chris' shoulder as they walked up the porch steps.

"No. I made Admiral," Chris responded as Mike opened the front door.

"I don't believe it."

"Nobody else does, either."

During the day smoke curled from the chimney. Sometimes the smoke plume grew longer as someone inside stoked the fire or fed it more wood.

Early that afternoon, Mike stepped through the front door and walked to Chris' rental car. He retrieved a suitcase from the trunk, then went back inside.

They reminisced over the years of service together. The service of any warrior is nothing more than an extension of his country's foreign policy. That's the way it had always been, whether the warrior carried a sword or flew an airplane. Mike knew more about Rhombus, the airplane, than anyone else in the world. Yet beyond the obvious, Rhombus was in the center of a sinister world of which he knew nothing.

Chris turned the conversation away from Rhombus. "Heard of the B-Two?"

"Sure," Mike responded. "It's the Air Force's new bomber. From what I've read, it must have some of the same technology as our airplane. Aren't they going to roll it out in a couple of days?"

"That's why I'm here," Patterakis responded. "I've been invited to the rollout at Palmdale. I want you to come with me."

Mike thought a second. "Wait a minute. Did you come all the way here to ask me to go to the rollout with you?"

Chris drew the fingernail of one hand under that of the other. "Yes, I did."

"Why didn't you just call me?"

"Because I thought I'd have to talk you into it."

Mike sat with his elbows on the table and his hands around his coffee mug. Wisps of steam spiraled away. "You thought I'd become a hermit, didn't you?"

"Well, you'd been through a lot, and everyone thought …"

"You thought I moved back to the woods to shut the world out."

"Yes," Chris looked at him. "That's what we thought."

Mike took a deep breath. "The best friends I have are my old military buddies, and they think I've walked away from them, don't they?"

"I talked with some of the guys. Nobody's heard from you. It wasn't like you to … I guess I'm here to see if you're OK."

"I should have called or written or something, but it has taken a while to reorder things. See this?" Mike opened his arms with a theatrical flare. "I built this." He held his hands over the table. "I built it with these hands. Darned proud of it, too." Mike ran his finger around the rim of his coffee mug. "Thanks for worrying," he said. He stoked the stove and re-filled their coffee mugs.

"Remember Brad Davis?" Mike asked.

"Brian's son? Sure."

"He was here last summer. Helped me build the porch." He sipped his coffee. "I'm helping him get through college. I guess you could say we need each other." He scratched a spot on the tablecloth. "First thing I'm going to do when I get to heaven is kick Brian's butt for bad estate planning."

Patterakis grinned. "I wonder if they have beer and hot dogs in heaven."

"If they don't, that's not where he is. Unless he's sponging lasagna from Kachina." He looked out the window toward the crosses. "When do we leave?"

"For where?"

"For Palmdale."

1988, TUESDAY, 22 NOVEMBER
PALMDALE, CALIFORNIA

As much as he loved his remote Appalachian home, Mike missed this world of technology and excitement. It was good to be back. He sat with Chris in the bleachers in front of the Air Force's B-2 hangar at Palmdale. The hangar was a huge metal building whose door was wide, but not very high. The bleachers were draped with rich-looking blue curtains and large reproductions of the Air Force seal. Off to the left, between the bleachers and the hangar, was a platform decorated with red, white, and blue bunting. Several people sat in chairs on the platform while one man spoke. The California sun sat low in the sky and filtered through a slight haze to cast soft-edged shadows against the concrete.

Mike was in civilian clothes, and so was Chris. Once in a while he smelled the sweet perfume of jet exhaust wafting across the concrete ramp. "Damn, I feel alive. Thanks for inviting me, Chris."

He wondered what it must be like on a carrier right now, launching off its deck into a misty ocean morning. He longed for the cockpit, seat, straps, and hoses that, even with their confinement, had given him the freedom of flight. The speeches and music of the affair were little more than background to his reverie as the minutes passed. An elbow nudged his side.

"You don't want to miss this," Patterakis said.

Mike's watched the hangar. The sound system played the "Ride of the Valkyries." The doors parted as though Moses had waved his staff. They opened ever wider to reveal a large shape that was indistinct in the shade of the hangar. Mike raised his hand to his forehead and squinted to see the Air Force's new miracle that hunched inside. A small yellow tractor huffed like the little engine that could as it pulled the massive shape into the sunlight. Mike's mouth dropped as the curtain of shadows withdrew from the B-2.

He fumbled for the binoculars hanging from his neck. Putting them to his eyes, he aimed for the Air Force's new Stealth bomber. He twisted the knob with nervous fingers. Finally, he got the focus sharp.

There it was, a massive low-profile shape with an unusual blend of sensuous curves and sharp edges. It was a giant black wing without fuselage and tail. Its cockpit sat in the middle of the wing just behind its leading edge. All in all, though, it looked like a giant black turnover.

Mike's binocular view paused on the cockpit for a moment, then fell lower and lower along the nose-gear strut. His breathing stopped. There, just above the compression collar on the nose strut, was the thin red line he had painted two years earlier.

"Hello old friend," he whispered.

The two men were silent as the car sped south from Palmdale to Los Angeles through the pass that separated the Sierra Madre from the San Gabriels. Sunlight streamed into the car. Mike stared out the window, his mind elsewhere in place and time. "Well, I know where I'm going. Where do you go, Chris?"

"Where do I go?"

"Where you going after you drop me off at the airport?"

"I'm driving on to San Diego. Heading for a funeral, sorry to say." Chris stared somewhere way, way, down the highway—somewhere in infinity. "How do you figure it? A guy swims in Haiphong Harbor with bombs going off all over the place and spends his career on missions that would make you and me cower in a corner. He marries a pretty little blonde and they have two nice boys. Then, one day, boom, he puts a nine-millimeter bullet in his head. Nobody knows why." Patterakis paused as he maneuvered around a slower car. "Did you ever meet a chief petty officer named Dick McIntyre?"

Mike rubbed his chin. "Name rings a bell, but I don't know."

"Navy SEAL. Great guy. I met him in Vietnam when I

worked with the river-patrol guys. I can't imagine … It's a mystery."

"Not a hint?" Mike asked.

"For the past five years, Dick seemed to be troubled by something he was unable or unwilling to talk about. He never abused his wife or his boys. She told me he just became quiet. He came home early one morning and was never the same. So, I have to bury another old friend."

Chris' aviator talent and training helped him weave through traffic with smooth movements.

"Thank you for today," Mike said.

"You're welcome."

Chris was terse, so Mike watched the traffic. Finally, "Tell me what happened, Chris."

Chris pulled himself from his thoughts, "Do I have your solemn promise you will not reveal what I'm about to tell you?"

"You do."

"I'll be brief. When I'm through, that's it. No questions. No answers. Agreed?"

"Agreed."

"I'll start with the airplane. That B-Two you just saw roll out was your airplane, you know."

"I know."

"That was pretty creative, painting the red line on the nose gear strut," Chris said. "Some of guys who saw you paint it are still on the B-Two program, and they'd kill to keep anybody from painting over it."

Mike chuckled. Chris continued, "It's taken more than two years to turn Rhombus into the B-Two you saw back there. The SID was removed and replaced with cockpit windows. In a few years you'll see the SID technology again. It'll be in the form of high-definition television. You may have wondered how we leapfrogged the Japanese and the Europeans in HDTV technology. Now you know.

"The MPP computer was removed. It's still being refined and tested. The next time you see it, it'll be playing against chess masters—and winning.

"The reclining ejection seats were removed, along with the joysticks. The ceramic CJ engines were replaced with conventional F-one-eighteens. Too bad about the engines. The one-eighteens have less than a fifth the thrust of the CJs, so the airplane now flies more like a conventional bomber than it does a fighter.

"The Aurora system. That's an interesting story. We shared the technology with the Soviet Union in order to restore the balance of power between the Super Powers.

"Right now, the secrets of Aurora are buried in two sites: a missile silo outside Moscow and a missile silo outside Little Rock. A force comprising both Soviets and Americans guards each. The silos are connected by phone to the Kremlin and the White House. Right now, things are looking pretty good, but should the Soviet Union come apart, what we do with the technology is anybody's guess. I would expect Aurora to leak out over the years in less capable forms. Give it seven or eight years, and you might start reading about electrically charged airplane coatings that will flash and flicker as a defense against anti-aircraft missiles.

"We thought the Rhombus program only cost fifteen billion dollars. It was much more. For years it sucked money from other programs, which were fronts for Rhombus dollars. Nobody in Congress knew about Rhombus. Nobody wanted to know.

"I knew that your target was going to be Chernobyl, but I couldn't tell you. You and Brian did great. After your attack, the Soviet Union changed. Most observers credit that change to the bungling of the Soviet bureaucracy in the aftermath of the meltdown. You know the rest.

"Meanwhile, we had ourselves a few airplanes we weren't supposed to have. We thought about scrapping them, but how could we account for spending that much money? Instead, we made something else out of them. We turned them into B-Twos. The CJ engines, the Aurora system, the MPP computer, the SID, the reclining ejection seats with their joysticks, and a hundred other things were removed, destroyed, buried. Meanwhile, all the airframes are now in storage. We'll bring them out of storage one by one as though each had just rolled off the assembly line."

"I'll always worry about some things," Mike said.

"You mean about Chernobyl?" Chris asked.

"Oh no. I'm at peace with that." Mike looked at the sweeping fly-overs that linked Interstate 5 to Interstate 405. "No, I'll always have a nagging question about what we had to do to keep Rhombus secret."

"Is that a question?"

"Take it any way you want it, Skipper."

"I don't know," Chris said.

"Pardon?"

"I don't know if anyone was killed or not, Mike. I do know that none of our guys leaked anything. We all made it through, and everybody who was, is, and will be involved is sworn to secrecy. Just like you."

Mike pictured the time in the high meadow when he almost told Kachina about Rhombus. "I guess," Mike said, "that some things are best not known."

"I guess so."

Chris pulled over to the United Airlines curb. The tires squealed on the shiny concrete gutter. Mike sat for a moment, then opened the door and stepped into the loosely gathered crowd around the skycap desk. He retrieved his hang-up bag from the back seat, then leaned into the open front door and held out his hand. Chris shook it. "Chris, tell me. Do you still like to hunt deer?"

"Haven't done it in years, but I enjoy it."

"I'll see you in the meadow next deer season," Mike said.

"Mike, tell me. Do you still like to fly?"

"Haven't done it in years, but I enjoy it."

Chris opened his mouth to speak, but Mike cut him off with an upheld hand and closed the car door. As the car's wheels turned away from the curb, Mike rapped twice on the glass. The two men waved. The car eased into the slow traffic, its top now one of dozens moving in the same direction. Raised above the moving shiny sameness was an arm, extended out of a driver's window, with a thumb pointing straight up. Mike smiled, returned the gesture, and turned toward home.

1988, CHRISTMAS EVE
HIGH MEADOW
NEW RIVER GORGE, WEST VIRGINIA

The sky was low and gray, surrendering to the night. The air was so cold it froze the moisture in his nose and hurt his head as he breathed. The wind blew gossamer knots of snow across the meadow like swarms of white bees over a broad white quilt. It was a night like this that he and Brian had flown just above the black river at the bottom of the gorge at the meadow's edge.

Mike stood on the porch, gloved hands thrust into heavy pockets. He watched the headlights come through the woods, causing naked tree branches to look like a hard spider web that moved toward him. He waved as the Bronco got closer, its tires crunching the powdered ice. A hand waved behind a crystal-framed windshield. As the truck stopped at the bottom of the steps, the driver's window lowered an inch or so. "Merry Christmas, bro."

"Merry Christmas, Scott," Mike grabbed a broom that leaned against the rail. He swished the broom from side to side as he descended the porch steps. He bent over and looked in the window opening at the woman who sat in the other seat. "Merry Christmas, gorgeous."

A smiling face was framed by a red and green woolen hood. "Merry Christmas, son." Laughter touched her words, as it always had.

Scott was not impressed with Mom's happy countenance. His breath puffed again. "It's colder'n a Norwegian well digger's—"

"Ah, ah." Mike interrupted as he waved a gloved forefinger. "You're the one who's been praying for a white Christmas."

"I'll have to be more specific next year." Scott stepped out. "I meant white as in the movies, not white as in Siberia."

"Hang on there, Mom," Mike said as Scott moved by. Mike swept a path around the vehicle. Snow bloomed from his labor, and the wind snagged the snow blossom's soft edges and pulled it into the night.

He opened her door. She steadied herself against him. With his arm around her back to guard against a fall, they walked up the steps and entered the house.

A Christmas tree stood in the corner. Its lights accented the soft flames in the fireplace and the flicker of the candles in the room. "Oh, Mike. I have something for you in the car," Mom said as she re-buttoned her coat.

He touched her hand. "That's OK, Mom. I'll get it."

The closing front door choked off the warm light that spilled across the snow on the porch. Bracing against the cold, he walked down the steps.

He opened the door of the Bronco and reached for a small printed bag clutched close at the top with thick yarn. With the bag in hand, he climbed the steps again and reached for the doorknob. He paused and cocked his head at a sound.

He brushed the snow from the flat wooden handrail by the door and sat the bag on it. He walked to the other end of the porch and looked into the gorge. Snowflakes blew around him as the gorge seemed to suck the storm from the sky.

He relaxed. The sound he'd heard was probably the wind blowing through a stand of white pines just over the crest.

But then it moved—fast—from north to south.

He stiffened and leaned forward against the porch rail, squinting at the dark. But all he saw were two spirals of snow, two small horizontal tornadoes about 200 feet apart that swirled with snowflakes and grew longer and longer as they snaked through the gorge together.

At the point of the tornadoes, the sound of whispering thunder moved, too, then disappeared toward Virginia, toward the Blue Ridge.

Snowflakes landed on his eyelashes and fell away each time

he blinked. His breath spilled around the corner of the house. He stood in the darkness for a while and watched the tornadoes drop into the gorge and rustle the naked tree branches.

When he opened the front door, light from the re-stoked fire swept past. At the meadow's edge, beneath the sugar maple tree, the light broke into crystal-sparked rainbows as it glanced off the snowflakes that lay on the three marble crosses. Mike stepped into the warmth of Christmas lights and pulled the door behind him.

But just before the latch caught, the door opened again. He'd forgotten the bag that sat on the handrail. He reached for it and missed. It tumbled. A jar fell out and thumped into the snow on the porch. The bag twirled between the banisters and flew away. He picked up the jar and brushed off the snow. The contents were dark purple.

He looked to his mother, who sat in the rocking chair beside the Christmas tree. The clicking of her knitting needles stopped and she lay her hands in her lap. "They're blackberries, son. You and Scott used to steal them from my pies and thought I never noticed." She smiled and returned to her knitting.

The door of the small house built on Arvel Neely's high meadow clicked shut.

Recent fiction from Huntington Press:

Timesong
by Bill Branon

Spider Snatch
by Bill Branon

Keeps
by Pete Fowler

About Huntington Press

Huntington Press is a specialty publisher of Las Vegas- and gambling-related books and periodicals. To receive a copy of the Huntington Press catalog, call 1-800-244-2224 or write to the address below.

Huntington Press
3687 South Procyon Avenue
Las Vegas, Nevada 89103